How to Love
in a
World Like This

Kipling Knox

A PRAIRIE STATE CREATION

Printed in the United States of America

First Printing, 2025

ISBN: 979-8-9871656-3-8

Prairie State Press,
Illinois
prairiestatepress.com

About the author: kiplingknox.com

Cover design by Marcus Lehto

The story "Downriver" was published in *The Madison Review* in March, 2022. Later that year, it appeared in the collection *Under the Moon in Illinois.* The lives of those characters continued, partly captured in the pages that follow.

ONE

Arthur and Morgan could never agree on what to call their little farm. After she left, Arthur, in a kind of comical tantrum, ripped a plank from an old shed, trimmed its edges, and etched the name: Failure Farm. He nailed the sign to a post he sank at the end of the driveway. That felt better, somehow, and set a tone he could live with, alone there on the outskirts of Middling. With that name, Arthur and his farm would at least meet expectations, and anything better was a victory.

Nature embraced his joke—it pounded the sign in autumn storms, warped it with freezing rain, cloaked it in snow, battered it with spring winds. Finally the sign popped loose and stuck into the mud sideways. Now, eight months later, if you read the sign your eyes would travel downward to the hard clay where nothing grew but wretched plants, where prior evils incubated, waiting for the moment to hatch.

That wouldn't do. The sign was only funny if you displayed it proudly, meticulously. One April morning, Arthur cleaned the sign and retraced the etching and fixed it to the post with two-inch screws. Work is always the best remedy for despair, and Arthur committed himself.

Mornings he rose at five, fed the chickens, tilled their compost into the gardens, planted early greens, made coffee, made plans. He walked the trails with a journal, recorded the proceedings of nature—the emergence of bluebells, the return of songbirds, the rise of the river. He collected the trash that blew into his hedges—wrappers and bottles and unopened mail. You couldn't think about that too much—the waste on these few acres multiplied by all the earth's acres. 16 billion acres of planet littered with trash. Who were they thinking would clean it up? I'm not your mother, he'd say, which made him laugh ruefully because his own mother used to say that, miming a teacher, when he left a mess, when he was young, when she was still alive. Ruefully—that was a good word. There was only one word for that. Well, probably there were multiple words for it in other languages, like German. It would be interesting to learn German, because then you'd have all these other words.

That was the farm work, and then there was Arthur's work work, building websites for local businesses. It was a little like farming, because you grew things from almost nothing, borrowing patterns from what had been grown before. After a shower and a lunch of sardines, it felt good to sit at the computer and write code. You didn't have to write code to make websites anymore. Arthur told his clients this. You don't really need me, he'd say, You can just pay a few bucks a month and choose a template and add some pictures and type whatever you want. I can set that up for you. Some of them did, but most wanted Arthur to do the work himself, because it felt more special—even if it were only another donut shop, or tire repair, or dog trainer.

What if one day he just stopped? Just stopped farming and website-making? That question always hung around, like an orphaned kitten, mewing through the window while you were busy. The honest answer to that question was dreadful, if you gave it your full attention. So Arthur ignored it, sometimes shaking his head sharply to regain focus. But always he was aware of a space, deep within himself, where a potent despair fermented. It was a spiritual infection, which you could manage but never eradicate, which erupted at vulnerable times, like the hours before dawn, or Sundays.

The second Sunday of every month, Arthur and Morgan had their regular 'check-in,' according to their separation agreement. That made it sound more official than it was—really their agreement was just how Morgan said things would go, based on a book she had read called *Beginning at the End*, which she sent to Arthur, who slipped it unopened into a drawer beside his bed. Once a month on Sunday they talked on the phone, mostly about practical things. Neither of them was a phone talker. They messaged each other sometimes, but most days passed without a word. Three out of four Sundays passed that way, and that was the worst. Because Arthur knew Morgan had the day off, up in Chicago, when another nurse came to look after Mrs Vogel. She had the whole day free, and she could reach out to him in so many ways, but she never did. He would feel better if she were doing it intentionally, because at least she would be thinking of him. One second Sunday he asked her, Are you not talking to me—I mean, do I not hear from you on Sundays, except for this Sunday, because that's how you want it? And Morgan said, Oh, well, not really. I hadn't thought of it much. It's my one day off, you know?

As Arthur stepped into the street to inspect his work, ensuring the sign was level with the horizon, he heard a cry from the woods. That was far away, across the fields, down near the river. He'd never heard a cry from there before. There was often gunfire, and chain saws, and engines roaring from unknown neighbors across the way. But never a cry. It could be a baby raccoon—sometimes their cries sounded human. Or a crow, probably a crow, so diabolical. But no, it was the cry of a human, asking for help. Ah, and there were new neighbors next door now, the Fuglesens. Nice people. Arthur left his tools and ran.

He saw them beneath two hackberry trees at the edge of the bluff. A long wooden beam hung from a rope over pulleys, six feet above where

Faulkner Fuglesen lay trapped between the two trees. His grip on the rope held the beam and elevated him a few inches from the ground. Nancy held the rope higher up, hanging her full weight from it. If either let go, the beam would drop on Faulkner. It was like a guillotine that stopped just short of its kill. Why do we think of guillotines so readily when they haven't been used for generations?

Nancy turned to Arthur, her face strained, and said, Oh thank goodness, Arthur, can you help?

Faulkner's head was at the far end of the situation, but he managed to smile at Arthur and say, Damn thing slipped. The thing is, if I scramble out, I have to let go the rope and then I think this beam might get the best of us.

The solution was obvious. Arthur said, Hold on a sec. He took the loose end of rope from under Faulkner's hands and tied it in a half-hitch around one hackberry trunk. The thing about the half-hitch, Gramps had taught him, was that you had to go the same way around both times. Otherwise it was a granny knot, which you couldn't trust. Now Arthur grabbed the rope above Faulkner's hands and said, Okay you can let go now—easy, if you can. Then he felt the weight of the beam, with Nancy's slight frame tugging above. Faulkner crab-walked out of the crook between the trees. Now you can let go, Arthur told Nancy. At the same time, he released the rope, and the beam fell and stopped, in the grip of the knot, just above where Faulkner had lain.

Faulkner stood, breathing hard, and swatted dirt from his pants. That's a neat trick, he said.

Yeah I learned it in the Merchant Marines, Arthur said.

The older couple studied him.

You were in the Merchant Marines? asked Nancy.

Nah, I'm kidding—my grandfather taught me that knot.

Well anyway, said Nancy. Thank goodness you were here.

Faulkner crossed his arms and put his weight on one hip. You know, he said, A well-tied knot can hold the world together.

Nancy gave him a look and sighed. She pulled a stick from his hair. Let's leave this for a while, she said. Let's go get something to drink.

Wait, no, first, said Faulkner, Let's get a picture in front of this disaster avoided. And so the three came together, with the wooden beam behind them, framed by the hackberries, and Faulkner took a picture with his phone.

So this was the Fuglesens, Arthur's new neighbors to the west, whose property also bordered the Sangamon River. They were middle-aged and empty-nested, semi-retired children of the 80s. They came out from Middling, just two weeks after Morgan left. That was a shame, because Morgan would have loved them. Maybe it would have made a difference? The day they moved in, the Fuglesens showed up at Arthur's front door with a loaf of banana bread, which was funny because Arthur had just made them brownies, but burned them, because Morgan had always been the baker, and he was considering trying again. When Arthur explained this, on his front porch, Faulkner said No no, I'm sure they're fine! And so Arthur brought out the dish and the Fuglesens each ate one, just to prove how fine they were.

In the days that followed the rescue, Arthur and the Fuglesens saw each other every day. It became hard to imagine not having them next door—curious how quickly friendship happens sometimes. That wooden beam was for a tree house Faulkner imagined, overlooking the river. Arthur helped get the frame assembled, teaching Fawk how you use a tree for support without harming it. They had dinners on the Fuglesens' deck. They had a fire on Arthur's bluff, overlooking the river, where the ghost farmer Hanacek sometimes strolled, where he and Morgan had liked to sit at dusk. Fawk brought a bottle of scotch that cost more than a pair of work boots.

Fawk was tall, with a long neck and oval head and springy legs that made him look like a human-sized cricket. Nancy was normal-sized, with a heart-shaped face and impressively big hair. She could have been pop star in an 80s music video. Interesting how sometimes older married couples seem so well matched, as if they fused like trees emerging from an old stump. Fawk and Nancy created a balanced whole. And curiously, their eyes were exactly the same color—green like English ivy.

As the fire died and the scotch disappeared, coyotes began to wail off in the woods. Nancy handed out blankets. They told their stories the way new friends do. Faulkner had built and sold a company that made sensors—cameras, accelerometers, microphones. Nancy had taught biology at Middling High for 20 years and then retired to paint scenes of dilapidated grain elevators. Arthur told them the story of Failure Farm. He told them about Morgan. How they went to college in Middling, and moved to Chicago, and then manufactured a dream of buying an old farm downstate in the country. It sounded like such a whim now, when he told it. Maybe if they had stayed in Chicago. He didn't explain why Morgan left. You don't just drop that kind of burden on a new friend. A barred owl called from some unseen perch: Who cooks for you?

Arthur, Nancy said, I want to ask you: Did you hear shooting last night? Across the river?

The question took him out of the moment. A sense of dread returned.

I did, he said. It was a nice day, so.

So, what? She tilted her head, listening, the teacher.

Well. They like to shoot a lot, the people across the river. Especially on nice days, after the weather's been bad.

Nancy winced a little, considering. You mean like as a way of celebrating?

Fawk put his arm around Nancy, an instinctual gesture neither seemed to notice. He said, Sounded like assault rifles or something.

Arthur looked toward the river. Maybe, he said. Probably. They seem pretty well armed.

I don't like it, Nancy said. It's very rude.

Do you know those folks? Fawk asked.

Not really, said Arthur.

Well maybe we need to change that, said Nancy.

Fawk asked, Have you gone over? Tried to meet them?

Arthur looked at each of them, then looked at the ground.

I guess I figure they might just stop one day. Or I'll get used to it. Or they'll move away.

How often does this happen, Nancy asked.

Often enough that you're always waiting for it, he said.

You know, Fawk said. He often started sentences with 'you know,' and typically followed them with aphorisms of his own invention, like 'On this world you must act, lest it act on you.' But this time he just said, It feels a little… peculiar back in the woods sometimes. Do you ever get that, Arthur? Like a strange vibe—sinister I guess.

Mmm, Arthur said. It seemed like such a pointed observation, but surely Fawk didn't know what had happened back there. Surely he hadn't seen Hanacek?

Nancy gave him a swat and said, Now you're just being superstitious. But let's figure out these neighbors, see if we can talk some sense into them.

Arthur said, So about your kids—you have two, right?

Our best work! said Faulkner. A matched set.

Sheila and Felix, said Nancy.

Where are they now?

Sheila lives in town—she's an independent journalist.

Arthur said, Oh I think I've read her blog.

Faulkner sipped his whiskey, now serious. That's the one. But she's taking a break. Legal problems. That's how the sons of bitches deal with journalists now—bury them in legal fees until they quit.

Oh it's not so bad as that, said Nancy. We have a friend, a really good lawyer up in the city—he's helping out. You'll meet him one of these days.

And Felix?

In Chicago, said Nancy. He's a government agent.

Like what kind?

Nancy and Faulkner laughed together, quietly, looking into the fire.

He could tell us, said Fawk, but then he'd have to kill us.

Overhead you could see the Milky Way through the bare tree branches. People used to think stars were holes in a great sphere that encircled the Earth. The Milky Way was a lot of holes. If that were true, who poked the holes? Was that idea stranger than what we believe now, these billions of balls of gas so far away they might be gone except for their light? What were they talking about? Oh yes, the kids.

Nancy broke their reverie. So Arthur, have you heard from Morgan recently?

Nancy had this gift—wouldn't it be nice to be like that. To be direct, but warmly. You felt like you could tell her anything and she wouldn't judge. Arthur had already said more than he thought he ever would. But not everything. Not the dark things.

Last week, Arthur said. Our usual call.

And you miss her now, Nancy said.

Well, sure.

You don't want to talk about this, said Fawk.

Not really.

Maybe I shouldn't have asked, Nancy said.

No, it's nice, said Arthur.

You should call her if you miss her, said Nancy. Tell her you love her. That can never hurt, just being honest.

Well now, said Fawk, the guy doesn't need to hear our advice.

Nancy looked at him, and that was enough. Fawk shrugged and studied his empty cup.

Nancy said, Arthur, do you want me to stop giving you advice?

I like your advice, he said.

Can I give you some more, then?

Yeah, said Arthur. But maybe he didn't, now?

Ask her to visit, said Nancy. Ask her to come down here.

Oh come on, Nancy, said Faulkner.

You shush, she replied. Arthur said he wanted my advice.

Well, I have asked her, Arthur said.

Not right away, said Nancy. That will make her feel smothered. Pick some later date. A date that seems far enough that it's easy to say yes. Ask her if she'll come down then—to meet us, maybe, to see the progress you've made on your farm.

Arthur stared at Nancy, for a moment unable to form words. There it was, in brilliant color, a complete vision of a day. It came as a full-body rush, like a potion in the veins. He looked back across Failure Farm, illuminated in little night lights, the house, the chicken coop, the goat yard, raised beds, the sapling trees, the planted prairie, the bird houses, the woods and the bluff and the river beyond. He saw, draped across this landscape, like some wonderful sparkling fabric, a thriving, bountiful, miraculous hobby farm, where rain would never fall til after sundown, where by 8am the fog would disappear.

Nancy said, Just a thought. Maybe it's not such a great idea.

Arthur turned back to Nancy, and knew his face must have looked enchanted, but he couldn't help it. He said, No. No, not at all. It's an amazing idea.

Fawk put his chin out, studying Arthur, and said, You all right there buddy?

Arthur looked at him now, his expression still glowing. He must be freaking them out, he should stop this. But still. What an idea!

Yes! he said. I'm absolutely fine. Better than fine. Outstanding. I'm gonna do this.

Sorry? said Nancy, with that tilted head again.

Like you said, Arthur said, I'll invite Morgan to come down and visit, later this year. Summer for sure—maybe August? Later in August, after the weather cools a bit but everything is still growing. That gives me plenty of time to get the farm in order—to do the things I've been thinking of doing. To make the name actually ironic, you know? Oh yeah, by August it shouldn't be any problem to get the gardens fantastic and the hens laying regularly and learn how to make goat cheese and the prairie will be high and a fox will slink through it but not kill the chickens…

Arthur was aware of how the Fuglesens were watching him, but he couldn't stop.

… and the house will be tidy, with the appliances fixed and cabinets painted—oh and I'll build the little lookout cabin on the bluff, with windows on the whole north side, and it will be full of birds. That's it, he said. You named it, Nancy. This is the thing. I'll invite Morgan and she'll come down and it will be One Perfect Day.

The Fuglesens waited to see if he were finished. Then Fawk said, You know: Reality divided by expectations equals happiness.

Nancy swatted his arm and said, You ought to write that nonsense on one of your river rocks.

Fawk shrugged. I think I might.

We don't need any more river rocks with sayings on them.

Fawk stretched out his arms. Why not? We've got the room.

What are you doing for dinner tomorrow, Nancy asked Arthur. Why don't you come over?

He looked at her blankly. He heard the words but his mind couldn't process them.

Dinner, she said. Why don't you come over and we'll eat outside. I'll fix some roast chicken.

Then it was like a massive turbine gradually slowing down, a descending note of Arthur's thoughts returning to the present.

Thanks, he said. That sounds great. But I'll have to see. So much work to do. Maybe another day? If that's not rude to say?

Nancy reached and put a hand on Arthur's forearm. We should let you get to bed, she said. If you change your mind, just come on over. We'll have plenty.

The next evening, after he ate and washed the dishes and crossed the day's tasks off the list, Arthur sat on his porch holding his phone. He had a text thread open—the last message to Morgan, from him, which said, *You free now?* That was from ten days ago, and she hadn't responded, and when they had their regular call on Sunday, she said she was sorry she must have missed it. Which is ridiculous—she never missed anything. So now, he couldn't text her again, or she would see the last lonely message, and that would seem pathetic. He had to call her. Maybe a video call, to make things interesting or create a sense of urgency? No, not a video call—that was clearly too much. Just a regular phone call, an old-fashioned call, a call like would come from an old phone, with a curly cord, like the kind of phone Fawk must have used when calling Nancy to ask her on a date. Arthur touched the profile image of Morgan—so beautiful, so stunning—and it opened her contact info. And there was the button to call. He put his finger above it. For some reason it brought to mind the feeling a surgeon must have when holding the scalpel before making the incision. Such a small action that could yield such dramatic results. Once he pressed, it would open up a pathway from which there was no return. It could be a fantastic pathway, a corridor to a fulfilled life. Or it could be a disaster, a ramp downward into some gloomy catacomb of despair. Like that infection inside him. Rotten.

With great care to not fat-finger something, Arthur closed the app, and then doused the screen, and set his phone on the wicker table beside him. He wouldn't call Morgan tonight. He wasn't ready for that. He would call when he felt the right moment. But still he was going to do it. Definitely. He had a goal now, and that wasn't going to change. He was going to create One Perfect Day. Inviting Morgan was just one step to cross off the list.

So he made some tea and walked into the back yard in the last light. The wind had subsided and now it was very cool. Mostly the trees were still bare, their branches groping skyward. He could smell the earth emerging from its slumber, the roasted fragrance of rebirth. He felt like he was walking aimlessly, and yet his path was straight—the path they walked on that last day, down the slope, through the hole in the forest where the trail entered. He went through the hole. Along the river, the forest floor was coming to life, a blanket of sprouts—cutleaf cone flower, nettles, bluebells. The morels would be up soon. Maybe he'd find them this year. Then he came to the place where the man had been. He didn't look at first, didn't want to give up the possibility that it would all be normal. But when he did look, near the shadowy bank, he saw clearly a patch of bare ground, in the shape of a man—in the very shape that man had lain, like a weird yoga pose, before Arthur had scooped him up. Nothing was growing on that patch. Did that make sense, biologically? Maybe it did. Maybe the corpse oozed something that acted as an herbicide. But maybe not. Probably not. It was very strange. But no stranger than the ghost of Hancek the old farmer with his two mules walking along the bank of the river, giving silent advice.

Arthur looked for Hancek now. It would be nice to have a visit. But he didn't see him. Just some notion of movement through the trees and across the river that was probably just his eyes failing where sharper animals could see. Like the great horned owl, who called at that moment, down the river to the west. It called again, a plaintive series of notes that echoed through the cold air. Some nights another owl returned the call. But not this night. Tonight, the owl called alone.

TWO

While Mrs Vogel took her morning nap, Morgan stood in the parkway of the old woman's mansion on Deming and prepared to spread mulch. Here was a fresh pile, just delivered, still steaming in the chill Chicago air. Gardening was a nice break from nursing, and it was good to be outside. She took a handful and let it sift through her fingers. She would have to figure out how to haul it back to the garden. She would have to find tools. But something distracted her from the task. Was someone watching? Probably not. Probably it was the house.

It commanded attention, the old stone mansion. You could feel it before you saw it, as you walked down the street. There was a sense that everything bent toward it, drawn by its gravity—the houses, the trees, the street lights, all leaning toward Mrs Vogel's mansion as if expecting some whispered proclamation. When it was built, in 1895, there were a lot of proclamations in Chicago, probably. Two years after the Columbian Exposition, in the shadow of the White City, when everything was possible and the world was inexhaustible. Limestone from Indiana, white pine timbers from upper Michigan. Slate roof on pointed turrets. Leaded glass. In the morning light the windows were just reflections of sky and branches, unseeing, like cataract eyes. It was hard to know what rooms went with what windows. In three months, Morgan hadn't been in all the rooms. You needed a purpose to go into rooms. The house didn't tolerate frivolous exploration.

Great structures made everyday things seem trivial. So did mountains and rivers and the Great Lakes. But still you did what had to be done. Like spreading mulch. When Morgan and Arthur did this on a larger scale, at their place outside Middling, it was so much easier. A truck delivered 10 yards, and they scooped it with their tractor and dropped it where they wanted. It was satisfying making fertile collars around all the trees. Here in the city, perhaps paradoxically, the job was so primitive. You could either buy plastic bags at a hardware store, or have a landscaping company dump a little pile of it on the parkway. Morgan chose delivery, because who wants to throw out all those bags, and she didn't have a car anyway. Now there was the question of how to get it in the back yard. Mrs. Vogel didn't have a wheelbarrow because—as Morgan recalled from her childhood—the hearty woman had shoveled her mulch on a tarp and dragged it where she wanted. It was the same with leaves in the fall. Well all right, it would have to be tarp-hauling.

How had Mrs. Vogel done these things before Morgan arrived, now that the old woman was bound to a wheelchair? She asked her that morning, while she braided the widow's remarkably thick hair, and wrapped the braids in a sort of crown that hadn't changed in all the years Morgan could remember.

How did you get the mulch down last year, Tante? Did you hire someone?

Mrs Vogel replied, as she did to most questions like this, by waving her hand dismissively. She said, Some assholes did it. I paid them too much—which was anything at all with the job they did. Trampling my jonquils with their big boots. My hostas—they suffocated.

Mrs Vogel turned to look at Morgan, who withdrew a hairpin just in time. And the machines, Mrs. Vogel said, —the wind-makers, what do you call?

Leaf blowers.

Yes! Leaf blowers, those god damned things are so noisy, you lose your hearing, what you have left of it!

Then Mrs Vogel patted Morgan's arm. Her hand had a weight to it, a strength that defied her apparent frailty. She said, But now I have my Nichte, for the time being at least, who can do a better job than those assholes!

Morgan resumed the hair dressing. She said, I wish I were your niece.

No this is better, said the old woman. You are Nichte by love, not by blood. Blood means nothing despite what they tell you. If your family is shit, choose a new one, I say.

Well I don't think your family is shit, Morgan said.

Mrs. Vogel turned again, abruptly. You say so?! When's the last time you see my family here? Ever?

Then she gave the dismissive wave again. They are dead, she said. Might as well be. Assholes, like those gardeners.

Morgan went to look for a shovel and tarp. The garage was originally a carriage house, where horses were stabled maybe? English ivy, leafless vines this time of year, gripped the stone all the way up to the gutters. The garage probably didn't like that—maybe she'd pull the ivy down one day. Inside, the smell was exactly as she recalled from how many, 25 years ago? This heavy scent of old wood and engine oil and damp concrete. There was a car in there, something low and wrapped in a faded cover, like a hospital gown for a car. Morgan remembered Mr Vogel loved fancy cars, but he died so long ago. If Arthur were here, he would peek under the cover, because he couldn't help himself, because he loved everything mechanical and beautiful. But she left it alone. Who cares about cars? They only get you faster to some other place you'd rather not be.

A tarp rested, folded neatly, in a corner by stacked ceramic pots. When she lifted its corner, mice scattered. Morgan jumped backward and let out a little cry, but nothing too embarrassing, and in a moment she was fine, reassured that it was only mice. It could have been rats. That would be another thing. She realized she wasn't approaching this task very wisely, that she really should have bought some gloves and suitable pants and shirt, rather than this corduroy dress with a jeans jacket. She would dress better next time. Now, she let the tarp fall open to see that any vermin were gone. She took a long-handled shovel from a hook on the wall, and went out.

Passing through the door, she felt a familiar wave of despair rush up from her stomach through her heart and into her throat. She couldn't breathe or swallow. She steadied herself on the doorjamb and thought, Feelings are happening to me. I am not my thoughts. I am not my feelings. But the wave persisted and she thought she might pass out and fall. She looked at the pavement, now cracked by so many winters, and imagined what that surface might do to her skull and the brain it contained. This brain was clearly at war with itself, causing all that despair in a rush of neurochemicals—but also, mocking her for having this rush of despair when obviously it was just feelings happening. How does the brain manage to do this, to be aware of itself? Is this what makes us special? Does this last after we die? It could be terrifying, thinking too much about your brain and whether you were it and it was you and consciousness might just be some clever wiring.

Then the wave passed, and Morgan went to the pile in the parkway. She spread the tarp on the sidewalk and shoveled mulch onto it. Funny how satisfying shoveling mulch could be, because it was light and easily scooped and it smelled so nice—the scent of possibility, of fertility and potential, before the bark faded and scattered, and the plants suffered under the cruelty of the midwestern summer. Before long, she had a proper pile. She laid the shovel across it, grabbed a corner of the tarp, and pulled. It moved, but it was heavy. The pile she'd created was too large, and it would get stuck in the narrow gate to the gangway. Another failure, oh well. There was no one there to judge her.

Then, without warning, came the familiar itch—the impulse to pull her phone from her pocket and search for news about the man she and Arthur had found. The internet had everything—surely there would be some new clue. But every time there was exactly one relevant result: An article Sheila Fuglesen had posted on her Middling news website, describing a missing persons report that Lupe Gallardo had filed with the county sheriff. That was eight months ago, three days after Morgan had left Arthur, on the day they had found that body. That could just be a coincidence. The body they found could have been some unrelated murder. But there were no reports of a murder—not on news sites or social media or neighborhood discussion groups or anywhere. But if it were unrelated, what happened to Lupe's husband? And what happened to the body they found? Arthur said it had just disappeared, in a flood. Then they stopped talking about it. Once you stop talking about something, every day it gets harder to bring it up. You don't want people to think you're obsessing.

If Morgan responded to the impulse every time it happened, she would be in a constant state of pulling out her phone, checking, and putting it back. She would be like an old-time mechanical puppet in a Christmas window, doing the same motion over and over, funny at first but then profoundly creepy. So you resist the impulse as often as you can. You breathe and let it pass. You return to spreading mulch.

Soon Mrs Vogel would wake up. She would need help getting to the toilet, and then Morgan would wheel her from the first-floor bedroom, across walnut floors and Persian rugs, through the parlor, and the grand kitchen with its archaic appliances, and into the sunroom. Morgan would bring her the black-framed spectacles, with lenses so severe they made the old woman's eyes enormous and bulging, like a squid. Then Morgan would retrieve for her whatever book she wanted, usually poetry these days because it was less tiring—often Rilke, in the original German. While she read, Mrs. Vogel liked a cup of hot water with a leaf of mint from the pot in the sunroom. While the old woman read, Morgan would take her blood pressure, and heart rate, and oxygen level. Sometimes the strong hand would grip her forearm, stopping her, and Mrs Vogel would say, Listen to this. And she would read a few lines aloud, sometimes in English, sometimes German, and then she would shake her head slowly and click her tongue in appreciation. Morgan would say, That's nice, or Oh how interesting, because what could you say about poetry that it didn't already say about itself.

All this would happen soon, just as it happened six days a week, every day but Sunday. It was nice not to have to think about what you were going to do every day, to just follow the itinerary set by a formidable old woman, survivor of her husband, estranged from her two children. Saturday nights were difficult, because she felt like you should go out with old friends, and Morgan still had old friends in the city. But their invitations came less frequently, because she so rarely accepted them.

Sundays were the worst, because you had to decide what to do. Once a month on Sunday she talked to Arthur. She looked forward to it, felt the lift of expectation, a kind of romantic simmer like the old days, and then their conversation always went badly. He was too curious, too needy.

Tell me about your days, he said so many times, I want to hear everything.

Every day is about the same, she said. Boring, but kind of nice.

Did you go out last night? he asked.

I did, she said.

Who with? I mean who was there?

Because Arthur was terrified she'd hook up with another man, even though they agreed they wouldn't date until they decided about their relationship, and Morgan found it very easy to honor this, because the last thing she wanted was to join the excruciating awkwardness of dating, but also because she was honest, mostly. But Arthur clearly didn't trust her and that was infuriating and made her want to punish him.

Just some friends, she said. It was fun. We were out late. I'm a little hung over today.

Then there would be silence between them, and she'd feel Arthur considering all the things he wanted to ask, but wouldn't.

Eventually, she said, How are things on the farm?

Fine, he said, sulking.

So she had to ask something specific, to draw him out, like, Have you planted yet? or Have you seen the new neighbors recently?

And that would work, because poor Arthur was like a dog, a very smart dog, like a border collie, but a dog nevertheless—all drive and instinct and yearning to please and be rewarded. And she loved hearing about the farm, despite herself, and she missed seeing the seasons pass, and she knew she would love the new neighbors, the Fuglesens, just as Arthur said she would. But she didn't say so. That would encourage him and he'd start talking about their relationship and making requests of her, which would be too stifling, so she kept her remarks shallow and pleasant, which she knew exasperated him.

So that all sucked. It was horrible. And if you thought about it too much you could conclude that there was no way it would change and they were just forestalling the inevitable—so you didn't think about it and hoped that life would surprise you somehow. Because sometimes it did, right? What could be more surprising than this—back in the old neighborhood, nursing Mrs Vogel, for goodness sakes? It seemed implausible, incredible—and yet, exactly right.

At lunchtime Mrs Vogel wasn't hungry. She was rarely hungry these days, and she had been losing weight. When Morgan helped her bathe,

the old woman's skin hung from her skeleton like a mother's dress hung from a little girl. Like the rhinoceros in Kipling's story. The aged human body can be an appalling thing to behold, unless you look at it like a prairie plant, where late in the season it dries and shrivels beautifully, suitable for a winter bouquet.

You have to eat something, Tante, or I won't be doing my job.

Mrs Vogel waved away the appeal. Eh, she said, I pay you anyway. You are my gardener now, not just my nurse.

Try this lemon cake, Morgan said, I made it. If you don't try it I'll be insulted.

The old woman reached out her hand, too large now for her forearm, this knotted oak-branch hand with fading dexterity—and she pinched the little yellow cake between thumb and finger and lifted it to her mouth and popped the whole thing in. She laughed silently as she chewed, tears forming at the creases of her eyes. She swallowed and held up a finger.

She said, When I was a girl, I ate like a pig! In Bremen we always had plenty to eat, don't listen to what people tell you about Germany then. Spätzle and cabbage and rouladen and cakes like this one. But I was never fat. I ran around too much.

Morgan poured her some apple juice. Why were you running? she asked.

From boys, of course! I was very beautiful. A blonde maiden with edelweiss in my hair.

Morgan smiled. Now you're teasing me, she said. Did you also wear lederhosen and make cuckoo clocks?

I had a bicycle, said Mrs. Vogel, as if that were a logical answer. But the boys did love me—that part is true.

I can imagine, Tante. Morgan wiped the woman's lower lip with a napkin.

How is your boy? Arthur, your tragic king. Last Sunday was your day to talk, yes?

He's fine, Morgan said.

Mrs. Vogel put her hand on Morgan's arm, and looked directly in her eyes. The irises were faded blue like a cornflower. She said, That's no answer. We can have real conversation, you and I. Americans always claim they are fine and good and great and can't complain. It's all bullshit and a waste of breath. You and I can have a real conversation. How is the boy.

I don't know, said Morgan. He's very busy working the little farm we had. Half the day he's building people's websites and the other half he's taking care of the animals and the gardens and fixing things. It's like he can't stop. So yeah maybe he's not fine. I'm worried I guess.

Mrs. Vogel wagged her head slowly, critically. She said, Then why are you here with me, instead of with him?

Morgan was surprised by a rush of emotion—it burst into her head without warning. It was like when you hear a certain song that triggers this incredible and yet delicious sadness. She began to cry and also fight against crying. Her face screwed up with the tension and she had to look away, to smear her wet eyes with her fingers, and take a breath.

Ah, said Mrs. Vogel. So it is that way.

Yes, said Morgan. It's that way.

During afternoon nap time, Morgan spread the mulch where Mrs. Vogel had told her to. This is how she made her living now, this is how she spent her days. Three months ago she was nursing post-op patients at Illinois Masonic. Five months before that she was driving the rental truck north from Middling with everything she cared to take, which wasn't much, not even books. She wished she had taken more books. Her apartment on Sheridan, in Uptown, echoed when she walked through it.

The late afternoon sun cast acute light across the quiet street, connecting the mansions and condos in shadows. A guy you could only describe as a 'gentleman,' who wore a tailored blue suit and fedora, walked a tiny white dog down the sidewalk. He crossed the street before he got to Morgan. People weren't friendly on this street, which is unusual in Chicago. They were more friendly when she grew up here, right next door, in a more ordinary house than most on the block, but still. Now perhaps they feel the pressure of the city around them, encroaching and threatening their peaceful enclave, and to be friendly is to open a seam in their defenses. It was too bad and probably not necessary because most people like the old streets with mansions. Don't they?

Sometimes you can trace your life in geography, even on a tiny scale, like on this sidewalk. In January, Morgan had made a serious mistake at the hospital. She lost track of a patient—an enormous man coming out of a hernia operation, recovering from general anesthesia. His wife was impatient, and Morgan released him, when he really should have been under observation, and she also forgot to explain his meds, which were certain to constipate him, and that could be very problematic for a hernia patient. No one knew she had screwed up, and maybe the big man was fine. But she knew, and realized that it could happen again and again, because she did not have her shit together. She had moments of dissociation, where she couldn't say where she was, and then looked for a familiar face from Middling Hospital, and then faked it when a patient called out to her, sensing some problem. Some moments she couldn't believe it was actually happening, the complete meltdown of her married life, the abandonment of all the romance and all the dreams—and also the absolute shame she felt for having failed.

So that day after work she took a bus down Clark Street and got off at the park and walked over to the old neighborhood, where she spent her childhood, before her parents' divorce, before she went to college and met Arthur, before everything. It was like walking in a trance, and she knew it was probably stupid, because what: were you going to knock on someone's door and have some revelation? No, it was sure to disappoint, but her legs kept taking her.

On the sidewalk between her old house and Mrs. Vogel's mansion, she saw a man in blue scrubs pushing a hunched woman in a wheelchair. The man was clearly a nurse of some kind, so Morgan smiled, because we should all be nice to nurses and teachers. The man smiled back, but it was a peculiar, insincere smile. He had a puffy body, like he ate too much processed food, and a carefully trimmed beard, and he wore crocs. His smile was severe, prissy, with a curt little nod. Morgan shrugged and looked away.

Then she heard, Morgan Deneau! Is that you, my darling?

And so it became clear that it was Mrs Vogel in that wheelchair, and they embraced with the awkwardness of a wheelchair hug. Mrs Vogel began to ask pointed questions: Why are you here, where are you working, didn't you get married, do people think that just because we have computers we don't need to write letters anymore? Morgan tried to answer all these questions, but the nurse made her uncomfortable. He sighed audibly, and when she caught his gaze, he forced a big smile like someone receiving a gift they hate. He kept checking his watch, and making a whistling shape with his mouth.

Don't mind Devin, said Mrs Vogel. He's rude.

The old woman turned to him and said, Go over there—beside that tree, while we talk a while.

Devin seemed astonished, but did as Mrs. Vogel asked.

Mrs. Vogel said, You're unhappy, dear.

Morgan looked away, unable to respond.

You don't like that job at the hospital. It's too soon for you.

Morgan clasped her hands, and looked down at the old woman. She said, Well.

Mrs Vogel said, Come back in two weeks, after you give notice at your job. Come work for me, dear heart. Until you get yourself together. I need to fire Devin anyway.

Then the old woman called to her nurse, You can take me inside now.

Morgan watched their backs as they went, as Mrs Vogel reached up an arm to wave, knowing Morgan would be watching. A cardinal sang from the bare maple above her—the first cardinal she'd heard that year, with notes precise and clear, piercing the late winter air, like the whistle of a train. How she missed the sound of trains in Middling.

So Morgan did what Mrs Vogel said. In two weeks she arrived at the mansion, where Devin explained the routine to her, because he wasn't so bad after all, though he deplored handling Mrs. Vogel's diapers and helping her bathe. He was squeamish about things a nurse shouldn't mind.

Morgan became one of two caregivers for the old widow. The other was Nakeisha, who came up from Bronzeville every evening and rang the gong-deep doorbell and waited on the step for Morgan to let her in. She dressed beautifully, in yellows and oranges and browns, and she always wore a hat, pinned to her beauty-shop hair. She had a smile like a buddhist monk, like she knew things. As Morgan raked the last mulch from the grass on the parkway, Nakeisha called her phone.

Happy afternoon, Hon, she said, How's the fairy godmother today?

Her usual self, said Morgan. Maybe a little feisty.

That's good, bless her heart. A fire in your belly keeps you going. A fire in her belly keeps us employed. Nakeisha laughed.

Morgan laughed, maybe too loudly? She wanted Nakeisha to like her. Some people always had clever things to say, even in small talk. It would be nice to have clever things to say. It would be nice to smile like a monk.

How are you, Morgan asked. What's up?

I'm sorry hon, I'm gonna be late. Cause my husband's late, because his shift captain is late, and on and on—you know how it goes. Like maybe an hour—is that okay? I'm so sorry.

It's fine, said Morgan. Totally fine. I don't mind.

Bless your heart, said Nakeisha. Devin was all right, but I like you better.

At bedtime, Morgan covered Mrs. Vogel in a quilt the old woman had made herself 50 years before. The quilt had an elaborate geometry, like an Escher drawing, and it played tricks on your eyes in the warm light of the incandescent lamp. On the walls of the old woman's bedroom hung oil paintings of picturesque but probably imaginary landscapes, created by some cousin who once lived in Strasbourg. They hung too high on the walls, above an average person's line of sight, perhaps because Mr Vogel was very tall and nothing much had moved since he died. But the height of the paintings worked with the 10-foot ceilings, and gave the impression of a room suited for giants.

She left the door ajar, and walked down the creaking stairs, and in the cool of the evening heard the boiler come on and steam clang through the radiators. You might think spirits were making an evening racket, banging out a melody to taunt the living. In the front hall, at the bottom of the stairs, she paused in front of a tall mirror wrapped in a rococo frame.

She was shocked to see a young woman who looked too pale, with dark eye bags, dark lips, black hair askew like octopus arms. The corduroy dress was too large and amplified her underweight frame. But that was her, Morgan Deneau, looking how she looked these days, drawing all the concerns from friends. She felt better than she looked, to be honest. So the looks might follow. It was sadly hilarious that Arthur would think she'd started dating—looking like this? She stepped close to the mirror and wiped her eyes and face with both hands and pulled back her hair and examined. She was normal enough, normal pretty—except for those eyes. They were the color of glacial ice, barely blue and almost white, with dense and dark lashes that set off the color. They were shocking eyes. When she met someone for the first time—even checking out at a grocery store or stepping on to a bus—she saw the effect of her eyes. People froze, sometimes recoiled, and then couldn't look away, despite their efforts. Her friends who said to men, 'Eyes up here,' they had no idea what it was like when the eyes were already up there—looking at her eyes like you might look at a chest of gold coins. Morgan's eyes were irresistible. They were a liability. They were terrifying.

Was someone watching? It felt that way. Maybe because other faces were watching her—the oil portraits of Mrs. Vogel's family, who hung from the walls in Teutonic severity, all of them now physically dead but immortalized through their portraits with pugnacious expressions. They observed and judged and followed you around the rooms no matter where you stood. They were unfazed by Morgan's eyes. They had seen so much more.

How long had she been looking in this mirror? Long enough to be strange, probably, because it felt like everything she did these days was strange. Morgan let herself check her phone. There was a message from Arthur, saying, How's it going? Plans tonight? She dismissed it.

When she looked back into the mirror, there was a large man standing behind her. Is that a painting, she thought, because that made more sense—but no, it was a complete man, without a frame, standing in the hall behind her. He was vaguely translucent, and seemed to be lit from within, so you could see the room through him. He must be nearly seven feet tall, with a mostly-bald head that seemed too large, even for his enormous frame. There were profound bags under his eyes, a fabric of folded, worn skin—but his eyes themselves, they were bright, searching, sad. He was looking at her, there was no question. He wore some fancy silk robe, with matching jammy pants and leather slippers and a wound scarf around his neck. It was the costume of an old-time rich man at bedtime, or maybe at breakfast, where servants brought everything on a tray with silver and a poached egg in the little cup. Why wasn't she alarmed by this? She looked at him, calmly, in a kind of subdued trance, as he looked back at her.

The man lifted one hand, a wave no higher than his hip, as if he were shy. This movement shook Morgan from her reverie, and she turned to look where the man must be standing behind her. She saw something, just the image of movement, like a smudge across space, a field of distortion where she looked—and then there was nothing.

The paintings continued watching, motionless. Morgan looked back in the mirror. There was nothing unusual. The tall man must had been imagined. In her state, at this hour, in this grave old house—of course she would have visions, flights of fancy, whatever you wanted to call them. She remembered her sadness, and let the idea of the man fade.

Morgan returned to her phone. She opened the browser and did her searches. Once again, she saw the story from Sheila Fuglesen. A missing persons report had been filed by Lupe Gallardo, whose husband had not been seen for three days, who had left in the evening to gather mushrooms in a park near the Sangamon River and never returned. The Middling County sheriff's staff were investigating. They cautioned that missing persons reports rarely yielded a person. Not alive at least, and not very soon. The article hinted that the sheriff's office were setting expectations before even trying.

Armando Gallardo had to be the man she and Arthur found near the river. Didn't he? Maybe not. Probably it was a coincidence. But what happened to the body? Did Arthur leave it there for vultures and coyotes? Or call the police? Was there heavy rain in the days after she left? Morgan couldn't remember. Could you find a record of what the weather was on days in the past?

The doorbell rang. Morgan jumped. She pocketed her phone and let Nakeisha in.

The nurse dropped her bag and put her hands on Morgan's shoulders. She smiled. Morgan felt a strange melting inside her, a relaxation of muscles such that she might fall down.

Morgan put her hand on Nakeisha's waist, wanting to exchange the kind touch, but it was awkward—were they hugging now? She let her hand drop.

Nakeisha studied her. You okay? she asked. You look like you just ate something bad.

I'm fine, Morgan said. I'm fine. Just tired.

Well I owe you Hon, Nakeisha said. How's our royal duchess? Anything I need to do right now?

It's no problem at all. She's sleeping—as well as she does.

You want to come late tomorrow? I can spell you, no problem.

No, thanks. That's all right. I'll be up regardless. I don't sleep in.

I get that, said Nakeisha. I don't even know what sleep is anymore.

Then they said good night, whispering, even though Mrs. Vogel was almost certainly awake. Maybe they whispered from the portraits, who so rudely watched and listened.

Outside Morgan smelled the warm and roasted fragrance of the mulch. That was a job well done. The scents of nature are healing. You don't get them so much in the city. It brought to mind her days in Middling, the breath of the earth after rain, the scent of moist loam along the river, where bluebells must be blooming now, where the body lay on the day she left Arthur.

THREE

Once he hatched his plan to create a perfect day, Arthur no longer needed an alarm. Each morning he woke a little earlier, roused by the excitement of all there was to do. He also awoke to the hope that Morgan had responded to his last message. But she was silent. Then on Saturday, a peculiar intuition awoke him, a sense that someone was nearby. Could it be Morgan? Had she driven down from Chicago overnight because she couldn't live apart any more? Of course that was ridiculous—she had never done anything like that. That was stupid thinking. On the other hand, maybe she would? In this state of mind, with hair askew, eyes still sleepy, and an erection making a tent of his boxer shorts, Arthur went toward the presence he felt, out the back door to the deck that overlooked the gardens.

There on the lawn, just a few strides from the house, stood the old farmer Hanacek with his two spectral mules. When Arthur appeared, the old ghost turned his head and stared beneath the rim of his broad hat.

Arthur instinctively covered his shorts with two hands and said, Hanacek! You're here!

Because he had never seen Hanacek anywhere but back in the woods, along the river, and certainly never right in the back yard.

What do you want? Arthur asked. He didn't expect him to reply—the old guy never did—but sometimes he moved or gestured in a way that suggested something.

Hanacek pushed his hat back on his head, like old-time farmers do on particularly hot days once the work is done. He put his hands on his hips, shirt sleeves rolled half-way up his forearms. And with meticulous intent, he took a long look around Arthur's place, in every direction. As he looked, the mules inched forward, grazing across the early clover. That is to say, they weren't actually grazing, because they were ghosts and the clover was quite real—but their prehensile lips reached out to grapple with stems and their jaws worked assiduously. Why was this necessary? Or were they grazing on ghost clover that Arthur couldn't see? And if that was so, were there other elements of the phantom world he didn't see, like ghost trees or maybe the relics of all of Hanacek's original buildings? It didn't add up, if you thought about it too hard, but then maybe the mortal mind lacked the constructs necessary to comprehend another dimension, like an alien world not based on carbon. Anyway.

Hanacek nodded his head several times, slowly, as if he were both surprised and impressed and he wanted that to be known.

It's coming along, said Arthur. Don't you think?

Hanacek dropped to one knee, dusted a bare patch of ground with the back of his knuckles, and then scooped up some phantom soil. He worked it between his thumb and fingers, allowing it to drift in the breeze, and looked up and across the land with drawn focus. He made a tossing gesture and lifted himself back to his feet. He nodded, as if making up his mind about something, and gestured for the mules to follow him. They went that way—old farmer nodding and mules following—back toward the river.

Thanks for coming by! Arthur said. Though, maybe call first next time?

The ghost farmer disappeared into the woods.

A voice came from the side of the house and Arthur jumped.

The voice said, You got company this morning, Arthur? Am I interrupting?

Faulkner Fuglesen walked toward the deck, carrying two cups of coffee.

No, no, said Arthur, I was just… talking to myself.

You know, said Fawk, a wise man said, A party of one always reaches consensus.

Fawk climbed the steps and handed Arthur a coffee. He leaned against the railing and said, Sorry, a little heavy on the cream this morning.

Are you the wise man who said that?

Fawk raised his cup in acknowledgement.

They sipped coffee and watched a pair of jays chase each other around the willow thicket, crying out in protest of some unseen atrocity.

Fawk said, What brings you out this early in nothing but your man pants?

Arthur looked down at himself. His torso was pale up to his neck and upper arms—beyond that, his skin turned deep red. That was the fate of a ginger in sun, Arthur, whose ancestors thrived under the clouds of the British isles. Here on the harsh prairie, he roasted, even this early in the spring. Morgan used to like it when he got a little color—it contrasted with what she called his 'North Sea eyes,' but then when it came to eyes she had no rival.

Maybe I'm getting eccentric, living alone, Arthur said. Do you think?

You mean like walking around in your boxers and talking to yourself?

Yeah, for example.

Not at all, Arthur. I think you're perfectly normal.

I think I'm going to plant today. Peas, kohlrabi, all the greens.

You're not worried about frost? The promise of early spring is for suckers, they say.

No you want to plant those things before the last frost.

Fawk closed his eyes and pointed toward Arthur. I have much to learn about this agrarian lifestyle.

Also, Arthur said, I got an intuition this morning. That it's a good day to plant.

And this is all part of your grand scheme, then? Still in the works?

Well, of course! Arthur paused. Was that rude? It just seemed strange that someone would think you'd waver from your plan, when it was as important as this.

But Fawk wasn't offended. He said, Well, great. Tell me about it, if you have a minute.

Arthur retrieved his phone from the railing and handed it to his friend. This is the latest, he said, I built this app to track everything. There you go. The one called OPD.

While Fawk studied the app at arm's length, so his aging eyes could see, Arthur explained. He had originally made a list on paper—all the things he wanted to complete for the One Perfect Day, when Morgan would visit and, hopefully, see the good in the farm again, and forget about the troubles, and consider moving back in together and—maybe— fall in love again. He immediately realized he'd need a set of tasks for each item on that list, and for many tasks he'd need a manifest of materials necessary for completion, and he'd need to identify dependencies between tasks, where one was contingent on the completion of another. He soon filled his pad with all these pieces of the plan, using an index at the back to cross-reference dependencies, and drawing a GANTT chart that didn't leave enough room at the end and so had to go up the margin of the paper like a hockey stick, which made it basically useless. And then Arthur realized—smacking himself in his pink forehead—that he had just written on paper what was properly a database and an application. And since web development was his line of work, he got to work making the

OPD app. Which now enabled him to track everything he needed to do, with tasks rendered across different views (list, timeline, geo-location), and priorities sequenced across the calendar, drawing input from sensors he'd installed around the farm. He even had a little module—not strictly necessary—where he employed AI to reason over images taken by his land camera, and to automate mundane tasks based on that reasoning. He took this module out of production when it dumped all the chicken feed into their water source. It was a forgivable incident, to be fair, because a rogue hen had climbed the coop right in front of the camera and, when she got stuck in the wire, flapped so fiercely that the system reasonably concluded that there were thousands of chickens in a state of starved apoplexy.

Fawk cleared his throat, and Arthur stopped talking. Fawk said, But other than that, it's been working pretty well then?

Oh yeah, said Arthur. I'd be lost.

Fawk said, Now hey. I can't really read this thing without my cheaters, but I'm interested in your original list—the main things, you know?

You mean my higher-order goals.

Yes, those. Read them to me?

And so Arthur did, as follows

REQUIREMENTS FOR THE PERFECT DAY
1. Organic gardens yield abundant food
2. Happy chickens lay lovely eggs
3. Jolly goats provide milk for delicious cheese
4. Birds of all kinds nest in native hedges
5. Bees hum busily among the forbs of the field
6. The farmhouse stands ship-shape
7. Friendly neighbors come for dinner, bringing wine and stories
8. Hanacek appears briefly
9. A fox darts down the prairie trail

That's a heck of a list, said Faulkner. Lots of adjectives. He crossed his arms and leaned back against the railing.

It could have been longer, but that's what needs to be done.

And the friendly neighbors—I assume that includes Nancy and me?

Well yeah, said Arthur. And a few others. I'll have to make some more friends.

Fawk smiled, his face creased like a dry stream bed. He put his thumb to his lip, thinking. He said, And Hanacek—who's that guy?

Arthur stared back. Why had he read that goal? He didn't talk about Hanacek to anyone except Morgan, who may have seen him but he couldn't be sure. Did he read that goal to Faulkner because he subconsciously wanted to talk about the old ghost? But if that were true, there were so many things he wanted to tell Fawk. So many things he wanted to tell someone, anyone, to let all that tension and worry flow out, like lancing the boil on your soul.

Fawk patted Arthur on the shoulder and picked up his cup. Tell you what, he said. Tell me about Hanacek another time. I should let you get to your planting. You know: Good friends pass the time, but true friends leave you to it.

The jays scolded Faulkner as he made his slow and contemplative walk home.

Arthur plotted out his vegetable garden with stakes and string. His plan, conceived with layout software, had curved rows of plants that weaved around each other. From above, it might have looked like a Peruvian geoglyph. The design provided sun exposure and wind protection optimized for each vegetable. It enabled transfer of nutrients among complementary plants—like the 'three sisters' of corn, beans, and pumpkins. It was all very ingenious and highly scientific and also likely to yield no difference in the harvest. The truth was, Arthur imagined walking Morgan through the garden on the perfect day. Curved paths just seemed more romantic.

He owned a seeder, which you could wheel along while gears and tines injected the seed at exactly the right depth. But this morning, Arthur preferred to do it by hand. The soil was cool and porous in his fingers. The sun warmed his back. Nearby, birds were staking claims among the nesting boxes. There would be two pairs of bluebirds, it seemed, and the English sparrows hadn't appeared yet. Fawk once said, Everything bad about America can be traced back to England, and that seemed kind of true, at least when you thought about birds. There was a mild breeze that rattled the high stems of the oaks beyond the gardens, drawing out their nascent buds. After a while, he stood up to stretch and look at his progress. The peas were planted now—they were the easiest and most satisfying. You put an actual pea into the soil, about an inch deep, and in a few weeks, plants would appear that would make peas just like you planted. It seemed too straightforward, too on-the-nose—but also miraculous. Every year when the seedlings appeared, Arthur was astonished.

What a day.

Then the gunfire began. Of course the neighbors started shooting, because that's what they did on nice days. Arthur pictured them waking up in union suits with the flap open, spitting phlegm, scratching their privates, staggering outside, tipping last night's bottle of moonshine, only to find it empty, chucking the bottle under the porch, looking up at the sky, and declaring, Nice day. Let's get the guns out.

Everything Arthur knew about guns he learned from his Gramps, who had a little truck farm outside Faire, IL, not far from the Wisconsin border. Arthur had spent most of his summers at Gramps's farm, especially after his mom died. On that idyllic 20 acres, he learned how to raise vegetables and prune trees and trap muskrats and catch bluegills and roll smokes. He also learned how to shoot. They shot starlings with a skeet-shot .22. They shot pheasants and rabbits with a double-barrel

20-gauge. They shot deer with 12-gauge rifled slug cartridges. And, for fun, they shot pumpkins in the fall with whatever gun was on hand.

Now, as a grown-up, it struck Arthur that they might have annoyed their neighbors with this shooting. It never occurred to him at the time, because to his nine-year-old self, a world beyond the 20 acres was inconceivable. But also, they always shot for a reason. And when that was done, they stopped shooting. They shot practical guns designed for farming and hunting. A gun was like any other tool, hung beside the shovels and axes.

These neighbors across the river, whoever they were, shot for some other reason. They shot assault rifles—you could tell by the staccato bursts of an automatic magazine. That was illegal, but laws didn't seem to matter. Don't tread on those guys. They shot some big guns, bigger than Arthur had ever handled—you could tell by the weight of the report, a boom not a crack. Sometimes it seemed like they were shooting at targets, three or four pops at at time, but then the shooting would turn willy-nilly, with several guns firing at once, and it was chilling. It drove Morgan away, those fuckers shooting. And it threatened the success of One Perfect Day, come to think of it, and so Arthur had to do something.

Right there, standing in his half-planted maze of a garden, he resolved to meet the neighbors. Just as the Fuglesens suggested he should. Just as he knew he would have to, but couldn't yet bring himself. Why was that? He wasn't afraid of them. Not specifically. He knew that with a quick conversation they would become actual people, like all people, not entirely bad, not entirely good. They would no longer be the monsters of his imagination. So why hadn't he gone over? Perhaps because that would mean acknowledging that the river, the back border of his property, was just like any other border, with neighbors, and not some wild frontier. Meeting the neighbors across the river was prosaic, and annoying, and that was not the best part of life. But it had to be done, for Morgan, for her Perfect Day.

The banks of the Sangamon River are host to a fast-growing, soft-wooded variety of maple. Some people called them 'water maples,' but that didn't seem right to Arthur. He kept forgetting to look it up. In any case, these maples were prone to splitting and dropping limbs in the river. Sometimes a tree would split right in half, right down the trunk, creating a kind of Jekyll and Hyde, or a Cloven Viscount, where the fallen half crossed the muddy waterway. These trees created great snags and dams, which collected more branches and debris during spring floods. You would see all kinds of human waste packed into the tangled mass of tree entrails. Some future archaeologist with access to these piles could reconstruct our culture in detail. After a season or two, the power of the water broke through the dams and created new ones somewhere else. And in this way the river was always changing, which was both good and bad, which is a heavy-handed metaphor for life, if you want to be judgmental.

Just such a snag persisted in the river bend behind Arthur's property, beside where he and Morgan had discovered the body on that fateful day. When Arthur carried the body with his tractor, he placed it beyond this snag, so it could float downriver. That was something not to think about. But the snag was still there. A water maple had fallen and it was particularly stubborn, so the whole river had to go through the sieve it created. Arthur hated this dam, to be honest, and he had fantasized blowing it up with the old dynamite Gramps always had on hand. The dam was in plain sight below the bluff where he wanted to build a little shelter for One Perfect Day—not a requirement but a nice-to-have. However, on this day, the damned dam provided a bridge by which Arthur could go visit the neighbors.

It was much more difficult to cross than you'd think. Most branches were soft and cracked under your weight. Twice he punched through and found himself straddling a log, his boot stuck in a tangle. So he switched to crawling, like the raccoons he'd seen down there. This worked better, but still his handholds sometimes broke and he dropped to his chest, staring down through the mess at an antifreeze bottle beside the head of a doll. But slowly, gradually, he made his way across the old river, where Abraham Lincoln had once envisioned a grand commercial waterway, where now there was a tiny, scrappy corridor of wildlife, decorated by the trophies of human consumption.

Once across, Arthur sat on the opposite bank and looked back at his bluff. The gunfire continued, in erratic bursts that made you think it might have finally stopped, and you relaxed a little, until it started up again. Even so, it was nice to see his property from this perspective. It was a scenic location, for this part of the world, and a shelter on that spot would be perfect for drinking wine and watching wildlife and maybe having a little chat with Hanacek. He would take down that creaky old swing and build a proper shelter. That is, once he got all the requirements done, which included subduing his neighbors somehow.

As Arthur stood up, his foothold on the bank slipped and he lost his footing. His phone fell out of his shirt pocket. When he picked it up, he saw that he had a message from Morgan.

A message from Morgan! Finally she had replied to him. Or maybe reached out about something else? This was monumental, thrilling, and also worrying. Arthur could only see the notification on his lock screen. There was a smear of mud over the camera, so the phone wouldn't unlock. As he wiped the screen and his hands on his shirt, he considered the possibilities. It was probably financial. Yes, probably—she always steered their check-in calls to this, the safe and sterile realm of their joint finances and practical shit. But maybe. Maybe she had been thinking of him and wanted to say hi. That wasn't too far-fetched—they were married for goodness sakes and she once loved him passionately. Or, at least with a little gusto. So it could be a simple 'hi, thinking of you.' On the other hand, it might be a message announcing her decision to divorce. A text would be a shitty way of doing this but maybe she had to because a conversation took too much courage. That was horrible. He would have no chance of creating the Perfect Day! What would he do then? Not to be dramatic, but what would he have to live for?

When the phone unlocked, Arthur saw the message.

Morgan wrote, *Have you seen this*

No punctuation, which she had started to drop since the separation. He didn't know why. She wrote, merely, *Have you seen this*

That was all. There must be a message missing. Cell coverage was horrible at his place, worse back by the river. He started to respond. He wrote, *What do you mean?* And then deleted it and said, *To what are you referring?* Which was awful. And then he just typed an ellipsis with a question mark, which he also deleted.

Another message came from Morgan. It was a link to their social app. He clicked it.

He scrolled through a long thread of posts, pictures and captions, organized under the hashtag #sangabody. The images were mostly of poor quality, pictures of a river, in every season. Each one showed a body floating in the river. An unrecognizable body, based on what he could see. But it was clearly a body, which assumed a variety of postures—sometimes it floated like a canoe, on its back, head pointed downriver. In other pictures, the arms and legs were bent comically, like a marionette. Sometimes the body was partially submerged, with the other half thrust out of the water, like an orphaned log.

Morgan wrote, *Look at the dates*

Then she wrote, *And the locations*

Arthur did as she said. For some reason, he began to write code in his head, creating a view that would take all these posts and put them on a map that also had graphical representation of time. Like an Edmund Tufte thing. If he did that, it would show a body moving gradually down the Sangamon river, from last fall through the winter and into this spring. The last post was from Lake Decatur.

Morgan wrote, *U there?*

Because he hadn't responded yet. Was he blowing it? He wrote, *Wow.*

That's it? Morgan wrote. *Just wow?*

He was blowing it. He wrote, *Sorry I mean wow this is crazy and thanks for letting me know. What do you think?*

You seriously don't get it?

No I get it, he wrote. *But, get what exactly?*

I assume you're joking

Do you think that's our guy?

'Our guy?'

Sorry, wrote Arthur. He tried to continue, but his fingers stalled.

Morgan wrote, *No I'm sorry. I'm freaking out and not giving you enough time to process this. Where are u*

Back by the river. On the opposite bank.

WTF are you doing there

Just visiting the neighbors.

You mean the shooters?!

Well, yeah.

You're friends now?

Oh no. I haven't actually met them yet.

There was a long pause and finally Morgan wrote, *Those posts show there's a whole meme out there, like a conspiracy group tracking sightings of a body on the river. And then also this…*

Morgan sent a link to Sheila Fuglesen's story about Armando Gallardo. This was Faulkner and Nancy's daughter. What did they know, then? Arthur scanned the article. There was a rush of anxiety. His mind slowed and became more acutely focused.

He wrote, *So last summer a farm worker Lupe Gallardo filed a report, which the cops ignored, and since then a body has been seen floating down the river.*

Morgan wrote, *Right - if you chart the movement of the body, you could track it back to our place at about the time. Like you could show this on a map*

I was thinking that too. Great minds. He added a smiley face.

Morgan didn't respond for a while. Then she wrote, *The thing is, they don't seem to have found each other. Like the #sangabody people don't know Lupe's story, and she hasn't seen them—or at least commented / posted*

Arthur couldn't tell what Morgan was suggesting, if anything. He wrote, *What are you suggesting?*

Immediately she replied, *I don't know I guess I'm just processing and wanted you to know*

It's good to hear from you, Arthur wrote.

Morgan didn't reply.

Arthur thought, fuck it, and sent her a heart.

Morgan did not reply.

The gun fire had stopped. Now, dogs were barking. At first, while he was messaging Morgan, Arthur ignored these barks. Dogs barked and howled through the woods all the time. So did coyotes. But these barks, coming from the direction of the gunfire, were more insistent. These dogs had an issue to protest, a bone to pick you might say, and their barks suggested they were working toward a common goal. These barks were coming closer, toward Arthur.

Then he heard human voices, calling low to each other, and commanding the dogs. They were close now—Arthur could hear them snap twigs on the forest floor. He looked back at his phone. Morgan had not responded. He considered, for a moment, turning and running away, scrambling back across the river and taking cover beyond his bluff. But why would he do that? That was insanity. He planned to meet the neighbors, and now that was going to happen, just in a different way than he imagined. He put the phone in his pocket, picked up a hefty stick, and walked toward the dogs.

FOUR

It was Mrs. Vogel's eighty-ninth birthday, and since there was no indication that any of her family would show up, Morgan and Nakeisha planned a celebration. Nakeisha had offered to pick some things up, but Morgan had insisted that she do the shopping. It was too easy to remain in the comfort of her apartment and Mrs Vogel's place. It took too much energy to get out into the city, still, and Morgan knew she needed to force new habits. People can get detached in cities—alone in a crowd, as they say. Standing at her door, showered, canvas bag in hand, Morgan felt the call of her bed. Come back, it said, you're safe here. No, no, Morgan said, I'm going. She turned the latches and went.

The Lawrence El stop was closed for construction, so she walked a few blocks from her apartment, up Sheridan, to catch the train at Argyle. It was already unusually warm for an April morning. The sun reflected off the weary pavement, and the air was so still and clear it made buildings look like hyperreal paintings. Trees glowed with green buds. There, you see? It's good to be out in the city. On a morning like this, it was easy to be hopeful, to be confident, adventurous, for tons of wicked little thoughts to merrily appear.

On the platform, as she searched her phone for new #sangabody posts, she became aware of a man watching her. It was strange how you could tell, peripherally, when a guy was checking you out. How you could tell if it was complimentary or creepy. This guy seemed complimentary, which was nice because, in her estrangement, Morgan had felt sexless and empty, like a spent cicada husk. She looked up at the man, ready to say hi or good morning, because that's okay in the Midwest, but saw at once that he was shocked by her eyes. Morgan was used to this, and so she smiled and shrugged, like yeah those are my real eyes.

The man, maybe ten years older, said, Sorry, I was just… I was thinking you were someone.

I am, said Morgan, last I checked.

She expected him to laugh, but instead he just looked uncomfortable. He kept sneaking looks at her eyes, and then glancing away, and then looking again. So he was one of those guys, who cast a spell over themselves. It was a shame, because in the lightness of the morning, she felt up for flirting. But these guys are too awkward to flirt. They're like rabbits who become aware a cat is lounging on the sundial. They assign a mystical importance to the encounter, and although that's flattering, in a way, it's not attractive.

When Morgan boarded the train, the man followed her and sat on the seat facing. Sorry, he said, do you mind? He had stopped looking at her entirely.

Have you decided if I'm somebody?

Oh, no. I mean yes of course. But no, not that somebody.

Shame, Morgan said, which was dumb because it was a flirt she didn't intend to pursue. But then also she knew he wouldn't respond. It was the last sputter of her morning randiness.

Morgan returned to her phone. There weren't any new #sangabody posts. She had been meaning to do a deeper search on the social app to see if she could find a trace of Lupe Gallardo. But the man's presence was getting to her, so at the Wilson stop she got off, walked up two cars, and found a new seat. It worked, and the man receded into the fabric of three million souls.

In Lakeview she walked to one of the last authentic German bakeries. What did it mean to be authentic? That was maybe a foolish notion, because cultures keep changing. You'd say an Italian restaurant known for its marinera sauce was authentic, but tomatoes didn't come to Italy until the 1500's so that sauce was new-fangled, relatively, and not at all authentic. Anyway, Morgan knew Mrs. Vogel liked the stollen from this place, which was called German Bakery. The girl behind the counter, who had a tiny bee tattooed on her cheekbone, asked How's your day going so far? And Morgan said, Just started – we'll see. And the girl said, Yeah I get you. Then she informed Morgan that they only made stollen around Christmas, so Morgan bought some strudel, which seemed cartoonish but it was the thought that counted.

Morgan got back on the Red Line and took it down to Fullerton, where she caught a bus heading west to Logan Square where there was a garden center that sold native plants. Not much time had passed since Morgan was a girl in this city, but even so her family would never have considered coming out to these neighborhoods. Now look at them! All spruced up and bustling, with trendy thrift shops, and mustache-grooming parlors, and two street poets sitting at a table on the sidewalk, wielding matching Remington typewriters, with a line of people waiting to order their poem. Who waits in line on a Tuesday morning to get a formulaic poem? Morgan does, that's who, because how could you not?

Her poet had one hemisphere of her head shaved, and from the other, thick, black hair down to her waist. One ear was riddled with piercings, while the other was unadorned. And so on. The girl called herself Janus, obviously. She asked Morgan a few personal questions and then said she could come back in ten minutes.

The garden center did have an impressive selection of native plants.

This was also crazy. When she was a girl, spending her summer afternoons in Mrs. Vogel's garden, it was all hostas and mums and hollyhocks. Now she was going to plant a pollinator's garden for Mrs. Vogel's birthday, which hopefully the old widow wouldn't mind too much, and right here in the city you could buy coneflowers and butterfly weed and a bunch of asters. Morgan filled a flat with more plants than she needed and went back to her poet.

Janus said, Do you want me to read it aloud for you?

That seemed too risky, exposing yourself in some streetside performance, so Morgan said, I'd rather just read it if that's all right? She took the poem, typed on an irregular-sized sheet of paper.

The poem read

Men die for your eyes
wicked lullabies, crows who loathe to fly
Welcome back to your city, cracked—a weary palm
read with aplomb, whacked until it stings
and when from your pupless den you sing
ancient seedlings resurrected, wish a life that's not dejected
too pretty to cry, too much of a hottie
the seedlings sigh
we hope you find your body

With the sun hot on her neck, Morgan felt her heart jump, a tingling wave spread across her skin. Of course it was a coincidence— that line about the body. Of course the poet, Janus, was just riffing on the theme of Morgan's appearance—of course it was a metaphor for Morgan coming to peace with herself. But still.

Janus waited, one eyebrow raised, the other shaved.

Morgan realized her expression might make Janus feel bad. She smiled and said, It's lovely. Thanks so much. How much do I owe you?

Janus said, Whatever you think it's worth.

But was it lovely? How do you know if a poem is good versus when it's drivel? Also, was this a poem or maybe rap lyrics, and also were those things basically the same? How can you really define a bunch of words in a certain order—isn't it all arbitrary?

Morgan realized that Janus was still waiting, and there was a line behind her. She realized she had no cash.

Do you take credit cards?

Janus laughed, holding out her hands, as if the answer should be obvious. Her partner, a blonde with tiny spectacles and a medieval dress, was reading a poem to another customer.

I'm so sorry, Morgan said, I'll come back.

Janus looked at Morgan's bakery bag with interest. What you got in there? she asked.

Oh, just some strudel.

I'll take a piece of that, Janus shrugged.

Morgan dutifully opened the bag, tore off the end-piece of the strudel, and placed it on one of the oddly-sized pieces of paper.

Awesome, said Janus.

Morgan stepped away, tucked her poem in her bag, collected her plants and pastry, and caught the bus.

On her way to Mrs Vogel's, a text arrived from an old high school friend, Ashleigh, who now lived in West Town. One of the few from her Whitney Young class who remained in the city. Since returning, Morgan had met Ashleigh once, for a Sunday brunch where they drank too many French 75s and reminisced, and summarized their lives, and then ran out of things to say. Afterward, Ashleigh kept inviting Morgan to do things, because that's how she was—a vast network of friendships kept aloft by sheer persistence—and Morgan kept declining, making excuses, drawing into herself.

Get a drink tomorrow? Ashleigh asked. *Some people I'd like you to meet*

The mischievous April sun shone on Morgan's face through the bus window. The mood of the day was so light, so deliciously peculiar, it was good to be out in the city. So Morgan wrote, *Sure I'd love to*

And Ashleigh replied, *Seriously???*

Morgan replied, *Don't be so surprised – I'm not a hermit*

To which Ashleigh sent an emoji of someone whistling, and although the intent was vague, Morgan added a laugh.

Ashleigh said *Okay meet at Sullivan's at 7 or whenever Miss Havisham lets you out.*

Morgan replied, *Nice*

And that was that.

Mrs Vogel rested in her wheelchair on the cobbles of the garden, while Morgan arranged the plants in one of the beds. The old woman's hair was done as usual and Morgan had tucked some baby's breath in it. Mrs Vogel had a mirthful energy, a bright and cheeky expression.

She said, You are the only one I would let plant weeds in my garden.

They're not weeds, Tante, Morgan replied, they're forbs. Native flowers.

Forbs, Mrs Vogel repeated. That's an ugly word. Vulgar in the mouth.

Morgan laughed. That's rich coming from a German.

Mrs Vogel said, So my garden will be full of bees now?

Hopefully!

And we are worried about bees these days? They are all dying? But your garden will save these bees?

Yes, Tante. If we plant these prairie plants in your little Chicago backyard, it will bring back bees all over the world.

Good, said Mrs Vogel. Then I approve.

Morgan opened the soil with a trowel, dropped in a coneflower, watered it, and returned the dirt. It felt cool on her hands. When she gardened, she felt connected to the planet, as if she were not some separate thing but rather a part entangled in the whole, sensing the pulse of life. If acupuncturists could detect illness by feeling your pulse, could you also feel the health of the earth by doing this? Also, it was crazy how the soil in this city lot was so nice, like original Illinois black dirt, while the ground back on their farm in Middling was horrible—infertile clay and rubble. Nothing is what you expect any more. Except a cardinal was singing from a sycamore next door. Cardinals were reliable.

You are quiet today, said Mrs Vogel. Are you thinking of your boy?

Morgan sat up. She dusted soil off her hands. Not really, she said. I was thinking about that cardinal.

You are not a city girl anymore.

No, I am. But maybe not. I don't know. Maybe I'm both. You ever miss the country?

I miss everything.

I suppose that's part of getting older. You get used to missing things.

Mrs Vogel reached up to adjust the baby's breath in her hair. She said, This is why we remember the good things. You remember helping in my garden when you were young, I think?

Of course, said Morgan. I learned a lot from you.

But you probably don't remember things with your parents so much. Why you spent so much time in my garden.

Morgan resumed planting. She didn't like where she had put a coreopsis, too close to a bergamot, so she dug it up.

I don't know, she said. It's hard to know what I actually remember versus what I've been told.

What do you think of your parents now? We don't talk about them, but we were neighbors all those years. It is a shame.

I don't talk with them very much, Tante. I've seen them each twice since I moved to the city. Probably I should try harder.

You didn't answer my question. Mrs Vogel leaned forward and peered at her.

Morgan staked her trowel and stood up to stretch. She crossed her arms then and thought, saying, Well unfortunately politics ruins everything now. My dad's so right-wing now I should despise him, but he's just an old rich dude and that's how they end up mostly. My mom is more complicated and maybe more despicable. She's very good at rationalizing things, making excuses for herself.

Morgan paused. The words were just coming out. Did this feel good? Was this cathartic? Would she regret it? It was hard to know, the energy of the day was so strong. She went on.

As far as I can piece together, my mom hooked up with another guy and she justified it by creating this story where she was miserable for her whole married life and my dad was emotionally abusive. But her narrative stuck—all their friends were like, Julian seemed like such a nice guy, a great philanthropist, but we guess he was tormenting Sharon the whole time. So then my dad got really sad, because he lost everything he loved, and then he got pissed and switched sides politically and made a bunch more money out of revenge, it seems like, and now here we are. But one thing I'll say about my dad—he didn't play to the stereotype, like getting a young hot wife or whatever. He just works all the time and lives with this sense of outrage.

Morgan was staring at a corner of Mrs Vogel's yard as she talked. There was a mulberry sapling back there she would need to cut. How was it possible to be confessing these horrible things while also assessing a garden? She looked at Mrs Vogel, and her tunnel vision expanded to normal, and she was embarrassed. Mrs Vogel still held her compassionate stare.

Sorry, said Morgan.

Mrs Vogel closed her hands into fists and said, There is nothing to be sorry for! You are having a hard time, and no wonder. But it's good for you to talk. Good to talk to your Tante.

That was too much. She turned and put her face into her sleeve, pretending she was wiping some dirt from her eyes. But she knew the old woman could tell.

Come, said Mrs. Vogel. Give me a hug on my birthday.

Morgan turned, and saw her Tante holding out her arms, and the sadness drained in a rush, replaced by the joy of having someone actually love you unconditionally. So she went to Mrs Vogel and hugged her down into the wheel chair, smelling her old lady perfume, feeling the softness of her weak muscles and the old bones beneath.

Afterward, Mrs Vogel said, Let's look at your weeds now. I want to know their names.

Morgan walked through them all, and the old woman listened with sharp attention.

You know a lot about this now, she said.

I guess I do.

You learned all this with your boy, down there in Middling, yes? You learned this together?

Yeah I guess we did.

Mrs Vogel nodded approval. She said, I learned about painting with Mr Vogel. We did that together and it was lovely.

Did you paint the portraits downstairs here?

Mrs Vogel dismissed this with a wave. No, those are by famous painters. She shrugged and added, Famous for their time.

Then where are your paintings?

Our paintings? What Karl and I did? Stowed away somewhere. I don't know.

Mrs Vogel was staring now at the corner where the mulberry grew. She continued speaking.

People think badly of Karl now, those who remember him, like your father. And he was very bad in some ways. But also very good. Like all men. You just have to decide.

Then Mrs Vogel came out of her thoughts and the merry look

returned to her eyes and she said, But you have met him, yes? Mr Vogel?

Well I remember him, but it's vague because I was so little.

No, said the old woman. I mean now. You have met him recently?

Morgan stared. Mrs Vogel's expression was inscrutable. Was she referring to his ghost? Were they having this conversation?

I'm not sure I follow, she said.

Mrs Vogel shrugged. Maybe not yet. But you will. Don't be afraid – he means no harm.

Morgan continued staring. There wasn't a good reply to this.

Mrs Vogel continued, But now I am tired. You take me inside for my nap, and then you can finish up here, and when I wake up, there will be bees.

At dusk, Morgan and Nakeisha rolled Mrs Vogel into the sun room where it was still warm from the fair day. They stuck a candle into the strudel and sang Happy Birthday. It was a mismatched duet—Morgan did her best but her singing seemed flinty next to Nakeisha's confident voice. As they sang, Mrs. Vogel moved her hand in time like an orchestra conductor, and smiled—but her eyes were moist. Then she leaned forward and puffed out the candle and they watched the smoke writhe up toward the antique light.

Nakeisha said, Look at you—old girl can still blow!

Then, when they considered it, they laughed like naughty coeds.

Mrs. Vogel pointed a gnarled finger at each of them in turn and said, I am not too old to get your drift. Don't forget people have always been saucy. Read Shakespeare—or Chaucer!

Nakeisha put her fists on her hips and smiled down at Mrs. Vogel. How's it feel to be eighty nine years old, Helen?

Mrs. Vogel raised a piece of strudel to her lips and her hand trembled. That was unusual. She chewed a while and then said, It feels exactly as it did to be nineteen, except that I'm stuck in this Scheisse old body. I still want to run. I still think of men in that way. It's all there. The spirit of a girl trapped in a corpse. God has some sense of humor.

Morgan put her hand on Mrs. Vogel's shoulder. She couldn't think of anything to say.

But Nakeisha, mercifully, always did. She wagged her head and said, But Helen, you're wise now! Every day I learn something from you. That's how God rewards us for getting old—he makes us wise. Then we can pass it on to young people—who don't listen!

Nakeisha and Morgan laughed again. But Mrs Vogel did not. She stared at the remaining pastry on her plate.

When you are old like me, she said, I hope you have good children.

It was clear what was on her mind. The daughter had sent Mrs Vogel a card, baroque and generic, with only a signature. There was nothing from the son. What do you say to that?

Nakeisha said, I'm sorry you don't hear more from your kids. There's no excuse for letting your mama's birthday pass. But you know everybody is so busy now. I bet they come around eventually.

When I'm dead? said Mrs Vogel, her eyebrows lifted.

Nakeisha shook her head sadly. Sometimes that's what it takes. But they love you, anyway. You just have to have faith in that.

Mrs Vogel snorted, and then took a large bite of the pastry. She said, mouth full, I'm too old for faith.

Morgan said, Oh gosh, I forgot about the tea! Should I make some tea?

Mrs Vogel continued, I have nothing now but memories and money and this old house. The memories will go with me. The money and the house… eh.

With that, she waved her hand bitterly.

I think we should have that tea, said Nakeisha. You put the pot on, Morgan, and I'll keep the birthday girl company.

Morgan left, relieved. But also disappointed she was so bad at difficult conversation. How do you get better at that. As she left the room she heard Nakeisha say,

Your garden looks nice. You and Morgan do that?

Mrs Vogel said, That was my Nichte. She's a good girl.

Back on the Argyle platform, the train was late. A breeze had lifted off the lake and Morgan pulled her jacket collar around her neck. A man in ragged clothes staggered down the platform toward her. Morgan took out her phone as cover. What did people do in these situations before phones? Smoked, probably. She searched for the usual things. No new #sangabody posts. But there—Sheila Fuglesen's article had been updated. Now there was a link. It went to the site of a Middling Attorney, Peg Hanrahan. There was a new post titled, *Have you seen this man?* There was a photo of Armando Gallardo—the first Morgan had seen of him. Sheila Fuglesen's original article left out any pictures, reportedly at the wife's request. But Lupe must have changed her mind. Armando had a grand, toothy smile creased into angular features. He had dense, black hair. He had copper skin. Morgan had seen this face before, though certainly not smiling. She had seen that face on the man dumped on their property near the river on the day she left Arthur. There was no doubt.

Peg Hanrahan's post asked for any information about Armando, whether he had been seen alive, whether his body had been found. Any tips would be of great help to the bereaved, she said. Any leads would be treated anonymously. Morgan tried to read more about Hanrahan. She was a defense attorney. She did pro bono work for the migrant community. But Morgan couldn't concentrate to read now. And where was the train?

Why was she so anxious about this? She let her arm drop, holding the phone, and looked down at the street. The man in ragged clothes had left the station. He shuffled down the sidewalk, past the bourgeoise shops and tidy bars. Why didn't she just reach out to Peg Hanrahan right now and tell her that she and Arthur had seen the body back in the summer? That would be the right thing to do. Then they'd know Armando had died. Then they could get the police more involved, maybe. Well of course that would be the right thing to do. But then, how would they explain that they hadn't told anyone about the body until now? You could say that you were in the middle of a marriage crisis and this incident kind of got lost in the shuffle, but that sounded lame. Who just forgot about finding a dead body on their property? There would be questioning, and Arthur would get dragged into it, and the farm would become a suspicious scene, and maybe she'd have to go down and answer questions too. And what about what happened after they found the body? Arthur's vague explanations would sound pretty weird to a lawyer or a cop. Who just left a body on the back of their property until a flood washed it away? She and Arthur did, apparently. So this is how normal people got drawn into criminal situations. No one is prepared for how to deal with these things. We wait, and we procrastinate, and we hide, and we turn away and go back to our lives.

As she messaged Arthur, Morgan had this foolish sense that she was creating a 'paper trail,' but she wrote anyway, *Look at this*, and added a link to Peg Hanrahan's page.

Arthur replied immediately, *Morgan! What a nice surprise!*

For fuck's sake, what was wrong with him. Morgan wrote, *Did you look at that link*

After a pause, Arthur wrote back, *Shit*.

Exactly, wrote Morgan.

Arthur didn't reply. She could see him typing and then stopping and then nothing.

I feel like we should reach out to Lupe, Morgan wrote.

Yeah maybe but what would we say?

Morgan typed furiously, making and correcting mistakes, *That we know where her husband's body is, dumbass*

Arthur didn't reply. Morgan waited. Her heart slowed down. She wrote, *Sorry, that was unkind. I'm just a little freaked out rn*

Understandable, wrote Arthur. *NP*

Then they both waited. Finally, Arthur said, *Faulkner my neighbor has a lawyer friend who comes down here sometimes. I could talk with him—just hypothetically?*

You trust him? Morgan asked. Just writing that, she realized the question was really whether she trusted Arthur.

Well he and Fawk are really close and I trust Fawk so

Morgan heard and felt the rumble of the train coming, finally. She looked at her phone, then up at the lights of the train.

You still there… Arthur wrote.

Sorry – trains coming, wrote Morgan

So, the lawyer—you think I should try him out – carefully?

As Morgan stepped into the train, she wrote, *Ok*

The train was crowded, but she found a seat next to a woman holding a French bulldog. The animal panted uncontrollably and looked at Morgan as if he expected something.

Morgan looked back at her phone. There were five new messages from Arthur. He wrote

Okay cool I will look into that, but don't worry I'll be cautious.

Not that it's your problem really.

No offense. Pls don't take that as shitty –just saying you don't live here so are removed.

You still there?

I meant to tell you—I met the neighbors. Across the river. They seem all right.

Okay, I guess we'll talk Sunday. Love you

Morgan locked the phone and closed her eyes and felt the rocking of the train.

FIVE

When Arthur told Morgan the new neighbors seemed all right, that was not strictly true.

Standing on the other side of the river, his hands and boots slick with mud, he saw the dogs come first. Two of them, leaping through the dried grass and bramble, what looked like a coonhound and a rottweiler. When they got within 20 yards, they stopped barking and trotted up to Arthur. The coonhound rubbed his head on Arthur's thigh. The rottweiler bowed and pranced in an invitation to play. Arthur scratched the dog's head.

Three men followed the dogs. The oldest, perhaps in his fifties, wore camouflage trousers and blaze orange suspenders over a t-shirt. He had a wide smile with gapped, stained teeth. A young man, probably his son, looked at Arthur critically, arrogantly. He wore a flat-brimmed baseball hat with a strange logo like an eagle. The third man wore black pastor's robes and Wellington boots. He lifted his robes as he walked, choosing his steps carefully. The other two tromped ahead of the pastor.

Don't mind the dogs, yelled the older man. They don't bite or nothing.

They all breathed heavily as they reached Arthur. The older man called to the dogs, Custer! Jackson! Go on, git!

The dogs steered away and followed some new scent along the river.

Arthur saw now that the older man and his son carried pistols in holsters, tight against their hips. The pastor clasped his hands behind his back and looked up at the tree canopy.

The older man said, You're lucky we didn't put a bullet in you, sneaking up on us over the river like that.

Arthur looked at the man's eyes to see if he was joking—hard to tell. The eyes were dark, nearly hidden between a heavy brow and fleshy cheeks. The man had a build like a troll, round and solid and neckless. The son was a replica, just younger.

Well, Arthur said, I guess you're also lucky you didn't shoot me. I mean, that would have been problematic you know?

The older man laughed silently and looked at his son and then at the pastor. The son released a sarcastic snort. The pastor smiled pleasantly and looked back the way they came.

The man said, I reckon you have a point.

He held out his hand and said, Bradley Martin. This is my son Donnie, and our new Pastor—Ravelin Magpie.

Arthur wiped his hands on his pants and then shook their hands, one by one. It felt like it took a long time. Bradley's calloused grip was like a vise. Donnie's shake surprisingly limp, an afterthought. The pastor's fingers were long and warm.

I'm Arthur Prendergast. I live across the way.

Bradley said, The old Hanacek farm. You've been there what—a year now?

Two years actually.

It was the first time Arthur had heard anyone refer to his place as Hanacek's. So many people had owned it since. Did Bradley know about the ghost farmer? Maybe all sorts of people did? It occurred to Arthur that you can't necessarily keep a ghost to yourself. That was interesting to consider but probably not now.

Two years, said Bradley. It seemed to interest him, and he nodded slowly, then turned his head and spat.

Donnie looked at his father. He said, I don't think you need me here I'm gonna head back.

Bradley dismissed him with a backward wave. Donnie shrugged, gave the pastor a tip of his head, and slouched back across the field. The dogs appeared from the river in great leaps and followed him.

Arthur said, I've been meaning to come by and say hello. He paused, then added, We didn't want to sneak up on you, you know?

Bradley reached out and clapped down on Arthur's shoulder. He leveled his gaze at him and said, Funny guy, there you go. You're all right.

Arthur responded with a kind of friendly punch, but partway lost faith in the gesture, and let his arm fall short. Why did he feel uncomfortable? It was annoying, to not be confident in these situations. His Gramps would not have been uncomfortable. He was the boss with all his neighbors.

Did you know Hanacek, the old farmer? Arthur asked. That was better—control the conversation.

Bradley laughed. How old do you think I am?

He turned to Ravelin and said, Pastor, how old do you reckon he thinks I am—a hundred?

The pastor looked surprised to be addressed. He tilted his head, considering, and said, Generally speaking, it's not good practice to speculate what's in a man's mind. Or in his heart, for that matter.

Ravelin's voice was extraordinary, carrying multiple tones at once—a smooth and fluid baseline with a sharp treble over the top. Like an excellent red wine. Did that make sense? Yes it did, to Arthur, but maybe it wouldn't translate to others, the way similes are sometimes only useful to whoever's saying it, but still—you wanted to hear more of that voice. He smiled at Arthur with profound empathy, the creases of his turquoise eyes meeting the dimples around his cheeks. He had curly blonde hair in need of a cut but stylish. It was a face that could be easily caricatured, like he should be famous.

Bradley squinted at him, disappointed, but he said, That's fair.

Sorry, said Arthur. Just that nobody really talks about Hanacek that I know of.

Well, said Bradley, that guy was kind of a legend, stubborn old fart, working the land with those mules. Made a fortune nobody knew about until his kids started to show it and moved away. That's what folks say anyway.

This was interesting. Arthur said, Hard to imagine anyone making a fortune on our place.

Bradley shrugged. He said, Lot of ways to make a buck. Lot of irons in the fire, I reckon.

The pastor was studying Arthur now. What's your profession, Arthur? If I may ask.

The question made him anxious. He never knew how to answer it. There was the way he made money, of course, but then there was the way he spent most of his time. It should be a simple answer—why did he complicate it?

I'm a web developer, he said. I make websites.

Bradley smirked. You one of those high tech millionaires?

The pastor looked at Bradley, curiously, then turned back to Arthur. That's important work, he said, Helping people share their message.

I guess so, said Arthur. But I'm definitely not a millionaire.

Immediately he regretted saying this. Faulkner had a saying about holding your cards carefully. Easier said than done. Faulkner also talked about how you learn a lot from people if you just encourage them a little.

Arthur said, Did you know the folks who lived on my place before?

Bradley looked over Arthur's shoulder, in the direction of Failure Farm. He said, There's been a lot of folks lived over there. The place is…

well… you must know.

Bradley narrowed his eyes and studied Arthur.

What must I know? Arthur asked. Sorry, I don't follow.

The pastor smiled, possibly amused. It made Arthur feel like he had done something well.

Bradley glanced at the pastor, then back at Arthur. Oh, he said, I shouldn't be bringing up rumors like a washerwoman.

That was a weird old-timey expression. Were there still washerwomen? Did they still gossip? Arthur smiled pleasantly and nodded, waiting.

Bradley made a dismissive expression, Lot of people passing through your place over the years, I guess. Hard to make a go of it since the old man passed away.

Arthur opened his face and continued nodding, as if this were all new and fascinating. Ravelin watched him, mirth in his eyes.

Bradley continued, You know people haven't cared for the old place much, some folks kind of considered it a dumping ground or what have you. You must have seen a thing or two?

Arthur thought of the body, and his pulse jumped. But no, he couldn't be talking about that. You wouldn't just bring that up. It had to be about all the junk that seemed to bubble out of the soil. Arthur said, Oh yes, lots of stuff. I've hauled truck loads of old junk off our place. But it's all right—some of it valuable old scrap. Extra income, you know?

A wave of incredulity passed over Bradley's face. Then he recovered. Well good for you, son! Good for you. Nice to have neighbors sticking it out. Keep the property values up, as they say. With so many undesirables coming down from Chicago or up from the border—you know what I mean?

The pastor cleared his throat and reached down, snapped a stem of dried grass, and inspected it. Bradley kept his gaze on Arthur.

This is the point in a conversation when you change the subject.

So is there a Mrs. Martin? Arthur asked.

After a moment of confusion, Bradley smiled, Oh yes, yes, Karen Martin. Donnie's mother, the true saint. Donnie's got four older brothers too, all of em off on their own. Except for one, who's dead.

How do you respond to this? On the one hand, you should express delight at the mention of Karen, and show interest in meeting her—but then there was the sudden tragic reference, so flippant, so weird. Arthur wanted to address each point, like a bulleted list, with appropriate responses for each one, until the list was complete, but conversation doesn't work that way, sadly. So instead he just let his head bob and said, I see. I see.

How about you, Bradley declared. Is there a Mrs….

Prendergast, Arthur said.

That's right—is there a Mrs. Prendergast?

There is, Arthur said. He felt a swell of other information come up to his throat, but he only repeated, There is.

Well maybe we get the missuses together some time, yeah? Have you folks over.

The pastor, holding the stem of grass between fingertips, drew in a breath. He said, Actually, maybe Arthur would like to join us at the Forest Service?

He exchanged a look at Bradley, who flinched, but then nodded slowly.

Good idea, Bradley said, A church service, Arthur, we have every year in our woods back here. It's a nice time. Coming up on a few weeks. Good opportunity to meet folks.

The pastor smiled in approval. All are welcome, he said.

Well maybe not all, said Bradley, and laughed abruptly.

The pastor shook his head, possibly in disapproval? He added, Only the willing.

Sounds good, said Arthur. Thanks.

The bark of a dog came through the woods, and Arthur saw the two hounds trotting back towards them.

Welp, said Arthur, I don't want to keep you.

Nice to meet you Arthur Prendergast, said Bradley. Next time, let us know you're coming, and you won't get any holes in you.

I like your dogs, Arthur said.

The two men paused to look at him. It was a strange thing to say, Arthur realized—it's just what he was thinking.

The pastor smiled. And they like you, he said.

Bradley turned, whistled to the dogs, and gave a low wave for Arthur to contemplate. The pastor put his hands behind his back and followed, looking up at the trees, stepping high in his wellington boots.

SIX

At Sullivan's it was loud. From the sidewalk outside the tavern's window, Morgan could hear them playing the Pogues. She could hear the roar of young people talking and laughing over the music. Sullivan's was one of so many Irish-themed bars in residential neighborhoods, brass and Kelly-green, on a cozy corner with apartments upstairs. Did Irish people own all these bars? Maybe they once did. Once Irish people were the victims of discrimination. Now everybody claimed to be a little Irish. The people in the window didn't look Irish. They looked pleased to have nabbed the window seats. There were empty pint glasses on their table with a set of darts in a case. They didn't notice Morgan. She could turn away and go home now, text Ashleigh with regrets and curl up on her bed with a book. Ordinarily that would be tempting, but now it seemed suddenly so depressing. Morgan pushed aside the plastic curtain in front of the door, and gripped the brass door handle, and went inside.

It was shocking—the noise and the heat and the scent of stale beer and perfume. People were lined deep around the bar and pressed among the tables. It had been a while since Morgan was in a place like this. Years maybe? Arthur didn't like places like this, though when he was forced to go he became the life of the party. His face turned red when he drank and his voice got hoarse. Arthur probably was a little Irish actually. But Arthur was in Middling now and if Morgan kept thinking about that she would not be in the frame of mind she needed for this night. There, in the back, at a high table, she saw Ashleigh with some friends.

Ashleigh waved merrily, calling Morgan over, and the friends looked up—two girls and a boy, and Morgan made her way, excusing herself, avoiding beer spilling on her coat, and finally got to the table, where they had saved her a stool.

Ashleigh's hair was pink now. It was hard to remember what her hair color was originally, in high school—probably a dark blonde? She introduced her friends. Katie and Maddie worked with her at a PR firm downtown. They had to shout, repeating themselves, and Morgan missed which one was Katie and which one was Maddie, and then it was too late to clarify. One was tall and dark-haired with Romanesque features. The other was round and cute and wore her blonde hair in a pixie cut.

And this is Lawrence, yelled Ashleigh, we call him Larry! He goes to our gym!

They moved so Morgan could squeeze into her stool, sitting across from Larry. He smiled and you could see his upper lip was slightly twisted from a scar. His hair was cut short but so dense it stood up, very black, and he was unshaven with equally-dense whiskers. People called that a five o'clock shadow, from the days when men shaved twice a day. Another word that described him was hirsute. Wasn't that the word? Another word that came to mind was swarthy, because of his dark complexion, but you weren't supposed to say swarthy now, right? Morgan smiled back at him and accepted a beer from the server, who let it splash as she reached over the table. Morgan drank half of the beer quickly.

I was just telling them, Ashleigh shouted, that you know every plant in the world! Like I can just grab a plant from the side of the road and say what's this, and you're like: that's blahblahopsolis crapolopsis!

Clearly Ashleigh was already drunk. She had started drinking when they were sophomores and hadn't stopped. Her tolerance was astonishing.

Morgan laughed and shook her head to deny Ashleigh's claim. She drank the rest of the beer and looked for the server. It didn't seem so loud or so warm anymore. This is why we drink—to tolerate intolerable situations.

She became aware of Larry across the table. He raised his beer glass to her and said, Getting down to business. He smiled again, and it was strange because she could hear his low-register voice more easily than the voices of the women. His eyes were brown like stained wood, with sleepy lids. But also bright, amused.

The girls were still talking about plants. Possibly Katie said, That's so cool that you know plants! It's like you live in a different world. I'm just like…Katie put on a dumb voice and said, That's a tree, that's a bush, that's a flower…

Oh my god, guys! said possibly Maddie, I got poison ivy once! It was the worst! And you know where I got it?

Ashleigh looked at her with eyes wide. Nooooooo, she said.

Maddie nodded and pointed down at her lap.

Shut up! Said Katie.

Seriously, said Maddie. I was on a picnic with Jaden in Caldwell Woods and I sat under a tree… It was not fun!

Morgan, Morgan! said Ashleigh, what's the official name of poison ivy?

Morgan squinted into her glass. She looked up and said, Toxicodendron radicans. It was just luck she knew this, because once she and Arthur looked it up, to see if it was related to virginia creeper.

See! yelled Ashleigh, and slapped the table.

You're just making that up, said Maddie or Katie.

Morgan shrugged. Look it up, she said. The girls studied their phones.

The server brought more beers. She had a tattoo of a tulip on the back of her hand. The beer was from a local brewery and honestly very good. It had been a long time since Morgan was drunk but maybe it was necessary. She saw Larry looking at her, kindly, and she wiped her lower lip and shrugged.

Just thirsty, she explained.

He leaned forward, and said, You don't need to shout. I can hear you.

Sorry, said Morgan. I'm not drunk, really. It's just the shock of transition from outside.

She was overexplaining again.

I know, Larry said. I can tell. You don't seem like the drunken type.

Morgan tilted her head and said, You might be surprised.

She took another long drink, keeping her eyes on him. Why was she doing this? It didn't make much sense, but neither did this whole situation.

So you're a biologist? He asked.

No, said Morgan. That's just a hobby. I'm a nurse, professionally. Or, technically.

Technically? Larry was able to smile and maintain eye contact while he sipped his beer. The scar creased his lip. He had an accent that was hard to place—a little drawly but also lilting.

I mean I'm not a nurse right now. I mean sort of. I tend to an elderly woman.

Morgan did not want to tell that story now, so she said, How about you? What do you do?

I'm an astrophysicist.

Morgan laughed. No really, she said.

No, I really am. I'm an astrophysicist. I have a grant right now, working at the Planetarium.

He was earnest, this Larry. Strangely humble, taking no offense at

Morgan's incredulity.

So you're not from Chicago?

Larry laughed. He drained his glass and set it down, leaning toward her. Not even close. I'm barely American. I'm from Louisiana. Lake Charles.

Ah, said Morgan. She received another beer over Katie's shoulder and placed it symmetrically on a Sullivan's coaster.

You know Lake Charles?

Of course, said Morgan. They looked at each other and laughed, though there was no joke.

Where is it? he asked. He was teasing now.

East of Houston, Morgan said. McNeese State is there. There had been an atlas of the fifty states at Mrs Vogel's, in her son's room, long ago. Sometimes it was nice to look at the far-away states and imagine going there. Once she spilled kool-aid on the Louisiana page and as she wiped it up, she noticed McNeese State, such a peculiar name. This is how we remember things.

Larry reached out and touched her wrist. His hand was warm. I'm impressed! he said. You know your geography and your botany!

It felt good to be praised, even though you shouldn't feel good just to be praised, because flattery is the easiest way to con someone. She scratched the top of her head with her fingertips—a habit from all her life. Larry noticed.

What's this? he asked, and pantomimed her scratching.

I don't know, said Morgan. You tell me. It made no sense but that was no longer necessary.

It's like a monkey, Larry said, and he scratched his head while the other hand scratched his armpit.

Morgan imitated him imitating her. She scratched her head and armpit. She made a monkey face and said 'ooo-ooo.' Why was she acting like a monkey with this guy? But it was fun and liberating—a contrast with all the heavy, repressed emotions of these past months. She felt the blood rush to her skin, a blush coming up on her face as they laughed together and their eyes watered. They were being monkeys together and everyone else in the bar had disappeared.

When that was over, Morgan asked, Why do you say you're barely American?

Larry's expression became serious as he gave that thought. Morgan heard Ashleigh blurt, Cause he's a Cajun! Larry the lonesome Cajun!

All three girls were watching now. I love that accent, said Maddie. Say 'I guarantee.'

Larry grinned and let his head wag, playing the part. He said, I gaire-ohn-tee, in a cartoon Cajun. He added, Laissez les bon temps rouler.

Oooh, French too, cried Katie.

Talk about, replied Larry.

We should road trip down there! said Ashleigh. Who's up for a road trip? Right now!

Let's do a shot first, said Maddie. Where's the waiter?

The girls turned their attention to hailing the server with the tulip tattoo.

To answer your question, Larry said to Morgan, I've lived in a lot of places. So I don't really feel American. Especially these days.

Like where? Morgan asked. It was nice to be just the two of them talking again.

Well, France is one place. I studied there.

At the Sarbonne? Morgan pronounced it with exaggerated French. It was the only school she could think of.

Larry peered at her. As a matter of fact, yes, he said. You have some kind of instinct?

It's the only French school I could think of, she said.

Ah, said Larry. You're honest too.

They looked at each other for a moment—too long. He didn't seem affected by her eyes, Morgan realized. She didn't want to be the first to look away, but eventually she had to.

I could use a smoke, said Larry. You want to join me?

You smoke? Like a cigarette?

Sometimes. Are you judging me? He narrowed one eye, and his lip creased in a smile.

Well I guess it's better than vaping—like, more authentic. But it will take years off your life.

That's your medical opinion?

That's common knowledge.

Larry was standing up, putting on his jacket. He had the pack of cigarettes in his hand. Standing up, he was only about her height—she had expected him to be taller. He said, A few human years are nothing, in astronomical terms. But a good smoke now, well that's something.

He tapped his hand on the table and eased his way toward the door. It was a hokey line to be sure. But also, if he were really an astrophysicist—which he probably was—he might actually feel that way. The universe doesn't care if we smoke. Morgan turned to Ashleigh and the two friends. They were playing a game where they put their hands in the center of the table and then tried to smack them with their free hand. They did something like that in high school, but Morgan couldn't remember how it worked. They paid no attention to her. It would be nice to get some fresh air. What would a cigarette feel like, after so many years?

She took her coat and followed Larry out the door.

SEVEN

Meanwhile, back on Failure Farm, Arthur stoked a fire in a stone ring near the woods. Under a gibbous moon, on a windy Saturday night, the fire glowed red on the faces of his guests—Nancy and Faulkner and their lawyer friend, Timothy Gardner. All three had attended Middling College together in the 80s, and Arthur could see the bond they had forged. Timothy was a solidly built fellow with a cherubic face and he had difficulty sitting still.

Maybe we leave the fire alone for a while, counsellor, said Faulkner. Here, have a little more whiskey.

Timothy looked with chagrin at the branch he was attempting to split with his foot, then set it aside and sat in a sling chair next to Nancy and held out his cup.

Nancy raised her hand and said, Wait, there's that sound again. Listen.

They sat in silence, witnessing the crack of the fire and the rustle of the branches overhead. Then the sound came again—a wheezing, growling panting from back by the river. It raised the hair on your neck.

What the fuck, said Timothy. His eyes popped in the firelight.

Maybe I should go get my .22, Arthur said.

Faulkner put his hands on his knees, Guns don't typically solve problems, he said, maybe we just take a look first.

Arthur turned on his spotlight and the beam cast a ray into the sky as far as you could see. Dust from the wind came through the beam. Arthur focused it where they heard the sound. He and Fawk walked to the edge of the woods, scanning. There was a crash of branches on the forest floor and then nothing.

Back around the fire, Fawk topped off their whiskeys. You ever hear something like that before, Arthur?

Not really, but you hear lots of strange sounds back here. Everything sounds more ominous on a night like this. But honestly it could have been a deer, like a sick one. Or maybe one of the neighbors' dogs.

Who you met? said Nancy. You were going to tell us about that.

Oh, right, Arthur said. He didn't feel prepared to talk about it— there were so many things he wished he had said differently.

Well, said Fawk, tell us!

Yeah, no, well there wasn't much to it.

Arthur told them about the encounter as best he could. It was tempting to revise it, to make himself seem better, but these were his friends so he stuck to his recollection.

Well that sounds a bit creepy, Nancy said.

Faulker was stirring the fire with a branch. Sparks flew up on the thermals and drifted into the night. He said, You tell a good story, Arthur.

Arthur squinted. Praise made him uncomfortable. It's just what happened, he said.

Fawk said, Maybe one day you write a little book about everything here.

Maybe. But I have plenty to do now.

Nancy pulled a fleece blanket around her shoulders. She asked, Did you talk with them about all the shooting?

I didn't. Sorry. Arthur realized that this was a failure not only in following through for his friends, but also in securing peace for his perfect day. If they started shooting while Morgan was there, well, that would be it.

One step at a time, said Faulkner. You know, men change their ways in increments too small to measure.

Nancy gave him a look. Not your best, Fawk, she said.

Timothy was back on his feet, trying to break the stick in half. I don't know how you guys live here, he said. I mean the land is great, but the people…

Well, that's America, said Arthur. Once he had said it, he wasn't sure what he meant.

A church service in the woods, Nancy said. That should be interesting. Good for you meeting them, though, Arthur. That took some confidence, with the guns and all.

Arthur shrugged, and drained his cup. He wanted to be done with this topic. They're just neighbors, he said.

It's a beautiful night, Nancy said. I'm still not used to it, living in nature like this.

Timothy balanced more branches on the fire and wandered toward the woods looking for more.

Fire's good for now, Tim! said Faulkner. Build it too high, you'll scorch us.

From the darkness Timothy called, For later. You always need more than you think.

Nancy tilted her head back, eyes closed, wind blowing her big hair. The light was flattering. She must have been a catch in her day. She was a catch now, really.

Nancy opened her eyes to see Arthur looking at her. She smiled. Are you missing Morgan?

Arthur shrugged. He held out his cup for Faulkner to fill.

It's okay to miss her, Nancy said. Okay to say so.

Leave the lad, said Faulkner. He filled the cup to the top.

Arthur drank. She would like this, he said. She always loved nights by the fire.

Nancy watched him. Have you asked her yet? To your big day?

No, said Arthur. He was going to explain but didn't. It was hard to imagine her saying yes right now. It was hard to imagine anything going right. Sometimes your mood comes down so darkly and so hard. Probably the whiskey didn't help. You should start meditating or something but who has the time.

Waiting for the right time, I'm sure, Nancy said. That's all right. She closed her eyes again and wrapped the blanket more tightly.

Timothy dropped a pile of branches near the fire and fell into his chair. There, he sighed, that should keep us for a bit.

They sat for a while, listening to a breeze in the treetops, and the rush of the river over the bluff. Arthur became aware that his front was hot from the fire, while his back was cold. The gibbous moon was now high overhead—how long had they been sitting there? The horizon wobbled, and Arthur remembered what he had promised Morgan.

Faulkner crossed his legs at the ankle and leaned back. He said, This business with the missing man, the farm worker, it's a damned thing.

Arthur's heart jumped. He felt a rush of sobriety.

Oh let's not talk about that now, said Nancy.

What missing man? asked Timothy.

Faulkner looked at Nancy, who shook her head in resignation. He said, A man went missing last summer, or fall maybe? He was pretty well known around here, a migrant worker, eccentric guy. His wife reported it but they came up with nothing—didn't try really, it sounds like—and he's still not found.

Timothy peered over his cup. Where was he seen last?

Leaving his trailer, I guess, early morning. Not far from here, in the park by the highway. His wife said he went foraging, which he liked to do.

Hmm, said Timothy. And they did a proper search, dogs and everything?

I don't think so, said Faulkner. Law enforcement being what it is.

They usually wait a few days, said Timothy, because most people turn up on their own.

Well, he didn't. Peg Hanrahan is on the case now.

Ah Peg, said Timothy. Haven't seen her for years. Pro bono, I assume?

Mm, said Fawk.

Nancy asked, Arthur do you know these folks?

No. I never met them. Alls I know is what I read in Sheila's article.

They were silent for a while. Now was the time, if ever.

Timothy, Arthur said. Can I ask you a hypothetical question?

Of course, said Timothy, and I guarantee you a hypothetical reply.

Well, Arthur said, it's just something I started wondering, after reading about it. About the law. It's weird, you know, how he just never turned up. Maybe he's dead now?

That's a safe guess, said Timothy. Unfortunately.

Right. So somebody must have found the body, don't you think? Well what if they found it and didn't know what to make of it. But then for some reason, they moved it. Just to some other spot. Maybe that's why he's still missing.

Timothy said, Interesting thought. What's the question.

Would the people who found the body, who moved it—would they be in trouble? Like legally guilty somehow?

Nancy drew in a breath. You have a vivid imagination, Arthur.

No, no, said Timothy. Great question. It's a tricky one. If they stole the corpse, intentionally, it would be considered Abuse of Corpse, which is a felony. But if they just moved it, and then left it, that's harder to prosecute, I'd say. Are we assuming it was a murder?

Arthur raised his cup to his lips and discovered that it was empty. He said, I don't know, what do you think.

Let's assume it was, said Timothy, for the purposes of our thought experiment. In that case, if it's murder, then there's a remote chance the people who moved the corpse could be considered accomplices. You know…

Timothy sat up straighter, his enthusiasm growing. He continued, But even if there weren't a conviction in criminal court, there could be a civil case involved—I love this one, not sure it's relevant, but I have to tell you. If the plaintiffs—say, family of the deceased—if they raised a civil case for murder they would only have to prove with clear and convincing evidence (not the more strict criminal standard). The burden of proof is less. And if it's the loss of a spouse—this is the good part—if someone kills your spouse, you can try them in civil court under the common law civil action of 'loss of consortium.'

Loss of consortium, said Faulkner. That is a grave loss indeed.

Okay, okay, said Nancy.

It is strange they haven't found him, said Timothy. In a small town like this.

It's a real shame, added Arthur. That's for sure. It was hard to know if he sounded sincere.

Arthur's heart was pounding, the pleasant drunken cloud lifted. Everything was hyper-real and clear. There it was, the verdict. They were fucked. How do you end the party now? He needed to walk, to think, maybe to text Morgan and tell her.

Faulkner looked at Arthur for a long time. Finally he said, You look tired, son. We shouldn't be keeping you.

Nancy was watching too.

Arthur said, Yeah, no, I'm fine. Sorry for the weird question. Sometimes your mind just goes on these things. After reading Sheila's article. Probably should turn in though. Thanks for coming guys. Thanks for sharing a fire with me.

And that was the end of the evening. Arthur, Nancy, and Faulkner carried in the chairs, while Timothy peed on the fire.

The next morning Arthur woke late with a hangover and an overwhelming sense of dread. Lying in bed was no use—he wouldn't be able to sleep. At these times, these lowest of lows, work is the only worthwhile treatment. You can always lose yourself and sometimes find yourself through difficult, prolonged work. So Arthur skipped breakfast and put on his stained clothes, falling once while pulling up his pants for lack of balance, and marched out to his farm. After feeding the chickens, and watering the early season vegetables, and filling the hummingbird feeders, he turned his attention to the goat yard.

He had recently acquired four Nubian goat kids. They were renowned for the butterfat content in their milk, and he hoped to make cheese in time for One Perfect Day—though in his haste, he hadn't researched when the goats would be of milking age. Why did he rush everything? Was that the source of all his troubles? Was his haste and impulsiveness to blame for the failure of his farm and his marriage? Maybe Morgan was right. Maybe she deserved better than him and he should just let her go. These goats were susceptible to all kinds of disease—he knew that, and he hadn't even arranged for a vet to examine them. Everything died at Failure Farm and it was probably his fault, all this death. Just look at those four kids, bleating loudly now in the goat yard, all spotted in brown and white, their famous ears flopping and drooping nearly to the ground as they cavorted in the grass. That was the only word for it—cavorting, and they had no idea what inept hands held their fate. Stupid Arthur Prendergast, the impulsive, incompetent, fool. And what was on his list today? Not calling the vet, not researching proper care for the goats, not any of the things necessary to ensure their well-being. No, instead he was planning to build three goat perches, which he would cover in sod, and water obsessively, so that when the goats were older they would climb up on the perches and make a quaint sight—like the goats you see on sodden rooftops in Norway or Door County. What kind of idiot was he?

He had to do better. Arthur sat on the ground in the goat yard, and let the kids butt against him, and clamber over him, and cavort in the unusually warm spring morning, while he pulled out his phone to look up vets. He saw then a message from Faulkner.

Fawk had forwarded a message from Timothy, which read: Sorry if I went on too much with your buddy last night re corpse case –the whiskey got the better of me, and I love a good hypothetical. But, seemed to be a buzz kill somehow. Didn't mean to end the night on that note. Tell him sorry for me would you?

Faulkner added no comment of his own, which was odd, but still. Did this change things? It was, after all, just hypothetical. Timothy implied it wasn't such a big deal. Arthur wasn't necessarily going to jail and neither was Morgan and he still stood a chance of pulling off the perfect day and getting his life back on track. Arthur reached out to scratch one of the kids on the head, and the goat instinctively pushed against his palm. A tufted titmouse called from the hedge—the cheerful three-note whistle. The sun was warm and the trees in full bud, and the daily report from his One Perfect Day app showed decent progress. Things were all right. He was still kind of an idiot—but a hard-working idiot and that might be enough.

Arthur found a volunteer service from the Vet Med school at the University, and he called and made an appointment, which was so easy he felt silly but also elated. Then he turned his attention to the goat perches.

Over winter he had dragged deadfalls out of his woods and had the trees milled into boards. They were mostly black walnut, which was heavy and dense to work with, but it was safer for the animals than treated lumber. He arranged his tape measure and circular saw and cordless drill and began construction. How gratifying it was to work so hard on this gorgeous morning. He was a competent carpenter, Arthur was, perhaps even a good one. When the frames were constructed like lovely, square benches, about five feet high, he took a break and went inside to make coffee and eat something. He drank a quart of water and took some vitamins and returned to work. He stapled plastic sheeting to the top of the frames. He covered them in dirt hauled from the river bottom, and planted native grass seed and watered it.

Then he rested, leaning against one of the goat perches, and watched a red tail hawk circle high above. Would that hawk go after one of the goats? No, they were too big. But an eagle might. This problem needed a solution. He added the work item to his app.

Then his phone rang.

At first he thought it was a wood thrush, early for the season, but then remembered that was the ring tone for calls from Morgan, which meant it was a call from Morgan, which reminded him—finally—that it was the second Sunday of the month. She had never before initiated the call. She always waited for him. But this day he had just forgotten. So she called. How interesting!

Later, Arthur wouldn't be able to remember all the details of this conversation, even though it was such a pivotal one. He remembered that when he answered, rather than exchanging mundane greetings like they usually did, he just started telling Morgan about the goat perches, and what he had accomplished that morning, and also about last night, the long fireside party with neighbors—and also, about meeting the Martins and the strange pastor. He remembered Morgan laughing, and he realized that he hadn't heard her laughter in so long—she had this kind of bubbling giggle, like a northern stream coming through stones. And the more he heard her laugh, the more encouraged he felt to continue with the stories, to bring her all up to date on Failure Farm. When she realized he had named it Failure Farm, which he only told her now, she had responded suddenly, Oh honey! in a sad but endeared kind of way. And how long since she had called him Honey? He couldn't remember but she did smell like honey and sometimes like clover under the sheets first thing in the morning. He remembered he felt himself rising, in his work pants, and liked it but also felt dumb letting that happen just because of a phone call, like he was in junior high or something. But also, maybe Morgan felt that way too? However that was with women, which was so mysterious to men, perhaps unknowable.

I'm talking too much, Arthur said.

No, said Morgan, it's nice. Nice to hear you doing well. And everything you have going on—that's great. Great for you. Not to sound patronizing, she said. I really mean it, Art.

She called him Art. It stopped him abruptly. He felt a surge of emotion rise up his torso, that wonderful sadness, that tragic jubilation—what the fuck was that? But anyway, it was good. She called him Art, which was her nickname for him, no one else's, and it reflected what she saw in him, perhaps an embodiment of Art, a creative person, a complicated person, capable of creative inspiration, one who manifests something lovely out of the base materials of life. She called him Art, and so he asked her.

Hey, he heard his voice remark, Maybe you should come down here one of these days and see it for yourself? No hurry. Whatever. It would be nice.

Then he thought of saying many more things, about how it could be so perfect, her One Perfect Day, how he was planning and tracking it all in a database, and working so hard. But he didn't say any of that. He just waited.

Morgan took her time. Then she said, Sure. Yeah. That would be nice. I'll look at my schedule.

And Arthur replied, Cool. Whatever works for you. Maybe wait a while, until things are green down here?

Oh that would be nice, Art, she said. Tell you what, how about late

August? I think I can get some time off then.

Late August, just as Arthur had planned. So there it was, after all the anxiety—so easy. The date was made and on the calendar. The rest was just execution. One Perfect Day.

He spent the rest of the conversation on a kind of autopilot, his thoughts racing, jubilant. But he was able to maintain enough focus to follow. She wanted to talk about the body.

I just saw a new #sangabody post, she said. I'll send it to you now. It shows his face clearly. It's definitely him, Arthur. It's definitely Armando Gallardo, Lupe's husband. From some place past Monticello.

What do you think that means? he asked.

Well, she said, I guess it means now there's a clear connection between Armando going missing near Middling and his body floating down the river, you know? So I'm guessing it's just a matter of time before somebody finds Peg Hanrahan's social posts about the missing person and this body that's been floating downriver since then.

And not decomposing, added Arthur.

Right, sighed Morgan. I noticed that too. It's so weird, like he's preserved somehow, and in all those strange poses.

I forgot to tell you, he said, I talked with the lawyer. Timothy.

You told him about us? She sounded irritated, for the first time today.

No, no. I made it totally hypothetical, that it was from a podcast or something. And everybody was drunk.

So you got drunk legal advice.

I guess. But it seemed legit.

What did he say?

Arthur considered telling her everything, but did not. He said, I guess the upshot is we should just keep it to ourselves and wait for time to pass—to blow over.

That doesn't sound like a strategy.

What's our alternative?

Okay.

Then there was a long pause. The kids pressed against Arthur's legs. What did they want? Did they think he was their mother? One of them made a loud bleat.

Morgan laughed. Is that one of the goats? What kind did you get this time?

Nubian, he said. They should work better, hopefully.

And not die, she said.

And not die.

Arthur, Morgan said. Can I ask you something?

Of course.

What happened to the body after I left that day? I mean, how did it get in the river?

Arthur paused. He felt a little nauseous. He said, I don't know. A flood took it, I guess.

But that doesn't make sense, because there was that huge snag through the river, and that was downstream from where he lay. Did it flood after that?

Yeah. It did. It kept raining—remember those storms?

Yeah, said Morgan. I guess so. It's just that it seems… implausible.

I guess the whole thing is implausible, right? I mean like how he's not decomposing and everything.

I guess, she said. Then after some silence, Morgan said, Well. I should let you go. Those kids need attention haha.

It was good to talk with you.

It was, she said.

Have a good day.

You too.

Okay, he said.

Then Morgan said, Arthur? I feel like I need to tell you something.

What? he asked. But his thoughts had returned to One Perfect Day, and how profound this moment was.

But then Morgan went silent again. And finally she just said, Oh it's not important, actually. Nevermind. Some other time.

He summoned all his courage and said, You love me.

And Morgan replied, You love me too.

And so ended their call.

Overhead the red-tailed hawk let out a high-pitched creeeee! And for a moment Arthur felt that he could see from the eyes of that hawk, down on his place, the old farm of the ghost Hanacek, along the banks of the Sangamon River, where nature was stirring in her womb preparing to birth another season of plenty, a bounty for the feast that he would create. He, Art, would create One Perfect Day for the love of his life.

EIGHT

In Chicago the early spring ended abruptly, with a merciless fog that hung for days and showered tiny beads of wetness that was neither rain nor snow. The mood of the city turned to resolute determination, to continue the work of living, to harbor no illusion of joy, to resign yourself to gloom and survival. It was inconceivable that the sun would ever return, that mild breezes would blow from the lake, that the Bears or the Bulls would ever win again, that your vandalized car would be repaired, that your landlord would fix the furnace. The thought of a sweet summer day in late August was so far off to Morgan that it was nothing more than a fairy tale, and at best, one that H C Andersen would write, where all the heroine could hope for was relief from suffering.

Mrs Vogel embodied the mood, slouching in her wheelchair, peering into the garden, eating so little she would soon waste away. She tried to make conversation, asking, Your boy—is it sunny down where he lives? I always heard they had more fair days, down there on the plains. And Morgan explained that it might be, but also the wind would blow so hard people's roofs flew off. I suppose this is just Illinois, Mrs Vogel said, you pick your poison. And Morgan, to lighten the mood said, I bet the redbuds are blooming down in southern Illinois, and Mrs Vogel replied, Maybe so, but that's not Illinois down there—that's Kentucky.

On the last day of sunlight, when Morgan had talked with Arthur, she had intended to tell him about Larry. Sitting with a cup of tea on her unmade bed, hearing Arthur tell the stories of the farm, with all his old enthusiasm, his hilarious and infectious energy, with none of the smothering urgency—his lightness made her want him for the first time in how long. In that moment, it seemed right to admit that she had made this friend, who was a man, and with whom she felt a special connection. But as time passed, she wondered why she needed to tell him that. Did she need to report to him on every friend she made? And why did she think of it as admitting something? You admitted something you'd done wrong. Like, for example, concealing information about a murdered body. There was nothing to admit about Larry, was there? Her compulsion to tell Arthur was a sign of dependence, a sense of unfounded guilt in an unhealthy relationship. If they had a more mature relationship, perhaps hadn't married so young, he would respect her independence. Friendships with men would be a part of what Arthur married. And yet, it still felt wrong somehow, or at least deceitful—sometimes thrillingly so.

Now that Mrs Vogel had surrendered to gloom, Morgan had more time to herself. She began to look at maps of the Sangamon River— satellite views of their farm, and the patchwork of woods that trimmed the river, winding like a contorted bowel in a southwestern path towards the Mississippi. Most of the #sangabody posts shared their location, where the corpse had been photographed.

The first was from Centerville, down the hill from the country church, in which the body was angled upright, the torso almost out of the river, the legs below the surface. His head was tilted backward, his face anonymous, staring up at a vast sky. That was last September, a month after they had found the body. The caption read, *Does anyone know where you report this?* There were a handful of 'likes' but no replies.

Another post, three weeks later, taken behind the Monticello Golf Club, showed the body with the arms straight downward and hands apparently clasped. It was as if he were putting, and indeed the caption read, *The back nine is a killer.* This one had comments including, *Dude you should report that,* and *WTF?? Not funny*

Then the body appeared in Allerton Park, on a river bend deep in the woods. He made a grotesque pose—arms pulled behind the back, head dropped to one shoulder. It brought to mind the sculpture, Last Centaur, commissioned by Robert Allerton 100 years before. The caption read, simply, *Ummm.* No comments.

In late fall someone shared a video of the body taken from the bridge where highway 32 crosses the Sangamon between Cisco and Cerro Gordo. Out there with nothing but farm fields and tiny cemeteries. The body had its limbs splayed, like Leonardo's Vitruvian Man, and was revolving in a circle under the bridge, chin lowered. The caption read, *This can't be real.* There were two replies: *Another hoax, yawn,* and *Obviously a mannequin – no sign of decay.*

And there was no sign of decay, in that post or any other. Just Armando Gallardo's clothed body and beaten face in so many impossible poses. The post that revealed his face in sufficient detail that Morgan was able to recognize it—this photo was taken just north of Lake Decatur, where the river bleeds out into marshy land. The author must have been using a zoom lens, with narrow depth of field, so that the face is in focus while the barren landscape is blurred. A bleak sun rises at the horizon. It was artful and horrifying. It said, *I've seen other posts like this now—should we be contacting authorities?* Comments were turned off, suggesting the person didn't like the replies. But there were 37 likes.

There were dozens more. Collectively, they began to seem comical, entirely detached from a gruesome tragedy. Morgan felt herself become numb, no longer surprised to see the body curled like a fetus along a grassy slope, or knee drawn up and hands praying at the chest like the yoga tree pose. Why hadn't Peg Hanrahan found these posts? How could Lupe Gallardo have missed them? Or perhaps they had found them and Morgan didn't know—they hadn't updated their website. The body could be found, for all she knew, and the case closed. The internet is a snapshot of all times at once—there is no linearity, no version history. Or maybe there is, in server logs. Arthur would know—maybe he could make sense of it.

Morgan and Arthur had been exchanging more frequent texts about the mystery. Despite her worries, it felt good to share this together. Secrets are the most intimate bonds between lovers. She and Arthur nurtured their secret like a foundling, often sending just a link, knowing how the other would receive it, no reply necessary. And yet, he was circumspect when she asked about plausibility—first of all, how the body had even gotten in the river, and also how the body managed to get past all the snags and oxbows, all the way to Lake Decatur. But Armando's body had gotten there, proven by a wintertime post in the lake, where the body appeared luminescent beneath the ice, as if it were looking into the world from another realm.

On the day she left Arthur, driving that rental truck out of a town she had called home, she realized she had forgotten the rental agreement. Those agreements were always confusing—presented to you, carefully folded, as if it were essential—but then never taken when you returned the car. Morgan couldn't live with this loose end: what if they needed that at the rental place in Chicago? What if she had to drive all the way back? So she returned to the farm. Arthur wasn't in the house or anywhere to be seen. She was surprised how messy she had left things—the pile of books, the wine glass in the sink—but she grabbed the agreement and ran back to the truck. In that moment, she heard the tractor rumbling in the back field. At the time she only felt relief that she wouldn't have to see him again, and didn't consider why he'd be out on the tractor in all that mud. But now she couldn't stop wondering why. These little incongruities in life stick with you, and surely they're a sign that your instinctual brain senses a break in a pattern that should be examined. But she hadn't asked about it, not yet. There was too much accusation buried in the question.

So in their phone call Morgan hadn't brought up Larry, or the tractor, and instead enjoyed the moment they had, just talking. When she heard the goats she wanted to touch them, to feel their taut hide and smell their muskiness. She wanted to drag her hand along the flowers of the prairie. To hear the oriole whistling and the river pulsing against the soft banks. How could they keep their marriage afloat until her visit, so she could experience the summer day she wanted so badly? Not by bringing up those inflammatory things, definitely not. But also. She needed to make a decision about their future. This limbo was at times annoying, other times agonizing. Always the sense of Arthur pulled at her, this persistent gravity. What would it feel like to pull free?

Morgan decided that she would make up her mind by the time she visited the farm. Then she would either commit or present him with papers. How did you get papers? A lawyer, of course. But she didn't know any lawyers. How do you choose a divorce lawyer? What if he hit on you? Mrs Vogel would know one. But maybe she wouldn't comply—she seemed to like 'her boy,' or at least the idea of him. Arthur would never drive all this to conclusion; Morgan had to. A deadline was somehow reassuring. It was a long way off. By then she would have a plan for her life. This job with Mrs Vogel wasn't sustainable either. But what would the old woman do? In the gloom Morgan lacked the energy to address all this, so she just kept going to work.

One morning she found Mrs Vogel sitting in the great hall downstairs, surrounded by all the family portraits and elaborate woodwork and stained glass. She had insisted that Nakeisha wheel her into that room and leave early. When Morgan arrived, Mrs Vogel kept staring at a corner of the room and said, I need to know when I will die.

Morgan said, Sorry, what?

Mrs Vogel said, I have arranged for some tests. Devin is coming to take me down to this town in Indiana where they do these things for people willing to pay. That goofy basketball player, Larry Bird, he is from this town. French Lick. What a name. They say it is fancy. Imagine a fancy town in southern Indiana.

Morgan asked, Why do you want to know when you'll die? How is that possible?

They have tests, Mrs Vogel replied. Science is very advanced now. If they know when the sun will explode and burn up the earth, they should know when an old woman will die.

Her expression was resolute, her focus on some distant point.

Morgan said, But Mrs Vogel, even if they can, why would you want to know?

The old woman turned to her and said, Wouldn't you like to know?

Then before Morgan could answer, she added, No, not when you're young—you don't want to know then. Possibility is what keeps us going. But when you are old like me, you no longer cling to possibility. You want to be able to plan carefully, to take care of the people you love.

Then Mrs Vogel's stern expression broke, and her eyes watered and she raised a curved forefinger to her cheek and wiped it away. She said, It's silly for an old woman to cry about these things, but I'm crying for the joy. The joy of knowing people. People like you.

Morgan went to hug her and felt a pleasurable sob rise up and she said, I'm so grateful you are back in my life. I should say that more often.

Mrs Vogel patted her shoulder and said, You don't have to say it, dear one. I know it every day you arrive at my door.

Then they collected themselves, and Morgan put a strand of Mrs Vogel's hair back in place, and they smoothed their clothes. Why do people smooth their clothes after they've been emotional? Clothes have so many more purposes than protecting our skin—it's weird to think about. Clothes on monkeys are funny, but not on humans, their primate cousins. When Morgan and Larry made the monkey gestures, god that was embarrassing, but still funny. And when is the sun supposed to explode? That probably didn't matter, practically speaking.

Mrs Vogel was saying, So now I want you to take this day off and do something for yourself. Devin will take care of me, that rascal has a good heart. I will wear my diapers. Mrs Vogel made a shooing gesture and said, Now go! I have a very busy day ahead and no time to sit here chit-chatting with you.

Morgan laughed, I can't just leave you alone in this room.

I'm not alone—I've been sitting here with Karl. We were looking at all these pictures of old fools, posing with so much arrogance. We were laughing about old times. You have seen him by now, yes?

Morgan didn't know how to respond. Mrs Vogel could be tricky.

The old woman didn't wait. She said, Okay, take me to the sun room—that is an ironic name these days isn't it? Take me there to wait for Devin. Then you go.

When Morgan had done this, and walked back through the house to leave, she paused again in the great hall. She did feel a presence—it must be the power of suggestion. But then, a vague and shimmering outline of a tall man appeared in the far corner of the room. He stood behind a table with a crystal lamp. He looked at Morgan as if he were pleading.

She heard herself say, Mr Vogel?

The man gestured, in what seemed like a sign language, bringing his hands together in a clap. He held the clasped hands out to her, as if to say, 'look at these!' and still his expression was deeply earnest.

Morgan looked behind her, and around the room. She said, I don't understand. What is this? She was talking to the man but also about the man. The whole thing didn't compute. She felt strangely normal, which you shouldn't if you were seeing a ghost. So probably it wasn't. Would Mrs Vogel pull a prank on her? This could be an old gimmick, like Pepper's Ghost, just a trick of light and mirrors. Was there a video projector somewhere around the corner? Why would Mrs Vogel do that? Well, she was a sly and mischievous old woman. But come on, after they had that emotional conversation, how could she do this trick? Maybe it was already set up and Mrs Vogel forgot. Or maybe it was Devin who set it all up? Mr Vogel continued to gesture and plead. He seemed stuck behind the table.

Morgan's phone buzzed in her pocket. Ah! She would take a picture. She pulled it out and saw that there were messages from Larry. Her attention shifted fully to this, her heart raced and her throat swelled. He had been to an art gallery and was sending her pictures of wall-sized photos that showed zoomed-in naked body parts. You could recognize the crease where a leg meets the lower abdomen, the curve of the spine just above the buttocks. He wrote, *Do you think Mrs Vogel would like these?*

Morgan laughed and wrote, *What are you doing today?*

Then her eyes caught a commotion from across the room. She looked up and saw Mr Vogel pounding his fists up and down in the air, his face screwed up furiously. It was a kind of tantrum. Well this had to be a trick. Or maybe it was real. She should show Larry. She switched to the camera and lifted her phone—but in that moment, the ghost was gone.

An hour later she met Larry at the Bean in Millennium Park. He appeared first as a reflection in the sculpture, comically distorted and wide, grinning at her reflection surrounded by tourists holding up cell phones. Even in the rain people flocked to this sculpture, named Cloud Gate. Always it created a marvelous view, like an Impressionist's painting in the city that exalted Impressionists. When she found Larry's real form in the crowd, he was shrunk back to normal proportions, perfect posture, but still a softness to him. He radiated contentment, always smiling, even now in the rain with a black slicker and hood up.

She went to politely hug him and they fumbled, not knowing which arms to put high or low, but they completed the hug. She could smell his cologne, something woodsy but with spices.

He said, Your eyes stand out even in the Bean—can I say that?

Morgan looked away. My eyes freak people out.

Larry feigned exasperation. In Cajun drawl he said, It must be such a burden being beautiful.

Morgan punched his shoulder. Why did she do that? She wasn't a shoulder-puncher.

He pretended that it hurt him badly and then laughed in a way that seemed to vibrate his thin body, So where should we go, mon amie?

They went to the Art Institute. On the way through the door, Larry let her go first and put his hand on the small of her back. It was a polite gesture, but she felt the pressure of the handprint for a while. He said, What would you think if we didn't look at a bunch of art, but instead just looked at one painting? To properly appreciate it—sometimes I like to do that.

Morgan said, I guess, but which one?

Larry put his finger to his lips and thought, then opened his eyes wide to her and said, I know the one! Follow me.

They sat on a bench in a room filled with Picasso paintings and fixed their gaze on Nude under a Pine Tree. In this scene, a heavy-set woman with cubist form reclines on rock in front of a pine. There is a line of mountains on the horizon. The woman is shades of pink and grey and the pine is dusty green. Your eyes follow the lines of her body, around and around, like a maze with no exit, until they rest on her face—such a primitive face, a rhomboid face, that stares at you plainly and without shame for her nakedness. You can feel the pressure of the rock under your skin. You can smell the pine. You can taste the nearby ocean and the sweat from the woman's armpits.

You see? Larry said.

I do, said Morgan.

Then they left the museum.

They went to a coffee shop in an alley that smelled like New Orleans in the morning after a rain. There was a long line because the coffee was very good and the shop felt like a portal from the Loop to some more exotic place. Larry said, Chicago is full of surprises like this—where somebody creates another world.

This became suddenly obvious and true. Morgan said, Like the White City. That was the biggest example.

Larry nodded, Like this city is always trying to prove itself, or reinvent itself.

They took the coffee and walked up Michigan Avenue. They paused at the DuSable Bridge, where Jean Baptiste built the first trading post along the river, where Fort Dearborn was later erected and then destroyed. The rain stopped and a strong breeze came in from the lake, down the mouth of the river, and ruffled Larry's thick hair. As workers and cars came across the bridge, he leaned against the railing and looked down to the river and the concrete that replaced its banks. A tour boat glided beneath them, the guide barking through the PA in her excellent local accent, pronouncing a's like a slap in the face.

Larry said, Hard to imagine what it was like, when the first people portaged through here, a bunch of shacks in the mud.

The river went the other way then, Morgan said.

You know, said Larry. The first Europeans here were Frenchies like me. We all got along great, natives and Frenchmen—trading, drinking, singing folk songs, cruising around in canoes. Things went to shit when the English showed up.

I think your timeline's a little off, Morgan said.

Larry made a dismissive shrug. In the twist of his lip, the scar showed. Eh, close enough, he said. The first part is true anyway.

He was kidding. Just when you thought he was serious, this peculiar wit popped through.

I'm starting to question your whole French bit, said Morgan.

Larry put his hand on his heart and opened his mouth, protesting.

Exactly, she said. I think you're an actor, not a Cajun, not an astrophysicist. I don't even know your last name.

He smiled, now sincere again. Celotte, he said. Lawrence Celotte. But don't look it up—it will just correct to Colette. Maybe my ancestors changed it. Maybe it was originally Italian, like Celotto, which might mean sky.

Those are lots of maybes, said Morgan. You're a shapeshifter.

I'm just quantum, he replied.

Whatever, said Morgan, laughing.

The bridge bounced with a truck rumbling past. The fresh wind off the lake was lovely.

I don't know your last name either.

Deneau.

What!? You're a Frenchie too? Why didn't you tell me? You got a secret side of you too.

This last part came in the drawl. Maybe it was authentic?

They put their hands on the rail and closed their eyes and let the wind blow their hair. Her hair must be huge now, a Medusa, but no matter.

How do you know so much about this city? she asked. Or pretend to. You said you'd only been here a year or something.

Larry considered the question, looking out toward the lake where a layer of blue sky appeared at the horizon. He said, It's a fascinating place. I think Chicago is the most American of all the cities. Everything is possible and everything is infinite and everyone can be rich. Anything less is a failure, so you better get to work.

He laughed when he said this last part. Morgan laughed too. It sounded like a line he had said before. But it was kind of true. Her parents were like that.

I can see it because I'm not from here, he said.

You think I can't see my hometown clearly? Morgan fixed her eyes on him, aware of their power.

Of course you can't and neither can I. That's how we can love them.

Then he turned and walked north up the avenue and she followed him.

They rented bikes and rode along the lakefront as the high pressure over the water rolled back all the gloom like a tarp and revealed a gorgeous blue. They ate brats at a place on Diversey, and watched people introducing their dogs to each other. He used his napkin to wipe mustard from her cheek. They continued riding north, and paused at Belmont harbor, where gulls were flying low and snatching something out of an old man's hand. They rode north to Montrose Harbor and walked through the Magic Hedge where songbirds gathered on a migratory stop. The birds reminded her of Arthur of course, and how he must be tracking all the migration on their farm, and so she insisted they get moving again. They checked in the bikes and went to an Ethiopian restaurant where they ate beyainatu with their hands. Larry explained his job to her. He was researching dark matter. Every month he went to a place in West Virginia where they had dug a hole nearly a mile deep so their sensors weren't distracted by other particulate matter and could focus on detecting this nothingness that was something and explained everything. They had to pump oxygen down into this tunnel and air condition it year round and if the systems failed you would probably die. Then they went to the Green Mill.

They bought martinis and because it was mid-week they got the banquette where supposedly Al Capone held court. It wasn't the 1920's any more, but no one had told that to the Green Mill, and so they sat among all the art deco under the dim lights and listened to a gypsy jazz band that wouldn't quit. Two young couples came in and started talking until the hostess kicked them out. The musicians were sweating. They played three sets and the crowd gave them a standing ovation. When Morgan and Larry came out into the street past midnight, it was so disorienting to remember where you were and what year it was and how you had to work tomorrow.

They stood under the light of the marquee, facing each other. Cars came by fast along Lawrence and up Broadway. How could there be so many people out this late? Where were they all going?

Larry didn't seem to know what to say. Morgan certainly didn't. What did this day mean? It was wonderful while it was happening but now that it had happened, it seemed more important than she wanted it to be. But there was no going back. They had this experience now, and were changed forever, together, even if they never saw each other again. Maybe they shouldn't see each other again. She might want that and then again maybe she wanted him to walk her home.

Thanks, Larry said. That was great. The whole day.

He looked like a boy now, looking at her, with those lidded dark eyes.

Words were stupid now, and so she went to hug him and this time they guessed the right position of their arms and embraced gracefully, and then Morgan rose up on her toes and put her cheek to his and kissed it and a moment later he kissed her cheek back and she could smell his woodsy cologne and the sharpness of gin on his breath and feel the stubble of his face. Then she pulled away. She swung her arms, and bobbed on her feet, and smiled at him, slowly walking backward.

Wait, he said. I'll call you a car.

I can walk, she said. It's not far. Then she turned and went, knowing he was watching her.

The headlights seemed too brazen, exposing her and yet making it hard to see. There was no one else on foot—just cars with dark-tinted windows cruising past. One enormous car that sat low on giant wheels approached from behind, barely faster than she could walk. She could feel the bass thump from its stereo through the sidewalk—she could feel it in her insides, this menacing heartbeat. People were shot, randomly, sometimes here. How quickly the vibe of the city could change. She walked faster and the car kept pace with her, booming, booming. So she turned up an alley just before Sheridan.

Now there was another sharp contrast—the alley was almost silent. Spring frogs chirped from window wells. A television flashed from a second-floor apartment. A jet flew low overhead, its roar rising and then fading. She walked steadily, but not too briskly—you don't want to walk like prey. That was a weird thing to think, something Arthur had told her, how people were just animals like all the rest and some were predators and some prey, depending on the situation, and so you wanted to seem like neither prey nor predator, just a neutral passing thing that didn't attract anyone's attention, that didn't trigger bloodlust or fear. Sometimes Arthur wasn't very smart but he was always intelligent. Larry was also intelligent but differently. Was that cultural? Arthur wanted to know everything about the natural world on Earth, and Larry wanted to know everything about the universe. What was more important? The idea of dark matter might seem totally dumb to people a hundred years from now, like the ether they once thought filled space.

Morgan saw movement along a chain-link fence between two garages in the alley. She stopped, and then remembered not to be prey, and kept walking, looking ahead but still watching peripherally. The movement stopped and she became aware of another human. Now she had to look. It was a young man—no actually, a boy, a full head shorter than Morgan. The light from the alley barely illuminated him, standing beside the fence. He wore an oversized Bulls jersey over a ratty t-shirt and pants about to fall off. He stared at her, so she had to say something.

Hey, said Morgan. That was stupid but it was something.

The boy reached behind his back into his baggy pants and pulled out a pistol. It seemed too large for him. He held it with both hands and pointed it at her.

Morgan stopped. They looked at each other. The boy's eyes might have been bloodshot but you couldn't tell in that light but still she couldn't see the whites of his eyes. What do you do in a situation like this? She had pepper spray attached to her key ring in her pocket but that seemed like a toy now. Also, you don't put your hand in your pocket when someone is pointing a gun at you right? She also had a loud siren on that key ring but also that was in her pocket. The boy kept the gun pointed. Was he trembling? Or was that just her eyesight because her blood pressure must be through the roof right now. This was just a kid. A kid with a gun. What the fuck. Kids with guns. They want to be rich like everyone else in this city. She should have let Larry get her a car. No, no, she was a big girl and didn't need a man to protect her. What would Arthur do in this situation? He was weirdly clever. He would probably make a joke maybe?

Morgan said, I hope that's a water pistol. Her voice sounded weak and strained.

The boy stepped toward her, now into the light. That can't be good, this willingness to expose himself. She felt now what he must feel, the power he held over this woman with weird eyes. Ah yes, her eyes! Were they helping or hurting? The boy looked right and left up the alley. What would it feel like to be shot? To have a bullet tear through your skin and hit a bone?

Now Morgan felt a rush of exhilaration. She really wanted to live, it turned out. Here she was facing possible death and she discovered that she didn't want that. This feeling—this wanting life—it had been gone a long time, but she didn't know until it returned. Just now. It was a good day, a beautiful day, and the rain was gone and she had a mysterious new friend and what would Mrs Vogel find out in French Lick and how would it go when she visited Arthur in the summer when the cicadas rattled from the locust trees?

Morgan stepped toward the boy and opened her eyes very wide so the light would reflect in them and said to the boy, Now I know what it means to be alive. Thank you!

The boy scowled at her and thrust the pistol into his pants and ran down the alley—a wild, scrambling run with untied shoes. She felt so badly for him. She wanted to say, don't run. I don't mean you any harm. Don't be afraid of me or anything, please. But the boy disappeared around the corner into the night.

When Morgan got home she couldn't hold her keys steadily enough to unlock the door. She rested her head against the wall and let her arms hang and began to sob violently. After a while, her hands steadied and she went inside. When she turned on the lights and saw her teapot on the counter and her record collection in the cabinet and the Kandinsky poster on the wall, the sadness of it all overwhelmed her. She sunk to the floor and leaned against the kitchen island and took out her phone and called Arthur.

It rang so long she thought it would go to voice mail but then he answered, Morgan! Are you all right?

How did he know?

She couldn't speak then. She just wept and shuddered into the phone, and listened to him say. Tell me. What happened? Do you want me to come up there? Are you at home?

But still she couldn't say anything. She tried but the trauma washed away any words and she just cried to him and he said, It's okay. It's okay. I love you. It's going to be all right.

Finally, Morgan said, Arthur.

Yes?

I'm sorry, she said. I'm sorry.

I know, he said. But it's okay. I'm sorry too.

She said, I'm sorry I'm sorry I'm so sorry, I'm sorry. And her breath came in gasps, which was embarrassing but pleasurable.

Then she pressed her phone off and went to lie on her bed.

After a while she could hear the El roaring off in the city, and the antique clock Mrs Vogel gave her ticked on her bedside table. She pulled the sheet over her head and put her fists up to her face. As she surrendered herself to sleep, she could smell the scent of Larry on her hands. She could feel the kiss he'd left on her cheek.

NINE

Many days passed and Arthur did not hear from Morgan. After she hung up that night, he sent messages, left voice mails, even tried email—all with no reply. Finally he sent a text saying *Can you just let me know if you're all right – I'm so worried I'm thinking of calling the cops.* To this, Morgan replied, *I'm ok – please stop.* And so he flung himself into work: caring for the farm during the day, building websites at night.

But still he couldn't stop checking his phone. He turned on notifications for everything, which was maddening but necessary. He left his phone face up on the ground while he planted 200 forbs at the edge of the field. Each time he heard the buzz, he grabbed the phone and checked—but it was never from her. When he woke during the night in a house too quiet to sleep, he tapped the screen beside his pillow—never her. In this long drought of words from Morgan, he looked for #sangabody posts and followed their discussions. It had evolved into a conspiracy, with speculation and debate about where the body originated, whether the body was even real. Some deduced that the body must have come from far upriver, possibly as far as Middling. Others wrote it off as frivolous AI. It seemed no one had found Sheila Fuglesen's story on

Armando Gallardo. No one saw Peg Hanrahan's posts, her plea for the case she kept alive pro bono, in the interest of migrant workers whose cause she embraced. But Arthur knew it was inevitable.

There were so many hours to think in the dead of the night. What if the community connected the body with Armando, what if they reached out to Peg Hanrahan? It was plain from the pictures that the body had been assaulted—it was clear this was foul play, possibly murder. And if Peg had proof it was murder, couldn't she get more attention from the cops? Once she could trace the trail of Armando, wasn't it a matter of time before they began to comb the banks of the Sangamon? Wouldn't they come around his place and start asking questions? How would he hold up under questioning? Arthur was a terrible liar. He would have to get better at that. Was there a way to practice lying, so you could do it well when the stakes were high? The stakes would certainly be high if they traced the body to Failure Farm and found evidence that he had played a part in disposing of the body—that was Abuse of Corpse, Timothy had said, and that was a felony. And also that Loss of Consortium crime—that could be proved too, maybe, and how would Arthur create One Perfect Day while defending himself in court? If there were teams of detectives and yellow tape all over his woods—not great. Maybe he deserved it, being indicted for his inexplicable crime. He probably deserved that. And if so, why didn't he just confess and let things take their course? Would that make a difference, in the big picture? Was it worth compromising his plans, his hopes for Morgan? It was exhausting.

Also, why had Morgan said she was sorry that night on the phone? What would have made her so upset? What was she sorry for? Maybe she was sorry for having left him—but that made no sense because she was ignoring him now. Maybe she was sorry for having married him, for making a terrible mistake, duping him into such a profound love for her, only to abandon him. They were so young then. So fucking young. She might be sorry about that. In his despair, he sent her more messages, and eventually it became an act that was numb and rote, something you did without hope, like a farmer during a drought checking radar for storms. Eventually he slept for a few hours, but still rose before dawn, because if you didn't maintain your schedule that was the beginning of the end.

One morning he took his coffee outside to walk the trails and discovered that his bee colonies had collapsed. From 20 yards away you could see that both hives were dead. He could tell by the absence of things—no blur of movement as the creatures traveled to early clover. No reassuring hum vibrating deep within the hive bodies. No sense of life. It was remarkable how you could feel the absence of life, like he did the moment he saw Armando's body on the river bank. Now the bee boxes had that same troubling emptiness. When he pulled out the frames, the delicate, intricate bodies tumbled to the ground like chaff in the warm breeze. The honeycomb, unattended, had become darkly discolored. There would be no explanation. The master beekeeper had warned him. He could only start again and hope.

Arthur leaned the frames against the boxes and sat on the ground. He muttered, Bees hum busily among the forbs of the field. This was Goal #5 in the manifest of One Perfect Day and the achievement score was now zero. Well maybe not exactly because he had planted forbs and they might do all right if the deer didn't devour them. Which would probably happen the way things were going. He would need to build a fence. That would be expensive and so would new colonies of bees and soon the taxes were due and Morgan might not pay half this time because she wasn't even talking to him.

He laughed and said again, Bees hum busily among the forbs of the field. He brought up a fist and bumped his head, what a dumbass he was, thinking he could do all this in one year, what a naive and pathetic fool. Just one of his goals was probably too much and he had committed to nine. He stretched a leg and kicked one of the frames over. Spoiled honey dripped on his boot.

He heard a voice behind him, Oh Arthur what happened?

It was Nancy, wearing Faulkner's high school track sweater, holding a tea cup with both hands.

When he looked at her, his face felt tight and all he could say was, Colony collapse.

Nancy sat down next to him. I'm sorry, she said. Can I help?

Do you have any spare bee colonies? He asked.

I'm afraid I don't, she said, and they laughed without mirth.

This was one of your goals, wasn't it, Arthur? The bees in the flowers of the field?

Past tense, he said. That's about right.

I'm sorry, she said. That is one of your goals.

Lots of people saying they're sorry these days, he said. He pulled a clump of clover from the ground and threw it. He was sulking now, like a spoiled child. That was rude. But it took so much energy to behave properly.

How do you mean, Arthur? She set her cup on the ground and put her arms on her knees.

That's why he acted this way—because she let him, which seemed unfair. He told her about Morgan's call.

And you know she's okay now? Nancy asked.

Well, she said so.

You know it means she still cares about you—you understand that, right?

Arthur shrugged, pulled more clover.

Of course it does, Nancy continued. A woman doesn't call a man at night crying and say she's sorry if she doesn't care about him.

Arthur looked in her green eyes—so much empathy. It would be stupid to cry now so he suppressed it.

Nancy said. I can't say what she's going through, but I have a strong suspicion she needs space. You've been doing that?

Arthur nodded with certainty. Yes, he said, I have.

It came easily, so maybe he was getting better at lying. There was that.

Nancy picked up her tea, sipped it, and poured the rest out. Cold, she said. Do you ever think about how we don't like cold tea when it's supposed to be hot, but other times we make cold tea on purpose?

I have thought about that, said Arthur. Many times.

What are you going to do about the hives? Fawk and I are here to help, if you think of something.

Thanks, Arthur said. I'm just going to have to start over. Maybe in another spot. Although this spot was supposed to be perfect.

Nancy reached out and put a hand on his shoulder. She waited for him to look at her. She said, Nothing is ever perfect, Arthur.

The remark stung. The whole point of things was to create a perfect day, and this little pearl of wisdom rendered it idiotic.

Evidently Nancy caught this and made the correction, Or I should say everything can be perfect, everything is perfect, in its own way, if you only let it.

Arthur laughed quietly. Now you're sounding like Faulkner.

After 35 years I guess he's going to rub off on me. Can I make us some fresh coffee?

Arthur thought about it. Caffeine didn't wake him up any more, not with so little sleep, now it only made him nervous.

He said, My grandfather used to drink just one cup of coffee, in this brown mug like they have in diners. He drank it standing up in his kitchen, after he finished his morning chores, like it was medicine. He stood at his back window and studied his land.

Oh? said Nancy.

Yeah, said Arthur. And in the summer, late afternoons, when he was sweaty from working outside, he stood in the same place and drank a screwdriver. He'd pour a glass of orange juice and top it off with vodka from a big jug and drink the whole thing at once, like it was medicine too. Sometimes he had sweat bee stings, little welts on his arms, that didn't seem to bother him. He'd say, Look, he got me, like it was wonderful.

Did he keep bees too?

He did, Arthur said. Five hives and not one of them ever failed. He had jars of perfect honey.

He gave Nancy a teasing look and said, Well, not actually perfect, of course.

Of course, she said.

Probably Nancy wanted to go and make coffee and get on with her day, but Arthur didn't want her to go. He continued, I learned from him that honey never goes bad or crystalizes if you store it correctly. You can't let any contaminants get in there, you know, and if you do it right, there are enzymes in the honey that keep it for as long as you like. I remember him holding up a frame dripping with such nice golden honey, and I was wearing a bee suit, but he just wore overalls because they mostly didn't sting him and when they did it didn't bother him. He was a huge man, you know, as tall as me but like a hundred pounds heavier and most of it muscle. He said, Honey doesn't crystalize in the hive—you see that? So no reason for it to go bad in the jar, not if you do the job right.

Nancy looked across the field at the trees over the river. She said, You're a lot like your grandfather I bet.

I wish, said Arthur. But not really. Too much of my parents in me.

Well that's a heavy statement, Artie.

I'm oversharing.

Not at all. I'll sit here all day and listen if you like. Did you spend a lot of time at your grandparents' place?

It seems like I spent all my time there. But just weekends, mostly. And holidays.

Nancy asked quietly, Did your parents come too? To your grandparents' place?

My parents, Arthur said, liked to go to conferences.

On weekends? What kind of conferences?

To be honest, I have no idea. I mean they were academic conferences I assume. Though I realize now that must have been mostly bullshit. My mom dropped me off at a fire station that was half way and Gramps and Grandma met me in their truck—an old Ford with wooden sides that said Prendergast Acres.

Can I ask, are your grandparents still with us?

No, Arthur said. Both dead. Like these bees.

Oh Arthur.

Sorry.

How about your parents? I've never seen them come around.

My dad lives in Arizona and my mom died five years ago.

He could feel Nancy looking at him, but he kept his gaze on the bee hives. She was probably tilting her head in that way, with that feeling in her eyes, and he couldn't face it.

He said, You know, I think I'll take you up on that coffee. We keep yakking here and this day will get away from us.

They stood up and brushed off their clothes. As they walked across the field, Nancy put her hand on Arthur's back, right at the shoulder blade, just for a moment, but that touch lasted with him for some time.

Arthur went to the farm supply store and bought fencing material and spent the rest of the morning constructing a barrier around his new plants. When Gramps built fences, he used lengths of wire that he twisted with his bare hands around the steel posts. These days you used zip ties that later you cut and throw away. Gramps never threw anything away. It seemed impossible to live like that now even if you tried. Gramps made an electric fence to keep an old mare he got in exchange for building a shed for Bob Grever, the township commissioner. Gramps never rode the mare—he was too big—and when she got lonely he bought a goat to keep her company. The electric fence ran off a marine battery fixed to the wall of the barn and inside the barn you could hear the converter clicking with each pulse of the fence. One time Gramps grabbed the live wire and released it, showing no effect. When Arthur tried it, the current shocked him and he fell on his ass. It turned out you had to listen to the clicks, and grab the wire between pulses. Later Arthur played this trick on one of his cousins, who cried until Grandma made him an ice cream float. There were so many birds back then, especially crows, who traveled in great trailing flocks at dusk toward some mysterious roost.

Arthur updated his OPD app—logging the construction of the fence and subtracting the score for the bee hives. There were so many more chores to do, but he had lost his gumption, so he walked back into the woods. He was drawn, as always, to the spot where Armando had lain. All along the river bank, cutleaf coneflower was sprouting in a carpet of green. But the spot of the body remained bare. Arthur had tossed seed there last fall, but nothing germinated—just a brown patch in the outline of a man, sprawled. What the fuck was that about? Just one more bizarre problem he didn't need—how would you explain this to the detectives when they combed your land? He dragged windfall branches to the spot and piled them up and lit them on fire. Now it was a burn pile, so he'd have an explanation. It was hopeless to expect life to spring from that spot. Sometimes you just had to burn.

When the fire reduced to embers, Hanacek appeared on the bank across the river, near the big snag Arthur had crossed the day he met the Martins. The mules flapped their ears and made the motions of grazing, walking along slowly, with Hanacek between them, hands clasped behind his back. Arthur watched as they moved gradually downriver until they disappeared around the bend. The old ghost farmer probably knew all the mysteries of that bend in the river and all the bends that followed. He just observed, and never interfered, and that was the way you knew things. You just observe and it comes to you. Like Gramps drinking his coffee—what did he learn each day as he observed?

Arthur decided to follow the river.

He drove to the first site where Armando had been photographed—Centerville, by the church. The river was lower than in the picture, due to the dry spring. In the picture Armando's torso tilted up from the water, his face staring at the sky. That seemed ridiculous now, looking at the current folding on itself. A dead body didn't just do that. Arthur took a picture and then drove down to Allerton park and hiked through the woods to where Armando had been pictured contorted like a statue. Several decayed maples lay across the water in a natural dam. A kingfisher chattered above the water, the first of the season. A dead body couldn't float past those maple snags—how long had they been there? He took another picture.

Arthur drove down to the bridge at Highway 32, where a video showed Armando revolving in the eddy—arms and legs splayed like the Vitruvian Man. As he looked at the video, and then at the water churning beneath the bridge, the #sangabody story seemed surreal—like a myth. It seemed ludicrous, this body floating down the river through impossible barriers, never decomposing. Whether it had actually happened or not, you could easily cast doubt on the whole conspiracy and maybe that would take the momentum out of it, maybe make it go away.

He sat on the tailgate of his truck and watched a tractor seeding a field a quarter mile away. A tanker semi sped past on the highway, shuddering Arthur's seat. He took out his phone and opened the social app and created a new account, called Hanacek321. He posted the pictures he had taken that day and tagged them #sangabodyhoax. He added comments pointing out how impossible the story was, how the river would never have yielded a floating human body. Then he put his phone away and poured coffee from his thermos and watched the tractor follow perfect lines across a field that had once been vast tallgrass prairie.

The coffee was cold.

TEN

The late-night call to Arthur was mortifying. The next morning, Morgan wondered if it had actually happened—so much that she checked her outgoing calls to verify that she had indeed made a call to Arthur at 1:17am, which lasted for a minute and seventeen seconds. That was a weird coincidence, the numbers, but whatever the important thing was that she had broken completely and prostrated herself to her husband from whom she was supposed to be separated—a separation that was supposed to help them understand their marriage, with the benefit of space and time and perspective. A blubbering call of weepy apologies was the last thing she should be doing. Arthur had been so kind and that made it worse. If you deleted the record of the call, would it erase the conversation from their memories? If only. Maybe one day AI would do that.

In the days that followed, the person who had made that call became a different person—an old Morgan, or a temporary Morgan—and she resolved to emerge a new self from that mortifying one and start doing separation properly. From pupa to butterfly. A fucking morpho butterfly with that shocking flash of blue.

Tante, she said, how long since someone cleaned your windows? You can barely see through them they're so dirty.

My window washer quit. He moved to Nashville to be a music star.

Well then I'll do them—do you have any old newspapers?

Tante, she said, today we're going to make spaetzle. You teach me.

No. I can't eat those rubber noodles any more. Ugh.

I bet you'll change your mind when there's a warm bowl in front of you. Where's that machine you use?

Tante, she said, let's get that old car in the garage running. Where are the keys?

That hunk of junk must be rusted—full of mice. Don't bother.

I'm sure it's a special car—wouldn't it be fun to go for a ride?

Ask Karl—he's around here somewhere.

Morgan became a catalyst, a dynamo, and while Mrs Vogel grumbled and worried, the activity was good for her. Every chore yielded stories. The work fueled their appetites. There's nothing hard work can't cure. If you keep moving, the demons can't catch you.

The city was enormous, infinite, teeming with adventure—millions of people in offices, workshops, alleys, pubs, apartments, game rooms, speakeasies, cafes, galleries. If you were bored, you must be boring. Morgan was many things but certainly not boring. People who move exhaust themselves, exhausted people sleep like the dead, the dead roam among us, inspiring more action, and the cycle accelerates. O Chicago!

Am I dreaming, asked Ashleigh. Is this really my introverted friend Morgan inviting me to go out?

Shut up, said Morgan. Let's throw axes. There's that place on Clark where you can throw axes.

I suck at axe throwing, said Ashleigh, giggling.

Well then you better start practicing.

The venue was called Second Axe, with a façade of rough-hewn boards and a wagon wheel out front. They played punk country music. Everyone wore flannel. The staff were serious about the art of axe throwing. The axes were very sharp. Morgan slid her wedding rings in her pocket so they didn't interfere with her technique.

Ashleigh arrived with a guy named Cody. He was bald by choice and had a precisely-groomed beard and muscles that burst through his flannel. But his eyes were gentle and he had a habit of touching Ashleigh's back, lightly, to protect her maybe? Cody was a gentleman. He bought them a round of beers and reserved a bay for throwing the axes.

Cody, said Morgan. Every guy at this place should be called Cody.

Maybe they are, said Cody. Seems like everybody our age is called Cody.

Western names, said Ashleigh. Very de rigueur.

Or fake Celtic names, said Cody. He winked and drank half his beer at once.

Touche, said Ashleigh.

When their turn came, the attendant brought a set of four axes wrapped in waxed canvas. He laid them with reverence on the spent bourbon barrel that served as a table.

Hi everybody, welcome to Second Axe, he said, I'll be helping you out tonight. I'm Kafka.

Morgan spit a little beer, laughing. No you're not! she said. Was it too rude?

He tilted his head, arranging the axes. Pretty sure I am, he said. Okay who's first? I guess with three, you'll just take turns?

What do you mean? Ashleigh asked. She took Cody's hand from her back and held it.

Usually people play teams—a foursome, said Kafka.

Morgan frowned. They should do this right. She said to Ashleigh, So Katie and Maddie definitely can't come?

Ashleigh shook her head, pulled out her phone. Hold on, she said.

Kafka looked back at the bar. You guys only have the lane for half an hour, he said.

I can pay for another, said Cody.

Ashleigh put away her phone. No it's cool, she said, I got a fourth. We can start and he'll catch up.

Sure enough, Lawrence Celotte arrived before Kafka had finished instructing them on the art of axe throwing. Larry wore a heavy green flannel and sturdy jeans. He looked freshly showered, his hair thrust back, mirth in his eyes, the scent of woods.

You remember my friend Morgan? Ashleigh said.

Of course, said Larry, and shook her hand. He greeted Cody with a bro shake—thumbs up, shoulders bumping. Did they know each other? Ashleigh must not know about her dates with Larry. Were they dates? Dates didn't have to be romantic did they? Was this a date—a double date? Morgan caught herself tucking her hair behind her ears, and then restrained.

Larry picked up one of the axes. Is this it? He asked, with mock disdain. Down the bayou we throw full-sized axes. Couldn't fell a fern with this thing. Guarantee.

He was laying on the Cajun accent. He ordered them all espresso martinis.

Okay let's see each of you throw, said Kafka. Then I'll leave you to it.

When Ashleigh threw, the others ducked, because she used her whole body and whirled her arm, but the axe stuck in the target. Cody hefted the axe, studied it like a pitcher scrutinizing his ball, and then flung it too hard, so the axe hit the wall sideways and skittered on the floor. Kafka suggested he use only his elbow and wrist. Considering this advice, Morgan tossed the axe lightly, confidently, and it sliced the bull's eye before dropping. Larry smiled in appreciation, kept his martini in his off hand, and threw the axe with a kind of carelessness. It bit the target and stayed, just off the bullseye.

Probably want to set your drink down, said Kafka. Anyway you're ready—have fun and godspeed.

Girls versus boys! said Ashleigh. I'll go first. There was no argument.

So you're a lefty, Larry said. He tapped Morgan's hand.

She held up the hand as if it were a specimen. Yes, she said, does that make me sinister?

No rings tonight, he replied. Has something changed?

Morgan patted her thigh. No, she said, just in my pocket. I take my axe throwing seriously.

Larry smiled. Did she notice a hint of relief? Or intrigue?

Cody still couldn't control his strength, and all his throws clattered to the floor. When Morgan threw, both axes stuck and scored points. It's strange how some things seem impossible until you learn the trick and then they are obvious, unremarkable. Another expresso martini appeared at the table when she was done. Larry nodded at her with lazy approval, his eyelids low. He kept his drink and flung both axes without hesitation, landing both.

You've done this before, she said.

Summers in Quebec, he replied, shrugging. Not much else to do.

Morgan squinted at him, tucked her hair behind her ear. She said, New Orleans, Paris, Quebec. The list is growing.

Just wait, said Larry. It's pretty long.

Oh! said Morgan. I can imagine. They caught each other's eye, held it, and laughed.

Break it up, you two! said Ashleigh. Your throw, sister. Let's not blow this.

Morgan looked back, smiled at her friends, turned, and threw a bullseye. The next throw was wide, but stuck. As she returned to the table, triumphant, she found her hand in her pocket, fiddling with her rings, flipping them over. Larry downed his martini, posed with the axe, and threw. It went wide and fell. Morgan fiddled more with the rings, nervously? Was it competitiveness, or something else? Her wedding band popped from her pocket and rolled across the lane. Instinctually, she rushed to grab it. Larry's throw passed by her head, whistling, just barely missing her ear, and stuck in the bullseye.

Morgan let out a small yelp and covered her head as if that would do something now. Larry was by her immediately. I'm so sorry, he said. Shit I might have hit you. He said it flatly, his accent vanished. Oh my god you are so lucky, said Ashleigh, hand over her mouth. Larry handed Morgan the ring, and she put it on her finger.

Kafka was there now, saying, Everything okay here? No one in the lane while throwing.

It's fine, said Cody, we're good.

Having escaped injury, Morgan felt exhilarated. It was like in the alley with the boy and his gun. Who was the warrior who could charge through the battlefield and never get shot? Washington? Alexander? Probably it was just luck, but to everyone else, they were special. Was Morgan special now? That was childish thinking. But it felt good, to be the survivor, to wave off the expressions of concern.

After that, Larry threw poorly. The girls beat the boys at the game. Their time was up.

Cody packed the axes in their waxed canvas, shaking his head. Just can't quite get the hang of it, he said.

Ashleigh hugged him from behind. You're cute when you lose, she said. Let's go back to my place. Axes make me hot.

Morgan and Larry stood on Clark street, illuminated by all the shop marquees, the headlights of passing cars. It was unusually warm out. The air was still and buoyant and made you feel like you could run with huge bounding leaps.

What now? Morgan asked.

How about a walk? I reckon this night isn't done yet.

His accent had returned. They walked east, toward the park, toward the lake. Morgan let her arms swing, touching things as they went—parking meters, mail boxes, brick walls, tree trunks.

Morgan said, So Ashleigh doesn't know we know each other now?

I guess not. He held out his arm to stop her from walking through a red light.

You didn't tell her we're friends? She would like that. It occurred to Morgan just now that she hadn't told Ashleigh either.

I don't know Ashleigh too well, Larry said. Mostly I see her in the gym and we talk about workouts.

She's kind of a cad.

That's a good word.

Or a rake.

I don't know about that one. Rakes are guys, I think.

You're probably right.

Honestly I know you a lot better than Ashleigh now, he said.

She's very smart, Morgan said, But there's not that much to know. No offense to her, but she kind of is what you think when you first meet her. I'm a little jealous of that to be honest.

Because you're not what people think?

Probably not. Are you?

They were in the park now, standing by the Conservatory. The park lamps glowed like planets on the steel and glass entry. Beyond that, the structure loomed in darkness. Larry crossed his arms and studied it. It was surprisingly quiet, just a rush of cars out on the drive.

Larry broke the silence. How old do you think this building is?

1890s I'm guessing, she said.

The Gilded Age.

Seems like a fun time to live. If you were rich. All these new inventions.

What do you reckon they'll call our age? Larry glanced at her, genuinely curious it seemed.

The question called for a clever answer. The first thing to come to mind was Digital Age, but that was boring, and also the digital state of things was likely to go on a long time, so in the future that term wouldn't distinguish their age from that present new time. It was kind of depressing, thinking about their age. But maybe it would seem romantic to future people? If there were future people? These days everyone seemed to be trying to escape the present, to make it either some nostalgic past, or some dystopian future. She had waited to answer too long.

Maybe the Virtual Age, she said.

Larry looked her in the face, thinking. He blinked a few times. That's good, he said. Most of the time our minds are spent in a virtual state—in these. He held up his phone. His accent had faded again.

Can I ask you, Morgan said. I mean, it seems like your accent comes and goes.

Was that a question?

She cocked her head. She was learning that he teased when he was uncomfortable. She didn't want him to dodge the question. His expression fell a bit, like a laughing person suddenly remembering a tragedy.

You called me a shapeshifter before, said Larry. You still think that? Like I'm a phony?

Sorry, it was just a question.

Well not technically.

Right. Well, sorry if that was too intrusive.

No. The honest answer is I don't know. Sometimes the Cajun comes out, when I'm feeling like that. Sometimes other places come out.

So you're really from Lake Charles.

Yes. But from other places too.

That's fair.

They walked down the path, toward the zoo.

What do I sound like? Do I have an accent?

You sound like you're from here, he said.

The zoo was locked and they put their hands on the bars of the gate, looking in. The scent of animals rose in the air. It was a melancholy smell, from a time when zoos seemed nice and you could eat hot dogs without guilt.

Do you like zoos? he asked.

They make me sad, she said.

Same, he said. I want to believe they're still useful—like, connecting people with animals so we develop some compassion and help with conservation and you know.

So the caged animals are like martyrs, helping all the free animals.

That's the problem, he said.

That's the problem, said Morgan.

They wandered around the zoo, now aimlessly it seemed. The park was confusing at night. Two people passed on bikes with their spokes illuminated in LEDs.

Morgan asked, Do you have good memories of zoos from when you were a kid?

Still walking, Larry rubbed his hands together, and dropped his head. He was considering something deep maybe.

He said, I don't remember good memories when I was a kid. Not to be a downer, but.

No that's fine, she said. Go on. I think I can relate.

I remember one time playing with some action figures. It's funny we don't call them dolls, because they're really dolls if you think about it. But anyway. I was playing with a set of Ninja Turtles in the sand by our house and I remember thinking at the time that this was probably the last time

I'd be playing with them because I would soon be too old to play that way anymore. I mean my childhood should have been happy enough—we were upper middle class and had everything I needed. Friends, etc. But still it was this profoundly sad moment of the end of things. That's what I remember.

What's your IQ, Morgan asked.

What? Larry laughed, surprised.

Sorry, I mean I was just thinking that maybe really high IQ people have more trouble being happy. I'm assuming you have a high IQ? Being an astrophysicist.

Never took a test. It was kind of passé when we were kids. Did you take one?

Morgan could picture the pages of a test on her parents' dining room table. Finding the shapes that corresponded with other views of shapes. It seemed fun at the time. She didn't realize she was being tested then.

No, she said. I don't think I did. Or I don't remember.

There was a bench beside the path, and Larry sat on it. She sat next to him. He put his head back and closed his eyes.

What a night, he said. I love spring.

Morgan looked at him, so resigned to the moment. He had a good face, a face worth drawing. Maybe all faces were worth drawing? Strange how each one was different, even between identical twins. It would be so nice to have a twin. Then: What was she doing here? Sitting on this park bench with this guy? Into the periphery of her awareness came notions of her life—the mansion, Middling… It was like they were on land and she was far from shore now. Untethered.

I wanted to be a musician, he said, his eyes still closed. I tried to play the violin and I was terrible. I was hard on myself. A very gloomy kid, honestly. I thought about death a lot and wrote some poems that were probably scary when my mom found them. Then my uncle from Montreal gave me a telescope.

He raised his head suddenly, grinning at her. This is going to sound cliché, he said.

No go on.

Seriously, it's very cliché. Can you handle it?

Things are cliches because they're true. Come on. She was grinning now too.

It was a really fancy telescope, he said, that you could program to rotate with the celestial sphere and look at very distant objects for long periods of time. When I looked into space, I was no longer sad. I just understood, implicitly, that there are no emotions in space. So that's where I wanted to spend all my time.

And then you went to the Sorbonne.

Larry laughed. Eventually, yes. I went to the Sorbonne.

That is super cliché.

I told you.

They sat for a while with this. It was nice that he had shared with her. That was probably difficult. Why do we choose to confide in people? Maybe it was better to not overthink this.

You probably want to go home now, Larry said.

I could walk a little longer. I'm not tired.

Espresso martinis.

They're the best.

Until tomorrow.

That's tomorrow's problem.

Okay let's walk.

They continued south down the path. You always knew what direction things were in Chicago.

Now it's your turn, he said. Tell me something cliché about your childhood.

Oh I don't know, Morgan said. I guess I went the opposite route, immersing myself in people's problems. Once I found a bird with a broken wing and I tried to help it heal. My neighbor saw this and said you should be a doctor. That stuck with me, but the thought of being a doctor stressed me out—the responsibility, you know? So I went into nursing. Is that cliché enough for you?

It's pretty cliché.

I wonder if we're using that term right. Maybe we mean trite.

Also trite. So you like nursing then?

I guess? It's just what I do. On a good day you tell yourself that you're relieving suffering. On a bad day you realize that all your patients are dying, bit by bit, or sometimes faster, and all your efforts are only temporary.

Well at least you aren't an escapist, like I am.

No, said Morgan. But Arthur is worse. She was surprised to hear herself say his name.

Your husband, said Larry.

Yes, my husband. He's even more committed to an impossible task that is certain to fail—the conservation of wildlife, the idea of restoration. I help people. He helps plants and animals, who are even more doomed than we are.

Morgan could feel Larry look at her.

Anyway, she said, and raised her arms. Springtime!

I hope I'm not bringing you down, with this conversation, he said.

No, yeah, no. I've been kind of pumped lately actually. But at the same time sort of numb. Like when you want to cry but can't.

Sometimes I listen to music that makes me cry.

Because you can't play it?

Ha. Good one.

Sorry, couldn't help myself.

I also suffer from numbness. You know what I do? I jump in a lake. Figuratively.

No, literally. I learned this from some Swedes I met in northern

Minnesota. It feels good to shock yourself.

Not far from where they walked, Lake Michigan swelled with power and mystery. This vast inland sea that brought so much pleasure and pain. Did she feel it calling to her? Can a lake call to you? She heard herself say

Should we jump in the lake now? She wasn't sure if she were bluffing.

Sure, he said. I'm always up for that.

They looked at each other, and there was understanding, and then they ran down the path toward North Avenue beach. They ran because if they allowed any time to pass, they'd chicken out, and talk sense into themselves, and miss this rare moment of carelessness. The only thing that mattered was to be in the cold water, despite all the daunting logistics as yet unsolved, despite all the consequences they might later regret.

At a park shelter, Larry stopped. He looked out at the lake, avoiding her gaze. The thing is, he said. We can't get our clothes wet.

Morgan began to shiver in anticipation. Her heart pounded—that was good. The adrenaline would help, if she was going to do this. No, she said, We should avoid that.

Okay then, said Larry. He began to unbutton his flannel shirt.

Morgan looked away. She said, You can't look at me, though.

Of course not, he said. I'll go first.

So she went through the process of disrobing, her fingers trembling so it was difficult to unzip, to unbutton. But then she was naked and shivering wildly. In the periphery she saw a flash of human racing out on the beach. She wanted to look but didn't because that would make this different from what she intended. Instead, she ran too. The sand pulled away beneath her feet, still warm from the sunny day, and then she felt the coldness of the water in the shallows, splashing up on her calves and thighs, and it was shallow for longer than she expected, so that she became aware of herself streaking across a beach in Chicago, and then she slowed down as the water rose to her butt—this would be the most shocking part—and when she was waist-deep, without hesitation she dove into the cold waters of the lake and then she was submerged in a bubbling quietness and she let her body propel through the water until it stopped.

Larry was treading water a few yards from her. Lights from the shore reflected off his thick hair, off his open-wide eyes.

See what I mean? he cried.

Morgan's jaw trembled in the cold, but she was adjusting to it. The water felt lovely, and reassuring. It was the first time she had ever swum naked. She treaded water and her heart surged and she said, Yeah but now I think I'm more numb!

Larry swam a few strokes further out, his head bobbing. Think about other things, he called. Think about science!

Science?!

All these water molecules. Millions of years old! Or older. Molecules that came from glaciers, molecules that were maybe in dinosaurs!

That was maybe a trite observation but also it was true, probably, water connecting all things through time. It didn't matter though. She became calmer, and turned to backstroke away from him, and then dog paddled in his direction, and then treaded water, looking at the lights of the buildings downtown. It all connected, everything. Good old Larry. What a guy, what a good friend. He had done her such a favor, this glorious night. She would like to hug him now, just out of appreciation. But of course she wouldn't, because she was naked.

Instead she said, I'm going in now. Give me a minute to get dressed.

Okay, but you can't watch me come out, he said. And hurry!

Morgan wasted no time.

ELEVEN

Arthur removed the last screw from the cabinet above the stove. It was nearly stripped, and he had to push hard for the bit to grip, then the screw lost its hold and Arthur felt the weight of the plywood box fall on him. It was too much for one arm and the cabinet crashed to the stove, which he had protected with a couch cushion. Probably it would have been better to move the stove out of the way, but that involved fussing with the gas line, and this morning he was eager to do some demolition—to see satisfying progress on this sixth goal for the perfect day: that is, The farmhouse stands ship shape.

He carried the cabinet out to the pile next to the garage, the door annoying him, flapping against his shoulder. It felt good to be strong enough to carry whole cabinets like they were cardboard boxes, like Gramps would. It was pleasing to hear the frame crack as it fell among the other demolished cabinets. Back in the kitchen, he checked that the stove burners still worked, that the gas line was intact, and then studied the plaster where the cabinets had hung. Squares of horrible burnt orange revealed a past paint job when fashion called for earth tones, contrasting with the linen white he and Morgan had painted, hastily, when they first moved in. Morgan, who persisted in her silence these days, Morgan who was lost no doubt in some new life free of Arthur.

There was water damage to the orange plaster behind that cabinet. When Arthur poked it with a crowbar, the plaster crumbled away. He hooked it, and tore some more, until the hole was the size of a cat, and found that the lath was black with mold and the insulation wet. So there must be a leak still, which meant there was a hole somewhere up on the roof, allowing rain to come down the inner walls, corrupting everything. There were ants, too, hundreds of them scurrying away. Carpenter ants, most likely, following the water.

Arthur sat on the linoleum floor and tapped the crowbar against his hand. It would be easy now to be overwhelmed, to succumb to despair, but if you made a little effort you realized all this was just information. He was merely importing data into his brain, where he would process it and devise a solution for the problem. Just information. Just data. Like Morgan's refusal to contact him—facts that required processing, all feeding into a plan. They were connected these things—fixing the kitchen would please Morgan, maybe more than all the farming and gardening, and so a solution to the rotten wall would yield a solution to the recalcitrant wife. This was the way to think about things.

That said. That said, water damage and carpenter ants could require massive excavation, and new framing, and a restored vapor barrier, and a repaired roof, and possibly new siding, and certainly new drywall. It could consume all his time, possibly, heading into the summer, when Failure Farm would need more attention. Worse yet, it could cost a lot of money. And Arthur was short on money.

If Morgan hadn't paid for the property with a fund her parents had given her, Arthur and Morgan would never have been able to afford the woe-begotten farm. But even so, the taxes were steep and the utilities were high and everything needed repair, and there was insurance and food and gas and animal feed and seed and mulch and… and… and.

He could barely cover essentials with his website business and so all the extravagance of Failure Farm went on a credit card. They hadn't talked about finances, he and Morgan, before she left or since. Neither had the stomach for it. He couldn't bring himself to ask because she had expenses of her own now, and nothing in Chicago was cheap, and after all she had paid for the farm.

An ant crossed the floor in front of him, scouting some new trail of scent. Carpenter ants weren't too hard to kill, supposedly. You just set a trap of sweet poison, which the workers brought back and fed the queen. Once the colony was dead, you just had to address the source of water, and repair the rot, and seal everything up, and your house was whole again. Strange how we celebrate nature when it's outside, but when it comes in our houses, we don't rest until it's destroyed. Well that wasn't entirely true, because outside you fought the deer and the groundhogs and countless rapacious insects and all the other pests. We cannot live peacefully with nature—not the way things are now. Or did we ever?

If he were honest with himself, Arthur hadn't worked very hard at the website business. He put in a few hours each day, tweaking sites he'd already built, responding to requests from clients. But often he forgot to track his hours, to bill them. And it had been months since he acquired a new client. This was unforgivable, really. For example, there was a prospective client—the Middling Café—who had reached out to him in January, and still he hadn't sent an estimate. And now, he sat on the floor of his demolished kitchen, watching an ant.

So he set the crowbar on the counter and took an apple and a handful of peanuts and went out to his truck and drove to the Middling Café. With luck he could sign a contract with the owner that afternoon. With luck he'd come home with a check. Actually, maybe he could sign a new client each week, and the payments would pile up, expanding with his business, extending into new markets—possibly much of central Illinois, possibly Chicago! With that kind of work, that kind of cash coming in, maybe he could hire a contractor to do the kitchen—no, just do all the water damage repairs and annoying tasks. Arthur would build the kitchen, beautifully, and Morgan would admire it.

The cafe was a single-story building painted the colors of Middling University, at a busy intersection on the edge of campustown. A tall marquee sign rose from the parking lot, picturing an Italian-looking chef holding a plate above his head, surrounded by light bulbs that had once flashed in sequence but burned out a decade earlier. The café was almost full, as usual, and at the door, the waitress called out to him, Sit anywhere you like hon. He found the one open booth along the rail that separated the dining area from the kitchen.

The café owner, Tristan Beardsley, was not in that day. The waitress explained that he had extended his winter stay in Florida. We don't really need him, she said, except to sign the checks. Arthur found Tristan's email and saw that if he had read it carefully, he would have known. Now he was stuck paying for a late lunch he wasn't hungry for. He took a picture of the row of seated customers and emailed it to Tristan Beardsley with the remark, *Love this place—can't wait to work with you on your website.*

When he lowered his phone, he saw someone wave from the end of the café. There were three men—he recognized them, but from where? Well, one was the deputy sheriff, confirmed by the holster bulging from his hip on the outside of the booth. His name was Myron something, or maybe Byron. Faulkner had introduced them once at the tavern. Or was it at a music festival? If you went somewhere in town with Faulkner and Nancy you met so many people. But who were the other two guys? The older guy called across the restaurant, beckoning Arthur to come over, and so he did.

He was preparing to fake it, but as he walked the aisle it came to him. Of course! The waving man—bald with a fringe, gap-toothed smile—this was Bradley Martin, from across the river. Beside him sat

Ravelin Magpie, the smooth-talking pastor.

Arthur smiled when he reached the booth and said, Hello neighbor. He held out his hand to shake, but Bradley gave him a fist-bump, which seemed strange for someone of his age. The pastor smiled warmly, with a bit of surprise, as if Arthur were a friend returning from some long adventure. The deputy twitched his head in the most minimal greeting, and stared away. He had delicate features, very pale skin, a black goatee.

Sit down, said Bradley, Join us. Move over, Myron, make room for the kid. This is my neighbor across the crick, from the Hanacek place—he's good people.

Arthur paused, indecisive. The waitress, passing with two plates, said, It's all right, I'll bring your coffee over hon.

The deputy stood up, adjusting his holstered belt, so that Arthur could slide into the booth. Arthur didn't want to join them, he had a sense of being trapped, but there was no stopping this string of events. Also, as Faulkner often said, you don't pass up an opportunity to visit—something good always comes from a visit, even if it takes a while.

The men had finished their meal, and their plates lay scraped clean in the middle of the table. The waitress filled their coffees, and Bradley said, Leave the bill open—whatever this young man wants. So Arthur ordered a tuna melt, which seemed to amuse Bradley, who looked at Myron, who made a wry smile and then looked out the window.

There was a painful moment of silence, then Ravelin leaned toward Arthur and said, Isn't this a gorgeous day? This whole spring has been… miraculous!

Yeah, no, yeah said Arthur. I mean, spring is always kind of a miracle you know? All this green material suddenly coming out of roots and trunks. Birds just knowing where to fly to start breeding. But yeah this spring especially.

Arthur had the sense that if he stopped talking, the table would descend into excruciating silence again. But Bradley broke in:

How's it coming on the old Hanacek farm, Arthur? You still hauling junk out of there?

Arthur felt a tremor in his stomach. Why had he named his fake social account Hanacek? It seemed funny at the time, but he forgot some folks still knew the name. Also, Morgan would see it and she would definitely not approve. Arthur considered going to the bathroom to delete the account—could you delete accounts?—but it would be too rude so he sat still.

Every day! he laughed. But you know, you keep at it. Little bit every day. How are things on your side of the river.

Oh you know, said Bradley, we keep at it. Always something to do.

Arthur recalled their conversation in the field, and turned to the pastor. Ravelin, right?

The pastor raised his eyebrows theatrically, lifted a finger, and said, Very good!

You were planning an event last we talked. Did that happen yet?

You know, Arthur, the pastor said, It hasn't. Not for a few weeks. Waiting for it to warm up. Hoping we'll see you there!

There was that voice—that beautiful, flowing pastor's voice. You didn't want it to stop. Bradley lifted a fork and pointed it at Arthur, saying, You should bring the missus.

Myron turned his gaze away from the window and squinted hard at Bradley. The older man looked back at the deputy steadily. He said, He's good people. Like I said.

When the sandwich came, Arthur ate, and the men waited in silence. The pastor tapped his fingertips together, gazing in peace around the café. The other two sipped their cups. Arthur wasn't hungry any more and it took effort to get the food down. He left the crusts, and washed his dry mouth with coffee, which made him jittery. How could they just sit there without talking? Lots of people did that in town, the old-timers. It made you kind of jealous, seeing how people could just sit together in silence, as if being together were enough and talking ruined the moment.

Finally Myron spoke, looking over their heads. He said, People are saying we could use some rain.

Arthur said, We sure could. The river's low for spring.

The deputy turned to him and asked, Why's that matter to you—how high the river is?

Arthur didn't have an answer. He added, Well, I reckon it's good that the farmers are getting their seed in.

You reckon, said Bradley, and the three men laughed.

Then he gave a side-smile at Arthur and said, You been spending a lot of time along the river? Looking for something special?

What could Arthur say to this? Would Bradley ask that just coincidentally, without knowing that yes actually Arthur had been spending a lot of time along the river, visiting sites where the body had been seen. But then maybe Bradley was just weird.

Arthur pulled his face back with that look of disdain that northern men make, and said, Who told you that?

Bradley looked at Myron, then Ravelin. Who told me that? he repeated.

Ravelin put a hand on Bradley's shoulder, with a look of kindness, and said, I think we might be making the young man uncomfortable with all this unintended subtext. It's just small talk, Arthur, just making conversation.

Bradley pulled away from the pastor's hand, and trained eyes on Arthur, suddenly intense. The dogs tell me, he said. They're awful gossips.

There was a moment of painful suspense, and then all three men guffawed. You don't hear guffaws very often, but these were definitely that. Arthur smiled and leaned his head like, Got me.

Then there was the sound of bells jingling as someone opened the café door. Bradley looked up over the deputy's shoulder and said, Well, shit.

Arthur turned to see a stout woman ignore the waitress and march down the aisle toward them. She wore cargo shorts and an outdoor fleece. She had tightly cropped hair and a face that was chubby and stern and pretty at once. The mood of the café seemed to change with her entrance. She came to their table, bumped the edge with her thighs, and pulled from her attaché a sheet of paper, which she lay in front of the deputy with a slap of her hand.

Your boss won't answer my calls, she said, so I thought I'd find you here.

Myron didn't look at the paper. He said, Hello Peg.

In an overly courteous way, Bradley began to introduce her to Arthur, but it wasn't necessary. Arthur recognized her—this was Peg Hanrahan, the attorney who had been looking for Armando Gallardo. The paper was a flyer, printed from her website, with the photo of Armando, alive and well. Arthur had seen this—but now, there was another photo. It was taken from a #sangabody post, the one that showed his face clearly, beaten badly, floating in the river.

Peg ignored Bradley and continued addressing the deputy. She poked a finger at the flyer, and said, There's your body. She paused for effect, and then continued, Our duly-elected Sheriff says he has no case without a body. Well, now he has one. And there are many more of these pictures. If you're unfamiliar with the internet, I'd be happy to assist you, Myron. Tell your boss we have a body now and I'll be filing with the DA.

Myron scratched his neck and turned his head away. He muttered, Well, there's plenty of shit on the internet – that don't constitute evidence of a crime. You know that, Peggy.

The attorney reached down and slid the flyer closer to him, and said, Tell your boss we have a body. Then she smiled to the others, resting her gaze for an extra moment on Arthur. Gentlemen, she said, and walked out of the café.

The waitress came to collect the plates and set down the check beside

Bradley and said, No hurry hon. Bradley took out his wallet and set cash down, paused to think, and set down another five-dollar bill. As he did this, he said, Have you heard about that, Arthur—that farm worker went missing?

Arthur struggled to focus his mind. He glanced again at the flyer and recognized the gruesome, injured face and recalled the body lying by the river that morning with Morgan and the sound the vultures' wings made in the woods as they flapped away. But there was another, parallel process running in his brain now, a clever self who forced Arthur to assume a calm, but curious expression, as if he were calculating a sum, or debugging some code on a website.

No, he said. I haven't. He looked at Myron and gestured to the flyer and said, Do you mind?

Myron sniffed his consent, and Arthur slid the paper toward himself and asked, What happened to him?

Who knows, said Bradley. Those people are always coming and going. Probably ran off with another woman up to Chicago. Or back to Mexico to blow all his wages. Doesn't matter. You know what I mean, Arthur?

Arthur looked at Bradley Martin. The older man didn't blink. Neither did Arthur, and he managed to keep that mild, curious look on his face. He asked, What do you suppose happened to his face?

The deputy continued looking out the window. The pastor studied a tiny New Testament he must have pulled from his robes.

Bradley didn't look at the photo. He said, That picture's a fake. To cause trouble. It doesn't matter. Do you know what I mean?

This time he emphasized the question, as an imperative. Arthur backed down.

I do, he said. And then on an impulse, he added, None of my business, anyway.

There you go, said Bradley. He reached across the table and slapped

Arthur's arm. There you go. Good people don't need to go looking for trouble.

They all stood up at once, and Myron gestured for Arthur to go first, and they walked out of the café in single file. Arthur looked to say thanks to the waitress, whose name he had meant to catch, but she must have been in the back. He thanked Bradley for lunch and promised to see them all around and went to his truck and sat. He heard Bradley's car start in a roar, and drive away. As he retrieved his phone, his hands shook as if he were being electrocuted. It was almost comical, trying to send a text. He kept typing and deleting, over and over, but then eventually he sent a message to Morgan.

He wrote, *I think I know who killed Armando.*

In less than 30 seconds, his phone rang.

TWELVE

Morgan saw Arthur's text just after she finished making a smoothie for Mrs Vogel, using powder the old woman had bought in French Lick. She was in the sunroom enjoying the afternoon. Morgan handed her a tall cup with its built-in straw and excused herself to make the call. Mrs Vogel nodded and stared at the drink as if it were some new adversary.

On the front stoop, Morgan touched Arthur's number and as it rang, she walked the path through the iron gate to the sidewalk. She had a rush of awareness that this was a gorgeous afternoon, the warmth of the sun drawing fragrances of spring from the soil and the trees. An oriole whistled from a sweetgum tree. Morgan looked back, on some instinct, and saw in Mrs Vogel's front window the form of a tall man looking out—peering around the drapes, beside the leaded glass. He disappeared as Arthur answered. All this took just a few seconds.

You must have seen my text, Arthur said.

His voice sounded strange, a higher pitch than usual.

Morgan said, Of course, that's why I called. What's going on?

Well I'm just sitting here in my truck at the Middling Café. Kind of freaking out—sorry.

What happened? Morgan felt her scalp tingle, her pulse quicken. Always there was drama with Arthur it seemed. The distance she had created recently made this more striking.

I just had lunch with Bradley Martin, Arthur said, and that pastor, Magpie, and a cop. Cripes, my hands are still shaking. Arthur laughed with a hint of lunacy.

Who are those people, Arthur? Can you start at the beginning?

Well you remember I met the people who live across the river.

Of course.

They're the Martins. The dad is Bradley. That's who I had lunch with just now. That same time back by the river I met the pastor too—wearing his robes, weirdly, but also some kind of muck boots. Maybe he borrowed them. They were with the deputy sheriff, Byron something.

Myron, Morgan corrected.

Who?

I think you mean Myron. The deputy sheriff is Myron Banks.

How do you know that?

Maybe 'cause I lived there for a while?

Are you being sarcastic? he asked. I can't tell.

Please just tell your story, Arthur.

Right. Okay. So I came by the café to talk with the owner who's supposed to be a new client of mine, but is actually down in Florida now—not that those things are exclusive, but I emailed him so hopefully he'll respond soon. Anyway that's not the point, sorry. While I was there, those three guys called me over—well actually Bradley called me over, and kind of insisted I eat with them. It was pretty weird TBH, I don't think I completely understood what was going on, seemed like a lot of subtext. But Bradley was extra nice and kept saying I was 'good people' and paid for the lunch. Anyway after I ate my tuna melt (which they seemed to think was funny. Not sure what's funny about a tuna melt?). After that, the door blasts open and here comes Peg Hanrahan, marching right to our table. I nearly shit my pants.

Morgan felt her stomach tighten. She said, Peg Hanrahan, like the lawyer?

Yeah, who's been investigating the Armando Gallardo case… or, situation, or whatever.

Oh Jesus, Arthur.

Exactly.

And she came for you? Why?!

No, no—she came for the cop, for Byron.

Myron.

Right. She came to give him a flyer, which had Armando's info on it and also some #sangabody pictures. She said that now they had proof of a body so the sheriff had to investigate. I guess he hasn't taken the case or made it official or whatever.

No Arthur, he hasn't, and Peg Hanrahan is pissed about that, and she's representing Lupe, the wife. You know this—it's all on Peg's site.

Yes, yes, I know. You don't have to patronize me. I'm just a little rattled right now, so.

Sorry, I don't mean to be patronizing—but your text said you knew who killed him, so…?

I'm getting to that. I just needed to give you context.

Arthur paused. Morgan could feel him pouting, that sad-boy expression on his big ginger face. There was a time when that face could get her to do anything, within reason, but now it was annoying. Immature. Down the sidewalk the gentleman in the blue suit and fedora was walking his white dog. The dog had to run to keep up, its tiny legs a cartoon blur. Morgan followed the man with her gaze, to see if he would acknowledge her. But he just proceeded. What a strange neighborhood this was, after all these years. Did that man live here then, when Morgan was a kid? He seemed familiar, but maybe the brain fabricates memories on frequent exposure.

Arthur said, Morgan?

You were giving me context, she said.

Arthur let the rest of the story out in a rush. He said, Well the point is that all three of them acted suspicious while Peg was talking and after she left they were even more suspicious and when I asked questions they made it clear that I shouldn't and I began to think that maybe they had something to do with Armando's death, since they live right there and we know someone came with a vehicle with a loud exhaust note and dumped the body and yelled Go go go—you remember all this…

Of course, Arthur.

So I was already thinking about how they might have been involved—maybe they knew who did it and had some reason to cover it up, and the sheriff or at least Myron was in on it. Well then we went out to the parking lot and while I was getting in my truck I heard their car start up and it was the exact same exhaust note as the one that dropped the body on that day last year.

Holy shit, said Morgan.

Holy shit is right.

You know your exhaust notes, she added.

I do know my exhaust notes, Arthur replied, And you always made fun of me but this time it's worth something.

Holy shit, she repeated. That was a weird expression—the two words together conjured up a strange concept. So the neighbors did it. They killed the guy she and Arthur found on the day she left him. That was a lot to think about. That was some serious holy shit. The gentleman with the dog turned at the stop sign down the block, holding his chin high.

Arthur, why? She asked, just generally, meaning many things.

You mean why did they kill him?

Well, yes. But also why did they dump the body on our property, and why did they act like that at the café? Like did they think you might know and they were trying to hush you up?

Heck if I know, Morgan. Arthur paused a moment—she could feel that he wasn't pouting anymore, he was thinking. Then he said, Why did you say you were sorry?

Morgan knew exactly what he meant, that night on the phone, the last time they talked. So that was his preoccupation, even in the face of this alarming news. He couldn't let things go. But to be fair, it had been strange and she would want to know too, if he had called crying and just said 'sorry' over and over.

What are you going to do? She asked. About the body and the Martins. And Peg Hanrahan.

Armando, he said.

Yes, right. About Armando.

Arthur paused again. Nothing, he said, with conviction. I'm going to do nothing, like Timothy, Faulkner's lawyer friend, like he said. Just let it blow over.

Timothy said that? I don't remember that. You said he just talked about the hypothetical. Arthur did you tell them more?

Well, no, Arthur said. He just implied it. Like, don't poke the bear.

This time Arthur seemed less sure. He had always been a terrible liar. She admired this about him—that he didn't have the constitution to lie well. But maybe that was changing. A furniture delivery van pulled in front of a mansion down the street and parked in front of a fire hydrant, hazards blinking. There was something about that act—of putting on your hazards to park anywhere you wanted, as if you were saying, 'oh my gosh I've had a sudden emergency in this illegal spot, so you can't ticket me.' Something about it crystallized her thoughts.

Arthur, why are we obsessing about this?

Arthur paused a beat and said, What do you mean? Like this isn't a big deal? It's kind of a big deal.

Yeah but why? I mean, what did we do, really? We saw a dead body, and later, it disappeared. We didn't do anything with it. That's not illegal.

Timothy's assessment, if I understood correctly, was all about if we had tampered with it. That was the felony. We couldn't be blamed for that if we didn't actually do anything except see it.

Arthur was silent.

You see my point, Morgan said.

Well, we didn't report it, he said, his voice weaker now. I wanted to, but you didn't let us.

Well maybe I was wrong. In that moment. Sorry. But now why don't we just go to the cops or Peg or whoever and tell them what we saw and explain that we didn't know what to do at the time but now that's it's out, we just want to do the right thing—just come clean and then we can walk away.

Arthur sighed, and said, Except that the Martins know that we know—or that we suspect it. They made that clear over lunch—to leave it alone and be good people. Also, there's the issue of property value, with our place being the scene of a murder. So.

Why do you care? She asked. Would you ever want to sell that place?

Well no, he protested. This is our home. We can't just give up on it.

What if I already have? She said, and knew it was cruel the moment it came out.

Don't say that, he said.

Morgan couldn't stop now, even though she knew it was cruel. Now that he had let those rednecks pull them into this hideous crime. It was infuriating. She said, When are you going to come to grips that everything has changed? We aren't going back to how things were.

Arthur raised his voice, I never changed from the way we were! You're the one who changed and created all this trouble.

The volume was painful and Morgan pulled the phone away from her ear. This was just bullshit, blaming her for everything, as if he were just a victim. She felt the argument escalate and couldn't stop it.

She asked, When's the last day we had together that was just really nice? Can you even remember? Cause it's a long time ago, long before all this shit. You know, in the last few weeks I've had some really nice days, and I remembered what that's like. Just to be joyful and adventurous. Just doing fun things without all this tension—we even threw axes…

Morgan stopped, realized what she had let out, hoping he had missed it.

We? he asked.

Oh just a friend, it doesn't matter.

Are you seeing someone?

I don't know what that means. We're married. Why would you even ask me that?

Those nice days, he said, was one the day you called and said you were sorry?

Morgan considered lying, but that was a bad habit. She wasn't a deceitful person, was she? She said, Yes. But so what.

What were you sorry for?

I don't remember. I was drunk.

You were drunk with someone. Tell me about this friend.

I don't have to tell you about every friend I do something with. You have to respect our separation—that's the whole point.

But you said we're married.

Stop it, Arthur! It was just an example, okay? We have to decide what to do about that body or just forget about it.

Armando.

Fine. We have to decide what to do about Armando Gallardo. I keep thinking about it, and it doesn't make sense to me—how we're so obsessed, and how he got in the river. I feel like you're not telling me something.

Arthur responded immediately, I've told you like a hundred times—it flooded and the river must have washed him away.

Past that big snag back there?

Morgan, there are so many snags that body got past—none of it make sense.

He was right—there were so many problems with the story. Then she remembered what she'd seen on the social app. She said, Oh my god that's right—why did you create that Hanacek account? If you want to lay low, why would you do that?

I don't know. It was stupid.

It was very stupid. People know that name. Why don't you delete it?

You can't delete accounts. But I deleted all the posts.

And that made it worse—with the conspiracy.

For now, yeah. Hopefully it will phase out soon.

Now he was pouting again—Morgan could feel it. There was a time she would have hugged him now. She was being too hard on him. They were both trying their best.

Look, Morgan said. I see your point. We're kind of trapped now. So we should just not do anything and be quiet and try to forget and let it play out.

Arthur cleared his throat and Morgan waited.

Why did you say you were sorry? he asked. It still means something even if you're drunk. That came from somewhere. What happened?

Morgan thought about it. The boy in the alley with the gun had so much fear in his eyes—what caused so much fear? Fear of her, a slight woman with freakish eyes, just wandering home drunk, basking in the glow of a wonderful day. What was scary about that? There was no good telling Arthur about it. But she didn't have to lie, either. There were many kinds of truth.

I guess I'm sorry that things have come to this. How we got to this bad place.

Because it was better before, he said. You're sorry about the contrast?

What does that mean?

If things weren't good at some point, you wouldn't be sorry when they turned bad.

Yes, okay.

And so things were good, and so we have that to strive for. That can be our goal.

Oh Arthur. There's no going back. I told you. We're both changing. You maybe don't even want me anymore.

I want you forever, Morgan. With all my heart. I love you.

He had spoken this so quietly, so tenderly. What do you say to such a thing? To say you love someone is the most vulnerable thing in the world. People say it every day, in passing, at train stops and airports and lobbies—in bed before the light goes out or on a late night call when you're away. This little profession of care, this contract of feeling, this raw and horrible vulnerability facing the risk that you won't hear it back. And Arthur said it with such sincerity. How do you respond?

I love you too, she said.

They waited on the phone. The delivery truck turned off the hazard lights and pulled away. Mrs Vogel called her name from inside the house. She rarely did this. There was a problem.

Sorry, Art, she said. I should let you go.

No I should let you go, he said.

They laughed at the old joke. Somehow now she didn't want to hang up.

I forgot to ask, she said, how is your business?

Not great, but hopefully I'll get that new client. The café.

Do you have enough money? To pay the bills?

He was silent. She said, I'll transfer some. I have plenty. Mrs Vogel pays me too much.

You don't have to do that, he said.

I'm happy to. We're still married.

She could tell he was crying now, though there was no sound.

I have to go, she said. I am sorry—about everything.

Arthur sniffed and said, We'll talk Sunday then?

Morgan had forgotten to tell him. The timing was terrible but there was nothing for it. She said, Can we say this counts as our call? Forgot to tell you I have plans Sunday. But it was great to talk now.

With your friend, Arthur said.

He knew her better than anyone in the world and no matter what happened that would probably always be the case. Now it was her turn to cry—not a full-fledged cry but a great pressure behind her face and a swelling in her chest and the taste of pennies in her mouth.

Talk with you soon, she said.

And that was all.

Back inside, Mrs Vogel had spilled the smoothie on her lap, and in trying to clean up, she had got her wheelchair stuck on the rug beside the kitchen sink. The emergency brought Morgan back into the moment. She brought a fresh dress down and together they changed the old woman in the chair.

I'm sorry, said Morgan. I must not have put the cap on tight.

Mrs Vogel waved her crooked hand with disdain. Oh, it doesn't matter. That snake oil they sold me—who knows what's in there?

The doctors at French Lick had also prescribed exercises, a spartan diet, and a wrist device monitored by an app on Morgan's phone.

Nothing has changed in this country, Mrs Vogel said. The same old medicine show—it just costs more money.

As the old widow shifted her weight, Morgan pulled the dress down to her calves and smoothed the sleeves. She draped a shawl over her and said, There. Better?

Mrs Vogel continued, I'll die when I die—I don't need some quacks to tell me the specific day.

Did they give you a specific day? Morgan had been afraid to ask.

I wondered when you'd ask me.

Well? Did they?

Down to the minute, Mrs Vogel said, They gave me papers to show their calculations.

I haven't seen these papers, Morgan said.

I told Devin to burn them.

Maybe we take a break from the protocol then, said Morgan.

Maybe, Mrs Vogel said. But you keep making the smoothies—I like them. Now that the crisis was over, the diabolical gleam returned to the old woman's eyes. She said, It's that time of day when the light is so nice. How about a walk?

So they went out during the golden hour and Morgan pushed her along the sidewalk, crumpled by the roots of the massive trees.

You like your time with me, yes? asked Mrs Vogel.

I'm very grateful for it. Morgan was feeling the lightness that comes after strong emotions. She added, Your house sometimes feels like the only place where I can, you know, just let down.

Maybe I give it to you, when I die on that specific minute they foretold.

Morgan laughed. Mrs Vogel reached back and grasped her hand, to show it wasn't necessarily a joke. Morgan wanted it to be a joke, to maintain the lightness.

Do you suppose your kids will want to live here?

They have their lives, by the oceans. Everyone wants to live near the ocean these days. After a pause, Mrs Vogel asked, Do you go to see your parents?

Morgan said nothing, just breathed in the heavy air of dusk. The street was getting busy with people returning from work.

Do your parents know you come to see me?

Yes, Morgan said.

What do they say?

Not too interested. They're self-absorbed, like a lot of rich people.

Do you remember when they stopped coming over? When we all stopped visiting?

Why did the old woman bring up these memories? Maybe she thought she was like a therapist for Morgan. Or maybe Mrs Vogel didn't understand herself.

I was just a girl, Tante, Morgan said. But here's what I remember. A morning when I got up and they both looked awful. I wanted to come and play in your garden and my dad said no. I had no friends then so I just sat in my room and looked down and saw you out there, raking leaves. Later I started to sneak over, and I figure they must have known but said nothing. Then for a while they went for meetings together and had long conversations in the parlor that I tried to listen through the vent but I didn't understand anything. We went to a church a few times—that Episcopal one on the corner, but the people there were like old hippies and very inclusive. It was a bad fit, so we stopped. Then one day they told me they were splitting up and they bought their matching houses in Park Ridge. Why do you ask Tante? Do you know what happened?

Turn at this corner, said Mrs Vogel. I want the last sun in my face.

As they bumped down a narrow street, the lights coming on in the houses, Mrs Vogel said, And now you are split from your boy. Do you think that's a coincidence?

It hurt Morgan abruptly and deeply. This was not a fair comparison. She said, What are you saying, Tante?

You still love him?

Yes.

Tell me why. Why do you love this boy.

Well, because, Morgan said. I just do. I love his passion for things, I guess. How he approaches the world like it's brand new and anything is possible even if it's ridiculous. He was the first boy who didn't seem freaked out by my eyes—he didn't mention that for months after we started dating, it was like he just looked into them, into my real self.

Mrs Vogel reached back and patted her hand. Let's turn around, she said. So your boy—he brings out what you value in yourself.

So maybe this was therapy. The old German was a sly one. Morgan said, When I got the job at the hospital in Middling, he moved with me there and embraced it with his whole self. He was just like, This is what we're doing now. And so we bought the farm.

Mrs Vogel asked, So why aren't you with him now?

Can we talk about something else?

No.

Morgan sighed, and said, Because his passion goes too far and he can never be satisfied. Okay? He can be such a fool in this shitty world. Remember the dog we had when I was young?

The greyhound.

Yes, Dr Watson. He kept eating chocolate and we kept having to make him throw up—and he was so cheerful about it. That's Arthur. Eventually, Dr Watson jumped the fence and ran across Clark Street and a cement truck hit him and he died. I couldn't catch him. The driver was so sorry—this huge guy with a moustache who cried and carried Dr Watson back to our house. I can't help thinking that will happen to Arthur.

Mrs Vogel clucked her tongue. You don't want to be there when he runs into traffic? But you are a nurse.

This comment stung too. She said, Maybe I'm just a shitty, broken person. I can only nurse strangers.

And what am I, Mrs Vogel asked, Liverwurst? They laughed and the old woman added, Why don't you go see your boy? Take some days off. Devin can come.

I'm going to see him in August. I get the feeling he has this big plan for the visit.

They were in front of Mrs Vogel's house again, the last light of day. As Morgan lowered the ramp, Mrs Vogel said, And your Arthur, down there in Middling—he's faithful to you?

Morgan laughed. I assume so. I can't imagine. Though sometimes I wish he'd find another woman he can smother, who appreciates him. I sure can't live up to his dreams.

You have him by the Hoden, says Mrs Vogel, squinting.

What does that mean? said Morgan, though she had an idea.

Mrs Vogel made her hands cupped. How do you say?

By the balls.

Yes! said Mrs Vogel. Maybe you should either let him go or do something nice with those balls!

They laughed. It was a relief. I know, she said. I'm going to decide by the visit in summer.

She wheeled Mrs Vogel into the foyer, and went back and shut the door. When she returned, Mrs Vogel was smiling, looking at the leering portraits of her family on the high paneled walls.

When Nakeisha comes, she said, I think we all have a beer together. You can stay late, yes?

Morgan paused. She looked at her phone. Larry would be calling soon. They were going to Sullivan's. Just as friends, of course. She could have friends, couldn't she. She was going to teach him to play darts. Like Arthur had taught her to shoot pool. Well, not like Arthur. Forget that comparison. It had been a long afternoon. A person gets confused sometimes. But still.

Yeah, no, yeah, said Morgan. That would be nice. I don't have any plans.

THIRTEEN

It was May now. Just before dawn, Arthur climbed the ladder to Faulkner's tree house, which encircled a massive hackberry at the top of the bluff overlooking the river. Inside it smelled of coffee and raw lumber. Faulkner had completed the house just in time to catch the end of migration season, using deadfall timber he harvested from his woods. He installed solar panels to power lamps, a heater, a record player, a coffee pot. There was a fold-out day bed for afternoon naps (and hopefully, Fawk confided, romance with Mrs Fuglesen). Shelves of books lined the walls, wrapped around Nancy's paintings and old photographs of Middling. But the centerpiece of the house was an observatory extending from the back, with chairs recovered from an abandoned theater, where you could watch stars at night and birds by day. Fawk said he weighed this investment against a fallout shelter and ultimately chose the optimistic path. He sat in the observatory, with coffee cup and binoculars, when Arthur arrived.

No Nancy? Arthur asked.

Afraid not, Fawk replied. She said the birds will still be there when she gets up.

Arthur muttered, That seems sensible. Sometimes I wonder.

Fawk patted the seat next to him and poured Arthur a coffee. You know, he said, a man's face is the executive summary of his disposition. So tell me.

On his way to the treehouse, Arthur had walked through his newly-planted prairie. He was expecting to see the progress of his forbs, now pressing sturdily upward, now extending the deep roots that protected them from fire and drought. Instead, the first light of day showed a field of shoots precisely nipped at the top. But only the native plants had suffered this assault. All around them, turf grass and buckthorn and hemlock and garlic mustard and every other possible invasive thrived. Overnight, the deer had surgically removed only the good plants.

So now, he told Fawk, I've had my bee colonies collapse and my forbs devoured. That's goal #5 in the shitter.

Faulkner peered through his binoculars into the woods. Sometimes it seemed like he wasn't listening to you, but it was only because he was thinking. He handed Arthur the binocs and pointed. There's a palm warbler right there, he said, in that big maple.

Arthur looked and found the bird. It was lovely to project your vision into space and watch such a delicate, perfect thing as a palm warbler. For a moment, the confines of the optics, the circular vignette framing a bird, chased away your worries. But only for a moment.

I'm wondering, Faulkner said, What percentage success rate have you set for your Perfect Day?

What do you mean, Arthur replied. He put the binocs on the sill and took up his coffee.

Faulkner cleared his throat and said, I mean, I assume you've estimated the likelihood of success across all aspects of your project and defined a target rate you can use to measure results.

Arthur stared at his friend flatly. He said, Like a business.

Exactly! Like a business. Like any endeavor.

Arthur felt an overwhelming weariness. He thought of Nancy, cozy in her bed, and wondered why he wasn't still in his. He thought of Morgan, possibly in bed with some other fucking guy. His stomach churned and he set down his cup and he thought of the dead bees like chaff and the snipped heads of the flowers and the leer of Bradley Martin and all the trash he had extracted from his property only to make more room for aggressive, toxic weeds. He barely had the energy to respond, but still he did.

One Perfect Day isn't a business, Fawk. It's perfect. So my target success rate is 100%.

Faulkner looked at Arthur for a long moment. Then he said, Hmm, and returned to studying the woods.

After a while, he said, Arthur, it seems to me we have a pretty good day ahead of us. The sun's just up over the horizon and we still have a little time to look at some birds. Then we'll have a quick breakfast with Nancy. Then we'll go to the farmers market, and we'll buy some little veggie plants to get in the ground by Mother's Day, just like the almanac tells us. Then we'll do some chores and I'll do some reading while you put in a few hours of work on Alfred Beardsley's website or whatever and maybe later we'll have a whiskey to cap off a pretty good day. Do I have that right?

That's the plan, Arthur said. It was hard to stop sulking, but now that felt embarrassing.

That's the plan. Exactly right. And some things are going to go our way, and some things won't, and that's all right.

Arthur took a deep breath. Sorry, he said.

What are you apologizing for, son?

I don't know, man, for just being gloomy. You're right. Let's look at some fucking birds.

Faulkner slapped Arthur's knee. There you go! Let's look at some fucking birds. There's a bright little fucker now—a redstart, if my old eyes don't deceive me. Look.

Arthur raised the binoculars and found the redstart, feeding on buds in a stand of willow. Well, there was goal #4, coming along perfectly on its own—Birds of all kinds nest in native hedges. That was something. Although it just now occurred to him that many birds wouldn't be nesting in August, when the goal was due, and so he should probably revise that statement to express a broader goal. Why had he only caught this now? That was probably a testament to his frame of mind and if he didn't get his shit together, the whole thing would collapse and it would be One Horrible Day. Still. There were birds in abundance in native hedges right now, and that was the spirit of the goal and that was on track. Although, what was native, really—technically, it depended on when you took a snapshot of the wildlife of a region. It was like a restore point on an operating system, and yet that metaphor broke because nature didn't exactly have factory settings you could go back to. At any given time, in any given place, maybe what was here was native, which made the word restoration a fool's errand, a quixotic lark.

Arthur! Faulkner whispered sharply. Dude!

Arthur resumed seeing through the binoculars and the redstart had gone and he was staring at another shrub no longer in focus. He blinked his eyes wide and shook his head and laughed. You only realize how wild your mind is when you tame it, for a moment, and that never lasts.

A family of wild turkeys came through the mayapple plants along the forest floor. Their goofy naked heads bobbed above the foliage, then disappeared, then reappeared again.

Fawk said, It's a mysterious place, this river, isn't it?

More than people could ever imagine, said Arthur.

What's the craziest thing you've seen down here? asked Fawk.

Well, a ghost, for starters.

Fawk turned to look at him. Are you serious?

Arthur kept looking at the turkeys, now nearly out of sight. No not really, he said. But there are nights you wonder, when it's foggy, at dusk.

Because I don't rule it out, said Faulkner. He kept his eyes leveled at Arthur, who turned now to look back at him. Ghosts are no crazier than a lot of things we take for granted, Faulkner said. So don't hold back on my account.

Arthur laughed uneasily. It seemed likely that Faulkner would have seen Hanacek by now, given all the time he spent building the treehouse. Unless Hanacek didn't want to be seen by Faulkner. He was probably the kind of old ghost farmer who might be frugal about exposing himself. But if anybody deserved to see him, Faulkner did.

What else? the older man asked. What's another strange thing you've seen?

Arthur paused for a while and finally said, Just a lot of junk, I guess. Once there was a huge plastic tank, maybe for fertilizer? I though it would be there forever, messing up the view. But one night the river just took it away. Or somebody came and got it.

Faulkner leaned back in his chair and folded his arms. He said, Have you seen the latest about that Gallardo fellow, the one who went missing? Pictures of his body floating down the river – on social media. Fair amount of gossip in town.

Arthur swallowed, but it was dry. His heartbeat surged to a manic rate—why does your body betray you when you need to be calm?

He said, In our river? This one?

Faulkner looked at him, waiting. Arthur also waited.

Finally Fawk shrugged, Surprised you haven't heard about it. It's the case we talked about with Timothy. Friend of mine, Peg Hanrahan, is representing the guy's wife.

Arthur swallowed again, looked down into his empty coffee cup. Peg Hanrahan, he said slowly, that's a great name. Do you know everyone around here?

Fawk laughed. When you run a business for thirty years, you can't help getting to know a few people in town.

Arthur pointed across the river. You didn't know the Martins, when I told you about them.

No, Fawk said. We're still strangers out here. Ten miles out of Middling is a whole nother world.

Arthur looked at his friend, and nodded slowly, That's what Morgan used to say.

The Middling Farmer's Market filled a city block, from courthouse to train station, a maze of vendors who came from half the state to sell produce and meat and soap and paintings and jam and ornaments and massages and jewelry and charities and potholders and politics. On Sundays they set up in the cold hours before dawn, and by the time Arthur and the Fuglesens arrived, the sun had warmed the crowd with its sharp, lateral light, and they were embraced by the fragrances of bread and lilacs and burritos and asphalt. Always there was the saxophone player, white-whiskered and skeletal, playing 50s television themes. Nancy dropped a twenty in his bucket, and Arthur gave a fiver, and it was like a donation at church—an obligation met with no gratitude. The sax man played on, and his honking notes wove with the hum of the crowd doing commerce and the sudden laughter of small talk and the thrum of generators behind food trucks, and the old train bell the butcher rang every time he sold a beef.

Arthur was eager to get to the other side of the market, where he would buy vegetable plants for cash off flatbed wagons. These were the plants too difficult to raise from seed—tomatoes, peppers, herbs—and many of them would be organic, meeting the requirement of goal #1 (Organic gardens yield abundant food). But the market was arranged such that you had to weave your way through each aisle, and pass every vendor, before you could get to the end and the bounty of those flatbed wagons. With the Fuglesens, this could be something of a gauntlet.

The first delay was the provost of Middling University and her husband, a florist, who called out to Nancy and Faulkner at the entrance to the market. A banner hung there, saying Welcome to the Middle of Everywhere. The conversation began before they could pass through.

The provost wore a broad-brimmed hat and matching jacket and pants. Her husband was similarly too-dressed-up for a farmer's market, with a turtleneck and tweed jacket that might have suited a 70s talk show host. Neither of them carried canvas reusable bags, standard issue for most shoppers—and in fact neither of them seemed to carry anything at all, not wallet or handbag or phone. They were unburdened and carefree.

I loved your latest post, the provost said to Faulkner. It was so, so clever—you have to keep writing those.

The provost's husband reached out to touch Nancy's arm delicately, And you, he said, I see your little painted cards are selling at the Art Cottage now—so darling!

Nancy and Faulkner accepted the praise without comment, and changed the subject. Nancy said, You must be in full swing for commencement now. Who's the speaker—can you tell?

The provost put the back of her palm against the side of her mouth, leaned forward, and whispered, Later. Not in public.

Faulkner said, Aren't commencement speakers always announced well ahead of time?

The provost's husband swatted at Faulkner and said, Not this year, silly! Where have you been. It's a doozy and it's a secret!

Arthur considered whether slinking away would be rude. Just then Nancy intervened.

I don't think you've met our friend! This is Arthur Prendergast. He is a true renaissance man—conservationist, gentleman farmer, computer programmer, and what else?

Country sage! Said Faulkner. And also a fellow alumnus!

Arthur shook hands with the provost, who burst with charisma, and her husband, who held Arthur's hand uncomfortably long and whose palm was wet.

In the pause that followed, another couple approached and Arthur's four companions cheered to see them. They truly, literally, cheered. How can people be so loose and unselfconscious? What must it feel like to be cheered for? Perhaps success and the comfort of institutions allowed this to happen. It occurred to Arthur, quite suddenly, that he wasn't aligned with any institution. He didn't even belong to a professional organization. He was entirely alone. No wonder things were so hard.

The new couple owned two of the major buildings in downtown Middling, and had some prior careers that must have been significant, but Arthur didn't catch that detail. He studied their clothes, which were overalls in the colors of the university. They might have looked clownish, but their confidence and enthusiasm made it work. The woman carried a wicker basket. The man held two coffees in paper cups. Arthur was introduced, but the conversation was impossible to follow. He felt himself sliding backward, as if he'd run out of strength on a mountain slope, and his companions had dropped his rope, and he was free to tumble backward, into his prosaic world of dead bees and decapitated forbs and possibly unfaithful wives. The moment became a blur of faces, healthy middle-aged faces, talking and talking, and hands reaching out for emphasis and connection, all together in a circle like a child's game that involves chanted rhymes and counting, or like a trick with strings around your fingers, a cat's cradle, a spider web. And still they hadn't entered the market.

Arthur took a step back to breathe. He touched Faulkner's arm.

I'm gonna go ahead, he said. Take a look at those plants.

Faulkner studied Arthur's face. Sorry, buddy, he said.

Arthur shook his head to say it was no problem and Faulkner nodded conspiratorially and soon the group was behind him and Arthur was immersed in the market.

He wove through the crowd, looking at each stall from a distance. Every one of them was interesting, but he kept his distance, to avoid getting drawn into conversation. Back in the good days, Morgan handled these conversations. She was a marvel at chit chat and showing interest. She could make friends while getting a bargain. Now Arthur drifted around the social bubbles, as if suspended between two magnets—one that yearned for human contact and another that was terrified by it. It was too late to be at the market. He should have come when it opened at 6am—when you had space, when you could talk without the pressure of all these people.

As he turned the corner where the food trucks were lined up, he heard the whump of an explosion, then shouts and a moan that rippled across the crowd—something had just happened to the right. One of the food trucks? Then Arthur was wrapped in smoke that obscured everything. He heard people call to each other to watch out, to be careful. He waved his hand in front of his face but it did no good—he could see nothing and felt his eyes burn and smelled charred meat and plastic. He put his arms out politely and began to walk, as briskly as he dared, in the direction he had been going. How could there be so much smoke so fast? And why did it seem to mute all sound? Arthur pulled his shirt up over his mouth and breathed through it. He kept walking, and then he found himself standing in clear sunlight in front of a small booth, where a short brown woman and a teenage girl sold honey and mushrooms.

The woman stood behind a table, hands folded across her apron front. She seemed to gaze with perseverance at some internal landscape. The girl arranged the honey samples in rows of white dixie cups, tweaking their order meticulously. There were hand-woven baskets of mushrooms along the edge of the table.

Would you like to try some honey? the girl asked.

Arthur stared at the cups. It seemed a shame to break one of the perfect rows. And yet, here was honey!

Do you make this yourself? he asked.

The girl fixed her dark eyes on him. The bees make it, she said.

She glanced at the woman, who did not move, and the girl resumed her ordering.

Arthur asked the woman, Do you keep the bees? Your own colonies?

The woman looked at the table, adjusted one of the girl's sample cups. She said, Maybe it's better to say the bees keep us.

Oh, said Arthur.

The girl drew a breath, and added, But we give them a home—and lots of red clover. Try some.

She held out a sample for him. Arthur tipped the cup back. It was too delicate an operation for his large hand and face. But when the honey met his tongue, when the fragrance rose to his nostrils, there was a rush of euphoria. The wonder of nature captured in this golden liquid. Those were fancy words, like a bad poem. But there were no proper words for this.

Arthur said. That's the best honey I've ever tasted. Once I had honey made from basswood blossoms in the UP and it was incredible, but this is better.

The woman nodded, and resumed her internal stare. Arthur held the paper cup awkwardly, searching, and the girl offered him a wicker trash bin.

Ten dollars a quart, she said. Would you like one?

Please, said Arthur. Can I ask you—how are your colonies? Do you ever have one collapse?

The woman squinted, as if just now seeing him. No, she said. Gracias a Dios. But one day it will happen, probably.

As the girl put a quart jar in a paper bag, she said, Do you know about bee keeping?

I've tried, said Arthur. It hasn't gone so well.

I'm sorry, said the girl. But don't give up on the bees. It takes time.

Arthur reached for his wallet, and in that moment his frame of vision expanded to the whole bee stand. He saw now a paper sign taped to the front of the table. It said, *Have you seen this body?* It was the flyer Peg Hanrahan had carried in the diner, with the grinning picture of living Armando, beside the horrifying snapshot of his beaten deceased face. Arthur looked up at the placard swinging from the tent roof. It said *Gallardo Fresh Produce.*

His heard surged, blood racing to the thousands of capillaries at the extremities—an exodus of blood from his core. He put his hand on the table to steady himself. His vision tunneled.

The girl set down the quart and asked, Are you okay?

Arthur recovered just enough to say, I'm sorry. Just lightheaded, I guess. Maybe the smoke.

The girl handed him a water bottle. Arthur took it and drank.

His instinct was to pay and walk away, to leave with a controlled gait, feeling their eyes upon his back, until he disappeared in the crowded market. Generations of instinct, reinforced over millennia—ancient habits, formed when we were scarce primates on a planet teeming with enemies. These habits accosted him. But that was a coward's way. Now in a world of primate domination our ancestors couldn't have imagined—in this world, our habits have become our enemies.

He said, Maybe I'll get some mushrooms too. Do you grow these? On your farm?

The girl arranged the mushroom baskets to be closer to him. The woman looked at him with curiosity. She said, Some we grow. Others we gather.

The girl tipped her head. She said, We don't gather so much anymore.

Why not? he asked.

The woman's expression darkened—was she insulted? The girl put a hand on the woman's arm. She said, My father was the gatherer.

Arthur looked at the sign, pretending to read it carefully. He said,

I'm sorry. How long has he been missing?

274 days, the woman said. The girl looked away, down the aisle to where a vendor had arranged a huge collection of balloons—it was the party store. A breeze came up in the morning sun and blew the girl's black hair across her face.

I'm sorry, Arthur said again, stupidly.

The girl smiled and there was empathy. Why is it so common for the victims of tragedy to take on the discomfort of other people? Arthur tried to reverse it and look back at her with compassion, but realized he was probably making a peculiar expression on his big pink face, like a sad mime.

The woman smoothed the flyer, tucking it from the breeze. She said, Have you seen him?

Arthur was horrified. Could she know? But maybe she was joking, in a kind of dark humor.

I wish I had, he said. Was that weird? He added, I'll keep an eye out for him now. And to prove it, Arthur took out his phone and photographed the flyer.

They waited. The woman crossed her arms. The girl tucked her hair behind her ear.

All Arthur could think to say was, I lost my mother not long ago.

The woman looked at him with profound significance and said, Did you ever find her body?

The girl winced, and sucked in her breath. The woman smiled, inscrutably.

What a strange, blunt joke the woman had made. This woman, who must be Lupe Gallardo. And this girl, who must be Sofia. They could easily be his friends, who shared the pain of loss, who knew the vagaries of bees.

He asked, Do you know what happened to Armando? If I can ask.

Lupe seemed to ignore him, but she waved her hand toward Sofia, who said, No. One evening he left to forage. That's the last time we saw him.

There was a pause, a silent communication, and Lupe nodded. The girl continued. He liked to go when the sun is low and the color of everything becomes like a painting. He said that's when he could see best, see the mushrooms down in the forest leaves.

Lupe added, He saw things no one else could see.

The girl began to wipe the table top, lifting each cup of honey in turn.

Arthur said, He sounds like a great guy.

Thank you, said the girl. He was. He always said he had found the secret of youth in the mushrooms. Every night at bedtime he ate mushrooms—just a very small amount, a few different kinds. It sounds crazy but also he did stay very young.

Arthur said, Mmm. Were they conning him? Impossible to know, with his nerves sizzling. He imagined Armando, roaming the woods at twilight—some crepuscular adventurer, friend of Hanacek no doubt. They would probably have been great friends. It wasn't crazy to think that mushrooms could keep you young. Or maybe even keep your body from decomposing!

He said, Are these some of those—the ones he ate?

Lupe shrugged. Sofia smiled. It's hard to say, she said. But they're very good.

Right, said Arthur. Well, I hope you find him. I hope you get some closure.

Lupe put her hands on the table and leaned toward him. What we want, she said, is justice.

It was the first time he had met her gaze. Can people really tell the truth in your eyes? Our expressions are so complicated. Can people really see into your soul? Arthur couldn't bear it, and so he rubbed his eye like something was in it.

That makes sense, he said. It was a lame response but what else do you say to that? I think I'd like to buy some more honey, he said. And some of the mushrooms?

How much? Sofia asked.

I don't know—three, four, maybe six jars? Do you have a box I can carry?

Sofia brought out a handle basket and began to pack the honey. She asked, What kind of mushrooms?

Arthur paused, studying the baskets of fungus. He said, Well…

Lupe stared at him brutally. You want the kind that Mando ate, yes?

Arthur looked back at her, innocently, and shrugged.

We have none of those. Only he could find them. But these, they taste good and you can't get them in the grocery store. We'll give you a bag of these.

Arthur paid. Seventy dollars. That was not in his budget. But with money from Morgan, maybe it was okay. He thought it would feel good to buy a lot from Lupe and Sofia, but it didn't help right now. Maybe later.

Holding the basket and sack of mushrooms, he made a kind of bow to the two women and said. Great to talk with you. And sorry, again. If there's anything I can do…

Lupe smiled at him, in a bemused way, a mysterious way. She waved off his offer. We don't need more people, she said.

Well, Arthur said, in any case, I live by the river, so I can keep an eye out.

Lupe turned her face up from the cash box, her posture frozen. By the river, she said.

It was a stupid remark, a mistake. Arthur tried to appear nonchalant, but his mind raced. He said, Yeah, well, in that general area. I just saw from the picture here he was in the river, so…

Now the two women stood beside each other, studying him, waiting.

Okay, well, said Arthur as he backed away. Right. Thanks again, Lupe and Sofia. Have a good day.

The two women stood still. He had said their names. They had never introduced their names to him. They must know it. He turned quickly, bumped into other shoppers with his packages, rejoined the crowd.

The steady breeze rose into a sudden gust, and the balloons from the party store detached and blew, in a vast bunch, like a monstrous jelly fish—toward Arthur and the crowd around him. Now they were surrounded by balloons, bobbing in festive colors, bound by yellow ribbon, and they struggled with the balloons in confusion, batting them away, trying to disentangle themselves, and apologizing to each other. Some of them were laughing. What a thing it was to get caught in a cloud of balloons at a farmer's market!

But Arthur wasn't laughing. He pulled away from the chaos, stepped on a balloon and stumbled, barely kept his balance and held his packages. He pulled hard away from the tangle, and snapped a ribbon, making some person yelp in reply, but he didn't look back to see whom he had hurt. He walked quickly, toward the end of the market, toward the flatbed wagons with plants that promised hope and what odds remained of One Perfect Day.

FOURTEEN

One night in early June, Morgan awoke to see the silhouettes of two men on the fire escape outside her bedroom window. One was tall and narrow, with flowing hair, a profile like an Afghan hound. The other was shorter and from his round head sprouted thick shoots of dreadlocked hair, as if he were a palmetto. They worked together, like tradesmen on a boring job. The short man ran a cordless drill into her wooden sash, while the tall one assisted. Morgan watched them with fascination—their approach was so ordinary, so brazen, that it seemed possible they were doing something legitimate. But when the short one handed the drill to the tall one, and lifted the steel security grate from the window, fear surged up in Morgan's throat and she couldn't get out the scream that formed within.

The two figures began to pry at the sash of the window, forcing it against its flimsy lock with a wrecking bar. The tall one paused, fumbled his pockets to find cigarettes, which he shared with his partner, like it was break time. Then, smokes in mouths, they resumed their break-in. In dreams you can't move when you need to—something scary approaches and you want so badly to move but you can't, your mind fighting your body, until finally you throw your full force of will into movement, but then you awaken and so you never really did move in that dream. Now, when Morgan was certain she was awake, she couldn't move. It was a strange sensation, this frozen state working against your best interests. Also, why were these guys so intent on breaking in? Why her apartment? She had nothing of value. What did they want with her? Did they just want her? That made her nauseous, but also it made no sense. Would two guys casually break their way into a woman's apartment like it was an odd job, taking smoke breaks, only to sexually assault her? Surely the world wasn't so crazy as that.

Arthur, Arthur, what would he say about this? The thought annoyed her—why did she have to think of him at her weakest moments? But he was so capable in these ways. He might fuck up a birthday card, but he could definitely save you from a burning building. And so she remembered the light stored in her dresser. It was, technically, a flashlight, but so powerful that it seemed like it should have a more special name. Arthur had bought it for her, this extraordinary yellow plastic-housed instrument shaped like a pistol, which could shoot a beam across a field and light up a great horned owl on a walnut branch. It held that ultimate power of illumination, eradicating all mystery while exposing something even more astonishing, the painful reality of things. Morgan grabbed the light and pulled its trigger. For a moment, the beam shot to her ceiling, so bright it seemed unsafe. In the next instant, she aimed it at the window, and some of the light reflected back, alarmingly, but most of it penetrated the glass and illuminated the two characters, whose smokes were now down to butts, whose faces winced in the glare. They both raised an elbow to shield their faces, turning away. And then they exchanged some brief conversation, leaned the security grate back in place, collected their tools, and walked down the fire escape. It was quittin time, apparently, and now they'd go to a tavern and drink their pay, and lament this night's failure, before returning to their bitter wives and leaking faucets.

At Café Voltaire, Morgan told Larry what happened. She tried to present it as a funny story. She made pistols with her hands and said, You know how it is—crazy times in Chicago! Bang-bang Al Capone!

Larry smiled but his expression remained concerned. Did they have guns? he asked.

Not that I saw, she said. They just had tools like your uncle would bring over to help you hang a picture.

Larry turned his espresso cup, carefully, with his delicate hand. He looked at her, heavy eyebrows low, and asked, Is your landlord coming to fix the grate?

I wouldn't call it a landlord, per se, Morgan replied. It's a big company. I filled out a report and some handyman is supposed to call me.

And you said this happened when…?

Three days ago.

Have you slept since then? Larry asked. He sipped his espresso and watched her reply.

Of course I've slept! said Morgan. But as he kept watching her, she revised it to, Well, on and off.

Larry rubbed the grain of the tabletop, studying it, and then abruptly looked up at her and said, Morgan, can I say something?

What? she replied. Hearing him say her name lifted her insides, like falling from a height. That made no sense—it was stupid. But his eyes were so dark, it could unsettle anyone.

Since I've known you, he said, It seems like you've been on kind of a… downward trajectory. So as your, well—mon ami, s'il vous plait?—it makes me worry.

Impulsively Morgan reached out and gripped his forearm. She felt warmth rising from him, the transfer of energy into her cold and skeletal hand—how could anyone have such a body temperature? She said, Of course! Of course you can call me your friend! Don't be silly, what a thing to say.

He didn't reply, just kept looking at her, and it was the kind of look people offer to the mortally ill, like I'm so sorry you have terminal cancer maybe if I look at you hard enough you'll feel better. Under this gaze, Morgan cracked, and found herself tearing up, and looking away, and smearing her cheeks with the back of her hand, and laughing with embarrassment, flapping her hand to dismiss her foolishness. Maybe it was just lack of sleep. But probably it wasn't.

She said, My husband and I, on the day I left him, we found this dead body.

Larry leaned forward and listened.

She continued, Somebody dumped it there, like right while we were fighting, and my husband wanted to move it or do something and I said we should just leave it alone, but pretty obviously it was murder or something very bad, this middle-aged guy maybe a migrant worker, just lying dead on our land by the river.

It felt weird to refer to her husband, like touching a live wire. That was dumb and a little suspect but you feel what you feel. She went on until she had told Larry the whole story, about the #sangabody posts and Arthur's encounters with the cop and the rednecks across the river and the lawyer Peg Hanrahan, about how they had obsessed about it, and fought about it, but also had come together over it, like sharing in a crime, like marriage, which can be kind of a crime, can't it, when it's not honest or someone is trapped, and also it wasn't clear whether Arthur was telling her everything, so much of it didn't add up—how can a body float down that crazy river, with all its twists and snags, and why would a body pose like that, and were they accomplices to murder, did she commit a felony, and should she get her own lawyer but if she did, wasn't that like an admission of guilt? Guilt, that was the word. Her whole self now was nothing but guilt.

When she stopped, breathless, Larry folded his arms across his stomach and rocked forward. His face drooped in concern and he said, I just feel so badly for you guys. Going through all that.

You do? she asked.

Of course I do, he said. He tilted his head in curiosity. Don't you think I should?

Feel bad for me? For us?

Yes. If one of your friends told you this story, wouldn't you feel for them?

Morgan began to reply, then stopped, and thought. If one of her friends had told her this story she would think they were… crazy. Or outrageously unlucky and confused. Maybe pathetic too?

Finally, she said, I think I've been oversharing, Larry. I'm sorry. We don't know each other that well.

He finished his espresso, set the cup in the saucer, and smiled at her, slowly, with a glint and a tease. She could tell he was about to talk in his Cajun accent.

He said, Well now there you go, pulling into your shell like a tortoise on an old log. I get that. But you don't have to be so self-conscious with me, you know. I don't judge.

Morgan began to fold her tiny cocktail napkin, neatly in triangles, one smaller than the other. She said, I think you're judging all the time.

Larry held his hand up, his fingers in a tube, and peered through it. I'm observing all the time, he said. There's a big difference.

Well then what do you observe now?

He dropped his hand and studied her face. She noticed now how unshaven he was. Or maybe he had shaved, but it just grew back so fast. Did you call that swarthy or hirsute? Were you supposed to say those words any more? He was kind of both.

As he replied, his Cajun faded, replaced by the precise enunciation of an academic. I'm observing a girl who has had a spell of rotten luck.

She thinks the universe is at odds with her, just now, and it's scary and frustrating. But she also knows the universe doesn't take sides—it just proceeds methodically toward entropy. And that troubles this girl most of all.

Morgan laughed and said, That's some abstract shit right there but believe it or not I think I know what you mean.

He pushed his plate of pastry toward her and said, Good. Now eat something. Have a bite.

The pastry did look lovely—the edges crispy, almost burnt, the apricot oozing from a slit in the center. But she wasn't hungry. She pushed the plate back.

Larry shook his head, lifted the pastry, and took an enormous bite. He breathed deeply as he chewed, making drama out of it.

Morgan laughed.

Larry crossed his arms. Look, he said. I'm just going to say. I know you're a strong person and everything. But this is a lot, what you're going through. Sometimes you need to ask for help. You know? Especially with the break-in.

Attempted break-in, Morgan said. I scared them away with a photon gun.

Attempted break-in, he acknowledged. Anyway, just know I'm here to help—if you need it. Whatever I can do. Yeah?

She nodded. This guy, this Larry fellow, master of astrophysics, seeker of dark matter, who hailed from the bayou, the city of light, who quoted Rilke—this guy was all right.

Larry smiled and winked. Who winks anymore? But it worked. He slid the plate back to Morgan and said, Now eat.

She lifted his pastry and bit into it. The apricot oozed into the corner of her mouth and she collected it with a finger and put that in her mouth and smiled at him.

There you go, he said. Better already.

He watched while she chewed. Then he said, So the body has been floating down the river all this time, not decomposing? That's crazy.

I know, said Morgan. It is.

The morning after the attempted break-in, Mrs Vogel knew something was wrong. In the days that followed, she kept asking Morgan, What eats at you? Tante knows when her Nichte has troubles.

Morgan deflected. She said, It's nothing—when the days start getting long I always have trouble sleeping. She said, Don't worry about me—I'm the one who takes care of you, Tante. She said, If you keep asking me what's the matter, something will be the matter, if you keep stressing me out like this.

Finally, at the end of the week, Mrs Vogel said, I think I will call your parents and tell them you need help. Bring me that phone and call your parents and give it to me.

Morgan laughed but then, seeing the expression on the old woman's face, her smile faded. They waited in silence, looking at each other. Mrs Vogel was leaning forward in her chair, her features compressed, her eyes fierce with concern. Morgan wept. It all came in an embarrassing rush that she couldn't control, just gasping and shuddering like a little girl.

There, said Mrs Vogel. Let it come. She held out her arms and Morgan kneeled in front of her and accepted the old widow's embrace, and then rested her head on her lap while Mrs Vogel stroked her hair. She told the story this way, in the comfort of Mrs Vogel's fading warmth, and when she was done she felt purged and clean and light. I don't think I can do it any more, Morgan said. I can't keep being afraid every minute.

Then she looked up at Mrs Vogel. I love that place, you know, she said. My little apartment. It's my space, you know? It's tiny and the paint is peeling and the radiator whistles and the kitchen faucet drips all the time like an old clock ticking, but I love it there. Or I used to love it but now I don't and that's kind of... heartbreaking, you know Tante?

Mrs Vogel gripped her shoulders and peered into Morgan's icy eyes and said, You come to live with me. Live with Tante for a while until you have your feet again.

Oh I can't do that, said Morgan.

Why? the old woman exclaimed. She waved her arm. I have so much room! You will have your space—you can live here in this mansion, which is like a fortress for your poor tired self and you won't even see Mrs Vogel unless you want to. There are so many stairs and doors to keep your privacy.

Morgan considered. She blinked and looked around the sunroom, as if that might provide an answer. What would it be like to live with Mrs Vogel, just for a while? It could be awful, always thinking she had to look after the old woman. A busman's holiday. But it was a fortress, but it was safe. But also the thought of sleeping in one of the remote rooms with its impossibly high ceilings and rococo mouldings and drapes—that made her squirm.

Oh, I can't, Tante, she said. That would be like running away.

Mrs Vogel thought. She put her finger to her mouth, and then pointed it at Morgan.

The attic, she said. You stay in the attic. Closer to the sky. That will let your heart soar a little. And there is the back stairs off the alley so it's like your own apartment. What is the difference living in your own apartment at the top of my house and some other place?

Morgan had no further argument. She was defenseless and drained.

Okay, she said. I will look up there after lunch.

Smart girl, said Mrs Vogel. Now let's play some cards.

FIFTEEN

Arthur took down the sign that said Failure Farms. He replaced it with one that said Prendergast Acres, just as his grandfather had called his little farm. That name—it had been a kind of brand up there in Faire, Illinois. Gramps made a stencil and painted it on the wooden rails of his pickup. He painted that name on the billboard that hung above their vegetable stand. He printed it on the blank side of old business papers, a simple letterhead, and made pads with rubber cement. Most memorably, Gramps burned that brand into a piece of white oak, and hung it with brass chains from a cantilevered sign post, and protected it with a small shingled roof. How did Gramps have time for this kind of thing? Maybe because they didn't have cell phones? Arthur had no time to build a roof for his sign—he just re-used the screws from the old sign and slapped it on a post of treated lumber. Arthur's sign would not last as long, exposed like that, but the fate of his Prendergast Acres would be decided sooner than wood could rot.

It was time to get serious. Time to get tough, to grow some bigger balls. It was almost the summer solstice for fuck's sake and One Perfect Day was 28% behind schedule. That is, according to Arthur's app, which didn't lie, which wasn't swayed by emotions, which forecast outcomes by calculating probabilities based on formulas reasoned over data. Gramps did all this by hand, wielding pencils sharpened with a pocket knife, on his home-made pads. He could tell you when to prune apples, when to plant tomatoes, when to fertilize strawberries, when to turn the chicks out from the incubator and into the yard. And it always worked.

Gramps didn't lie awake worrying. He never left the goat gate open, freeing the animals to devour every row of cruciferous seedlings. He never forgot to switch the rain barrel valve and so his basement never flooded. He never backed the tractor into the chicken shed because he was lamenting his wife who had left him. Because Grandma had never left Gramps because why would you? A fucking awesome guy like that? Gramps's wife never left him and Gramps never dumped a corpse into the river for no reason either. Partly because he had no river and, as far as we know, no corpse. But even if he did, he wouldn't have done that. He would have called the cops, because he knew the cops, and they generally did what he asked of them, even though he gave them slightly insulting nicknames. He would have called the sheriff and said, Shitkowski, you got a body over here. Send one of your lackies before it starts to stink. And Zaskowski would come by that afternoon with the coroner and it would all be over by the time Gramps was showered up, sitting on his balcony with a can of Old Style and a .410 shotgun to pepper starlings. And because none of this would have happened to Gramps, he also never would have stumbled into the market stall of the widow of the man he dumped in the river, and he wouldn't have engaged her in stupid conversation and let slip that he knew more about her than he should have, making him look suspicious, when he was already suspicious, because the internet was tracking the body to his property, to a precise spot on the river bank where nothing would grow. And even if all this had happened to Gramps, he would have befriended the neighbors, who would have kept their mouths shut and protected him, because they were a little afraid of him, in addition to being his friend. When Art Klewer build a duck blind on Gramps's side of the marsh, he and Arthur drove out there with a stick of dynamite and a spool of wire, which they unwound away from the marsh and sheltered behind the old Farmall tractor while Art Klewer's duck blind vanished in an eruption of mud and cattails. Afterward, Martha Klewer sent over a rhubarb pie as an apology, and Grandma threw away the pie and made a proper one because Martha's crust was soggy.

That's how they were, Gramps and Grandma. They were serious and tough and had big balls, because you had to be that way, before the internet. So now it was time for Arthur to get his shit together and follow in that tradition. He had no excuse, unlike the soft peers of his generation, those watchers of bratty cartoons, collectors of participation trophies, helmet-wearing, energy-drink drinking, cell-phone addicted poor children of the millennium. They didn't have the benefit of Arthur's anachronistic childhood—they could be forgiven their softness and anxiety. But Arthur was another story, held to a higher standard. And so on this very night, on the day when he re-christened his hobby farm, he would attend a 'service' across the river, at Bradley Martin's, because he had accepted Bradley's text invitation, because it was the ballsy thing to do. Faulkner had accepted too, telling Arthur: You know, knowledge is always a good thing, if you don't take it seriously. Then Faulkner added, And how could we not?

The drum beat began at 8pm, an hour before the start of the sunset service. The pitch was as low as distant thunder, like a wooden mallet on an oil barrel, which it probably was. One beat per second rolled through the woods from the Martin's place. Arthur heard it from the Fuglesens' deck, where he drank whiskey with Faulkner and Nancy. He felt the beat in his chest, matching the rhythm of his heart. You found yourself anticipating each beat, wanting it to come sooner, expecting the tempo to speed up, and in this way it drew you toward it, with this suspense—how long could it go on, so perfectly, so persistently?

Nancy shuddered. You couldn't pay me to go to that, she said.

Fortunately for you, you weren't invited, said Fawk. He sipped as he peered into the woods, toward the river, down below his house.

Nancy crossed her arms and stared that way too. I'm not so sure you should either, she said. Don't know what you're getting into.

That's true, he said. But we don't have much choice. We can't just cower here wondering what's going on.

Arthur said, It's our god damned neighborhood and we'll piss where we like.

Nancy and Fawk turned to him. She said, I'm not sure I follow you, Art.

He was still full of the spirit of Gramps, though not sure how to use the old expressions. What did that one mean? It didn't matter. He shrugged and drained his whiskey.

They listened to the beat. Ordinarily there would be a chorus of crickets and frogs and maybe an owl. Tonight the wild things were silent and there was only the drum.

Fawk said, You reckon we should drive or walk?

Arthur made a grimace, looking into the woods, and said, I'm walking straight toward that god damned drum. He held out his glass to Fawk.

Fawk said, Son I'm not sure you should have another just yet.

Arthur shrugged again, and said, Don't matter--that whiskey ain't worth the powder to blow it to hell.

Fawk laughed and said, What?

Have you been reading something? Nancy asked.

Arthur looked at them looking at him, and suddenly laughed, breaking character. It was a welcome release, this laughter, and he realized he had been straining for days. So maybe it was okay to relax. But he would need to resume that character. It was the only way.

He said, It's just something my grandfather used to say. We should walk. You can still get across that big snag.

Yeah but what if we need to make a hasty exit? Faulkner asked, his smile inscrutable in the fading light.

Arthur shook his head, and said, Let's just go.

The fires were visible from the river—blazes erupting from oil barrels and lines of tiki torches. Through the trees you could see dozens of people, their shadows cast obliquely in the firelight. As Arthur and Faulkner got closer, an electric guitar joined the drum, madly distorted, playing repeated licks that made no song. As they got closer still, they could see that the people were wearing masks that covered their heads and necks. They had the faces of animals.

In the light of the golden hour, these figures appeared authentic— human bodies with animal heads. Or perhaps animals with human bodies. Not that humans aren't animals, but still. Most of them wore camouflage clothes, but some were dressed in more formal attire. A man with a lion's head wore a tuxedo. Another man with the head of a wild boar wore only a thong, his thighs massive like easter hams, his belly and breasts sagging perilously. Most of the masks appeared to be rubber, like you'd find in a costume shop. There were many rams, with red eyes and Fibonacci horns of some hard resin. Wolf heads were also popular, as were bald eagles, whose beaks curved ferociously, flashing in the last rays of the sun. But also the heads of cougars and beavers and roosters and rabbits and bears and snakes and—atop an unusually tall body clad in robes, the ovoid noggin of a science fiction alien.

But some masks appeared to be the real thing, heads severed from their beastly forms, immortalized through taxidermy, fitted neatly on the human celebrant, creating a hybrid so convincing you asked yourself why not? And here came one of these painstaking creations: The head of a white-tailed deer, boasting 12-point antlers, walking rapidly. He greeted Faulkner and Arthur as they stood at the end of an aisle that led between rows of folding chairs to a stage. The great buck waved one hand, and raised a canvas bag that said *Where America Shops*.

Hey neighbors! the buck said. Glad you could make it. I've got masks for ya—guessing you didn't bring your own?

It was the voice of Bradley Martin. And it was strange that the mouth of the buck didn't move—somehow you expected it to. That mouth was fixed, barely open, showing teeth behind black gums, and a tongue just visible, as if the animal were panting.

I picked out a couple, he said, Hope they suit your fancy.

Faulkner accepted the bag and held it open for Arthur. When Arthur searched Fawk's eyes, the older man nodded consent, so Arthur shrugged and pulled out the head of a fox. Faulkner reached in and produced an owl's head. He returned the bag to Bradley.

So, Faulkner said, sort of a masquerade?

I know, the buck said from his frozen mouth, it seems a little strange. But this way we set aside our everyday identities. It makes us all equal, as we are in the eyes of the Lord.

Faulkner donned the owl's head and adjusted it. Immediately, he took on a watchful, almost haughty demeanor. Fair enough, he said to the buck.

Bradley added, Besides, it's better than white hoods, right?

The owl turned and stared at him, his thoughts obscure.

The buck exclaimed, Kidding! Kidding of course. Come on in, gentlemen, make yourselves at home. Get some punch, find a seat— Pastor will kick things off pretty soon now.

Arthur put on the fox head and tried to align the eye holes. From inside, he heard himself asking, How do we drink punch in these masks?

The buck laughed from his panting mouth. You'll see, he said. You'll see.

Then the buck, and Bradley Martin inside it, made a kind of bow, lowering the great rack, and turned and marched back up the aisle, calling out to attendees by names you couldn't quite hear over the noise of the drum and guitar.

The fox mask narrowed Arthur's field of vision so that he felt detached, disoriented. He kept thinking he would trip, or walk into someone. The eyeholes were too far from his eyes, a deuce of portals, out of alignment, revealing a grotesque scene in the woods. When he pulled the mask tight to his face it was better, so he did that as they walked toward the refreshment tables. Faulkner the owl turned and saw Arthur pulling back his mask.

Don't do that, Fawk said. It looks silly.

Arthur dropped his hands, but protested, I look silly? Like this whole fucking thing isn't silly? It's as silly as shit through a goose.

I don't think that's the expression, Faulkner said. He leaned his owl head over to Arthur's foxy ear and added, Maybe we shouldn't call attention to ourselves. You know?

Arthur did know. There was a sense they had been admitted provisionally, and were under scrutiny, a kind of trial. He tilted his head back so the mask fell against his face and the eyeholes fit better. He imagined this gave his fox a curious look, like it was sniffing the air for trouble, and that seemed fine.

At first everyone was a stranger, anonymous creatures out of some contemporary Greek myth. But gradually you realized that you could recognize people by other clues. There was the bartender from the Good 'Nuff Tavern—you could tell by his barrel torso and slouching shoulders. He wore an alligator mask. There was the electric company lineman, whose steel-toed boots were flecked with orange paint. He had the head of a monkey. There was the crossing guard, who had a hook for a hand, standing in the aisle with a mallard duck head.

The refreshment tables, draped in gingham cloth, held several large bowls of red liquid—presumably punch. There were also bowls of what appeared to be pudding. At the end of the table lay piles of turkey basters and piping bags. Once Arthur's eye holes aligned properly, it became clear. He saw the deputy sheriff do it first—Myron, betrayed by his shiny shoes, whose head was a badger. The deputy took a baster to the punch bowl, drew up some liquid, and then tilted his head back and poked the baster into his rubber mouth and deposited the refreshment. Then he went to a bowl of chocolate pudding, scooped the treat into a piping bag, and maneuvered that into his mouth the same way. Scanning the crowd around the table, Arthur saw many people doing this—sating their thirst and hunger through these cooking devices, through the rubber masks of animals. What the fuck.

Faulkner the owl gave Arthur the fox a quick nod—stern and wise. They took basters and sampled the punch. It was strangely delicious. Arthur was expecting something sweet and synthetic, but it tasted like a blend of real fruit and exotic spices. There was a kick at the end, some pure kind of alcohol. The baster spilled inside Arthur's mask before he could get it to his mouth. He reached inside the mask to wipe it. Why did he feel like he couldn't just take off his mask and use a napkin like normal? Because this was all not normal. You found yourself doing things because that's what everybody was doing. Because it was so excessively weird, it made it easier to go along. So he left the sticky punch on his chin and went for another baster.

He felt a hand on his shoulder and heard the voice of the owl say, Careful son. That stuff is dangerous.

Arthur considered whether he would try the pudding with the piping bag. It seemed too messy to be worth it, but then it must be good because everyone was taking it. And you might as well try things once.

Just then a short, stout person approached with the mask of the Cheshire Cat. The cat was wearing cargo shorts and sensible hiking shoes. It reached up and put a hand on each of their shoulders, and said,

Fancy meeting you here.

It was a woman's voice, but a very low one. Who was that voice? He had heard it before, and it made him nervous, that voice. Before he could inquire, the cat vanished into the crowd.

The owl whispered in his ear, Peg Hanrahan. Very gutsy of her to come. The only woman as far as I can tell.

Arthur put his muzzle to the owl's ear. He said, How did she know it was us?

We all have our tells, Fawk said. Which makes me wonder why she's here. Can't imagine she's part of this crowd.

Should we find her and ask?

That could blow her cover, Mr Fox. If she is indeed incognito. Also, you can't just find a Cheshire Cat.

Arthur looked at the owl who had been his friend. There was something delicious about the surrealism of this situation. It made you feel high. Morgan liked surrealism. She always went to that room in the Art Institute. Thinking of Morgan seeing him now brought a sudden wave of shame. That wasn't fair. He was on a man's mission here—reconnaissance. Maybe some of that pudding would help.

Then the drum and instruments stopped. A spotlight shone on the stage where the lectern stood, and here came Bradley Martin the buck deer, tapping on the microphone. There were curtains at the back of the stage and Arthur saw movement behind them, something frantic. The crowd didn't seem to be paying attention, but Faulkner was also looking that way with strigiformian interest. Shapes moved into the curtain, bowing it out, lifting the hem. The deer cupped his hand over the microphone and swung his ponderous head and antlers and said something fiercely to the offenders behind the curtain. Then the deer recovered his composure and tapped the microphone again, this time loudly for attention, and spoke over the PA, saying, If you would all make your way over and take a seat. That's it, very good. Fine fine, fill your basters—you can take them to your seats. We'll start momentarily.

The creatures were more orderly than a typical crowd and soon they lined the rows of chairs, an impressive taxonomy of fauna holding turkey basters, their attention turned on the stage. It was dark now and the light of the fires dappled their faces and illuminated the canopy above with spectral shapes. Bradley Martin introduced someone who 'needed no introduction,' and stepped down off the stage and slunk behind the curtain.

The science fiction alien took the stage with slow steps, his long cranium bowed, his hands clasped in front of him. He came to the lectern, arranged his robes, lifted the microphone to its limit, and held his palms over the audience to calm them. He held the pose for some time, past when the crowd went silent. There came a chorus of crickets and frogs, a barred owl, and then—from a distance—the shrieking yip of coyotes. How had he arranged that? Surely it was a recording. But no, there they went again, a pack of coyotes hollering the way they often do in these woods. The alien nodded, approvingly, the ghastly face frozen in a look of astonishment—huge eyes almond-shaped, mouth tiny, nose vestigial.

Then the alien reached up and grasped its face with both hands, pulling the cosmic flesh away from the skull, lifting it—and the mask came off. It was the pastor, Ravelin Magpie. Some of the audience reached to their masks, but the pastor stopped them: No, no. Leave them on. Tonight you are creatures of the forest, all equal in the eyes of god. I am only here to speak a few words, and then I'll cease to be here. You might say, I never was here, and so the mask is unnecessary. Also, who can take me seriously wearing that thing?

There were chuckles from the crowd, and you could see the pastor's smile, shockingly sincere and charming. His eyes turned down at the outer corners and his cheeks turned up into dimples. His eyes were turquoise in that light. His golden hair unfurled in waves like a Roman statue. And that voice, so lovely, so layered. His look and his sound were so extraordinary, it was hard to pay attention to what he said, but you believed in it still.

The owl tilted his head over and whispered, That's some top-shelf snake oil right there.

The pastor remarked that a year had passed since the last Forest Service, since he had begun to lead the flock at the Most Redeemed Church. He shared words of gratitude—about the lovely night, the gracious hosting of the Martins, the fellowship among all gathered there, the delicious treats and clever instruments for enjoying those treats. He continued in that way, words flowing like honey over a sore throat, making you sleepy and euphoric. Then Arthur woke up a little, and began to comprehend as the pastor said…

"… all these cities, built on shorelines, built on swamps, on earthquake faults and mountainsides—none of them will stand, none will bear the test of time. They will sink, these cities, and melt as they approach the Earth's molten core, like the heat from the heart of God, they will melt into a shameful state of matter—neither liquid nor solid—just a demonic plasma of filth and sin, evaporating from the heat of our Lord Savior. But here! Here in purified Righteous towns like our own beloved Middling, here we shall be spared of that great meltdown. Our towns will rise like exalted citadels on hills, the chosen cities of God, where the people are pure and true and unadulterated, unhomogenized, unvaccinated, unpasteurized, un…"

The pastor paused, as if searching for another word and unable to find it. He placed his palms together and brought his forefingers to his lips and continued…

"Here we will continue to serve the Lord and live out our days and receive what is owed to us, what we are entitled to, what is our birthright—a heaven on Earth, a trailer for Heaven, a prequel, a delicious appetizer before the feast that is the Rapture, the big ball, the championship game, the ultimate trophy of God shining in our case of righteousness!"

The crowd of animals erupted in applause and hoots of approval. One enormous, camo-clad body with the head of a Holstein cow stood up and clapped bombastically, sending a ripple of energy that brought the rest of the crowd to their feet, clapping and hooting and banging on their chairs. The pastor held out his hands, palms down, calming them. The crowd silenced, but remained standing. Arthur pulled his mask back so he could see better and looked behind him. All the heads of beasts facing the pastor in awe, their gazes fixed, flashing in the firelight. A gorilla saw Arthur looking back and shoved him, yelling Turn around! Pay attention! For the first time that night, Arthur felt a wave of fear. He turned and dropped his arms. He felt a hand on his shoulder, steadying. It was the owl, Faulkner. The pastor went on.

"Now! Now, now, now. It's not so easy as that though, is it? There is work to be done. Because the sinful residents of those doomed cities aren't stupid. No, no. Don't underestimate them. The devil comes in many forms but he is always clever. He is always diabolical, hence the Latin root, etymologically speaking. Those residents will want to escape—they already want to escape. They are already escaping and seeking refuge in places like our town. And while we may welcome them, as did the Son of Man, and not cast them away, we will require of them good behavior! We will expect good manners and respect for property and adherence to our codes and ordinances!"

A cheer erupted from the crowd again, some throwing back their pagan heads and howling, slapping the backs of seats before them. The pastor quieted them again.

"That's right," he said. "Just as you would not build a shed without a permit, you will expect that these intruders—these aliens, if you will. You will expect that they won't break laws or dirty our streets or corrupt our children or generally make a scene in situations that call for good manners and proper decorum!"

Proper decorum! Someone shouted from the crowd, and there was more applause.

"Yes, yes, yes, proper decorum indeed. And so! So it is incumbent on us, the heirs to the throne of Heaven, to set an example for these interlopers and send them a message vis a vis the behavior we are expecting of them! With that, I leave you. I return the pulpit to our brother Bradley Martin to conduct whatever he has planned. Of which I have no knowledge, of which I wash my hands, prophylactically speaking. And remember!"

Here the pastor threw his arms out violently, pointing his fingers at the adoring crowd, waiting for their silence. After some moments, he concluded, in practically a whisper. "Remember, my brothers and sisters. Remember. I was never here."

And with that, he pulled on his alien mask and flowed off the firelit stage in a smear of monochromatic robes, vanishing into the night.

Bradley Martin the buck deer jumped on to the stage, pulled the microphone down to his muzzle, thanked the pastor and praised God. He said, And just as Pastor said, we need to set an example and send a message to those intruders who disrespect our way of life!

He turned to the curtain, now rustling again with movement, and said, Bring him out! Bring out the interloper!

Two husky men, wearing masks of bloodhounds, burst through the curtain, holding the arms of a smaller man whose head was wrapped in cloth. The man's wrists were secured by zip ties, his posture as if he had struggled mightily and finally given up. In contrast with the pink arms of the bloodhounds, you could see that his skin was darker, copper-colored, and his hair blue-black and long. He wore loose, filthy trousers, and basketball shoes torn and unlaced.

Careful, said Bradley, cuidado! We treat our sinners with respect, that they might repent and spread the word. Then he turned to the crowd, gesturing toward the captive man, and said, This fellow was apprehended stealing raspberries from the thicket around our church—raiding it at night. Berries intended for an ice cream social, in honor of our elderly members. Those seniors were deprived of their raspberries because of this man's greed. And so we have held him, for a few days, to consider his offenses. Now, we turn him loose, to return to his people, with the message of a peaceful, harmonious community—just as Pastor Magpie described so eloquently!

Bradley thrust a fist into the air and the crowd cheered. Then he turned and stood at attention, facing the bloodhounds and the captive man, and cried, As Honorable Chamberlain of the Holy Society of Beasts, I declare this man's freedom! Release him! Then he pointed to the man and said, Dile a tu gente! Dile a tu gente!

One bloodhound snipped off the zip ties, while the other unwrapped the man's head. Then he was unfettered, blinking in the fiery light, squinting at the crowd, then turning toward his captors. He rubbed his wrists and stood.

The buck laughed. He said, Well don't just stand there! Go! Vamos! Adios!

The man began to walk to the edge of the stage, sideways like a crab, looking at his captors to see if there were a trick or game. When they remained still, he jumped off the stage, staggered a few steps, and ran down the aisle. As he went, the crowd closed in on him, animal-headed humans shouting in his face, pointing at his eyes, shoving him this way and the other, as he ran faster, and escaped into the woods.

Then through the same aisle came the buck and the bloodhounds, yelling Clear the way, clear the way! The crowd parted, settled down, and just as the three came even with Arthur's row, he heard the buck say, sharply, Follow him—make sure he gets back. But don't touch him for christ's sake. No more fuckups!

The bloodhounds ran into the woods, toward the river, where it bordered Arthur's farm. Then there was chaos, as Bradley returned to the stage, and all the Society of Beasts chattered and high-fived, and made way to the punch bowl. In this confusion, Faulkner the owl gripped Arthur's arm, and said into his earhole, Let's go—while we won't be noticed.

They wandered, nonchalantly, to the edge of the crowd, to the perimeter of the firelight, and stepped into the dark woods. They removed their masks and pocketed them, to leave no trace, and ran to the snag over the river. The way was rough, through honeysuckle and briar, and they slipped down the muddy bank. Arthur expected to see the man here, and maybe the bloodhounds, but there was no one. They stood there panting. Faulkner seemed to read his mind.

They must have led him east, to the little bridge the Martins have over the river there. That's the only logical way to go.

They crossed the snag like chameleons across the branches, feet and hands clutching, feeling the unstable flex of the rotten bows, fearing at any moment they might crack. But then they were over, on the other bank, scrambling up the mud, grabbing exposed roots of water maples. Once across, now on Arthur's land, maybe 50 yards from where he had found Armando's body nearly a year ago, they sat on the ground and panted.

Finally, Faulkner said, Well. That was not what I was expecting.

Arthur breathed deeply, trying to slow his heart rate, which pounded not because of exertion but because of worry. He asked, What were you expecting?

Faulkner laughed, almost silently, perhaps bitterly. He shook his head in wonder. He said, Good question, Art. I guess I'd say I was expecting anything but that. But now at least we know.

Know what? Arthur's voice came out too high pitched, his throat strained with tension.

Well, what happened with Armando Gallardo, of course. Obviously he was one of their victims—their 'examples' or 'messengers' or whatever the fuck those assholes call it. And it must have gone badly. Did you hear Bradley at the end—what he said to his thugs?

I did, said Arthur.

So that explains it, I guess. Peg must know by now too, if she stuck around.

Yeah, said Arthur. So they must have killed Armando.

Faulkner shook his head in disbelief. Christ, he said. I guess you know this kind of shit happens all the time, all over the place. But still. When you see it.

It's horrible, said Arthur. Do you suppose, he asked, the guy they released tonight—do you suppose we'll ever see him again?

Faulkner stared, looking deflated. I can't imagine, but who knows. None of his options are good.

They sat, considering.

Fawk looked down into the river. There's one thing, though—one thing doesn't make sense.

What's that? Arthur asked, his voice barely audible.

How did Gallardo get downriver? said Faulkner. I mean, if they dumped him in the river, it would have been by the bridge, right? That's the only decent access for miles. And the pictures on the internet, they show the body nearer than that. So how'd he get past this snag? Right? Any ideas?

There were lightning bugs flashing in the space over the river. Arthur looked toward the older man's face, but in the darkness his expression was lost. There was only his breathing, and his waiting, like all the people waiting for Arthur to do something right for once, and not disappoint them, and not fall short of the potential he had been given, the terrible failure of a wasted life.

He stood up and dusted the seat of his pants with the fox mask. No, he said. I have no idea.

SIXTEEN

Larry helped Morgan load her belongings into a rental truck, which they double-parked in front of Mrs Vogel's mansion, hazard lights blinking. It was late afternoon, and Nakeisha had agreed to switch shifts with Morgan, who would stay through the night. From the passenger window, Larry looked at the house.

Hoo eee, he said. That's a right proper mansion. Talk about...

Larry was extra Cajun this afternoon. But also, he had obviously shaved, and his cheeks glowed. His thick hair was combed carefully, and he wore a plaid button-down short-sleeve shirt, like a southern teenager prepped for church. Did Morgan read too much into people's details? Probably, but that wasn't going to change and sometimes it was helpful.

Well, she said, it feels even bigger inside. Plus it's haunted, so brace yourself. But first you have to meet my ladies.

Nakeisha and Mrs Vogel and all the paintings of her ancestors were waiting in the parlor. Nakeisha stood beside the old woman's wheelchair.

Morgan said, Sorry we're running late—this is my friend Larry.

He went forward to hug Nakeisha, but she stopped him by extending her hand, which he shook. And then, bending awkwardly, he reached out to Mrs Vogel. She let him take her hand, but only stared at him grimly.

Good of you to take the day off to help my girl, said Nakeisha. She had her fists on her hips, studying him.

It's no big deal, said Larry. My schedule is flexible.

Mrs Vogel made a backhanded gesture at him and rolled her eyes.

What kind of job do you have? Nakeisha asked.

He paused, then said, I work at the planetarium.

What kind of work? Nakeisha asked. You put on shows for the kids?

Larry smiled at her and blinked. He had the dumbfounded look of someone who doesn't speak the language, but doesn't want to show it. Finally, he said, No, well, research.

He's an astrophysicist, Morgan said. He's studying dark matter. It was annoying how skeptical Nakeisha looked, how unwelcoming Mrs Vogel was. Why would they have a problem with poor Larry.

Mrs Vogel kept her eyes trained away from them, peering out the window. She muttered, Hocus pocus.

Must be nice, Nakeisha said, having your own schedule. She smiled then and put a hand on Morgan's arm. She was trying. She said, Ya'll need some help with your stuff? They're gonna ticket you parked out there too long.

We've got it, said Morgan. She looked at Mrs Vogel with intention. The old woman just lifted a hand slightly, dismissively.

Okay you just let us know, said Nakeisha. I'll be right here hon. Nice to meet you Larry, Mr Dark Matter. She laughed and then Larry laughed, too loudly, too obviously relieved.

It took longer than expected to unload the truck, even though Morgan didn't have much. Most of her things were still back on the farm in Middling. Each time they came into the house, Mrs Vogel was there, watching them pass. Larry was unaccustomed to this kind of work, and Morgan had to instruct him. As they carried her mattress, she said You take the bottom half up the stairs because you're taller—here we go, step,

step, step… When he brought her reading chair, he was confused in the doorway, and she helped him set it down and rotate it to the narrow side and ease it through the frame. He was focused, studious, treating the movement of old mismatched furniture with the kind of earnest dedication you'd apply to a geometric theorem or a crossword puzzle. When they arrived in the attic, and set the piece down, each time, he let out a breath and grinned with their success. He was flushed now, a little sweaty with the effort.

It's kind of fun, Larry said, moving house.

Haven't you ever?

He looked wily. Not really, he said.

You had people? She asked.

You might say. Well, he corrected, my family did. And my place now, it came furnished.

They sat in the attic in her two café chairs beside the tiny round table. Morgan couldn't remember where that table had come from. Arthur must have bought it. Had he refinished it, years ago, back at the beginning? She couldn't remember. She was busy with work then. You couldn't remember everything, could you? There was no shame in forgetting some things.

Your place sounds nice, she said.

It is, Larry said. He considered for a moment. But it's kind of… sterile. Lifeless.

Do you have plants?

Plants?

Morgan laughed. Yeah like houseplants. Do you have any? Is there good light?

Lots of light, Larry said. And a deck on the roof.

You have to have plants, Morgan said. That way there's the symbiosis of life in your home—you and the plants, exchanging oxygen and carbon dioxide. She paused, and then said, Too much?

No! Larry said. He reached out and touched her shoulder. Not at all. I'd like to learn about plants. Maybe you can teach me.

Morgan wiped dampness from her brow with her sleeve, and then gathered her hair and pulled it back with a rubber band. Tell you what, she said. When I get settled here, we'll go to your place and I'll help you get some plants.

Larry rubbed his hands together and looked out the high window of the attic, where the houses across Mrs Vogel's street were illuminated in the last glow of a long day.

I would love that, he said.

It was amazing how Larry could sit with so much equanimity. He was like the frog from Buddhist fables, content to just sit, until action became necessary. And he was a little soft at the edges too like a frog, but in a handsome way. It was okay to observe that he was handsome, wasn't it? It was just an observation after all. Morgan, by contrast, felt like a ground squirrel—always twitchy, darting glances, having to move, to be busy. Her restlessness was no doubt a way to stay ahead of her anxiety and profound worry. But even in good times she hadn't been able to sit still. Larry calmed her down. He had a heavy energy that blanketed his space. Like a front porch surrounded by live oaks covered in Spanish moss. It made her drowsy sometimes.

Still, there was work to do. She had to arrange her new room and move aside some of the things the Vogels had stored up there over the years. Mostly it was boxes—so many boxes! They were all marked with dates and some code she couldn't decipher. Did Mrs Vogel know what was up here? It could have been decades since she had seen this space.

What's in all these boxes, Larry asked.

No idea, said Morgan. She ran her hand over the top box of a stack. It was secured with scotch tape, now yellowed and brittle.

You want to look inside? He asked. He raised his eyebrows and shrugged, that crafty expression that foretold some adventure.

It's not really my business, Morgan said. But her fingers slid under the tape and the box top released with a pop.

Larry came over and pulled the flaps wide, carefully, like you might expose a relic.

The box was full of papers, typed manuscripts. Morgan pulled out the first one, three-hole-punched and bound with copper fasteners. It had a cover sheet that said, *Reflections of a Wayward Soul, Part XXV.*

Larry read it aloud. Part twenty-five, hoo eee, that's a long memoir.

He reached out and turned back the first page, as Morgan held the manuscript. She flipped it back. No, she said. I don't want to read this. We don't have a right to read this.

Larry shrugged, and drifted away. Probably right, he said, now looking at a stack of boxes where the rafters came down. These have a different label, he said. What you reckon's in these?

Open it, Morgan said, if you're so curious.

Larry tucked his fingers under the taped lid, and looked up at her, smiling. Then he pried the box open. He peered inside, boyish, curious. Paintings! He said. He put his hand inside. They're really jammed in there—this guy was prolific.

Morgan sighed. It felt wrong, but also, so intriguing. She rubbed her eyes, opened them, and became aware of a human form barely visible in the opposite corner of the attic.

Oh for fuck's sake, she said.

Larry looked up and then followed her gaze to the spectral form. He yanked his hand out of the box, and backed toward the table where they had sat. He had the look of someone whose picnic has just been carried away by crows.

Morgan sighed and said, I told you this house was haunted.

Larry glanced at her, and back to the ghost, and back at her, incredulously. No seriously, he said. What is that?

Morgan shrugged. As far as I can tell, that is the ghost of Mr Vogel.

The ghost of Mr Vogel began to move, then, behind the row of boxes—his face turned toward them but his body sideways so he could walk. When he got to the sloping rafters, he turned and walked back toward his original position, still facing them. He was translucent and very tall, slightly stooped like an emeritus professor. He wore a mustard-colored cardigan over a shirt and tie. His thin hair was combed back neatly. As he paced, he worked his hands together in the manner you'd expect from an old-time detective. He was clearly agitated, as he had been every time Morgan saw him.

He's harmless, she said.

Larry continued to look back and forth, his expression compressed with doubt. Wow, he said. We're actually seeing a ghost right now... is what you're saying.

It's my best guess, Morgan said. Larry's worry infected her, and now, as she watched Mr Vogel in his state of concern, she grew nervous herself. It was a supernatural thing, after all, even if she had grown used to it, even if she had learned to accept the ghost as part of the old mansion, a fantastical place born of the spirit of the old days, when everything was possible, when the White City glowed downtown. But now, seeing it through Larry's eyes, it was unnerving.

Larry stepped forward, cautiously, and studied the spectral form. Is it possible, he said, that it's some illusion? Light can do crazy things under the right circumstances. Are we maybe seeing a reflection?

Mr Vogel stopped walking. He stood to face Larry. He corrected his posture so that his head nearly touched the beam.

Oh, said Larry. He took a step back. I've offended it.

Him, said Morgan. You've offended him.

Larry continued inspecting the image. It was nearly dark in the room now, and yet the spirit was visible, as if he projected a faint glow. Larry said, Could it be that what we're seeing is a shared hallucination, because of...

At this moment, the ghost of Mr Vogel raised his arm and pointed a finger at Larry. He held the gesture, and then flicked his hand toward the window. His expression was severe, authoritative. Once again, he pointed at Larry, and then toward the window.

God damned Mr Vogel was ruining the day. The god damned ghost of Mr Vogel was ruining a really nice time Morgan was having with Larry and possibly poisoning a nice night, between friends of course. It was infuriating.

Stop it! She said to the ghost. That's rude!

Mr Vogel turned his focus toward her, and shook his head in judgmental disappointment.

Morgan stepped around the table and strode toward him, tripping once on her mattress, but recovering and going toward him in a kind of rush. Get out of here! she said. Seriously, go on. I live here now. Find another room to haunt, creepy old man.

Mr Vogel moved backward, flinching, and then stopped and fixed a look on Morgan of such terrible despair it took her breath away. The sadness of the old man burst throughout the room and reverberated among the old rafters and floorboards. It was agonizing, to feel this dark emotion, the worst sort of depression brought on suddenly and Morgan managed to look back toward Larry and see he felt it too—was he crying even? And then just as quickly, Mr Vogel disappeared and with him went the sadness and Morgan was left with a peculiar confusion in her mood, like waking from a bad dream.

Larry stared at the place where Mr Vogel had been. His dark eyes reflected the street light through the window, and he raised his eyebrows high, his mouth agape. He looked at Morgan with this same amazed and entertained expression, and then he exclaimed, Ha! Oh my gosh! Then he began to laugh, with wonder, with relief. He walked toward Morgan, his arms outstretched. Look at you! he said. It's like you've seen a ghost!

Morgan shook her head and laughed too, but silently. His accent had evaporated and now his tone was dear, sweet. She let Larry wrap his arms around her, his head the same height as hers, which still felt strange in a boy, and he drew her into his warmth and softness. She could feel him chuckling still through his ribcage, deep from his lungs and heart, and all this relief flowed up from their embrace, closing the space between them until it felt like there was none.

Larry released her and put his hands on her shoulders and held her that way, looking into her face. What a strange and wonderful day, he said. I mean, there must be some rational explanation for this, but still. Thank you for sharing this with me.

Sure, Morgan said. She wasn't able to say more.

What would it be like if he kissed her now? She let her lips part and looked into his face and wondered if he would do it. She could feel his breath, smell the sweet staleness of it, like straw in a barn. When he looked at her it was with respect and curiosity and gentleness. And also maybe love? That was all right, wasn't it? Love was always all right. What if he kissed her? Would she kiss him back? What would he taste like, would it be exotic or familiar and would he kiss passionately in the way you'd think would be too rough but actually you liked, with the tongue and everything, and if they kissed that way what would that lead to? There was a mattress lying right here—how easy and natural it would be for that kiss to melt their legs so that they dropped to that bed and then how long until she felt the nakedness of him, skinny but soft, and so incredibly warm, and also she could imagine he'd be shockingly firm—you definitely shouldn't think of that, but what if that was just love thinking and love was always all right. Wasn't it? Didn't she love Arthur that way? Oh Arthur, what are you doing here now? Always Arthur, you poor dumb dog some day you'll run across the road and get hit. Arthur might be on the road right now, driving north, while Larry holds you, breathing a little heavy, his brow wet, his eyes gleaming. What if he kissed you right now?

We should move the truck, Larry said.

Morgan pulled back from him and shook her head. She dropped her face into her hands.

Are you okay? He asked.

Morgan looked up, feeling bright with affection, but nothing more. That's what you're thinking of? she asked. We just saw a ghost and you're thinking of the truck?

Maybe we saw a ghost, Larry said. And maybe not. We'll never know.

Morgan smiled at him, curiously. She said, Always the scientist.

Larry walked to the window and dropped down so he could look up at the sky. He said, Actually my kind of science makes me more likely to believe in the possibility of ghosts.

Morgan joined him at the window. She said, Because of the theoretical, and the unknown. Because you know how little we know.

She felt him turn and look at the side of her face. He said, That's exactly what I meant.

Moon, Morgan said, pointing. It had appeared between the chimneys of the house across the street, ticking up the night sky with celestial precision.

A waxing gibbous, Larry said.

I never liked that word, gibbous, said Morgan. People say it like it makes them seem smart but actually everybody knows it's called that. And it feels weird in your mouth.

Larry said, Just because things feel weird in your mouth doesn't mean you don't want them there.

Morgan looked over and their faces were close. What exactly do you mean by that, sir?

Larry looked back at the moon. Soon it will be full, he said, and we'll all become lunatics for a night.

There are worse things.

Can I tell you something, about the moon? I mean, you probably already know it, but.

Try me, she said.

Well, I remember as a boy my mother explained to me that the moon and the Earth are locked in a kind of whirling dance. Our gravitational fields act on each other. The moon pulls at the Earth, and creates the tides, and the Earth pulls at the moon. And over billions of years, that gravity—that constant pulling—has deformed the moon so that one side has a concentration of mass. That's why we always see the same side of the moon. It can't spin away from us any more. Always the same face—it can't look away.

Mmm, said Morgan. I didn't know that. Not all of it anyway.

After a while, Larry said, Will you be all right here? With the ghost and… everything?

I think so. It feels right.

When will you come over and see my place? Teach me about plants?

Soon, Morgan said. Very soon.

SEVENTEEN

It would be too hot to work outside on this day. You could feel it at dawn, in the fierce rays of the rising sun, the oppressive humidity. It was the kind of day people say It's gonna be a hot one, as if that set your expectations and made it more tolerable. After he watered the animals, Arthur returned to his office, closed the blinds to contain what coolness remained, and got to work. He finished the website for the Middling Café. It looked nice—very professional, with a hero image of the restaurant, edited to make the building look more fresh, less dilapidated. Now customers could order meals to go, which might bring more business, which might make things more predictable for the staff. Arthur sent an email to Tristan Beardsley, with a bill that was fair.

The rest of the day he would dedicate to the kitchen. It was ridiculous to set a goal that the farmhouse would stand ship-shape by Morgan's visit in August. There was no objective measure of 'ship-shape,' anyway—that was measured only by how Arthur felt about the place, whether there was no more work to be done. And on a hundred-year-old farmhouse, there was always work to be done. A house is a kind of living thing, imbued by the spirit of its occupants. This is why old houses deteriorate so rapidly when left vacant. All you could really expect was to keep a house in good repair, forestalling its decline over the years, as your body slowly failed, until you died and handed the house off to someone else. Was that depressing? Not really. It was just the way things are. But still, it was possible to remodel the kitchen by August. It was worth trying.

Half of the old cabinets still clung to the wall where Arthur had left the job. The hole remained in the plaster, exposing the water damage. But it seemed the carpenter ants were gone. Poor things. Today he would gut the kitchen—that was the best approach. Once he had it down to the studs and floorboards, he could update the wiring and the plumbing, and hang fresh drywall over it, and install new cabinets with a knowledge of the structure behind the walls. He got a discount on materials from the lumberyard, in exchange for doing their website, so the budget was reasonable. He had a lead on a used stove and fridge that were a lot more attractive and efficient than the olive green appliances they had now. It was all just work.

The remaining cabinets came down easily and Arthur added them to his pile next to the garage. He was soaked with sweat in just a few minutes outside. But it felt good to sweat. He paused in the yard—all was still. No sounds of birds or tractors or highway or guns. A dragonfly perched on tall grass. An absolute stillness as the land rested under the heat. Back inside, the cool felt good.

Some previous owner had installed paneling around the cabinets, and someone else had wallpapered over that, and on top of the wallpaper were layers of differently-colored paint. It made it more difficult to demolish the old walls, layer upon layer clinging to its substrate, unwilling to accept its fate. But Arthur persevered, with wrecking bar and hammer and an old iron rod. He wore a bandana over his face to keep out the dust. Gramps did that. Cowboys did that, supposedly. Although, it seemed like most of the cowboy myth had turned out to be fantasy. Gramps was real though.

Arthur sat on a stepstool in the kitchen and drank a root beer. What was real? That was a good question. These days, it was hard to tell. Bodies floating down rivers in strange poses, never decomposing. People wearing animal masks for church services in the forest. Ghosts of old farmers. It all defied common sense. It didn't seem real. It was surreal. Did that word mean 'south of real?' In Spanish sur meant south. But the latin prefix meant above or beyond, which made more sense. Probably the Spanish thought of the sea as beyond. But all those things had happened to Arthur, sure enough, and he had witnesses to attest. So, it was just life. Probably you should be grateful that things are so interesting and inexplicable.

In the far corner of the kitchen, built-in shelves nested in the wall. Arthur and Morgan had thought they were charming—those glass-paned doors. But now, with the rest of the studs exposed, the shelves looked shabby. The hinges were cheap and bent. That should come out too—Arthur could make better ones. He removed the doors, carefully, and then tore out the shelves. The wood was thick, heavy, must be pretty old. When somebody made these shelves, they were proud, probably. They put their china there, when people had china.

When he removed the last board, along the floor, he found a notebook wedged behind. It had a brown cardboard cover and thick-stock pages yellowed with age. It was a sort of ledger. Inside the front flap, an inscription: Roy Hanacek, 1938. Arthur sat down on the stool again, breathing hard from his labors, and paged through the ledger.

There were rows of entries, in pencil, in a precise capitalized script. Accounts of expenditures, like *chicken feed – $.15*, and *16-penny nails - $.75*. Also lists of tasks, like *tilled south field*, and *repaired grinder*, and *made sauerkraut*. The days went by like this, in the ledger, the quotidian events of a small farm in Illinois near the end of the Depression. Arthur felt a compulsion to read the ledger through, line by line, maybe out of some communion with a fellow caretaker of the land, or maybe out of some respect for a life mostly forgotten. But also, he found notes in the margins.

The notes came in a different script, a woman's hand mostly likely, the lovely cursive of a day when handwriting was a matter of pride. Often the notes came at the top corner of a page, and they said things like *Wishing you a good day, darling*, and *Lovely sunny morning*, and *Thanking the Lord for his grace*. These notes appeared on most pages. Sometimes there were comments, pointing to ledger entries, like *A job well done*, and *Penny saved is a penny earned*. Under each of these notes, a thick line in pencil. Arthur imagined what had happened here—Hanacek's wife adding her sentiments to his days, and Hanacek underlining each one, as it came. Probably he couldn't give voice to these notions, but he appreciated them, and the act of underlining completed their shared endeavor.

Or was that too sentimental of a read? It was easy to fall prey to nostalgia, thinking about these old times. There was a lot of bad shit back then. Robber barons. Fascism. Polio. But how else could you read this ledger, this artifact of the Hanacek farm? Arthur tried to imagine another explanation. Maybe she was taunting him, and each time he underlined her phrase, he called attention to how much he resented her mockery. Maybe he was plotting to kill her? No. It just didn't hold up. The ledger was honorable, and true. Toward the end, the notes stopped. There was a day when Hanacek had only one entry—it said, *Made arrangements*. So maybe Mrs Hanacek had died.

Arthur closed the book and sat with it in his hands, on his lap. If only Morgan could see this old book. She would love it. How could she not? Then, maybe because of the heat or because of fatigue, he grew dizzy, and felt himself lifting up out of himself and looking down on himself, in this gutted kitchen, hunched on a stepstool, cradling a faded ledger. Why did that guy, that Arthur guy, so out of his mind all the time, so impulsive and frantic—why did he want to show the book to his wife? Was the idea that she would see this nice old couple, sharing a life together, and think, Oh, we should be like that—I should move back down from Chicago and return to our idyllic life on this hobby farm? That was definitely part of it. But also, and to be fair, he just thought it would bring Morgan a little joy. You can try to be cynical about these things, but sometimes they're just nice.

So the question became: Should he show her the book? Because on the one hand, it almost certainly would bring her joy. But also, she would question his motivation. And she should question his motivation, because it was often…

Arthur sneezed. It blew his bandana outward. He untied it and sneezed again. And again, and again. A sneezing fit. Christ when would it stop? He pinched his nose and got a glass of water and then he was all right, his eyes tearing with all that sneezing. He took the ledger up to his office, and put it in a drawer, and returned to the kitchen.

Now the flooring could come up. Here too there were layers. The black-and-white tile, and under that linoleum, and then another layer of tile. Hardwood beneath that. No wonder the counters had seemed so low. Who puts flooring down like this? It contradicted the notion that people always did things better in the old days. Well, maybe they were saving money not ripping it out. By the time he was finished, and all the flooring was hauled out to the pile, and the solid old floorboards were revealed, running crosswise through the kitchen because they were more sturdy that way—by this time, the sun was low near the horizon. It was so huge and orange resting there, like the sun over the Olduvai Gorge in the days of the first humans. Arthur remembered a picture of that from a children's encyclopedia. Olduvai Gorge. It felt good to remember that name. What country was that now? Kenya probably. Or Tanzania? He should learn African geography better. But also weren't these boundaries invented by imperial powers carving up the continent arbitrarily?

It was exhausting to be thinking all the time. Arthur made a peanut butter and jelly sandwich on top of a cooler he'd set in the kitchen. He took the sandwich outside with a can of beer and sat on the steps to the back deck and watched the sun set. It was dazzling, outrageous, these shades of yellow and orange and purple—the last rays bursting up behind low clouds. If you weren't from Earth you would think this wasn't real. You'd think it was surreal.

He watched a flock of crows flap overhead, silently, and disappear beyond the river.

EIGHTEEN

The mail came early that morning and Morgan heard a package drop from the letter slot and echo in the foyer. She looked up from her coffee and met Mrs Vogel's surprised expression. Nakeisha saw the alarm in both of them.

What? she remarked. It's just the mail.

Morgan said, She never comes this early.

Nakeisha laughed, You're like a couple of old biddies with your routine.

Mrs Vogel stared toward the foyer. She said, She's doing her work before the storm.

What storm, asked Nakeisha.

Morgan and Mrs Vogel turned to her incredulously.

A bad storm is coming, said Mrs Vogel.

Supposed to be a derecho, said Morgan. Don't you check your weather app?

Nakeisha laughed and set a smoothie on the tray in front of Mrs Vogel. She said, The weather's gonna be what it's gonna be. Checking a weather app won't make any difference.

Mrs Vogel glared at the smoothie, but didn't drink.

Morgan went to check the mail.

The package was from Arthur, a manila envelope fat with something. She recognized his handwriting on the envelope, the letters formed carefully but primitively, like a child's script on school paper. Handwriting is so revealing, such an intimate view into people—how can each one be different? Billions of people and billions of scripts. But we can tell, immediately, who it is. There was Arthur, lying on the wooden floor, so plain and vulnerable.

Morgan took the package out to the stoop and leaned against the iron railing. She could feel the storm coming—the sky was weird, dark, almost green, and the air was still and pensive. No birds sang. She had lived here long enough to know that it was going to be what the weathermen called a doozie. She slid her finger under the flap and tore open the package.

First she pulled out a book, a collection of Mary Oliver poems called *Why I Wake Early*. A literary friend once made fun of Morgan for liking Mary Oliver and that always brought a twinge now, but Arthur loved those poems and he used to read them to her in their first mornings in Middling. How did he know that she wanted these poems, but couldn't bring herself to read them anywhere but in that worn copy? Probably just a coincidence. Or maybe even it was a gesture of rejection, like Here's your book I don't need it any more. That was an ungenerous thing to think. The way we project our worries on other people, it was horrible sometimes.

The package also contained a business letter marked with the logo of Middling Hospital, addressed to her at the farm, care of Arthur. So they knew she didn't live there but that Arthur still did? There was a sense of dread, like a bill unpaid or a call to witness for some malpractice. She tore it open. But the letter was not malicious at all. It was a job offer, sent from the head of HR herself, with a specific description of Morgan's talents, a plea to consider the offer, and the promise of a handsome salary and even a signing bonus. A signing bonus? Who offered that to nurses? But there it was. And although the promise of good money was welcome, what struck Morgan at that moment was the thought of all the patients in need of care—physically, yes, but also emotionally. All the patients not being treated so well right now, or perhaps not at all. And then came that familiar rush of emotion, rising up from her abdomen and choking her throat. Oh, Arthur. Arthur you fucking guy, you piece of work. How could you send all of this?

A blast of wind came down the street and nearly pulled the papers from her hands. It was as if someone had switched on a continental fan, some malevolent god savoring the inevitable destruction. Morgan slipped the precious things into Arthur's envelope, tucked it inside her robe, and rejoined the ladies.

Well you were right, said Nakeisha, it is going to be a doozie. School's cancelled, but so's my husband's work, so he's got the kids. I can stay with you biddies for a while and make sure you don't blow away.

They sat around the kitchen table listening, at Mrs Vogel's request, to WGN on the radio. If those people are still talking, she said, we must be safe.

But the broadcast served as a regular reminder of the fierce winds approaching and the damage they were sure to cause. When they looked at their weather apps, the radar showed a 700-mile streak of red, an open wound across the plains, from Dubuque to Nauvoo, marching toward them on 80 mile-an-hour winds.

The house shuddered and the panes in the old windows rattled like Halloween teeth. Branches struck the windward side of the house with abrupt reports that made the ladies jump.

We should go to the basement, said Nakeisha.

Right, said Morgan. I'll fill the bathtub.

What? asked Nakeisha.

Oh nothing, Morgan replied. Kind of a joke. Something we always did and I never understood.

Nakeisha turned to Mrs Vogel, Honey, you want us to take you down in your wheelchair or have me carry you down, baby-style?

Mrs Vogel crossed her arms and lowered her chin. You will do neither of those things. I will stay. This house has always protected me. You can go to the basement if you wish, but I will stay right here and be safe. The people are still on the radio.

Okay, wheelchair it is, said Nakeisha. Morgan you get the top and I'll get the bottom, cause you're too skinny to go down first.

Morgan unplugged the radio and set it in Mrs Vogel's lap. They eased her down the basement stairs, one creaking step after another, and set the wheels on the concrete in the dark.

Where are the lights, Tante? Morgan asked.

I don't remember, said Mrs Vogel. It's been too long.

Morgan felt around the corner of a wall and found a switch in a bare metal box attached to conduit. There it is, she said, and switched it on.

They were greeted by a host of eyes staring from makeshift shelves along the seeping walls. They were the eyes of dolls, wooden dolls whose paint had faded, whose hair had disintegrated into mangy clumps, whose legs outstretched like polio victims, whose arms hung limply as their torsos listed to one side or the other. Nakeisha yelped.

Oh yes, said Mrs Vogel, my dolls. They don't look so good do they?

After a pause, she said, Plug in my radio! We need to see if the people are still there!

Morgan found an outlet and the broadcasters continued their storm coverage. Did she remember those dolls from when she was very young? It seemed like she could, but that also seemed like a dream. Sometimes strange experiences conjure memories with no basis in the past. Those freaky dolls could make the soberest judge insane. She asked Mrs Vogel.

Certainly, said the old woman. You carried one around, a German peasant girl with braids. Your momma made you leave it here and you cried. Karl and I made these dolls together, if you can believe it. He was an okay woodworker and I could paint, make clothes. It seems so innocent now, doing that together. Of course we stopped around the time your parents divorced and I put all the dolls down here. You can understand why.

Morgan did not understand. But Nakeisha was watching the two of them, holding Mrs Vogel's smoothie cup, and the time did not seem right to pursue it.

Drink, said Nakeisha.

Mrs Vogel pushed away the cup. What's the point, she said.

Honey you haven't had a thing to eat or drink all morning and that makes me a bad nurse. I don't want to be a bad nurse, do I make myself clear? You gotta drink some of this or your blood sugar's gonna crash like a plane with cotton wings.

Mrs Vogel took the cup, pretended to drink, and then pointed toward the corner. She said, Get that table and set it over here. We play cards. We play the euchre game, like old times.

Nakeisha looked at the dusty card table propped next to a shelf of dolls. I'm not going over there, she said to Morgan. You get the table and I'll get some cards.

Morgan said, Wait, but we can't play euchre, there's just three of us.

Nakeisha pointed upward with her thumb and said, Maybe the old man'll come down here from the attic and be a fourth.

Mrs Vogel laughed suddenly, her eyes watering. Morgan smiled and shook her head.

Then the old woman resumed her serious command. No, she said, I will play two hands—one partner for each of you.

Morgan protested, Yeah but then you… Why was she arguing as if she were a child obsessed with fairness, with competition. Who cares if the old woman played two hands? Morgan said, Right, that makes sense.

They sat at the leather-wrapped card table, among the eyes of the dolls, and Mrs Vogel dealt—two cards, then three, then two—in the old tradition. Just as they lifted their hands, the power went out.

It was a moment of pure darkness and silence, down in the pit of the mansion, where orphaned dolls bore witness to the passage of lives and waited for some cruel rapture. All three women stopped breathing. But there wasn't time to react—in a moment Morgan and Nakeisha's phones lit up with alerts, casting their faces in light like the sinister dancers of Toulouse-Lautrec. Morgan went to look for candles while Nakeisha searched for batteries for the radio.

There were dozens of candles, partly burnt, in a pantry drawer, but there were no batteries that fit the radio. Back at the card table, Mrs Vogel's hands trembled with the cards. She said, The people are gone from the radio—it is our last hours, so we might as well play.

They sat and picked up their cards, now illuminated by candlelight.

Nakeisha played an ace of clubs, the trump suit. She said, Mrs Vogel, are you a Christian?

Mrs Vogel took the suit with the left bower from the partner hand for Morgan. She said, I am a German. We invented Christianity.

Nakeisha laughed and said, I think you're playing better for Morgan. And everybody knows Jesus invented Christianity.

Mrs Vogel led with the ten of clubs and Morgan took the trick with the right bower. Morgan said, Pretty sure Paul invented Christianity. Jesus was just trying to straighten out Judaism.

Morgan played the nine, Mrs Vogel took the trick with the king, and they won the hand. Mrs Vogel said, Well. Then the Germans perfected Christianity. Then the English ruined it. Now Americans make it worse.

Despite her defiance, Mrs Vogel's hands still trembled. She kept looking up at the stairs, and then sideways at a shelf of dolls. She pointed toward Morgan's phone and said, Does that thing play the radio?

Morgan tried to find a stream for WGN but the signal was too weak in the basement. It was perfectly calm down there, embraced by the earth. But you could hear the storm pounding the windows upstairs. She showed Mrs Vogel her phone and said, See they're still there—I just can't get the broadcast down here in the basement.

Mrs Vogel pushed the cards across the table in anger. Why do you try to trick Tante? she asked. I am not some child. The French Lick doctors were wrong about my day of death—I can feel it, this is that day. I can't play any more of this stupid game. I must prepare.

Nakeisha went and put her arm around Mrs Vogel's shoulders. She touched her hand. Honey, do you want me to pray with you?

Mrs Vogel waved her free hand dismissively and said, If you must. But then she held Nakeisha's hand in both of hers and closed her eyes. Nakeisha began to recite the 23rd Psalm. Mrs Vogel moved her lips along with the words.

Morgan sat. Why did praying make her feel awkward? It would be so nice to be religious, such a comfort. But she knew that if she tried to pray with them it would feel false and almost like tempting some curse. She studied the dolls and tried to remember which one she had carried.

When the prayer ended, Mrs Vogel opened her eyes and found Morgan with a glare. In the candlelight, her features were ancient and the cataracts of her eyes glowed dully like some unknown fish from the deep.

She said, as if in accusation, You don't pray, Nichte.

I listened, protested Morgan. It's a nice prayer.

You don't pray because you have too much guilt. This guilt you get from your mother and your father. That is their sin, but yours is that you are not curious. You don't care. Always about yourself, Nichte. You leave that boy of yours by his lone self down in that home you abandoned. You flit around with this other boy. And you don't care—not about Tante, not about what happened there…

Mrs Vogel pointed in the direction of Morgan's childhood home, next door. You could just see through the window well the red brick of the wall that separated the properties.

Mrs Vogel continued, And not about what happened here. She pounded her wheelchair.

The three were silent, then, shocked by the outburst and rattled by the wind upstairs and embarrassed under the watch of the dolls. A siren began to howl from the neighborhood—it meant a tornado or winds of a dangerous speed.

Nakeisha patted Mrs Vogel's shoulder and smiled with compassion at Morgan. Maybe I'll see if I can make us some tea, she said.

No, said Morgan, and the abruptness of her response surprised her. I'll go, she said. I need a break. She left without looking back at Mrs Vogel and walked up the stairs, numbly.

The storm called to Morgan. It said, Come out, little human woman. Come outside and feel what it feels like to be alive. Feel how fragile your world is—see the beauty of my destruction! Feel the relief of knowing that you are nothing, see the wonder of a city laid to waste! Hundreds of years of careful construction, brick upon brick, branch from branch, all of it rubbed out with my loving lashes. Shall I reach into that fortress, little human woman, and pull you out? Or will you come to me of your own will and know the exhilaration of courage and absolute forfeit?

I'm coming, Morgan replied, Just let me put the kettle on.

The gas range still worked and so she filled the kettle and put it on and then walked toward the foyer. In the parlor, there was Mr Vogel, which seemed expected somehow. He was stooped badly, staring out the window, his hands entangled and writhing like mating serpents. His worry was palpable, a wet fog in the room. When Morgan walked by he looked over, and from his eyes came that profound sadness she had felt in the attic with Larry—a sadness that left you reeling and empty. Morgan looked at him, shrugged, and opened the front door.

The wind slammed the door open against its frame and she heard the leaded glass shatter. The force of air sucked her breath from her. She adjusted her breathing, a labor to draw in and blow out, and she leaned against the wind, holding on to the railing. She made her way down to the sidewalk, somehow just a little safer there, and witnessed.

The trees bent in a gruesome pose—too far over to hold their roots, it seemed. Perpendicular trees, cantilevered like illusory sculptures, all that xylem and phloem stretched to capacity—oaks and maples and sycamores not trained to withstand such abuse. Morgan wanted to help them, she wanted to cry for them. But there was nothing to do, for the wind also brought garbage of every kind, skittering down the street like hordes of rats, and shopping carts and wrecked umbrellas and roof shingles and lawn chairs and someone's stained wedding dress, clinging for a moment to a light post, then departing beyond sight toward the east.

But also, here came a jogger, in wispy shorts and tight shirt, leaning into the wind, pausing briefly to check her smart watch. And here came the man in the suit, carrying his little white dog still attached to its leash, the man holding down his fedora and grimacing vaguely as if it were any old inclement day. Ah Chicago.

After a few moments, the wind eased slightly, but you could tell. The air pressure changed, and it began to rain. Enormous drops, crashing like Christmas tree balls into the street, stinging Morgan's face. It came down harder then, in smaller drops, a downpour so complete someone might have released a pregnant tarp from above. She felt submerged, with water in the eyes and ears and mouth. Oh if there were a god she would thank her, that fucking rain felt so good.

And then it passed. Morgan became aware that she was a little human woman standing on the sidewalk in a deathly storm, her hair flat against her scalp, her clothes saturated and heavy, her weird eyes a bright beacon to survival, surrounded by so much wreckage. She thought of Arthur.

Oh god I hope you're all right, she said. She took her phone out, and began to text him, but then stopped, and instead checked the weather in Middling, and saw it was okay there. Maybe she would call him later. It must be cozy in the house on the farm, listening to the rain.

Robins began to chirp, drunkenly, from down the street. She saw one flit down and seize a worm flushed out by the rain. It must be over. The birds know.

Inside the kettle was screeching. She put some tea in the pot and poured it and carried the pot with three mugs downstairs.

Nakeisha looked up and said, Girl! Where have you been? How long does it take to make a pot of tea? And how'd you get so wet?

Sorry, said Morgan. She put the mugs on the card table and then began to pour.

Nakeisha shook her head and clucked, You are one weird girl. I'll take some sugar.

Mrs Vogel's head was down on her chest and Morgan realized she was sleeping. She pointed and said, How …?

Nakeisha smiled diabolically and said, Oh, I gave her a little help. I always keep a few.

But she wasn't drinking, how'd you get her to…?

Mmm-mmm, said Nakeisha, Not sharing my secrets. You got to learn on your own.

They sat and drank tea. Morgan's clothes dripped on the concrete floor. Suddenly all of life was still there, the bad and the good, and it seemed like anything could happen now. Like you could do anything, because the slate was wiped clean. It was hard to describe how this felt, this complete openness and possibility. But also it was silly, just because there had been a storm. Life wouldn't change much, once people got back to their TVs and phones.

Morgan said, Nakeisha, can I ask you something?

You just did, she said.

Well then here's another: How do you manage all these things in your life and still seem so… I don't know, so… cool? Like your kids and your job and your marriage and your church—you just do it all like it's no big deal and you don't complain.

Nakeisha chuckled, deeply, and sipped some tea, and set her mug down, and said, Well, thank you. I appreciate you saying that. You might be frazzled, but you're a smart one and you have a big heart. So I appreciate your opinion of me.

Morgan nodded, self-consciously. You always wanted compliments until you got them.

Nakeisha continued, The truth is, I'm not always cool at all on the inside—sometimes I'm just freaking out, you know? But I try not to show it, and then it goes away. And what's left is my faith and my contentment. You know what contentment is?

Morgan said, I'm gonna say I don't.

Most people don't. Contentment isn't happiness. Contentment is simply wanting what you already have, bad or good. It's just being okay with right now. You know?

Well, said Morgan, I think I understand.

There you go, said Nakeisha. Things are gonna be what they're gonna be and you just do your best. And don't want too much. Then you'll be content.

Morgan wanted to touch Nakeisha, to make some contact to express her gratitude but she held back. Nakeisha stood up.

Now come on and give me a hug, she said. I know you want it.

In Nakeisha's ample arms, Morgan felt tiny and melted. She thought of Arthur.

Nakeisha said, Now let's get the fairy godmother up to bed. I gotta get home and see my babies, make some supper.

And your husband? Morgan said.

Yeah, him too.

Up in her attic apartment, Morgan could hear crickets outside and an occasional whoosh of a car. Down the block someone was working a chain saw, clearing fallen branches, but that went silent. How much she would like to hear an owl right now. Like the owls back by the Sangamon River. She picked up her phone and before she could stop herself she called Arthur.

He answered immediately, saying, I've been thinking about you.

You too, she said.

Are you all right? I've been watching the news—seems like it was bad up there.

I'm fine, Morgan said. Which is more than you can say for Mrs Vogel. She really freaked out. Thank god Nakeisha was here.

What happened? asked Arthur. He sounded genuinely interested. Was that new, or had she been misjudging him?

She said, Oh I don't know, she gets very superstitious sometimes and she's got some kind of grudge against my parents she won't tell me about.

That's too bad, he said. Have you asked her about it, like directly?

You mean like a normal, well-adjusted person would do?

Yeah.

No, she said, I haven't. I probably should.

Don't be hard on yourself, he said. 'Should' can be a shitty word, sometimes.

All this wisdom I'm getting today. Morgan realized her fingers were in her hair, twisting it.

Oh? he asked.

Yeah Nakeisha had all this advice for me—it made me think, I guess.

Like what?

Just about contentment and how to be… content. Morgan slid down in her bed, crossed her legs and rubbed one bare foot against the other. It was good to be dry. Hey, she said, I got your package.

Oh, you like my package? He said this too quickly, and she knew he regretted it. So she laughed and said, A lady doesn't say.

Then after a pause she added, It was really sweet, Art. I mean the book—I've been wanting that book.

I'm glad, he said. I thought you might.

It was nice to hear him say this. He was just being nice—you couldn't interpret it any other way. Morgan let out a sigh she knew he could hear. That was enough of a response.

He said, What was the letter from the hospital? Kind of a mystery!

Oh nothing, she said. It was just a thing.

Arthur didn't ask any further. She could hear him clink a dish in the sink. Maybe he was pouring a whiskey. How long would they talk?

She said, How about you, what's been going on?

A lot, he said. A lot. Been working on the kitchen. Also, we went to this crazy church service thing in the woods at the neighbors across the river, the Martins.

Tell me about it, Morgan said. All the details.

She listened to him tell the story, which was horrifying. He described it all so well—the animal masks in the firelight, the drums, the bizarre pastor, that poor man they released into the woods. The story made her stomach upset, a little. There was a small jolt of adrenaline like she used to feel when there were creepy noises in the middle of the night, or in the mornings when they discovered junk the neighbors had dumped in their field or maybe just came up out of the field—they never knew. And yet, also, Arthur's story was beautiful in a way, in how he told it carefully, passionately. It had a fairytale quality, not so sinister as before but more cartoon-like. Like a fictional world with fictional villains, but also good people, a world that's tempting in contrast with your own harsh and often lonely world. A world in which you might find yourself… content.

And so the body, Morgan heard herself say. You think the Martins put it there?

Oh I know they did, he said. They as much admitted it.

Morgan paused, then asked, And how did it get in the river?

He cleared his throat—had he sipped his whiskey wrong? The flood, he said. Like I said—that's all I can figure. It rained a lot after you and I found the body.

I see, she said. I guess so.

They both let the subject drop, knowing it could ruin this rare conversation.

Arthur asked, So you're all settled in now? You like it?

I do, she said. It's pretty weird, I know. But it feels right to me.

She added, For now.

I was wondering, he said, how'd you get your furniture and everything moved? I felt like I should come up and help you but, you know.

Morgan swallowed. She brushed her hair back from her forehead and looked at the rafters of her bedroom. Some friends, she said. Some friends came over to help—it was easy, really. Nice of you to think of it though.

Arthur was silent. She knew he had more questions but kept them to himself.

I'm so tired, Art, she said. All of a sudden. All of a sudden I'm just pooped.

Well I'm not surprised, he said. Braving a storm all day. I'm amazed you're up this late.

I didn't brave a storm, she said. I just survived it.

I would give you more credit, said Arthur.

I know you would, she replied.

Then they agreed to hang up, and maybe to talk again soon, and they said they loved each other, and it felt like they really meant it for the first time in so long. Morgan left the phone by her pillow, now warm from the long call, some silly proxy for her husband, the cheerful nerd, the accidental storyteller, the goofy dog. She thought about going to get the envelope he had written on, and the book of poems, and hold them with her warm phone in her bed. But she was too tired. Instead, she fell asleep, into a shallow half dream, where she and Arthur walked together through a field of flowers along a river's edge. Did that really happen, or was she just half-dreaming about a dream? It doesn't really matter, because life is but a dream. Once they paddled a canoe down the crooked Sangamon—was she dreaming that now? They row, row, rowed that boat gently down the stream. They were rowing now, merrily, merrily, coming around a bend where some hawthorn trees blossomed. And what was that up there, jutting out of the river, blocking their way? Was it a tree trunk? Some farm machinery? No. That was a body, the body of Armando Gallardo, jutting rigidly from the water like a road sign in a flood, and his face was looking at her, looking into her, where all her secrets cowered.

Morgan sat up in bed, wet with sweat, her eyes open and frantic, and the old house breathed around her.

NINETEEN

The night after Arthur talked with Morgan, sleep teased him. He had visions of a diabolical sprite, who cooed sweetly from shadows, but when Arthur approached, a wicked face leaped out screaming. Arthur woke with pounding heart. Since Morgan left, he had only slept on his side of the bed, leaving hers made. Every morning he made his half, with the pillows the way she liked. He hadn't washed the sheets, because for a while they smelled of her skin but that fragrance was long gone and now he could only smell his solitary odor, the reek of a lonely bachelor.

In the wee hours of the morning, he walked down the hall and got Hanacek's ledger and brought it back to bed, reading by the light of his phone. It told the story of such a deliberate, honorable life. Mr and Mrs Hanacek, making the best of difficult times, living off their humble farm, complementing each other's unique outlook. It was impossible to imagine the old farmer planning some extravagant day to impress his wife. Well, surely they weren't perfect. There must have been disagreements, maybe some fights. But the days you saw recorded in that ledger were so… consistent. That must have been a satisfying way to live. Was it possible for Arthur to live that way? Not to impress Morgan, but just to be a good person. Probably Arthur was too hard on himself. But he was too hard on Morgan too, wasn't he? It would be nice to have a do-over. Now he was so deep in the mess he had created—you can't just turn the page on that, can you? These are the thoughts that arise alone in the dark in an old, groaning house.

In the first light of morning, the rooster crowed. Why did he keep that rooster? It was a pain in the ass, that bird, chasing all the hens around, agitating them from egg-laying, waking the neighborhood with its cartoon song. Gramps once had a rooster, mistakenly included with a batch of chicks. When it started to crow, Gramps beheaded it with a machete and Grandma served it for dinner. The smell of it reminded young Arthur too much of the hen house, but he ate it anyway, for fear he would be scolded, but later he was sick behind the toolshed and to this day he didn't like roast chicken. So why then did he buy that rooster? Because it suited his vision of a perfect farm, that's why. A fool's vision.

He made coffee and, on a lark, splashed some whiskey into it. The drink fortified him and he put on his dirty work clothes and went back to the field to repair some deer fencing. The sun glowed through the hedge, its light diffuse in the bottomland fog. A house wren sang merrily. Grasshoppers leapt as Arthur walked the dew-damp field. Well, this was like a morning on a perfect farm. These were the mornings that made it all worthwhile. He managed to repair two sections of the fencing, then rested, drinking coffee and whiskey from his thermos. But then as the earth revolved and brought the sun above the trees, wind returned. By nine o'clock it whipped fiercely from the south again, hot wet air from the oily Gulf, and Arthur could no longer hold up the fencing.

But there, across the field, walked an older couple, holding hands. It was the Fuglesens on their morning stroll, with their mugs and binoculars. Faulkner stumbled on a hillock and Nancy caught him, laughing, her hair enormous in the wind. They saw him, and waved, and he waved back, and he walked toward them. But then they turned and looked, and waved toward the house, and there came another figure—a stout woman with close-cropped hair and cargo shorts, trotting across the field toward the Fuglesens. There was no mistaking—it was Peg Hanrahan. And now that he had been seen, Arthur had no choice but to join them.

Well if it isn't the Cheshire Cat, said Faulkner.

Ah so you did recognize me, said Peg. She crossed her arms and stood solidly. Her face beamed confidence in the sun. Morning, Arthur, she said.

So she remembered him. Arthur waved a hello and nodded.

That was a bad business, that service in the woods, Faulkner said. And ballsy of you to infiltrate their ranks.

Oh not really, said Peg. People like that have so much hubris, they don't notice much.

What were you doing there—can I ask? said Nancy.

I got a tip, Peg said. I was just confirming the evidence.

On the Gallardo case, said Fawk.

Indeed, said Peg. It's a pretty steep hill to climb, getting to the truth on this. So we want to be really sure.

Peg wiped sweat from her hairline and breathed heavily. Then she held out her hand to Nancy and said, Hey, congratulations to the newest member of the Hospital Board!

Well, Nancy said, I hope I can be useful.

I'm sure you will, said Peg. And they need it--so many unfilled positions.

True, said Nancy. We'll do our best.

They all paused in silence, considering the problem. Arthur put on a smile that took considerable effort. The thing about smiling using fewer muscles than frowning—that was bullshit. Smiling felt weird when you didn't mean it. It was like a grimace, like an angry baboon.

You'll have to convince people to live in Middling, he said.

Well that shouldn't be hard, said Faulkner cheerily. He gestured to the landscape. Just look at this paradise!

Peg peered out toward the river. She said, It's a hard balance, isn't it? You want to root out our problems, but also you have to cheerlead a bit.

Fawk sipped his coffee. I try to stick to the cheerleading, he said with a small laugh. You know, he said, A stone must conform to its river.

What the fuck does that mean? said Arthur. It didn't come off right at all. His god damned insomniac brain was making him behave badly. He forced a broader smile.

Nancy looked at him with concern, then put her hand on Peg's shoulder. She said, I'm thinking of compiling all of Fawk's sayings and selling them as bathroom books. We'll make a fortune, don't you think?

Absolutely, said Peg.

Faulkner turned to her and pointed his cup. So what brings you out here this windy morning?

Mmm, said Peg, nodding. I was hoping to take a look around. Maybe connect a few dots.

Arthur felt a chill run up his back. The dots, once connected, could quite easily lead to him. But this wasn't the time to let guilt overcome you. This was a time to act most naturally. He heard himself say, Peg, what's your interest in the Gallardo case? I mean, isn't it kind of stale now? Not that I know much about it.

Peg put her hands deep into the pockets of her cargo shorts and rocked forward on her toes. Well, Arthur, she said, I guess I think about Lupe—Armando's wife, and her daughter, Sofia. The limbo they're in now, not knowing what happened, and the shame they must feel in the community, like they're not important enough to enjoy the benefit of the law. It seems to me we have to help people like that, the underprivileged. That seems worth a few hours of my time, doesn't it? But it's not just some kind of altruism—it's self-interest too. If we allow people to be abused like this, it makes cracks in our society, and too many cracks mean it will collapse. I don't want a collapsed society, Arthur. Do you?

No, he replied. He couldn't think of any other words to say. Something bit his neck and he swatted at it.

I think, said Peg, that we could be the happiest, most prosperous country in the history of the world. Why not shoot for that?

Totally, said Arthur. He looked to Faulkner and then to Nancy, to draw them in. But it seemed Peg was only addressing him.

I'll never have kids, said Peg. That's just the nature of my life. But I have nieces and nephews. I want a good world for them. Long after I croak. I want to do everything I can to leave the world a little better for them.

Yeah, said Arthur. He nodded and looked at his boots. They were matted with seeds from the wet field. He was trying to make the world better too, wasn't he? With his nature restoration and everything. Maybe he should say that. But it would probably sound lame. Like, Oh you recycle—I recycle too!

After a moment, Peg turned to the others and said, Is Sheila still looking into this? She did such a nice piece on Armando. I haven't seen her post for a while.

Fawk and Nancy looked at each other. Nancy chewed her lip. Fawk said, I think… she doesn't want to interfere, with legal action pending and so forth.

Peg lowered her brow. She said, That hasn't stopped her before.

Nancy touched Faulkner's arm, It's Peg, hon. It's fine.

Then Nancy drew in a breath and said, To be honest, Sheila got some threats. Very violent threats that seemed credible. More than in the past. So she's taking a break.

Fawk blinked a few times, and his voice faltered as he added, The Yeshevsky business—that was bad too. And when this new guy, Ravelin Magpie, replaced him—just as harmful but probably more effective— well that took the wind out of her sails.

I'm sorry, said Peg. Maybe I shouldn't have asked.

No, no, said Nancy. It's a good question and Sheila wrestles with it all the time—what's the right thing to do, the courageous thing.

Courage doesn't matter if you're dead, said Arthur. It had just been a thought, but he said it.

Actually, said Faulkner, sometimes it does. That's the hard thing.

Peg nodded. Exactly, she said, exactly.

Fawk clapped his hands suddenly, brightening. Well! he said. For what it's worth she's doing PR for a conservation company now, I forget the name.

Soil Keepers, said Nancy.

Right! Said Fawk. Stewards of Dirt!

All four of them laughed and the dark mood drifted away in the persistent wind.

Counselor, said Fawk. How can we help you today? Anything you need.

Well for starters, said Peg, you can give me permission to walk the river.

Be my guest, Faulkner said. Just watch for the nettles. And poison ivy. And the banks can be slippery.

Peg turned to Arthur. He realized the request was for him too. The others waited. He squinted and scratched his head, and looked back toward his stretch of river. Why was he pausing? That looked guilty. He said, Oh, yes. Yes of course.

It was a terrible time to return to fence-building, but Arthur did it anyway. He sank the poles deeper, working with a pickaxe to get around the rubble in the clay. He tied lines to the posts and tried to create a system of lifting the netting by means of a pulley, like sailors did on the old ships. But of course the hot southerly wind tugged at the netting and knotted his lines and ripped out the pulleys and in the end he ruined what little progress he had made that morning.

The ground where he worked was littered with deer shit—piles of soft, brown pebbles every few strides. Those vermin must shit constantly. All the native plants were nipped to their stalks, while the invasives thrived. Deer shit fertilizing noxious weeds—insult to injury.

Arthur sat on the ground and tipped back his thermos. It was empty. What was the point of all this? Even if he were successful in creating the Perfect Day, the day after that, the struggle would continue. And one day he would be dead, and the land would succumb to the onslaught of this unbalanced world, and everything he had nurtured would die, and probably someone would buy the place for a dollar and build some storage facility for people with too much shit to store more shit. That was the way of the world. Peg Hanrahan and all her idealism, her happy prosperous world—why did he let her patronize him like that? What a bunch of horse shit that was. Gramps would have said something like, Peg, you're so full of shit your eyes are brown.

Arthur realized that he could, if he wanted, just sell this place and walk away. He could even not sell it and walk away. Just one morning get up and put on his boots and start walking, just walk north until the air was cool and the forest closed around him and he could sit by a mossy stream and listen to the wood thrush sing. In fact, he could start walking right now. Like John Muir, with a crust of bread tucked into his belt, walking out to some glorious, glorious landscape, climbing some giant fir tree in a storm, watching a little dog run over a glacier, studying a water ouzel for hours on end until you became that marvelous bird. Why didn't he just do that now, Arthur, following the steps of John Muir.

He considered it, sitting in his deer-beshatted field.

Morgan. That's why he didn't do it. Morgan with her delicate fragrant skin and her unruly hair and her infectious laugh and her startling intellect and those ice-blue eyes that never seemed weird to him, they just seemed right—little portals to a soul without whom he could not go on. Arthur found himself singing, in a whisper, an old folky song they liked: You are my sunshine, my only sunshine, you make me happy when clouds are grey. God he was tired.

He would forfeit the field. You had to make cuts in any large project. It was a necessary part of the process. Some tactics had to be abandoned for the higher-order objective. He took out his phone and opened the OPD app and deleted that goal. 'Bees hum busily among the forbs of the field'—deleted. Perhaps some of the forbs would survive, and perhaps his bee colonies would recover. But if they didn't, there was no shame.

Arthur became aware that he was hungry. Ravenous, starving, a deep, aching hunger from every cell. He rolled up all the fencing and flung it behind the shed and went into the house and made himself a ham and havarti sandwich and ate it standing up, on the back deck, and then drank a can of beer in one go. God damn, that was the way to do it.

But the calm and satisfaction did not last. Arthur began to think of the patch of woods by the riverbank where Armando had lain. The burn pile he made there would probably cover the weird fact that nothing would grow in a body-shaped patch of woods, but what if the pile had blown away? What if the ground were bare again, in that unmistakable shape, squarely on his property, an irrefutable piece of evidence in the case against him? There was no question—he had to assess that risk, the greatest threat against One Perfect Day.

He jogged across the field and down to the opening in the woods and followed the path to the scene of the crime. There was the burn pile, still intact—a mound of ashes and some charred branches. It seemed okay. But could you tell that it was a strange shape, elongated like a man? Arthur snapped a branch of honeysuckle and broomed the ashes around, making the site look more messy, more natural.

He felt a presence. Across the bank stood Hanacek, arms crossed, flanked by his two mules. He fixed his spectral gaze on Arthur and held it in an expression of profound disappointment. One of the mules shook his head, flapping ears like propellers. Hanacek reached out and patted the beast's head, calming it, but he kept his eyes on Arthur.

What? Arthur called. He was exasperated. This stupid ghost with his cryptic appearances, and his perfect life, fuck that guy.

What do you want? Arthur said. Are you judging me? Seriously, how could you judge me of all people? Me the only guy who's still trying to do something about your pathetic piece of land? Your precious woe-begotten land. Yeah, I said woe-begotten. I went to college. Did you, you old fart? What do you know? Looking at me like I'm some disappointing son or something.

Hanacek slowly turned his head away, and then his body followed, walking, trailed by his mules, as if he had never noticed Arthur. As if he had been looking through him, at some scene of the old farm long past, visible only in the realm of spirits.

Wait, Arthur said. I'm sorry.

A twig snapped behind him and Arthur heard someone say, Am I interrupting?

He turned and saw Peg Hanrahan, just on other side of the burn pile, where the double-track dirt road ended. She smiled at him, inquisitively. She must have heard him scolding Hanacek, maybe she saw him brooming the burn pile. He needed an explanation. He shook his head and affected a rural drawl. He said, Well, yeah, you caught me talking to ghosts.

Peg looked surprised, amused.

Arthur said, My dog, I buried him here. Sometimes I come out and talk to him.

It must get lonely here, said Peg. She added, By yourself.

That was cruel. Did she know about Morgan? Lawyers knew everything, the blood suckers. But Arthur couldn't get angry now, not standing there with the imprint of Armando's body between them. He remembered Faulkner's lawyer friend, Timothy, once talking about how he coached people going to trial. You don't take the prosecution's bait, instead you deftly change the subject with your reply—throw them off the scent.

Everybody gets lonely, he said, still with the drawl and an aw-shucks tilt of his head. You finding what you need out here?

Peg crossed her arms and tapped a finger to her lip. She peered at the river and said, I'm not sure. The thing is, we know the Martins must have done something to Gallardo. You were at that masquerade the other night—you saw what they do to migrant workers. Maybe they tried to scare him and something went wrong. Maybe he fought back—he was a kind man but also a defiant man, not the kind of guy who took abuse. Maybe when he fought back, they lost control of the situation and killed him, accidentally. Do you follow?

Arthur stared at her, and nodded.

Right, Peg said, so that's all hard to prove without concrete evidence. We could search their place for clues, bits of cloth, maybe get some samples. The sheriff won't grant a warrant for that, of course. But if we could find his body, maybe there would be something that would persuade a judge—a federal judge who isn't sympathetic to the old-boy's club.

Peg paused, and bit her lip thoughtfully.

The thing is, Arthur, we don't have a body. We have sightings of a body, supposedly, all these pictures on the internet of Armando floating down the river. Have you seen those?

Arthur rubbed his eye and looked at his finger, buying time. What should he say to that? Instinct told him to play stupid, but reason told him that you tell the truth as much as you can right up to the point where you don't—where it could incriminate you.

Yeah, he said. I mean, who hasn't. Pretty disturbing pictures.

Very disturbing, said Peg. And in many ways, inexplicable. Because if you study this scene—here, where the Martin land comes to the river, it doesn't add up. Maybe they chased him through the woods, and maybe they beat him to death back in there. But you can't really get to the river from their side, can you? It's too steep, and that time of year—the time of his disappearance—the brambles are too thick. They would take that body somewhere else. But let's say they did that—put his body in a car and drove it somewhere. There aren't many places to back up a car and dump a body, are there? If you had just beaten a man to death, by accident let's say, you'd want to get rid of it as fast as possible. You'd want to dump it somewhere away from your property but not too far, where someone would find him and they'd have to deal with the situation. If you're the killer, you want to pass on the burden of your crime to someone else as fast as possible. Am I making sense?

Arthur's face was hot. He could feel his heart beat in his throat. He was never cool in stressful situations. Why was he so bad at that? Why hadn't he learned to meditate or something? Too late now. He said, I guess so but not sure why you're telling me all this?

Peg reached down and grabbed a stalk of grass and began to twist it around a finger. She looked at him. Well because Arthur I'm just wondering if you might have any insights. Since you live here, and you spend time in these woods. Maybe you see something I've missed. Maybe you have some idea how that body got in the river?

This was too much. Who did she think she was, barging on to his property, where he worked so hard, day after day, trying to make things better? She had no right—she wasn't some official person, and she wasn't a neighbor, she wasn't even his friend. She was Faulkner and Nancy's friend, and why were they friends with this pain in the ass? Gramps wouldn't put up with this shit on his property. Arthur felt a wave of embarrassment, then a surge of outrage. He did what Gramps would do.

I think, he said, that you talk like you've got a paper ass. And I think you're trespassing on my property.

Peg gave him a look of innocent surprise. She let the twisted piece of grass drop. I'm sorry, Arthur, she said. I thought you gave your consent.

She looked at him, waiting. He stared back at her. That was a stupid thing to say. It probably made no sense. Well, now what? Fix it, that's what. Fix it for Morgan.

Arthur laughed. He forced it out and it sounded maniacal, but he smiled as sincerely as he could, and said, I'm kidding you! I bet you get a lot of that, in your line of work.

Peg tilted her head. She said, I don't recall ever being told I have a paper ass.

Oh it's just an old expression. From my grandfather. I don't really know what it means.

I should let you go, said Peg. Thanks for your time. If you think of anything, let me know. I'd appreciate that, Arthur.

She gave him a low wave and turned to walk away. It wasn't a good ending. She was upset with him. That wouldn't do. She should like him. It was important to be liked. He should do something that showed her he was nice.

Wait, he said. Peg turned around. Was there a spark in her eye?

Gallardo's wife—Lupe, he said. Like you said. I feel for her. Is there something we can do?

Peg put her hands deep into her pockets, and looked down at her shoes. Well, she said. I suppose you could ask her. Peg turned up her eyes toward him. She's usually at that little farm stand off County Road 800. You know it?

Sure, said Arthur. I'll stop by and give her my best. See if there's anything we can do.

Peg nodded thoughtfully, and turned to walk away.

And I'll let you know, Arthur called. I'll let you know if I think of something!

The farm stand off County Road 800 stood on a treeless plain of waist-high corn. It was a plywood box, painted white, with a sloped roof.

There was a neat, hand-painted sign that said Gallardo Farm Stand, and another that listed: Honey, Pies, Produce. An old generator sputtered outside, powering a small refrigerator that had the futuristic, art deco look of 50s appliances. Lupe sat inside on an aluminum lawn chair, reading a paperback book. When Arthur walked up, she looked at him, inscrutably, and waited.

Hola! he said. Buenos dias!

Hello, she said. She set down her book and stood up, hands folded.

I'm Arthur Prendergast—we met at the farmer's market.

I know, she said.

Arthur looked over the counter at the baskets of lettuce and radishes and jars of honey. It was all very tidy, an expression of meticulous pride. The south wind beat the plywood walls in a constant shudder. It was the kind of scene an art photographer would love, for its honest beauty but also for its sadness.

So what are you selling here? Arthur asked.

Lupe's mouth turned in a smile, but her eyes contradicted it. She pointed to the sign.

Ha! He laughed. Of course, obviously. So, pies. What kind of pies do you make?

A white pickup rumbled along on the road and Lupe followed it with her eyes. She said, Right now, strawberry and mushroom.

Mushroom! Interesting. I remember you said Armando used to gather them.

Yes, she said.

Well it sounds good, Arthur said. I don't think I've ever had a mushroom pie.

You can try one. I have samples. She remained standing, her hands folded, her eyes fixed.

Was it rude to say yes or to say no? It would be a hassle for her to cut a pie, and also maybe a waste. No thanks, he said, I just ate.

She looked at him, waiting. It's so easy to project your own mythology on someone, but it seemed like Lupe's expression had an ancient quality to it, like she was the embodiment of millennia, of workers through the ages, whose expectations matched reality, who lived to merely live, without question, unaffected by the miseries of the present age.

How are things going? he asked.

She gave him a confused expression. Finally she said, It's windy today.

Yeah, he replied. Really windy. I wish it would stop.

Lupe shrugged.

It was clear that Lupe didn't want to talk. Why had Peg sent him? Was this a setup? And what was his plan anyway? Arthur had thought he would ask her if there was anything he could do to help, but of course that was an absurd idea, because the one thing he could do to help her— to explain that he had dumped the body of her murdered husband into the river—he could never say that, because that would mean certain ruin for him, and maybe for Morgan, and also if he went to jail it would hurt Prendergast Acres and the wildlife he was nurturing there. That was too much of a tradeoff, wasn't it? Yes, but still it felt wrong. To confess to Lupe felt like the right thing, the courageous thing. But probably that was just the delusion of his insomniac brain, and the whiskey and coffee, and the god damned wind.

I'll take some pies, he said.

What kind, she asked.

I don't know—all of them.

All of them, she said.

Yeah, I'm having a party.

Lupe stared at him. She began to speak, and then stopped. Then she said, What did you do with the honey?

It took him by surprise. The honey? Oh yes, the jars that still rested on his kitchen counter. Arthur said, I ate it.

You ate all that honey already, she said.

Well I shared it with some people. It was delicious—thank you so much.

Lupe put her hand on the refrigerator door. Then she turned and said, You're sure you want all of the pies.

Definitely, he said. He looked around and asked, Sofia help you here too, or just you? It was just small talk but immediately he wanted it back.

Lupe let go of the fridge and turned, her arms hanging loosely, her shoulders back. That's not your business, she said. Are you here for pies or questions?

I'm sorry. Just the pies, please.

She pulled six pies out of the refrigerator, each held in a tin covered with aluminum foil. She placed them on the counter. Arthur paid her, and then lifted two pies, and considered for a moment stacking the others, but that would smash them, but it would be awkward to make three trips to the truck.

I'll help you, said Lupe. She carried four pies, balanced on her forearms and set them on the back seat.

As Arthur shut the truck door, Lupe stood on the shoulder of the road. Cornflower grew up through the gravel around her feet. She seemed even shorter, standing here in the wind.

Okay, Arthur said, and smiled, slouching in her direction.

So you live by the river, said Lupe. Something had changed in her expression—barely perceptible. Was it vulnerability? Despair?

I do, he said.

Did you ever see my husband around there? Did you ever see Armando?

Arthur looked at Lupe and blinked, the wind riffling their hair. His mind was strangely blank. You'd think visions would appear, memories of bad things, but he was just there on county road 800, with a truck full of pies.

I don't think so, he said. I'm sorry.

Lupe turned to face the wind and closed her eyes for a moment. Then she said, Have a good day, and walked back to the farm stand.

Arthur did not reply.

Driving back into town, what would he do with those pies? He couldn't eat them. He might never eat again, his stomach felt so tight. He had to do something good, to redeem this wretched day. He would go to the soup kitchen, and donate these pies. That felt right. He drove there with windows down so he could feel reality more keenly.

The soup kitchen, a modified storage shed that stood by the railroad tracks, was closed. When he got back in the truck, flies buzzed in the cab. He saw one walking primly along a seam in the aluminum foil of a pie, looking for a way in.

Clearly, it was time to be done with all this. Clearly, he had to come clean. He had exhausted all the possibilities of escaping from the burden of his guilt, and now just one path remained—the way of the truth. It felt good to know this—a lightness Arthur hadn't felt in such a long time. He turned on the radio, playing some choir music, and left the windows down, and drove fast enough to give vent to the hot air, and the flies, and the scent of mushroom pies, and the weight of a life nearly wasted.

TWENTY

When the call came from Arthur, Morgan was wearing Larry's clothes. She felt the phone buzz in the pocket and her pulse quickened, because she knew it was Arthur. How did she know? How do we know any of these things? How do we know that it won't rain despite the forecast, that fledglings in the garden nest will die, that the person who offended you in traffic is heading to the same shop? Just because we don't know how it works—that doesn't mean we can't sense these things. Morgan knew Arthur was calling, even though he rarely called, even though she had been getting lots of scam calls, and so she excused herself and went into the bathroom and answered.

Arthur, she said.

Morgan, he replied.

What's wrong, she asked, Why are you calling?

He sighed. Then he said, This morning I would have asked you why I couldn't call just to say hi, but I'm not doing that any more. I'm tired, Morgan. Either we're going to be honest about everything or I don't know what.

Arthur, what happened? She said. His voice had a kind of strength, but also a richness and complexity. His voice reminded her of walnut wood. That was weird, but it was so, and she traced the grain of the bathroom door with her finger. It was not walnut.

Arthur laughed, so quietly. That's the question, isn't it? What happened? I can't even remember how this all started, and how one thing led to the next, and everything. It seems so strange, that we're here, after what we were, when things were hard but good—I mean, great. It's like I just woke up and it was all a dream, which is a cliché, but there isn't any better analogy, and actually, maybe we have been dreaming, in a sense, and now it's time to wake up.

He laughed the quiet laugh again. I'm not making sense, he said. I sound insane.

Well, yes, Morgan said, But maybe I understand, kind of.

She realized she had been running her fingers through her hair, over and over, letting it fall down her face, and then scooping it up and back again. Her hair must be a wilder mess than usual. She moved to look at herself in the oval mirror. Her hair was enormous, like a spirea bush, but what she noticed was Larry's white dress shirt—the open collar hung down below her collarbones. What was she doing?

Look, Arthur said, This is probably a conversation that we should have in person. Maybe I should come up there. I just thought of this, sorry. Should I come up there?

She felt her defenses lock up—it sounded like a sure disaster. Why? It didn't matter—she just knew. Morgan pulled the collar together at her neck and held it tightly. She said, I don't think that's a great idea—not today. I've got a lot going on right now.

Arthur paused a long time. A rich, wooden, silence.

Sorry, Morgan added.

Are you bullshitting me? he asked.

Morgan was, of course. All she had going on today was spending time with this lovely, peculiar, and at times frustrating man who was not her husband. All she had going on was being there in his apartment in the late afternoon, wearing his clothes while hers rumbled in the dryer, which deferred to the rumble of the El, which roared supreme just behind Larry's building, every 20 minutes. Every 20 minutes, she and Larry had to pause their conversation, and just smile at each other, until it passed. It could be infuriating, but somehow it was welcome, because in those moments of overwhelming rumble, you got to pause and think about what you were saying and not rush to say something more. What if we had devices that did this for conversation—forcing you to pause every 20 minutes to consider?

Arthur why don't you just tell me what's going on… Morgan said, but it was lost in the arrival of the train. She could hear that he was saying something but she couldn't understand.

When it passed, she said, Sorry, just the El. Can you say that again?

Where are you Morgan? Not at Mrs Vogel's I guess.

No I have the day off. I'm just… at a friend's house. The El goes right next to it. I don't know how you could live here honestly. But that's not important—tell me why you're calling, Arthur, please. Did something happen?

She hadn't lied, but she had deceived—and was there a difference? Morgan had to remind herself that she had every right to be with whomever she pleased, so long as it wasn't actual cheating, and she had no obligation to tell Arthur about it. This kind of freedom was the point of separating, wasn't it?—living their own lives for a while and seeing how that was. Really, she should be angry with Arthur for making her feel badly, because he was so jealous. Even if the current circumstances did look incriminating, her wearing Larry's clothes in his apartment.

Morgan didn't owe anyone an explanation, but there was one. She had finally accepted Larry's invitation to come over and set up some plants in his apartment. Which they did. Just simple, easy-to-grow plants like philodendron and spider plant and a peace lily. They looked good, arranged on his glass shelves, among his white walls, with the light streaming in from high windows. It was great to put plants in such modern spaces, such a contrast. And of course when they were placing the last pot—a pothos at the top of a partial wall—Morgan tripped off the footstool. Fortunately, Larry caught her in his wirey arms, but neither of them could stop the pot from crashing down on them, raining wet soil over their selves. And then Morgan's blouse and jeans were too dirty to wear, so she put on some of his clothes while hers went in the washer. For some reason, standing in front of Larry's well-organized closet, while he laughed at her careful consideration, Morgan chose dress clothes—a white oxford shirt and gray slacks. After her shower she tied the shirt tails around her waist, and cinched the pants with her belt around her hips, and with her hair still wet and eyes aglow, she looked hot in that outfit, she had to admit, admiring herself in the mirror. It was all good fun, at the time, before Arthur had called and spoiled things.

Now she felt silly in these clothes, like a child caught playing dressup, and she couldn't wait to get hers back on.

I bought six pies today, Arthur said. Six pies from Lupe Gallardo, from her farm stand on County Road 800. A few weeks ago, I bought all the honey she had at the farmer's market. That's pretty fucked up, Morgan, you know?

Well, I guess, she said. I mean, why? Why'd you buy all that stuff.

Guilt, of course! I wanted to help her somehow, because I felt guilty about what happened to Armando, what we did—what I did—and there isn't really much I could do. Or to be honest, I couldn't bring myself to do what would have been helpful, so instead I bought a bunch of her stuff and then had to throw it all away. That is just nuts, that I did that. I have to stop all this. That's why I called.

You mean you're calling to tell me that you bought pies and honey, or that you've decided to stop buying them?

Come on. I'm trying to be honest here, to start a new path.

There was a light tap at the bathroom door, and Larry said You all right in there?

Morgan muted her phone and cracked the door, smiled at him through the crack, and pointed at the phone and shook her head like it was just something annoying. Larry made an exaggerated, surprised 'O' with his face, and then smiled graciously and gently pulled the door shut.

Morgan? Arthur asked. You still there?

I am, she said. But I have to tell you I'm kind of busy at the moment. Could I call you later?

No, Arthur said. No, Morgan. We have to talk now. We have to get all this out in the open.

Arthur, what the fuck are you talking about. You sound crazy. Like, more than usual.

Oh, he replied. So you think I usually sound crazy—that's what you're saying.

Well, yes, I am saying that. I mean, you have to admit you've been kind of off lately—for a while, actually. I mean, no offence, but…

No offense, Arthur mocked. Like that absolves whatever you say before it. Like You suck, you're a horrible person. No offense.

Arthur did you call just to fight?

Morgan heard Larry pop a wine cork in the kitchen. That would be nice. It might be necessary, after this call. Hopefully her clothes would be dry so she could put them on before they sat with a glass of wine and admired the new plants and watched the light change at sunset.

Arthur sighed. He said, I'm sorry. I was just expecting a different conversation. But that's my fault. Listen, I have to tell you something. I should have told you a long time ago.

Morgan knew immediately what he was about to say. You just knew things sometimes and it didn't matter that experts couldn't explain why. She knew he was going to tell her something about Armando's body, something only he knew and had been hiding. She realized she had known all along, and she felt nauseous waiting for it to come. Her palms sweated and her face flushed—she confirmed it in the mirror—little capillaries rising in her cheeks.

God damned Arthur. Of course he did it. That land ruined him. This is the guy who shot a flock of grackles, just because they had eaten strawberries, and let the birds lie by the path to the woods.

She realized he was talking, saying, It's not that I think Peg's going to figure it out, or that she has already. Or that the Martins might say something if they think they need to. Or even that Fawk or Nancy might turn me in, if it comes to that. I mean, yes, they're all kind of circling like vultures, along with the #sangabody people. But the thing is, I realized I don't like the person I've become and I want to be someone better, and that means telling the truth, even if it has awful consequences, and so I'm starting with you. Because you're still my wife. Technically.

That statement touched a string inside her, and its vibrations filled her body and came up into her face, crumpling it. Don't look in the mirror. Don't look in the mirror and see yourself cry—then you won't be able to stop.

Arthur continued, I guess there's no way to say this but just to say it, Morgan. After you left, so suddenly, I didn't know what to do. Should I run after you? Maybe I should have but I couldn't bear the idea that you'd reject me again. A guy can only handle so much rejection, and also maybe it wasn't fair for me to keep chasing after you—maybe you really did want to leave without talking any more. So I was there, standing in the woods, next to this dead guy, this body that wasn't breathing. I could feel him begin to decay. It sounds crazy, but I could. I imagined his juices dripping out of him and onto the ground, onto that rich soil down by the river, just kind of defiling it, you know.

Morgan retched at his description, but held the sound at bay, and then another sob came up from her diaphragm and she closed her eyes as Arthur went on.

We didn't kill him, Morgan. We didn't do anything. We just wanted to have our small farm, and leave the world a little better than when we came. So I had to get rid of the body, I just had to get rid of that… rotting corpse.

Armando, Morgan managed to say.

Armando, yes, I understand. A real human person, Armando Gallardo, a good man with a wife and daughter, a lover of the woods, an expert on mushrooms. Of course. What I'm telling you is that at the time it was just this horrible thing defiling our land and you were leaving and it was my duty to get rid of it.

Your duty, Morgan whispered.

Or my job, or responsibility—whatever. So yeah, so I just got the tractor and went down to the river and scooped up Armando's body and dumped him in the river. That's what I had to tell you. I'm sorry.

Arthur's voice caught. He must also have fallen into emotion. Morgan said, On the other side of the snag.

Yes, Arthur sniffed. On the other side—that's how he started to float downriver. I watched him. Hanacek did too.

Hanacek watched him, she said. The ghost.

Believe what you want, Arthur said. I'm not trying to make you believe or be anything you don't want to be. Not anymore. I'm just trying to tell the truth. I'm really sorry, Morgan. I'm sorry I've been lying.

Then the weight of the lie began to press down on Morgan. Her husband, Arthur Prendergast, had committed a bad deed, and instead of taking responsibility for it, he had shared the burden of the deed with his wife—her, Morgan Prendergast. He had drawn her into his shadow of guilt and anxiety and pinned her there, shared with her all the horrible consequences, the sudden flashes of worry while you're having a nice day, the surreal nights of catastrophizing. How could he have done that to her—loaded his crime onto the shoulders of his wife, who he said he loved? And now he says he's sorry, but it's too fucking late for that, all the days she had suffered had already happened and they weren't coming back. How different things might have been if she hadn't carried this worry all this time. And to think that she had started to love him again, and that last phone call was so sweet.

Now she looked at herself in the mirror. She didn't bother smoothing her hair, or give a shit about the streaks of tears making clown marks of her mascara. She leveled her formidable gaze and looked at herself and thought, Fuck this.

Fuck Mr Vogel standing in his jammies. Fuck Mrs Vogel and her worrying hands and her premeditated death date. Fuck that guy in the nice suit and fedora who walks his tiny dog. Fuck Janus the poet-for-hire who said 'we hope you find your body,' fuck all the boxes in the attic and all the leering dolls in the basement, fuck the derecho, and the El, and those guys who tried to break into her apartment, and fuck the houseplants and fuck Larry, and fuck Nakeisha. No. Not Nakeisha. Leave her out of it. But fuck all the rest of it. But especially, fuck Arthur Prendergast.

Morgan? Arthur asked for the third time. Are you there? Maybe this is too much. Please please know I'm sorry and I'll try to make up for it, somehow.

Morgan cleared her throat, preparing to talk. It made Arthur quiet, and so she let him wait for a while in the still, digital air of a phone call.

Then she said, You don't need to do anything. We're done.

A long silence, then Arthur said, Wait, what?

We're done, she said. We're done, we're done, we're done. What about we're done don't you understand?

Yeah, but done how? Like done with this phone conversation? Or done like... more.

I'll let you figure that out, said Morgan. And she ended the call.

Now would be a good time for a cry—how badly she wanted the release and the rush of neurochemicals that would soften her whole self and the lightness afterward, the drained, purged lightness and the new vision you get after a good cry. But that would have to wait, because Larry was right outside that bathroom door, another dumb man with suspicious motives and patronizing concern. Morgan rinsed her face and smoothed her hair and hiked up Larry's pants around her waist.

He was sitting on the arm of the couch, head down, looking at his hands. When he saw her, he stood up and smiled. Then his expression changed, now with the inscrutable look of a man who senses trouble. She knew her appearance must be shocking. She saw her clothes folded on the table beside the couch. He had touched all her clothes, folding them like that. Larry took a step toward her, and Morgan stepped back, holding up her hand.

I have to go, she said.

Are you okay? He asked.

Of course I'm okay, Morgan said. Do I look not okay?

Just that you were in there for a while. Can I help, or something?

What could Larry do to help? Hadn't he done enough already, seducing her these many weeks, drawing her into his life, confusing her? He knew she was married—what did he expect would come of all this? No, he hadn't seduced her. That wasn't fair. She was a part of this questionable relationship, this ill-defined friendship. But that was too much to think about right now. It would be just like a woman to immediately start blaming herself when she'd been so horribly wronged. The point was that Arthur lied, and turned her life upside down, and that's what needed dealing with right now.

I'm going to change, said Morgan. As she gathered her clothes, she could feel the tension between them. Why do we feel the presence of other people so strongly sometimes? Do we give off some kind of force field of emotion? Could it be measured? Could it be controlled? Or was it all a matter of perception, something she was constructing in her moment of confusion?

In the bathroom she put on her clothes. She could smell the fresh linen scent of his fabric softener. She folded Larry's clothes perfectly. She would need to show composure.

I'm sorry to leave so suddenly, she told him. She handed him his clothes and their hands touched. Larry received them and took a step back. His eyes were—what was the word? Beseeching. His eyes were beseeching, searching for an explanation of her mood. He would have to live without an explanation. He was a scientist. A minute after she was gone, he'd forget, his analytical brain turning to the contemplation of dark energy, the vast inexplicable phenomena of a universe that renders our lives immaterial.

Don't forget to water, she said. The plants. The soil should stick when you pinch it. If it crumbles, you need to water.

Will do, said Larry.

Morgan stood at the door to his apartment. She looked at Larry. He was like a little boy now, who has just witnessed some bad part of life for the first time—a little boy who had just seen his parents fight, or a squirrel get hit by a car, or a playmate fall from a tree.

I'm sorry, Morgan said. It's just that something's come up.

Was it your husband on the phone? Arthur?

She found it hard to explain this directness. Larry did it sometimes, and passed it off as a socially awkward academic, or maybe a simple country boy. But she wondered if it was actually a form of manipulation, maybe to dominate you, possibly just for sport. You couldn't trust southerners. Even worse were people posing as southerners.

Yes, she said. It was Arthur. We had a fight. It was a lot. I have to think about things.

I hope you guys work it out, he said. He started to say something else, but stopped.

I know you do, said Morgan. Thanks for a nice day.

As she grabbed the door handle, Larry said, Morgan.

She turned.

Larry gestured toward her, politely. Your shirt, he said, It's buttoned wrong.

Morgan looked down. He was right—the buttons were off by one, twisting the shirt. She couldn't go out like that. Morgan turned away from him. For a moment she thought she might not be able to rebutton it, her fingers trembled so badly, but she got the job done and said goodbye without looking and left.

On the street the El came again and its roar obliterated her thoughts and all the other sounds of the city. It was evening but still so very hot. All the concrete and steel of this massive city radiated an unbearable heat, respirating waves of polluted air, stirring a soup of all the anguish of the three million souls who labored here. How nice it would be in Middling right now, in the cool shade of an oak tree, with your bare feet in the grass, where you could hear the evening crickets chirp and see the lightning bugs flash in humid fields. But that was not for her. It was all gone now.

Morgan clenched her fists and glared at the cars on Lincoln Avenue. What do you do with all this anger? She wanted to punch something. She wanted to yell at someone, to break them.

Morgan took out her phone and found her last message with Arthur.

She wrote: *Just so you know – I've been seeing someone.*

Then she backed through the letters, deleting them. But no, actually, why not. She wrote again: *FYI, I've been seeing someone. Also, forget the visit in August. I'm not coming.*

Morgan sent the message.

She turned off her phone and put it in her pocket. She hit the crossing button with her fist. When the light turned green, she walked east toward the lake.

TWENTY ONE

After he received the message from Morgan, Arthur turned off his phone and set it on the deck railing. He looked at the device, resting there, so benign and yet so sinister. He thought, That thing only brings me bad news. He had no more use for it now, because he had just one thing to do and that was to walk. Arthur began walking. A person in good health could walk a long way—much longer than people realize. We are made to walk and what's weird is that walking is a form of continuous falling, where with each step you stop your fall, and then begin falling again from the other side. When we walk we are metronomes to the world's piano practice—tick, tick, tick we walk, and the world fumbles out its crude melody. It always feels good to walk, but especially after a devastating loss. The feeling of having lost, utterly and disastrously, can be delicious, can't it? You have this lightness—like, what shall I do now? Walking enhances the sensation—you are high from the release of worry, since your worries have played out, and you can drift along on a cloud of unburdened possibility. That is, until the sadness comes, which Arthur knew it would, but he set that aside until its time.

Now, where to go? Arthur knew where his walk would take him, ultimately, but there was no hurry in getting there. Grandma used to say 'let's take the scenic route,' when she didn't want to drive their pickup on the highway. It felt indulgent, taking the scenic route—the luxury of having extra time to immerse yourself in beauty. Arthur heard himself say it aloud, Let's take the scenic route. His voice sounded surprisingly chipper. Let's see if Hanacek is around.

Arthur's legs took him through his field toward the river. On his way, he walked the meandering rows of vegetables. They were doing remarkably well, these vegetables. Not that it mattered now. The lovely meandering rows had been a stupid idea, because watering and tilling and weeding were nearly impossible. But there were the vegetables, rising above the weeds, bearing their tasty fruit. Who would eat it now? Probably the ground squirrels—what a bounty for them! Bon appetit, ground squirrels!

On through the restored prairie. What an optimistic name! The field was neither. But some of the forbs had come back since the deer nipped their delicate heads. They were stunted now, meek little flowers. Arthur had deleted that goal from his list—about the bees and the forbs of the fields. Technically, now, he could delete the remaining eight goals. He reached for his phone—but then he had left it behind, sensibly. It would feel good to delete them, to delete the app, to scrap all the code and images from his server. But it would also be meaningless. Now, the only meaningful action was walking.

The path into the woods, where he had shot those grackles. He shouldn't have shot those grackles. They had only been eating strawberries. He felt badly for the Arthur who shot those birds. He also felt bad for the birds, of course. Imagine if your neighbor started leaving fresh hamburgers on your porch and then, when you ate them, he shot you. So that was pretty bad. But still he felt sympathy for that Arthur who was still so attached to goals and outcomes and who thought he could make a difference in this world. It seemed as if that Arthur were dead now.

Speaking of which, here was the patch where Armando lay.

It was still an oblong pile of ashes and charred branches. Why did Arthur expect that something lovely would be growing here now? As if his confession to Morgan would make that happen? Clearly that wasn't enough, but maybe once he was finished, maybe the patch would spring new life again. No, that was transactional thinking. Arthur would do what he had to do without expecting any outcomes in return.

There was time to sit on the swing in the woods, so he did. Here, where he had sat with Morgan, drinking wine, listening to the sounds of the night and the creak of the swing's chain. Where they had first seen Hanacek. The swing was weathered now—maybe unsafe? Had it really been that long? It settled under his weight, but it held. Ah yes and here comes Hanacek.

The old ghost farmer strode through the brush, purposefully, dragging his reluctant mules behind him. When he came to the river bank across from Arthur, he stood on his feet and crossed his arms and looked. The mules came just after and sat on their haunches, skin shuddering under the assault of flies. There was no doubt that Hanacek was looking at him. His expression was clearly, Well now you've done it. That felt unfair. The old fart was exasperating.

What do you know? Arthur called out to him. How could you possibly know what just happened?

Saying those words brought to Arthur's awareness what had happened. It was too awful to rest your thoughts on that for long. He probably shouldn't have sat. He should be walking.

Well anyway, he told Hanacek, I'm done with the place. You can have it back. Or maybe you always had it. Maybe you're the reason things are so fucked up here. I don't know. I don't care.

Hanacek's expression grew more sad. He wagged his head slowly, keeping his eyes on Arthur. One of the mules took a step toward the water and the old farmer held out a hand to steady the beast, but his eyes remained on the young man across the river.

Arthur said, Don't give me that. I'm not falling for your bit any more. I'm sick of this stupid oracle thing. You're probably a figment of my imagination. My mind playing tricks on me, because of some indigestion—you might be bad mustard, or an underdone potato. There's more gravy than grave about you—ha! No seriously, you're like a bad Steinbeck character who never actually does anything. So see you later, Hanacek. I have nothing to lose any more. I'm just gonna walk now.

As Arthur stood up, Hanacek removed his hat and ran his fingers through his wispy spectral hair. His expression had changed once again, to a man at his wit's end. Those grey eyes—what was the word for it? Beseeching. Hanacek's expression was beseeching. Well, too bad. Fuck that guy and fuck this accursed shred of land—Arthur walked.

Darkness was falling in the woods. A great horned owl hooted once, and got no reply. Lightning bugs flashed beneath the canopy of walnut and oak. Arthur needed to cross the river while he still could. There was the snag that remained since Armando's death—the snag that proved Arthur's guilt. At some point that snag would be gone. A flood would lift the logs up and cast them about like bones. It was probably too late for this year—the heavy rains were over, just hot days until October. He crossed the snag without difficulty and leaped to the steep bank on the other side.

Now he was on Martins's land. Far through the woods, he could see the light of their house. He walked that way. This could be dangerous. Who knows what man traps the Martins had set? Couldn't their hounds be out patrolling the woods? If the Martins heard a human tromping through the brush, wouldn't they shoot first and ask questions later? And when Arthur lay in the tall grass, gut-shot and bleeding out, they would call the deputy sheriff—what was his name, Myron or Byron? And the deputy would write up the incident as self defense and Arthur would die in vain. Would Morgan come to his funeral? Probably not. Fawk would—Fawk and Nancy, what good friends. Friendship didn't make up for a failed marriage, but it helped.

But none of this came to pass. Arthur made his way through the dense brush on the Martin side of the river and the world didn't notice him. He passed the makeshift auditorium, where walking got easier, where the Martins groomed the forest floor for their animal masquerades and strange rituals. The moon was rising, yellow-faced through the arcing branches, and he was able to stroll along with that incredible lightness of having lost everything. Not far away glowed a picture window in the back of the Martin house and he could see, just barely, there were people in there. No dogs around, as far as he could tell, so why not have a look?

The Martin house was a sprawling ranch, brown-bricked with deep eaves, a monument to 70s architecture. In the back there was a patio, with a fountain that wasn't running, and beyond it the picture window that glowed into the warm, dark night. Arthur approached just to the edge of the light. Bradley Martin sat with his wife—was it Karen? That seemed right. They sat in dark blue recliner chairs, their legs outstretched, their laps balancing TV trays of dinner. It looked like a balanced meal—fried chicken, some corn and peas, crescent rolls. Cans of Fanta pop—she had grape and he had orange. And on a separate plate, a big hunk of pie. It looked good. Arthur had not eaten since… he wasn't sure when.

The Martins were watching a 24-hour political channel. The television extended from floor to ceiling, so bright that no other lights were necessary. The two had nearly identical posture—although they reclined, their heads bobbed forward toward the TV, their necks at a sharp angle, a hump forming in their upper backs. They didn't appear to taste their food, so spellbound were they by the television. Poor things. Should Arthur turn them in, for the death of Armando Gallardo? He might not get them convicted but he could certainly cause a lot of trouble. Maybe. But not yet. You had to get your own house in order first, if you want to be liberated from this endless cycle of suffering.

Arthur held out his hand toward the window, in the gesture of a pastor blessing his flock. See you around, he said. Then he felt a pressure against his thigh, and a moment later a wetness on his hand. There, at his side, was one of the Martins's dogs. And here came the other trotting over to greet him. They should be barking at him, fiercely, and he should be running in a terrified panic. But that's not how it was. Instead, he petted the animals, who were so innocent—they hadn't picked their keepers. He scratched their heads behind the ears, both his arms extended, and whispered affection to them. They pressed closer against Arthur's thighs, and he was reluctant to leave. But he had to. It was time to walk again.

Around the house, along the sidewalk, under the light of the moon, with the dogs at his side, Arthur left the Martins. He walked up their long gravel driveway, with its rows of callery pears, to County Road 1250. Here he bid goodbye to the dogs, disciplined beasts, who knew their boundaries. And so he walked east.

The road was recently chip-sealed, crunching under his boots, smelling of new tar. It was only one road over from where he had lived for years now, but Arthur had never been on 1250. There was no point in hiding the reason why—he had been afraid to go down this road. From across the river had come so many threats—random gunfire, midnight chain saws, screaming motors, the beat of the Martin's drums. For years Arthur had turned away from this stretch of properties, flinching and ignoring, but always aware and always afraid. These people had scared away Morgan, you could say. They were the enemy.

Now, of course, it just looked like normal rural houses, set back from a quiet county road, with mailboxes and gardens and lawns. He had known this for years, knew that he should just go down that road and see the people for the uninteresting, righteous folk that they were, maybe even meet them, like Gramps would have, but Arthur's imagination had been too powerful, and so he conjured monsters across the river and then cowered from them.

But no more. Soon, he was at the end of 1250, where it intersected with 300, at a farm with a sign that said Fresh Eggs. Oh shit! Who would take care of the chickens? Or what about the goats? Arthur's pulse rose for the first time that evening. He should have brought them all with— that would be funny, the hapless hobby farmer leading a procession of his animals. But it wasn't funny! It was irresponsible, this walking, this wanton perambulation, this pointless peregrination, when there were creatures who on Arthur depended! And why did he sometimes think in this ornate prose? The words just formed themselves, and you had no control over them.

But the animals would be all right for now. They had plenty of what they needed. They were spoiled, honestly, and could go a day or even two without Arthur's care. But he would need to get back, and he would need to find new homes for them. Oh for fuck's sake it was going to be a pain unwinding from Failure Farm—all the things that would need selling, all the cleanup, all the paperwork, all the explanations, the story he'd have to tell. He would find new homes for the animals and then, well, he would find a new home for himself.

Now the walking was ruined. It had been great, for that little while, to walk without obligation. Maybe one day he would walk that way again, after all the unwinding and divestment and explanation was done. Still, there was a whiff of the equanimity and freedom he had felt, in those few hours, and Arthur was able to hold it as he walked, metronome to the world's piano, down 300 and over to 1300, now toward his ultimate destination.

Here, as you left the forested corridor of the river, it was section after section of corn and beans, and here a farm house, and there a machine shed, and little stands of blue spruce around the houses to break the wind. The land rose slightly here, and it was open, and the sky was enormous. The yellow moon was high but still there were stars, arranged in constellations that had no basis in the organization of the universe, but were rather human constructs—three-dimensional, actually, as constellations have depth too. Ancient civilizations, who presumably didn't talk with each other, made up similar stories about the constellations. Orion was a hunter over many lands, even though it's just a sloppy rectangle. That was strange but probably everybody knew this—didn't they? Orion was below the horizon now, it being summer, but there was Scorpius, stretching in languorous repose low in the sky. It looked more like its namesake.

Arthur was tired. How far must he have walked? He calculated it, to keep his mind alert, adding up the segments of his walk—probably 5.2 maybe 5.3 miles so far? He had a ways to go. The thought of stopping was unwelcome—without the reassurance of walking, who knew what his mind would do? If he walked far enough, maybe he'd pass out. There were downsides to that. Come to think of it, Arthur didn't have a plan, per se. He had a destination, but not a course of action. Well, it would come.

His senses played tricks on him. Flashes of movement in his peripheral vision, shapes that emerged and disappeared in ditches, strange figures way down the road ahead, peculiar scuffling sounds behind. There were ghosts everywhere, probably. If you believed in Hanacek—and how could you not?—then you had to believe in everything. There were the legendary ghosts, of course. Not far up the highway you could find Resurrection Mary in her lovely flapper dress, shoeless, hitchhiking for victims. But also all the anonymous ghosts, farmers who toiled these fields only to find at the end of their days that everything they had grown had been eaten or discarded, and if they hadn't grown it someone else would have, so what was the point? But also the animals remained as ghosts, because if Hanacek had mules there must be all the animals. Come to think of it, there must be ghosts of extinct animals. Right here, on this glaciated plain, there must roam the ghosts of mastodon, lifting their heads in a church-bell wail. That was fucking awesome to think about.

But Arthur didn't want to join them, all these creatures with unresolved energies—when he died he wanted to return peacefully to the soup of molecules from which he had come. He just had this sense that for that to happen, he needed to set some things straight now, and leave no trace of wickedness behind.

Finally, here was County Road 800. Just another mile now, a section, and the road descended a little, and the walking was even more like falling. And finally, in the darkest of the night, after about 8.6 miles walking, Arthur came to the farm stand. No one was there, of course, but still he checked. He knocked quietly at the plywood door. No answer. That was fine then. He could just rest now, here on the slope above this drainage ditch, with his head up and his feet down. Poor feet, so badly treated. Poor Arthur and also poor Lupe and poor Armando and poor Morgan, and poor everybody else. Good night all you poor souls.

He awoke, not to the light of the sun but to the sunlight being broken—broken by a shadow, or rather by a person making a shadow, over Arthur, where he lay in the ditch beside the farm stand.

The silhouette said, Time to wake up.

Arthur shielded his eyes and groaned.

The person said. I have to open the stand now. Get up.

It was embarrassing for someone to wake you up when it was so late in the morning. Arthur remembered the sound of Gramps's tractor when he was still in bed and how he had leapt up and run out of the house without breakfast to beg forgiveness and earn back his place in the morning chores.

He sat up now, shielding his eyes, and saw Lupe Gallardo. He had not pictured it going this way. Lupe stepped around Arthur, so he didn't have to look into the sun, and handed him a cup that steamed against the blue sky. It was a battered diner cup, but the black coffee was delicious.

Thank you, he said. I'm sorry.

Nevermind, said Lupe. Finish your coffee and then go. I have work to do.

Lupe walked back toward her stand. She wore a dress with a tiny flower print and sensible brown shoes. It was interesting how people who really did the work in the world didn't need to wear special costumes. It was the same with her car, a red Saturn wagon she had parked on the shoulder. How was that still running? Lupe went to the car and pulled a bushel out of the back. You could see the greens flop over the edge of the bushel as she bore it on her hip.

Arthur walked to the stand. Lupe was inside, and she hadn't yet opened the metal rolling window to do business. He set the cup on the ledge of the window. Maybe he should just leave? Maybe that would be better for everybody. No, of course not. Arthur tapped on the metal of the window. A moment later, it rolled up, startling him. Instinctively, he reached out to help raise it.

Leave it, said Lupe. It gets stuck. Why are you still here?

She turned her back to him and began taking the greens from the bushel, arranging them on piles on the worktable in the back.

Because I need to talk with you.

You talk a lot, she said, but you don't say very much.

I know what happened to Armando, he said.

Lupe stopped working, and kept her back to him. How is it that when someone is perfectly still and quiet, we can feel their emotions? Now wasn't the time to ponder these things. After a while, Lupe reached for an old cloth calendar now used as a towel. She wiped her hands with it, and then raised the towel to her face, and held it there. Her torso expanded and relaxed, in a great breath, and she clutched the towel in her hands and turned to face Arthur.

I know, she said.

You know? How?

Lupe stared at him, testing whether he was serious. Then she compressed her lips, and let her eyes wander beyond his shoulder toward the fields.

You wear your guilt like a big hat, she said.

Like a big hat?

Like the hats kids wear at their birthday parties at Tres Hermanos.

Was she messing with him? Arthur felt himself blinking, looking at the counter.

Lupe said, Tell me about Armando. Esta bien.

It seemed like they should be sitting—he imagined them sitting on chairs at a table—but instead he stood outside at the counter, like a customer, and she stood inside, listening. It would have to be this way, then.

Arthur began: We… then he stopped. There was suddenly too much emotion to speak, and also that was the wrong word. After he composed himself, thinking about Gramps's tractor for some reason, he began again…

I found him, Armando, on the bank of the river in the back of my property. He was… passed away by the time I got to him—I'm so sorry. Someone had left him there, I heard the car drive away and people shouting. Can I tell you who I think it was?

Lupe looked at him, waiting. Finally she closed her eyes and nodded.

It was the Martins, who live across the river from me. Bradley Martin and his son Donnie and maybe his wife, who I think is Karen, and probably some other of their people. I'm 99% sure it was them. There was this party, where everyone dressed in animal masks—oh that sounds crazy. I'm getting off track.

Lupe continued looking at him, enigmatic, but for an instant she bit her lower lip.

Arthur continued, What I'm here to tell you is that I'm almost certain that the Martins are responsible for Armando, your husband's death. That's the first thing. The next thing and I'm really sorry about it, but that I put Armando in the river. After I found him. It seemed like the right thing to do.

This was too horrible—why hadn't he prepared something to say? Why had he walked all night like a selfish fool and slept in a ditch until this poor woman found him? What was wrong with him? The grand confession he had envisioned became idiotic.

But now he saw, in Lupe's eyes, a vulnerability and a recognition of him. She had been steely, her eyes fixed on some middle distance, but now she focused on Arthur's hapless face.

She asked, Was he badly beaten?

Arthur could picture the scene exactly, how you could tell even from a distance that the face had sustained vicious blows. And then there were all the pictures on the internet of that same face. You wanted to tell people what they wanted to hear, you wanted everyone to feel better about this awful life, but sometimes that was the cowardly thing to do.

He said, His face, yes—someone hit him. It must have been hard. Hopefully he didn't suffer much because of that.

Lupe's eyes were full of wetness now, reflecting the light of the morning sun on the fields, but still she did not cry. She raised the towel to her nose, wiped, and clutched the towel again at her waist.

She said, What about his body?

I didn't see it, Arthur said. He was wearing clothes.

Lupe took a deep breath and then said, I mean, where is his body?

I don't know, Arthur said.

Lupe responded with exasperation, her shoulders dropping, her head tilted.

I mean, said Arthur, I think he's somewhere down river. That's the way he went after... after I placed him in the water. I put him on the other side of the snag behind me and he just, he just floated away, peacefully—sorry, that's probably the wrong thing to say.

Lupe listened. Then she said, You've seen the pictures online.

Well, yeah, I have.

Are they real?

Arthur considered this. He had assumed they were, but maybe not. How do you know if anything is real?

I don't know, he said. But I think so, even though so much of it doesn't make sense.

Lupe turned and resumed working, arranging the greens in individual baskets.

She said, The mushrooms he ate—he said they would make him live forever. He never got sick. So that's why his body looks the way it does in those pictures, probably.

They stopped him from decomposing, Arthur said.

Lupe paused in her work and shrugged, looking at him.

Okay, he said.

When she was finished, Lupe wiped soil from the counter and then folded the towel into thirds and then again in half, and set it on the counter. She put her hands on the towel and looked at Arthur and said, Is that it?

Sorry, he said, Is what it?

Is that what you came to tell me?

Well mostly, I guess. I mean I wish I had said it better. What do you want to do now? Do you want me to tell the police, or Peg the lawyer? Or what—anything you want.

Lupe studied him, then she leaned out the window and looked down the road both ways. There were no cars, no humans at all. It occurred to Arthur that she might have a gun behind the counter. Well, that would serve him right.

But instead, Lupe said, It's gonna be slow. Let's sit for a minute.

They went around the back where there were two folding chairs with metal frames and worn wooden seats. Lupe brought more coffee. They sat in the shade looking at the hazy fields and hedges. Arthur drank and waited for her to speak.

Lupe said, Thank you for confessing to me.

She sighed, and sipped her coffee and looked at the land. Then she continued,

I knew the Martins did it. From Peg Hanrahan, but also I know where Mando used to roam. They are dangerous people, and not very careful. Also I knew you were involved somehow. How could I not? You should stay away from crime—you're bad at it.

Yeah, said Arthur. The cops probably won't be surprised when I tell them too.

Lupe crossed her arms and pointed her chin. Her eyes were dark as she seemed to think aloud. She said, The police, Peg Hanrahan, all those people—they can't help me. Don't bother talking to them. It's not what I want.

What do you want, then?

Lupe looked at him, now with a formidable gaze, a kind of haughtiness. She said, I want you to tell me why you came to tell me this today.

Oh, said Arthur. And then he told her.

Once he began, it was hard to stop. Lupe listened, leaning forward, her elbows on her knees and her hands folded. Sometimes she looked at the ground beneath her sensible brown shoes, sometimes she looked up and peered beyond the fields toward the horizon, sometimes she turned her head to look at Arthur. Her eyes held a thoughtful concentration, and she nodded now and again, as if she were considering the terms of a business proposal.

Finally Arthur said, So it's probably too late, you know, for me and my marriage and the farm and everything—but I'm hoping it's not too late to set things right and clean up the mess I've made.

He stopped abruptly. He had run out of words. What a pleasant feeling.

Lupe looked at him, and then at her hands. She said, You have a very strange life.

Arthur laughed, and it surprised him. Lupe laughed then too, but quietly, a tremor in her shoulders. It was the first time he had seen her smile. Then a tear dripped from the corner of her eye down her sun-creased cheek and she wiped it quickly but still smiled.

Arthur wanted to hug her. Such a nice person, Lupe was. Kind of scary, yes, and mysterious, but also so obviously kind and good. As he thought this, was he back to his old ways, romanticizing everything, so high and then so low? Maybe Lupe was just a normal person. Or maybe, probably it was too soon for Arthur to make a judgement. But still, you could feel kindness toward a person, couldn't you? You could give their character the benefit of a doubt. He couldn't hug her, of course. Could he?

Lupe said, So you're giving up then, on Morgan, and your perfect day.

Arthur rubbed his eyes. He was suddenly so tired. His thoughts murky. He said, Yes, I guess I am. But it sounds easier than it will be I suppose.

Lupe looked at him. She said, Why would you give up on someone you love? The person you married and swore you'd spend your life together.

That was hard to hear. Arthur had to push it away, this hard question. Also, here was Lupe whose husband was murdered and who he dumped in the river—she was talking about his life, Arthur's life. It was wrong and selfish of him to let it go that direction.

Arthur said, Is there something I can do for you? Anything at all?

Lupe's gaze trailed away from him, and she shook her head.

Arthur had an idea that came in a great rush—a glorious idea. In an instant, the whole thing was clear and symmetrical and made perfect sense.

Why don't I give you my farm? He asked.

Lupe pulled back her head in a bemused expression. She replied, Why would I want that? You said it's cursed and nothing grows there.

Arthur saw the idea crumbling now. He said, Well that was kind of an exaggeration.

Lupe shook her head, continuing to consider the stupidity of the idea. Morgan owns the farm too—you can't just give it away to someone.

Arthur crossed his arms, shrugged. Eh, he said, It was just an idea.

All the coffee had made him jittery—he was exhausted and agitated at once. He needed to sleep but knew he couldn't. There was nothing he could do for this woman. What would he even do once the conversation was over? Where would he go?

Lupe said, There is something you can do for me.

Oh? he asked. What?

Before I tell you I want to say: I won't promise you anything. I don't know if I will forgive you. With your stupidity you caused a lot of grief and sorrow. Still today. Maybe there will be a curse on you, maybe not. You don't know me or my family. So if you do these things, I can't promise anything.

I don't care, said Arthur, and he meant it. Tell me.

Two things, she said. First, have your party—try to do your perfect day, even without your wife. Invite your neighbors, including those Martins. I will come too, and bring some things to eat. I'll help you make your party and we won't talk about it.

Arthur nodded, Yes, okay. Yes of course. I can do that.

It was good he hadn't deleted the source code to his OPD app. It was good he hadn't yet done anything rash.

And the second thing? he asked.

Keep looking for Armando, she said. He needs to come home.

Okay, he said, I will.

A car appeared over the rise down county road 800. It seemed to break the spell of their morning. There were other people in this world. Arthur had a lot of work to do.

Now go, Lupe said. I have customers coming.

TWENTY TWO

Morgan began to rise before dawn, and step lightly down the attic steps, holding her shoes, while Mrs Vogel and Nakeisha were still asleep, before the day got too hot. Each day she walked through the tunnel on Fullerton, where bodies lay motionless in blankets and tarps, where the scent of urine and diesel hung, and then she came out into the brisk and fishy lakefront air. From there she'd walk north sometimes up through Belmont Harbor, or south other times along North Avenue beach, out to the pier, and from there you could see the towers of downtown emerge like a mythical city through the haze—a city you could walk toward for days and never reach. Frank Baum once lived here, so that made sense.

Like a tavern at midnight, the dawning city had its regulars. The joggers, the dog-walkers, the speeding cyclists, the car commuters in light suits, the wandering souls who hadn't slept, who bore a crust of filth, shoes on their last legs. Morgan got to know all of them, and some of them acknowledged her—sometimes with just an upward glance from their phones—and she nodded back seriously. We are the early risers, the children of the stackers of grain, tool makers, players with railroads, hog butchers for the world—we come up with the sun and stoke the fire of the city and keep the world rotating through the traction of our steps every morning.

Dawnwalking is how Morgan remained steadfast, after she severed the line to Arthur. People who get up early have their shit together. Early risers don't break down—they don't waver or tremble or cry, or ask for help, or plead for forgiveness. Not here, not in the city of the big shoulders. And so by the time she returned to the mansion on Deming, Morgan greeted her colleague and their benefactor with a breezy confidence and an air of no nonsense.

All that exercise can't be good for you, Nakeisha said. If you keep that up, you better eat more doughnuts, or start smoking.

No, said Mrs Vogel. She pointed a finger at Nakeisha and said, I know you joke, but exercise is good for the girl. The walking, the gardening… Mrs Vogel thumped a fist to her chest… They make a strong woman. No. The problem is Nichte doesn't eat. I wonder the lake breezes don't carry you to Canada, you're so skinny.

Nakeisha clicked her tongue and set a smoothie down on Mrs Vogel's tray. Not supposed to talk about a lady's body, she said. There's no shaming here.

Easy for you to say, said Mrs Vogel. She looked down at the smoothie suspiciously. Then added, You look like a healthy woman.

I'm gonna take that as a compliment, Sweetheart, said Nakeisha. She rinsed the blender in the sink. Now if it's all right with you two ladies, I'll leave you to the day and go home and see my babies before I put this healthy woman body to bed for a few hours.

Morgan caught her in the hall. Can I talk with you? she asked.

Nakeisha checked her hat in the hall mirror. She always wore a hat, in any kind of weather. She said, You're talking with me now.

They went to the front stoop, where the humidity was already beyond comfort.

How do you think she is? asked Morgan.

Another day closer to death, just like the rest of us. Nakeisha glanced at her buzzing phone.

No I'm serious. Does she seem a little off since the storm?

Nakeisha put her hand on Morgan's forearm. Of course she is, she said. She's a very old woman, who carries a lot of sadness and regret, and some quack told her the exact day she's supposed to die. Anybody would be a little off in those circumstances.

Morgan nodded. It wasn't exactly what she was getting at. But what was she getting at? It all seemed slippery now.

Nakeisha lowered her head to look into Morgan's eyes. The real question, girl, is why you've been a little off. I'm not gonna get into your business, but I see you. I know something's up. You can talk with me, but you've known the old lady a lot longer. Maybe you try her.

Nakeisha smiled with sly meaning. Then she tilted her hat, to shield her face from the sun, and walked down the street.

Back in the kitchen Mrs Vogel sat with her smoothie unfinished. I am done with these, she said. If God intended us to live on these things he would have given us mouths like goldfish.

Morgan made scrambled eggs with sausages from the German butcher. It was too hot in the sunroom these days, so they ate in the dining room. The great mahogany table could seat twenty people—its expanse required three chandeliers of leaded glass. The canvas walls bore paintings of ornate ceramics and overripe fruit, with impish monkeys hanging from the ceiling, delicate hands poised to steal. Morgan and Mrs Vogel shared one corner of the table, and kept their voices low because of the echo in the cavernous space.

I need to tell you something, Morgan said.

Mrs Vogel looked up from her plate, still chewing, a bit of egg on her lip. It was strange how our bodies keep needing fuel, how we can pack it away even after our systems practically fail. Funny how we lament about old age when really we should be in awe that things still work.

It's about your boy, Arthur, I think. Mrs Vogel raised one eyebrow and pressed her napkin to her lips. Despite the beastly nature of her eating, she was still a lady.

It is, Tante. I have broken it off.

What does this mean—broken it off? You are getting a divorce?

Well, not exactly. Just that I told him we're done and we haven't talked since.

Mrs Vogel stared at her empty plate and spoke as if to herself, scolding, That is a messy situation. That is not done. You are done when you have decided about the legal status, about the future, about finances.

You're right, Tante, said Morgan, It's a total mess.

Her voice broke at the end and she found herself crying, just for a few moments, and then regained her composure. She was an early riser.

But Mrs Vogel had seen. The old woman held out a hand and said, I'm sorry Nichte. I am so sorry. Come here.

Morgan scooted over to the corner of the great table and leaned her head against the top of Mrs Vogel's head and put her arm around the old woman's loose kindling shoulders.

He's just such a fool, she said, He means well, he has a good heart, but he's just such an idiot. Everything he touches turns to... something bad.

Mrs Vogel reached and petted Morgan's hair. Probably you are right, she said. But maybe also the boy just needs some luck. You were probably his best luck, and now he doesn't even have you.

That was too much, and Morgan pulled away and wrapped her face with her hands and let it come until there was no more.

Mrs Vogel clucked and consoled, patting Morgan's back. She said, That was too harsh, saying that. It is not always good to say the honest thing.

Morgan wiped her eyes with her napkin, and pulled her hair back into a ponytail, and then let it fall. She drank some water. She said, Actually Tante your honesty is the best thing right now. That's what I need—just people being honest and plain. I'm so exhausted by all this guessing, all this gamesmanship of humans.

Mrs Vogel considered. You speak of us like we are animals like any other—calling us humans.

Well, aren't we?

Mrs Vogel nodded, thoughtfully. We are, she said. You are wiser than you know, Nichte.

Morgan stood up and began gathering their plates. As she worked, she said, So now I have to figure all this stuff out—to clean up the mess…

Mrs Vogel gripped her forearm. Sit, she said. The dishes will wait for us. You must not run so quickly when it gets hard.

Morgan let out a huge sigh, and sat. She said, I have a job offer too. At the Middling Hospital. So there's that.

Mrs Vogel's expression darkened to concern. But that is down there in the town with your Arthur, who you are done with. How are you considering it?

Well, I miss it, to be honest. But I know it's a disaster of a situation. And of course I can't leave you now, Tante. It's just that I realized I wanted this job, kind of, more than I would have thought. So that just adds to my confusion, to my mess.

Mrs Vogel lifted her fork and tapped it against the table, contemplating. She said, You will return to work again. If not in Middling then here. You said the hospital here would take you back in a boiling minute.

A hot minute.

Yes, hot minute. What does that mean?

I don't know, Morgan said. Arthur would have something to say about this—that it was funny to describe time with temperature, but also maybe meaningful.

We should not say things when we don't know what they mean. Words are too powerful.

I know, I'm sorry—it's lazy.

Oh, no! said Mrs Vogel. I did not mean to insult you specifically. I meant to insult all of us—the humans.

On behalf of the humans, I apologize, Morgan laughed.

Then they sat in the quiet of the house. The grandfather clock in the hall ticked time—long, cool minutes. A truck rumbled down the street and its roar trailed away in testimony to Doppler. Morgan's stomach churned loudly, unused to the large meal. It would be nice to sit here for a long time, in this moment of reprieve from all the torment of the day. And couldn't she? Couldn't Morgan just sit there quietly, in the kind company of this old woman, this adopted great aunt, merely living in the now, moment after moment, until it was time for lunch, and they would have sauerkraut and ham, maybe, and some green beans boiled until they were soft. People used to live this way, didn't they? Now they were gone, so they might as well have.

Mrs Vogel's hands were flat against the table. Her lips were puckered, her eyebrows lowered. She had the demeanor of an executive about to announce a decision.

Well, Nichte, she said, Now I will share something with you. I have been waiting for the right time. Or maybe I've been waiting for you to ask me. Some things, there is no good time. It must be done with.

Morgan folded her hands in her lap, and leaned forward. Her Tante was troubled by something, that was plain, and so she deserved a kind and open face. As Morgan smiled, gently, in this way, she remembered her eyes—did they freak out Mrs Vogel, even now? They could. If you knew someone with a tiny unicorn's horn, even after you knew them for years, and came to love them unconditionally, you would still think the tiny horn was weird. Morgan closed her eyes, and smiled her face, and listened.

Mrs Vogel told her story, like this: In the autumn before your parents broke off from us, my sister was dying. She lived in Kenosha, and her husband was a drunk, so no use to her. She had leukemia—blood cancer—and the treatments then were even more brutal than now. So I went up to see her, as often as I could, so at least she would have someone near who loved her. Karl was busy with his writing then, so I went alone. I didn't like seeing my sister—each time she looked more like death. But I liked the drive up there, through those hills that roll, and the last few dairy farms. For some reason, I dreaded the drive back. It made me nervous, all the traffic coming into the city. But also I did not look forward to seeing Karl. He would hug me but our bodies together were cold. Like two wooden dolls that you make hug. So you see, I knew something, in the way we know.

Morgan's eyes remained closed, but she heard the old woman sigh, and then continue.

One day my sister died. I was with her and she didn't fight it. The doctors wanted to give her another treatment, but she knew better and she shook her fist at one of them—poor young doctor—and said Fuck off with your poison, dummkopf! So he left us alone so she could die. I held her hand until it was cold, the nurses were very patient. Like you would have been Nichte. Then I walked out of the hospital and just drove home. I didn't talk with my sister's husband because there was no point. I didn't call Karl because I didn't want to speak with anyone. I think I worried that he wouldn't care, he wouldn't say the right things.

It was dark when I got home and I didn't like to put the car in the garage when it was dark so I left it on the street. I am glad now I did. I walked up to the front door and removed my shoes—I must have known what I was doing—and I walked quietly down the hall and up the stairs and down to our bedroom door. It was open and I could see there was only candle light in there. Also, there was music, rock music that I never cared for and neither did Karl, so he said. I stepped into the doorway and looked into the room. On the bed there were two naked bodies. My Karl, and a woman. They were tangled together in a position—it doesn't matter. I remember I thought of the expression *in flagrante delicto*. What a strange thing to think, this latin expression, when you are seeing your husband having sex to another woman. Maybe it helped me to think of it this way, to turn it into an observation, so I was not a part of it.

The woman was your mother, you are probably guessing. From her position with Karl she saw me in the doorway and she screamed. She pulled herself from him and wrapped herself in the sheet. Karl was left there, naked and stupid-looking.

I stepped back from the doorway and put out my arm, showing the path for your mother. She gathered her clothes and ran out, still wearing the sheet. I have not spoken to her since.

Morgan opened her eyes. Her heart pounded violently. Mrs Vogel was staring past her, toward the doorway to the dining room. Morgan turned to look, and there, for a moment, was Mr Vogel—or rather the ghost of him—with such brooding sadness you almost pitied him. Then he vanished.

Now it's been said, said Mrs Vogel. Now you know, and I am very sorry.

Then Mrs Vogel pointed her chin toward the doorway and called, She knows now, Karl! We are all in the open. No need to skulk around any more. We can be friends now, the three of us.

Morgan looked around the room, which seemed to be tilting, first one way and then another. It made her nauseous, this rocking of the floor and ceiling, like a boat crossing the tide. She put her hands down on the table to brace herself, to slow the motion of the room.

Mrs Vogel said, Are you okay, Nichte, you look unwell. Maybe this is too much for you – I am so, so sorry.

When the room righted itself, Morgan looked at the old woman. Why would you be sorry? She asked. You were the victim of all this.

You've had to live with it for all these years—there's nothing for you to be sorry for.

It felt good to advocate for Mrs Vogel, to stand in her shoes, and postpone thinking about herself. But it didn't last. What a dumb bitch her mother was. What a selfish dumb bitch—selfish Sharon shagging the neighbor. When her mother's affair had been a mystery, Morgan had sometimes pictured a swarthy, intriguing gentleman who treated her like a queen and so created a contrast with Julian the bully, Julian the child. Morgan could almost rationalize her mother's choice to have an affair when she was trapped in such a marriage. But she wasn't trapped, was she? She had her own money and could leave any time. In fact, she eventually did. So why sleep with the next-door neighbor, one half of a couple who are supposedly your close friends, a man what 30 years older? Well, maybe it was love. You can't get mad at love. You can only shake your head like, aw that's a shame.

Mrs Vogel was still watching her, pensively. Morgan asked, Do you think they were in love?

The old widow laughed abruptly. I asked Karl that, some months later—did they love each other? I will tell you what he said. He said, 'There is no right answer to that. If I say I loved her, that will diminish our love. But if I say I didn't love her, it will make it a careless, indulgent act.' But eventually Karl told me that no, he never loved Sharon and as far as he knew she never loved him, but there was a magnetism between them that eventually he couldn't control and he had to find a release for it. Shortly after that he got prostate cancer, wouldn't you know, and the surgery made his parts not work any more and so that was his last hurrah, as they say.

Who says that? asked Morgan.

Isn't that an expression: last hurrah?

Morgan laughed, It is—I was just kidding.

Oh good, said Mrs Vogel. You seem okay now.

Morgan thought about that—was she okay? Well, of course she was. There wasn't really any new revelation here—she already knew her mother was a complicated, selfish bitch, and she knew Mr Vogel was problematic in many ways. That they hooked up—well, it kind of made sense. What was left was just sadness—for Mrs Vogel, and for her dad, and for herself, even, picturing her little girl self sneaking into the Vogels' garden to play alone, despite her parents admonition not to—and in fact knowing that her parents knew she was there but didn't even care enough to enforce their own rules. That all made her weary and sad.

Morgan put her hand on Mrs Vogel's hand. She asked, So, have you forgiven them? Mr Vogel and my mom?

Mrs Vogel pulled her chin back righteously. Oh yes, yes long ago. A grudge hurts no one but the grudger. I let that go. Karl tried very hard to make it right. He tried much too hard—look at all those boxes in the attic! Frustrated artists—they think creation is atonement. They think some small success will justify who they are. Karl had no success. But his effort helped me forgive him and continue loving him. Before he died, I told him that I only needed to tell you one day, and that would be that. It hurt him, to think of you knowing, but it was his penance, he knew. But your mother—she never said another word to me, not a sorry or anything, and I think that was worse. But people like her, they give us a gift—you know what it is?

Mrs Vogel looked at Morgan pointedly, and gripped her hand. Morgan waited.

They show us how not to be, said the old woman. Then she nodded once, punctuating the statement, and watched Morgan.

And now it made sense, the way the old woman had been treating Morgan—her cryptic references, her sudden criticism, the sulking, the rant of insults she threw at Morgan during the storm. But all these things alternated with affection and loving gestures, so that Morgan didn't know which Tante she might find when she came down from the attic. But now it made sense. Mrs Vogel worried that Morgan, like so many of us, was veering toward repeating the mistakes of her parents. It's a little vortex, these dark habits of our ancestors, swirling us down toward a drain of hopelessness, and we have to swim very hard to pull free of the current—to make our own way.

Morgan crossed her arms and looked at Mrs Vogel with the full force of her eyes. I'm not seeing Larry, if that's what you're suggesting. I'm still married to Arthur and I respect that commitment until we decide.

Mrs Vogel held up one crooked finger and smiled. But now you see how right you are, she said. Now you have the example of your mother to see that these affairs diminish us as people.

Morgan shrugged. That was probably true. Well, that was definitely true. The notion of her mother creeping over to the neighbor's house for little trysts—it made her feel now very cold and business-like with Larry. The giddy veil was lifted.

Now Mrs Vogel was looking out a tall window of the dining room. With a modest smile she said, Men are very interesting. The doll-making—I don't know where that came from. One day Karl started making those dolls, and since we had been painting together, I just began to paint the dolls instead, as soon as he made them. He bought some expensive tools from Germany to make those dolls. He was good at it from the start. But we never sold them. All this happened while he was bumsen with Sharon. Aren't men strange?

Oh Tante, that is so creepy. I mean those dolls gave me the willies before, but now… I'm never going down in the basement again.

Mrs Vogel peered at Morgan, the old mischief back. She said, But you are going down there, Nichte. How else will you get rid of those dolls for me?

Late that afternoon Morgan walked down Webster into the setting sun, as the heat radiated up from the pavement and a westerly wind carried dust from the plains. She pulled behind her a tarp, folded into a sack, stuffed with wooden dolls. It was heavy, this load of faded dolls, none of them ever used except for one. Morgan had to lean into the effort, switching from one hand to the other, while swinging the other arm for momentum. It was hard crossing streets before the light changed and twice cars honked at her and swerved past. But no one seemed to actually see her, to acknowledge what a bizarre mission this was, this young woman with ferocious hair and startling eyes, pulling two dozen old dolls in a tarp down the sidewalk. That is, until a city truck pulled up alongside her.

Inside the truck, a man with a beefy face and tremendous moustache. He looked at her flatly. You need help? He asked. You don't seem like da the homeless type so I thought I'd ask.

Morgan was trained to suspect any man who offered her help, but this guy seemed legit, and not particularly interested.

No, thanks, she said. Yeah, no, I'm good. I got it.

The man shrugged, tapped his rear window with a calloused paw. He said, We could chuck whatcher carrying dere in the back and I can drive you. Last chance…

He raised his eyebrows, waiting.

Morgan smiled, and waved to him. No, it's fine. I need to do this.

The man took one last look at her, and her burden scraping the street. He said, Suit yerself, and drove away.

Where Webster meets the north branch of the Chicago River, there's a small cluster of trees along the bank. It's called the Webster Wildlife site. It didn't look like a place where wildlife would gather, but maybe. The point was that it was shaded and easier to access the river from here. Morgan paused to catch her breath. She looked around to see if anyone were near.

When she folded the tarp open, the dolls lay in all directions, some facing down, some facing up. It looked too much like a massacre. So

Morgan lined them all up, side by side, facing the sky. Then it looked too much like dead soldiers after a battle. She tried to sit the dolls upright, to approximate living things, but they were too old and the hip hinges too decayed, and they fell to one side or the other. Well, what was the point anyway—they weren't staying there.

One by one, Morgan set the dolls into the river, face up. It was like releasing fish after you caught them, dropping your hand down into the water to minimize the disturbance, letting the current carry away the liberated creature. Soon there was a flotilla of dolls, floating down the river, to join with other rivers, and eventually the biggest river, and then the Gulf, with all its oil slicks and forlorn birds. But for now, the dolls enjoyed a float together, on a warm summer evening, no longer confined to a dank basement but rather enjoying the sensation of being supported by water because of its rare molecular properties. The last one she released, of course, was the German peasant girl with braids, the one she had played with as a child. She thought this would be an emotional part, a sentimental gesture. But not really. That doll floated like all the others, bobbing over a wake left by a few geese, turning, turning in the current, until it found its way again headfirst downriver away from Morgan and all the memories of betrayal.

When the dolls were out of sight, she folded the tarp and walked home. She saw the man in the truck coming back on the same street. As he passed, he lifted his fingers from the steering wheel to say hi. Morgan almost asked him for a ride. She was tired and thirsty. But no, it was better to walk.

TWENTY THREE

With just a week to go, it was hard to imagine getting everything ready for the party and the perfect day. You don't necessarily have to stick with that day, Nancy said. And that was true, because Morgan was no longer coming. Faulkner said, That's true, Nancy, and I don't want to contradict you, but there is something nice about Arthur making the original date—undaunted, you know? Arthur listened to both of them, with a new patience and equanimity, but the reality was that he didn't have any other plan, so he might as well stick to the original.

There was also the question of his nine goals. When he wrote them, back in the spring, his intention was atmospheric—they were like brush strokes on a painting that would enchant Morgan into coming home. Now, they sounded silly, and also not parallel in their construction. On the one hand, he had farm-oriented goals: gardens, chickens, goats. On the other, unpredictable circumstances: Hanacek appearing, a visit from a fox. And in the center, he had planned a dinner with friends. A reasonable person would now focus primarily on that dinner, the party that Lupe had asked him to have regardless. But Arthur put his best effort into all the goals, just as he had for months now.

The difference was that Arthur no longer clung to a desired outcome. It was a subtle difference—although he wasn't trying to win back Morgan, he was still trying to make all the goals happen and the day perfect. He worked hard, but now without expectation that anything would come of it. But the difference had a profound effect on his outlook. Or was it that his outlook had a profound effect on the difference? When his thoughts veered into these philosophical traps, Arthur wanted to laugh, but kindly, at the remnants of the anxious fool he was only days before. When people change, you assume it happens incrementally, methodically, but instead it happens in leaps that punctuate long stretches of stasis. Wasn't evolution like this, now that we understand it better? Anyway, he returned to his task, because the doing was all that mattered at this point. The doing was enough.

The first goal took a lot of doing. *Organic gardens yield abundant food.* That could mean a lot of things, but Arthur interpreted it to mean his dinner could only serve produce he had grown, more or less in an organic fashion. It was funny to interpret a goal you had written yourself. But that was the way with words—as soon as you wrote them, they became their own thing, and you had to work at clarifying them or they might turn on you.

Raccoons had just discovered the gardens, giving this goal the most urgency. Arthur had built fences around the gardens—he wasn't stupid. But they were six-foot wood frames and cattle panels and were, therefore, perfect ladders for raccoons. So maybe a little stupid. On their first night, the raccoons raided the sweet corn, pulling down ears and shucking them neatly. There was plenty of corn left, but another night could wipe it all out. Clever, wicked little raccoon hands. They had to be stopped.

It wasn't difficult to string electric fencing around the top of the wooden fence. Faulkner held the spool with his large clever hands, while Arthur pulled the wire and strung it from one insulator to the next. In the humid heat, sweat ran down his arms and into his gloves. Sweating made you feel alive, part of the water cycle. You drank water, and it went into all your nooks and crannies, and then came out your skin. When they connected the wire to the energizer, and the energizer to the marine battery, and the battery to solar panels, the fence came alive. It clunked with each electrical surge, each pulse, a steady beat.

They listened together, admiring their work, drinking beer from cans before they cleaned up. Faulkner made a spooky grin. He said, That pulse… it reminds me of the drum the Martins beat that night at their masquerade. Wasn't that fucked up, that night, Arthur?

Arthur nodded, thinking. He tipped back his beer, and then said, I invited them, you know. The Martins.

Faulkner looked at him. Arthur could feel it, but didn't look back. The electric fence pulsed.

Faulkner said, You don't say. Well, all right. All right, then.

As for *Happy chickens lay lovely eggs*, that was hard to measure. How do you know if chickens are happy? It seems to me, said Nancy, that if they're calm and eating their food and laying eggs, they must be happy.

But what if happiness isn't a thing with chickens, Arthur replied. What if the state you're describing is just regular existence, which contrasts with irregular existence, which is when they're scared or sick. But not necessarily happy in the way we define it.

Nancy tossed compost into the chicken yard, and asked, Didn't you write that goal, Arthur?

He considered, and said, True. We'll go with your definition.

The hard part of chickens was the automation. If he did everything manually, it was easy, just a lot of tedious work. But that took time, which Arthur didn't have to spare. Come to think of it, time had been his adversary since they bought this land. Always rushing to finish something before time stole away the opportunity. Time was like an annoying teacher, rapping your head with a pencil, counting out seconds, while you tried to take a test. It never stopped, this relentless tapping of seconds, even while you slept. So Arthur fought back with technology and ingenuity. Automation could let the chickens out of their house in the morning, and beckon them in at night, and pour precise allocations of cracked corn, and ensure fresh water, and scan for predators, and sound the alarm when necessary. It was wonderful when it worked, which it did mostly. But when it failed, what a pain.

They tested the predator monitor. While Arthur watched the camera on his phone, Nancy walked a stuffed fox into view. The system didn't recognize it—just a question mark and an annoying chime. Let's try pulling it with a string, Arthur said, It's probably seeing you and getting confused. Nancy attached a string to the stuffed fox's neck and pulled it, but it kept falling over. The system briefly matched the fox with a cat, but then resumed its question mark.

Arthur watched the chickens peck at insects in the grass of their yard. They croaked gently, then snapped their heads to scan for threats, then resumed pecking. Didn't they seem happy?

Nancy asked, Have you seen foxes recently?

I wish, said Arthur. Nothing for months. I'm not so sure about that goal.

So you want to see a fox on your perfect day, but you also have to protect your chickens against the fox?

Exactly.

Isn't that just like humanity, Nancy laughed, and pushed her hair back from her forehead. She said, Is it crazy to ask whether you might just turn off the predator monitor, since it's been causing so much trouble?

Not crazy, said Arthur. But I don't want to give up on it yet. Let's try this.

He pointed his camera at the toy fox and scanned it, then labeled it as a fox predator, and updated the system. When Nancy pulled the fox again, the alarm sounded and the sprinklers gushed, herding the chickens back into the house, door shutting with the last one inside.

There, said Arthur, now we're protected from stuffed foxes.

The goal Arthur had written for the goats was unreasonable and ridiculous: *Jolly goats provide milk for delicious cheese*. And yet, it was still possible to achieve. Just a few days ago, the goats' milk had come in. They were still young—maybe seven months—but heavy enough to start producing. Milking goats was easy—the hard part was catching them. Arthur had not mastered that. And because they seemed so carefree and independent, he had let them go a little wild. It was a pleasure to see the goats leap up on the perches he had built—they did look jolly, peering over the fence, always chewing something.

But they were strong, these goats, especially for creatures less than half his weight. He could coax them with a chunk of iceberg lettuce, but when he set down the bucket and stool, they kicked and gamboled away. Arthur had read in *The Lonely Goatherd* magazine that goats become more cooperative when you treat them like pets. So he named them: Up, Down, Charmed, and Strange. But it didn't seem to matter, and also it felt weird to call out, Come on Strange! That's a good girl. He had always been bad at naming, particularly with his farm.

Fawk and Nancy could hold a goat while Arthur got the stool and bucket underneath it. But when he grabbed a teat, she squirmed free like a walleye over the side of the boat. Every time, the goat pranced a few feet, looked back, and bleated in a jolly fashion.

Then Faulkner, on impulse, dropped to all fours and stared at Charmed. He looked deeply into her golden, slit-pupiled eye, and bumped his head into hers. Charmed bumped back, mildly. Fawk pushed forward. Charmed pushed back. Nancy stepped away, her hands outstretched just in case, but not touching. Finally Fawk and the goat reached a kind of equilibrium in their butting, and Arthur scooted underneath and did the milking and there they had it—goat's milk.

Then it was just a matter of adding vinegar and lemon juice, and straining in cheesecloth, and adding salt—they had goat's cheese! What a miracle to be able to achieve this, just days before the perfect day! Also, who first figured out you could do this? Does all of cooking come from some Neolithic accident? There would be time to consider this after the work was done.

Meanwhile, there was only one downside to the goat trick: Charmed began to follow Faulkner everywhere. So strong was her desire that she learned to leap from her grassy perch to the top of the fence, balancing acrobatically for a moment, and then descending to freedom. From next door Arthur heard Nancy exclaim, Your girlfriend is back—if you don't break things off, you're moving in with my mother.

But your mother's dead, Fawk said. No offense.

Nancy said, Exactly.

The birds, of course, were a delight, and it seemed that they would achieve their goal without any intervention from Arthur. When he wrote that goal in spring: *Birds of all kinds nest in native hedges*, he was enchanted by all the nesting to be seen in his fields and woods. He forgot that the perfect day would happen in late summer, which is not the classic bird nesting time. One particularly mopey day, he told Faulkner that he probably needed to delete that goal.

Au contraire! Fawk said. Many songbirds have second or even third broods through the summer.

And goldfinches, Nancy said. Don't forget about them.

Sure enough, when the thistle was high in the field, the goldfinches descended, eating their seeds and gathering thistledown for luxurious nests, hidden in the hazelnuts at the forest edge.

Do you remember, Arthur asked, how Morgan could imitate the goldfinch sound?

Nancy tilted her head. Well I don't Arthur, she said. I haven't met Morgan.

Right, he laughed. It just seems like you have.

I hope to one day, said Nancy.

She couldn't whistle properly, he said. She did it with her tongue against her teeth, but it was exactly like goldfinches.

She's missing out, Nancy said, not coming to your party.

Maybe, he replied. But maybe not. I guess we'll see.

Nancy put her arm around his shoulders and said nothing, because she didn't need to.

Arthur had deleted the fifth goal: *Bees hum busily among the forbs of the field.* After his bee colony collapsed and the deer ate all the forbs, what was the point? He left the hive boxes barren and the fence around the prairie fell. Sure enough, as soon as he stopped caring, a cloud of bees began investigating the hive, and little flower heads emerged on the prairie. Nature cautiously returned. By the big day, it looked like there would be honey in the hive, produced from the nectar in the forbs of the field.

So now the question was whether Arthur should reinstate that goal so he could mark it as done? Was this manipulating his own system? Yes it was. Did he care? Not particularly. Morgan would say, Give yourself a break. Take the win when you can. But if the situation were reversed, would she follow her own advice? No she wouldn't. Arthur shook his head to get his mind off that track. But Morgan would love the new honey. In the mornings under the covers she smelled like honey. He shook his head again.

Arthur stood alone in the kitchen, admiring his work. The new tile floor was cool underfoot, the cabinets hung true, the counters gleamed, the appliances shone. He had built a little table for two out of walnut he salvaged from the old floor. It was beautiful, just as he and Morgan had imagined it. Did *The farmhouse stand ship-shape*, as required of that sixth goal? Of course it didn't. Time had shifted the foundation, torqued the frame, cracked the plaster. But this remodeled kitchen was kickass.

Arthur took some pictures with his phone. The light was good and the pictures could be in a magazine. Morgan should see this. Just because things had ended, it didn't mean she wasn't still interested. Or maybe it did. But people spend so much time worrying about what other people think, how they might react, how everything was imbued with hidden meaning and calculation—that was no way to live your life, was it? When you were going to die eventually, and maybe soon—who knew?

Standing in the kitchen, sweat drying on his neck, dirt under his fingernails, Arthur sent the pictures to Morgan. He followed with this message: *Thought you'd like to see the kitchen, since so many of the ideas were yours. I think it turned out pretty well. I'm not asking you to respond or anything. Honestly. Just thought you deserved to see. I hope you're well and I'm still sorry about everything and I wish you the best.*

It wasn't his best writing, but it was time to get back to work.

He put his phone away.

The seventh goal was really the main event, and all the other goals were in service of it. That seemed right, given the significance of the number seven. Arthur didn't love the phrasing: *Friendly neighbors come for dinner, bringing wine and stories.* It was obsessive. God it sucked to read your own words sometimes. It should have been more like, *We have a nice dinner.* Whatever. It wasn't like he was going to publish this list. On the other hand, your words did make a difference, especially when they defined your goals. From that perspective, this goal seemed achievable and likely to happen.

What to serve? Arthur didn't like descriptions of food, or menu lists—it gave him the willies somehow. He would serve fresh greens, sweet corn, pickled beets, new potatoes, grilled chicken… enough, enough! He couldn't stand the fussy, cloying words any more. Oh also, he would have Lupe's pies. What kind would she bring? Hopefully dessert, because he had none.

Being so busy, he hadn't been thinking too hard about Lupe. Or that she would be there with the Martins. The awkwardness that would create. Possibly quite a scene. Arthur felt a surge of the old anxiety. It wasn't just a matter of the day not being perfect—it could be a catastrophe. And he would be the catalyst. Well, it would be what it would be. All these months of worrying and freaked-out living, it was just exhausting. The only cure, it seemed, was to keep moving forward, doing the things you promised you'd do, and let what happened happen.

Nancy wrote the menu items on recipe cards, so they could keep track of things. The words didn't give her the willies.

Oh we need a vegetarian entrée, Arthur added.

For whom? She asked.

Right, he said. Never mind.

The eighth goal was stupid. *Hanacek appears, briefly*. Umm, okay. He was about as likely to attract the ghost as a fox. And Hanacek was a stubborn old prick anyway. If he knew Arthur wanted something (that is assuming ghosts can 'know' in the way we do), he would be sure not to do it. He was useless, the old fart with those dumb mules. Fuck that guy.

Nevertheless, it was an item Arthur had committed to. So he proceeded. Down by the river, when he knew Nancy and Faulkner were away, he sat on the squeaky old swing, and waited for Hancek. The woods were silent except for the wash of the river through the snag. After almost an hour, Arthur decided on a different approach. He began to speak into the woods, as if he were on stage.

All right Hanacek, you old bastard. I am here to invite you to a dinner, three days from now, on a long table in my backyard. Or, your backyard, depending on your time frame. Dress is casual—overalls and a straw hat will be fine. Animals must be leashed, or better yet, left at home. I guess you have a loophole there, since my party is technically in your home. Whatever—bring the mules. But please appear only briefly, and in such a way that you don't cause a disturbance with the other guests. To be honest, I only wanted you to come so one person could see you—Morgan, of course, you know who that is. I only wanted Morgan to see you, so she would have to admit I'm not crazy. She has since sent her regrets, I'm sorry to report, Hanacek. So now there isn't much of a point to your coming, but I'm inviting you anyway, because it's on my list. No offense.

Arthur laughed to himself, because there was no one else. It felt good to be weird. What was that moving there, over the river, beyond the stand of hawthorn? Was it the rump of a mule? There were dark shapes for sure. But then, nothing. Oh well. Arthur tried.

A fox darts down the prairie trail... It was a nice goal, coming at the end, kind of poetic. But also, it kind of slid off the list, like an arbitrary thought, a non sequitur, some incongruous postscript. But that was fitting because it seemed unlikely that this goal would manifest on the perfect day. Which made the day imperfect. Wow, perfect was an outrageous adjective to label the day, to be honest. He had known this, implicitly, for a long time, so why hadn't he changed the name of the day? It's impossible to make a day perfect, even with a clever app. Unless… unless you defined perfect as just how things are. Every day and every moment is perfect, because they are miraculous. The nearly infinite web of events—from the interaction of subatomic particles to the wobble of the earth—all contribute to this very moment, and so this very moment is indisputably perfect. Every day is a perfect day. The one Arthur was preparing for was just a day he chose to celebrate the perfection of every day. Right?

Then the epiphany was gone, like a dream before waking, like vapor over a pond at sunrise. What had he been thinking? Oh yes—how to attract foxes. They say you put out smelly bait, like fish, but only very small portions, to keep their interest but don't become dependent on your feeding. So Arthur put out individual sardines on the path in the woods near the river, where foxes surely roamed. He mounted a trail camera at the bait station. Woodland creatures arrived the very first night, and paraded in a display of biodiversity—raccoons, skunk, coyote, possum, house cats, mice, and even a mink. A mink for goodness sake! Wild minks still roam free! But no foxes, not a one. So much for perfection.

So that was that. The list was done, basically. Or rather, the prep for it. Now all Arthur needed was luck and execution. He sat near his fire pit on an Adirondack chair he had built. The chair wasn't quite square, and rocked a bit, but was otherwise solid. Nancy and Arthur sat beside him. They hadn't yet lit the fire or opened the bottle of wine.

Arthur held up a hand. Wait, he said. Sorry, I'd just like to sit for a minute, before doing any thing more.

Mmm, said Faulkner.

Right, Nancy whispered.

So they sat. The cicadas rattled. The scent of fertility rose up from the banks of the river. Nighthawks circled in the dusky sky. On cue, a Great Horned Owl hooted once. No reply.

Okay that's good, said Arthur. Now let's drink.

TWENTY FOUR

For her whole life, Morgan had looked away from people. She didn't look them in the eyes, not for very long, because it seemed too rude and shocking. Even looking in the mirror sometimes she was like, Oh god! Then immediately looked away, at her hair, at her neckline, whatever. But after she broke up with Arthur, after she learned about her mother's infidelity, after she released the dolls in the river—Morgan began looking people in the eye. Nakeisha noticed immediately. She said, Oh yeah girl, you're bringing those headlights now! Mrs Vogel met her gaze in a kind of staring contest each morning, and then forfeited, laughing, so obviously pleased with her Nichte. On her early morning walks, Morgan looked plainly at her compatriots passing—to her surprise, they didn't recoil. They just said, Hi.

It was the week she was supposed to visit Arthur. She had wanted to forget it, to just have a normal week. But now, she didn't feel the need to forget. There it was, in blue pen in her pocket calendar, and also on her phone calendar. It said 'Arthur' on August 28. She should reach out to him, and just acknowledge that it was an important day for him, perhaps a difficult one. Without apologizing, without backtracking, she should show that she still cared for him. Which she did. Of course she still loved him—those feelings don't just dry up do they? Or maybe they do. You never know what's happening on your first time through. But anyway these days it felt like a wistful, nostalgic love. It wasn't hot and angry anymore. It was like the fading sweetness of autumn, which was coming soon.

Arthur's message with the pictures caught her by surprise. When she saw the preview on her phone she felt the familiar skip of her heart— what now? After she'd ended things so abruptly, after they hadn't spoken for a while, she expected an angry retort, or something dry and bitter, maybe a cold reference to a bill unpaid. But the pictures of the kitchen, so beautiful, and the message so plain, the reassurance that he held no expectation—what do you do with that? She studied the pictures carefully, and saw all the detail in his craftsmanship, how he had brought her ideas to reality. It must have taken a lot of effort, no doubt originally planned for her visit, but then just carried out without that motivation. He was just living his life, earnestly—no tantrums or histrionics. Maybe, even, he was learning to live without her? Morgan felt no right to be upset by the idea of him moving on, since she had ended things, with good reason for sure but also rashly. Also, duplicitously, claiming she was seeing someone else, which she wasn't actually, was she? Oh Arthur, so shockingly simple he became mysterious. Morgan gave each picture a heart, and said no more.

Devin was coming to visit Mrs Vogel. They liked to play backgammon and argue. So Morgan had the morning off.

As she cleaned Mrs Vogel's breakfast plate, she said, Now don't be too mean to Devin—it's good of him to visit.

Mrs Vogel waved her hand, It does him a lot more good than me. I'm the only girlfriend he'll ever have.

Morgan kissed the old woman on the top of the head. She had

started doing that. Why had she started doing that? Somehow the old barriers were gone. She said, I'll see you this afternoon. I need to talk with you about something, okay?

Mrs Vogel looked up at her. They fixed their eyes on each other's until Mrs Vogel relented, laughing. Then she grabbed Morgan's wrist with surprising strength. I have something to talk with you too, she said.

At the door, Devin stood in his scrubs. He hugged Morgan lightly, then whispered, Did you change her? You know I don't do diapers.

Morgan laughed, adjusted her purse on her shoulder. She said, I think she'll hold until I'm back. Just don't give her too much tea.

When she arrived at Café Voltaire, Larry was already there. There was an apricot danish on the table, opposite him, and as Morgan set down her purse, the barista called out, Cappuccino for Morgan?

Aren't you being nice, she said. When they hugged she felt his bony back, a dry coldness like steel springs in winter. That was a good sign, how she felt about the hug. Perfect timing, she declared, and retrieved her coffee. The foamed milk formed the shape of a swan.

It's been a while, Larry said. The least I could do. He sipped his sweet tea and looked at her over the rim of the glass.

Morgan looked back, unflinching. Would he notice? He smiled the jolly Larry smile. How was the conference? she asked.

He shrugged and flicked his eyebrows in resignation. What can you expect when you get two hundred astrophysicists together in a casino in Las Vegas.

Morgan laughed. Honestly I have no idea, she said.

Well to our credit, he said, no one gambles—probably because we can calculate the odds pretty easily. But other than that, it's mostly politics like any conference.

Did you give your presentation? I remember you had a presentation.

Larry's face lit up. I did! he said. It went really well I think. I mean behind my back I'm sure they were making fun of it, because I included music and added some drama. But I could see them perk up when I got into the math. Do you know what it's like when you really have people's attention? Like they're… oh what's the word for it?

Rapt?

Yes. They were rapt. Et voilà!

Larry continued to explain the results he shared in the talk. Morgan became aware of the café. It was noisy. You could hear other conversations—two fancy women were talking about trouble with a contractor. A group of business people huddled around a laptop—they had taken stools from other tables for their meeting. Looking at it now, Café Voltaire was a little bougie for her taste. She looked back at Larry.

I'm sorry, he said, I'm boring you.

No, sorry, she said. It's just a little hard to hear.

Larry looked hurt, just a quick flash of it, and then he smiled again and sipped his tea.

Then they spoke at the same time.

He said, How are things with Arthur?

She said, Listen I have to tell you something.

They laughed. Larry said, You go.

Well first, Morgan said, I'm sorry about how I acted at your apartment last time. That was kind of rude.

Larry waved away the comment and then winked at her. Still with the winking. He said, To be honest, you were a little crazed. I was worried I had done something.

No, Morgan said, It wasn't about you. You were very kind. How are the plants?

Thriving, he said. I can hardly walk around, so bountiful is their growth.

Morgan laughed, I bet.

Should she be doing this, she wondered. Was she about to throw away something precious? She let herself feel—was there anything there, like before? No, nothing. That was good, like how you don't crave something after you've quit it for a while. It's just gone.

So I want to clear the air about something, she said. I hope it's not weird, but I think it's important. I'm trying to clean up some things up in my life.

Larry made an alarmed face, miming comically. No sorry, he said, go ahead.

This thing, Morgan said. This thing between us, you know? This tension we've had for a while now, this unspoken thing, right?

She focused her eyes on his, but now he was inscrutable, listening, scientific.

It's been fun, I totally admit that. But I think it has to end. I just want to acknowledge it, so it doesn't get too weird, and we can just be friends. You know?

Larry squinted. He looked over at the business people laughing too loud. He turned back to her and said, Sorry I don't know what you're talking about, Morgan.

Was this an honest response, was he pretending? She pressed on, Come on Larry, you know what I'm talking about.

I don't, he said. In his face there was genuine confusion. He might have been looking at nonsense equations from some crackpot academic.

You don't know what I'm talking about.

I don't, Morgan. Aren't we just friends?

Well yes of course, but also…

Morgan stopped herself. Suddenly she was very warm and she could feel blood rush to her face. Her hearing went dim and the café was awash in vertigo. Was it possible he hadn't felt a thing, all these months? Could it only have been Morgan's perception, a one-sided notion of tension? Like when you dream about someone and see them later and wonder if they knew you had dreamed about them, and you knew that wasn't possible but still it seemed like they had to know, but of course that was ridiculous but still? She wanted badly to leave the café. It was excruciating. But there was no more running away, no more looking away from frightening things. But how to get out of this situation?

Larry was turning his glass on the table, his fingers draped over the rim, turning it click click click like a stopwatch. He retained this confused expression—or maybe bemused?

Well, Morgan said. Great. That's great then. I had thought we had kind of a… romantic situation brewing, but I guess not. Sorry.

Larry's face exploded in a laugh. He put his hand out on hers—a hand too soft, too little scarred from life. He said, Morgan, I have a girlfriend! Well, two, maybe. But not you. You have nothing to worry about.

Morgan studied him. Was he bullshitting her? Two girlfriends? He hadn't mentioned anything like this before, so maybe he was inventing it because he was embarrassed. Or maybe he was as odd and diffuse as he had always seemed. Maybe he did have two girlfriends. But still, Morgan knew he had acted like more than just a friend, there was no question of that. You have to remind yourself sometimes that your perspective is legit, even if it's unreliable. But then maybe she had missed some signals along the way and should let it drop. But no, she had invested too much in this guy to let that stand.

So, two girlfriends? You never mentioned that.

A shadow passed over his face, but he recovered. Well, he said. Maybe not girlfriends exactly. I mean, what does that even mean these days? But dating, for sure. Dating a couple girls. So yeah you have nothing to worry about.

His Cajun accent had disappeared.

I wasn't worried, she said. There's no worry.

It was probably time to stop talking. She had done what needed doing. And now, it was clear it was the right thing to do.

On impulse she held out her hand to him, across the table. Larry looked at it for a moment, then took it, and they shook hands.

Friends, she said.

Friends, he replied, grinning.

She ignored his amused expression. She took her napkin and carefully wiped crumbs from the table, then folded the napkin.

She said, Now what do I owe you for the coffee?

Walking back to Mrs Vogel's, it was hot and the air felt charged. They had been predicting thunderstorms for days now and they never came. When she turned on Deming, Morgan realized that she couldn't remember getting there. The streets, the people, the buildings, the cars, nothing. How do we do this—walking or driving or biking—without any attention because we're so lost in our thoughts? Humans are amazing. And also fucked up. But as the embarrassment of the encounter with Larry faded, it left behind a kind of clean elation. That was done, now. And honestly, it could have gone much worse. He had made it easy for her, whether he was pretending or not. Probably not. Or, probably? If he did have girlfriends, it was weird and shitty of him to not mention it— that was suspect. It stung a little, to think that he felt no sexual tension with her, but that was just the ego talking. And the ego is a bratty child who needs to be ignored until it behaves.

She stood at the top of the stairs by the front door. She was earlier than she had planned. Now she could collect her thoughts. It was time she got back to work. Not the Mrs Vogel work, but her actual profession, healing people and contributing to the chaotic hive of a hospital. It was exciting to think about it now, the thrill of a hectic day, the grim camaraderie of a medical team, the satisfaction of repairing a body, or sometimes a soul. The delicious exhaustion at the end of a grueling day, earning the reward of a glass of wine, a proper dinner, a comfy bed.

Without warning, she ached for it. Now every day spent not doing it was excruciating.

Down the street came the man in the suit and fedora and tiny dog. He crossed to the other side of the street. What the heck? It was annoying.

Hello! Morgan called to him. She waved dramatically.

The man stopped. The dog kept walking until it met the end of the leash. The man tipped his hat back and looked around until he saw Morgan up on the stair.

Oh! he said. Hello. Didn't see you there.

The man tilted his head and smiled. Now Morgan didn't know what to say.

She said, Just saying hi!

Oh great, great, he said. You know Mrs Vogel then? How is she?

Could it be possible he had never noticed Morgan before? He seemed genuine, and much older now that she could see him plainly. She said, She's doing fine. I'm her caretaker—or, one of them.

Oh good, good, the man said. He raised his arm in a weak wave. Well, have a good one.

Morgan waved back, and the man walked on behind the dog.

You just never know with people.

Morgan could probably go in now. She wanted Mrs Vogel's advice. She also wanted her approval. The old woman would support her going back to work. But what if Morgan wanted to take the job at Middling hospital? That seemed crazy, to move back down there, with things ending with Arthur, maybe. But somehow the idea wouldn't go away. After she got the letter, she called the attending who said they'd have a job for her whenever she wanted it. It made a difference when people wanted you like that. But there was the job at Illinois Masonic too. She could stay near Mrs Vogel that way. Chicago was her home, right? There didn't seem to be a right answer. There didn't seem to be a wrong one either. Like people said, it was a good problem to have. Easy for them to say, when they didn't bear the weight of the consequences. So maybe Tante could help her think it through.

When she went inside, Devin and Mrs Vogel sat at the kitchen table with the backgammon board. Mr Vogel stood at the old woman's side, studying the board. He was very faint now, his ghostly form vague and flickering. Could Devin see him?

Devin was complaining, You can't do that! It's cheating.

Mrs Vogel pointed her gnarled finger at him. That is not cheating. That is the rules. I have played this game for twice as long as you have been living.

Devin saw Morgan in the doorway. Fine, he said. You win. Again. Mrs Vogel always wins.

The old woman sat back in her chair, satisfied. You can put away the board now, she said. Morgan is here.

Mr Vogel drifted backward and was gone.

On his way out, Devin touched Morgan's arm. She seems better, he said. More of the old spark—what's got into her?

Morgan shrugged merrily, everything was a mystery. Thanks for coming today, she said. I owe you.

Take me to the dining room, said Mrs Vogel. I have something to show you.

There was a stack of papers on the long table. The old grandfather clock ticked in the hallway. She told Morgan to sit at the papers so she could read.

It was Mrs Vogel's will, obviously. Morgan began to read down the long preamble, but it was hard to focus. Why did they make some words in all caps? Lawyers did all these things to make it all seem official, immutable. But everything was made up, and only worked because we all agree to it. Money was like that too. Why couldn't Morgan focus? The meeting with Larry, and then the old man, and now Mrs Vogel with this cryptic and formal presentation.

It is my will, said Mrs Vogel.

Right, said Morgan. I can see that.

Maybe I just tell you what's in it.

If you want to, Morgan said. I don't feel like it's my business.

I am leaving the house to you. The old woman stared at the papers. She said it solemnly, perhaps sheepishly. She turned her eyes up at Morgan, and Morgan looked back at her, directly, trying to pull her thoughts together.

But your kids, she said. They should get the house.

They will get plenty, said Mrs Vogel. And they will deserve none of it. Only you deserve the house. Only you will appreciate it. And now that you know everything, all the things that happened here, there is atonement. After atonement people can start fresh, and places too—they are also reborn after atonement.

I can't, said Morgan. She couldn't say more then, not if she didn't want to cry. She didn't want to cry.

Nichte! The old woman scolded. This house is worth a lot of money!

Morgan breathed, in and out. I know, she said. I mean, I don't know, really. But I can imagine.

You will never have to work again, said Mrs Vogel.

Morgan flinched. But I want to work, Tante! I have to work.

Mrs Vogel shrugged. It seemed like she might pout.

And also, Morgan said, just practically speaking, if you think I will appreciate the house I can't sell it and if I don't sell it then I would still have to work, right? I mean it just doesn't make sense, is what I'm saying.

Mrs Vogel crossed her arms and lowered her head. That had been callous of Morgan to say. It was just too much.

I'm sorry, she said. I'm so sorry. I should be saying thank you. Thank you so much, Tante. But I just don't know. It's a lot to take in. I love that you did this for me and I love you.

The old woman turned up and there was joy in her face. I love you too my dear Nichte. I have always loved you and I always will.

Sometimes you realize, in an enormous rush, just how fortunate you are. Here was an extraordinary woman who loved Morgan unconditionally. Here was a remarkable house that could be Morgan's. There were two wonderful jobs that Morgan could have. There was Larry, a fun friend, maybe a devious friend, possibly creepy, but a fascinating friend. There was Nakeisha, the reliable sage. There was the man with the suit and the fedora and the tiny dog. And there was Arthur, who loved her still, despite all that had happened, who would probably always love her, who wanted nothing more than to be with her, to impress her, to make her happy.

As if reading her mind, Mrs Vogel said, Who knows—maybe your boy can move up here and live with you. He would like the city, I think. The garden here is much more manageable than that farm you have told me about.

Ha! Morgan laughed, surprising both of them. Arthur back in the city, she said. That is quite a thought.

She put her hand on the will, such a stack of papers. Why did it take so many words? Our language is so imprecise, so ineffective, we have to pour out thousands of words just to try to approximate meaning, and even then it's not close. Maybe it's asymptotic. Maybe it gets very close. Larry would think that was funny. But Arthur would actually understand.

What are you thinking? asked Mrs Vogel.

I was thinking about words, to be honest.

That is a strange thing to think when someone has left you their mansion in the best neighborhood in Chicago.

Morgan laughed, and Mrs Vogel laughed too. Suddenly they were relaxed.

Can I ask you, Morgan said, Can I ask you for this not to be final until I've had a chance to think about it? I don't want to sound ungrateful—because I am so, so grateful to you—but I just want to be able to think for a while, about things in general.

Yes, said Mrs Vogel. You think. But don't take long because the day of my death is soon.

Morgan shook her head disdainfully. You don't believe those doctors really do you? I wish you had never gone down there.

I do too, said Mrs Vogel. But now the box has been opened. I know what I know.

They sat now without speaking, as the clock ticked seconds. It made no sense to ask Mrs Vogel's advice about the job now. Despite all her good intentions, there was no way she could be impartial about Morgan moving to Middling. And also, it was crazy for her to think of taking that job in Middling, with a good job here among friends and a free mansion. That was too crazy to suggest to her Tante. It would be embarrassing.

And yet. The thought would not leave her. She so badly needed someone to talk with, someone who would understand her fully, someone comfortable with crazy notions. Well. She knew who that was.

TWENTY FIVE

So this was the day.

Arthur awoke hours before dawn—was it some violent sound outside? He crept to his deck to look but there was nothing but the slumbering neighborhood. He went back to bed and lay there, listening to the ticking and creaking of the old house. When he fell asleep, he dreamed he was alone in an ancient castle. The stone walls were cold and damp. Outside across the moat a vast army was assembled, men on horses holding banners. Where was Morgan? He ran through the empty halls of the castle looking for her. There were rats the size of racoons and they brushed past his legs. He came into a cavernous hall with wooden chandeliers bearing unlit candles. A round table stood sturdy in the center of the hall, circled with high-backed chairs. Why was he dreaming this? If he could ask this, was he actually awake? How can you be both awake and dreaming, how do our minds do this?

When Arthur came to, sunlight shot through the bedroom window on to his face. The sun couldn't be there, that would be late in the morning—how could it be late in the morning? But it was, and that meant Arthur was already terribly behind on this day. He jumped out of bed, let the pillows fall to the floor, and went to the front door to look out. As if to confirm how late it was? He didn't know why he had gone to the front door, he was just manic. He had a dinner to serve people today. He had never served a dinner. It had to be nice for everyone—they had all kindly accepted his invitation. He couldn't host a dinner for nice people and then have it be bad. On the front step there was a tray, with a coffee carafe and scones wrapped in a gingham towel. There was a note from Nancy, saying, A little breakfast for your Perfect Day. Call if you need help!

Nancy's handwriting calmed him. All right. He could have some breakfast. He sat on the rocker on the step and drank the coffee and ate a scone, thinking about what had to be done. Yes this was the way to do it—be methodical. If you thrash about, things actually take longer. Where the heck was his phone?

It had fallen to the floor when he got up. There were no new messages on the phone. Was this a good thing? That meant no one had cancelled, that was good. On the other hand… Well that was stupid. Of course he wouldn't hear from Morgan on this day. Why should he expect that? He opened his OPD app. Everything was good, just as it had been yesterday.

The morning was what they call fair. Funny that fair could mean very nice weather—you might even say perfect—but also mean just okay. Like 'fair to middling.' Anyway the sun was out and the sky was blue. It was a little hot, kind of stuffy. The forecast said there was a chance of thunderstorms that afternoon, but these days there was always a chance of thunderstorms and they never came. The weather would cooperate, Arthur decided.

The dinner would be at 2pm, a midwestern dinner time. When you called this dinner it meant the later meal would be supper. He didn't like the word supper. Why? It didn't matter because he was serving dinner and if they ate again later that would be great because it would mean people were enjoying themselves and they could call that meal whatever at that point. Maybe they would all be drunk, staggering arm-in-arm down through the field, singing songs. Wouldn't that be something.

Nancy and Faulkner had offered to help prepare, of course. But Arthur declined, repeatedly, because he wanted them to just be guests. I don't want you to feel responsible for this going well, he said. I just want you to have a nice time. He meant it sincerely, but also he wanted to stay busy. If the Fuglesens came to help, they might get done early and then he would have to wait, idle. It was the doing that mattered. Not the result.

It felt good in the kitchen, doing the meal prep. He played John Coltrane and that circle of fifths, going round and round, made a kind of rhythm to his work. See this was nice, the infinite revolutions, nothing special, just revolutions, like the moon around the earth and the earth around the sun. Just another day. He put a marinade on the chicken, and cut up the beans, and shucked the corn, and mixed the salad, and seasoned the potatoes, and opened the jar of beets. All of it now arranged in serving bowls, filling the fridge to capacity.

Outside he loaded the grill with charcoal and arranged the grilling tools. He dragged a long table into the yard and covered it with two tablecloths Nancy had loaned him. One was gingham and the other had a flower print. They didn't go together. Also, they divided the table into two sections, so people would be either in one section or the other. Would that bother the conversation? When they were doing carpentry, sometimes Gramps would say 'we're not building a church.' That meant that if it were a little off, it was all right. It gave you permission to not be perfect. Well, the table setting certainly wasn't a church. Arthur cut some flowers and put them in vases along the table, and then set out the plates and silverware and it looked great.

The chickens were in their yard—the automation working as expected. The goats were on their perches. Up butted with Strange and knocked her off. Charmed looked toward Faulkner's house and bleated.

Down stared toward the river. Jolly goats. Jolly good goats. There were the goldfinches over the field, flying in parabolas, making the chirps that Morgan could imitate. The gardens looked cool, actually, with their impractical wandering paths. If you stood still you could hear the bees. There was one on a bergamot flower. No fox, of course, and no Hanacek, but what did you expect? It was all right.

An hour to go before the guests would arrive, and there was nothing else to do. Arthur sat on his deck looking down at all of it. He reached for his phone and then put it back. Where would the guests sit? They didn't all know each other very well. That could be awkward. Faulkner and Nancy would be great. Jamie and Vicky from across the road were super nice people. Timothy Gardner the lawyer could talk with anybody. And Alfred Beardsley from the Middling Café and his wife Jennifer, they always had stories to tell. But the Martins, that would be weird. It had to be done, because Lupe had asked him. And Lupe, how would she handle being at this dinner party with the people who probably killed her husband? This question had tormented Arthur for days now, lurking in the back of his mind, pushed away again and again. Maybe they wouldn't come. Oh, it would be so great if they didn't come. But the Martins said they would and so did Lupe, who was bringing pies. Maybe she wanted to forgive them, to put it all behind her? Man that took courage. Lupe had no lack of courage. You could learn a lot watching people like Lupe. Anyway, there was nothing Arthur could do about this now. The day would just have to unfold. He closed his eyes and breathed. The air smelled like hay.

The doorbell rang. Arthur had just installed that new doorbell. The chimes were a weird scale that sounded medieval. Like long horns at the front of a cavalry, with banners, like the army from his dream. Good lord, the party was starting already.

Lupe stood on his front stoop, holding two large reusable grocery bags. She wore a neat outfit—kind of professional, black slacks and a white shirt. She seemed very calm, steady, as if she could stand there, holding the bags, for hours. She said, I'm early. In case you needed help.

Oh yes, hello, said Arthur. Good to see you – come on in, let me get those bags.

I'm fine, she said, and walked through the doorway into the kitchen. She set the bags on Arthur's shiny new counter.

So, you came! he said.

Lupe turned, put her hands on hips, tilted her head. You can relax, Arthur, she said. She looked about, curiously. This is a nice kitchen. Did you do this yourself?

I just did, yes. Thanks.

You're welcome, she said.

She began to unload her bags—pies, napkins, cups, a gingham tablecloth. She said, I'd like to help today, with the hosting, so you can pay attention to your guests. No need to make a fuss, introducing me. Is that okay with you?

Arthur said, Well I don't know, Lupe. I mean you're my guest. I want you to have a nice time.

Lupe put her hands on the counter and looked at them. She said, It's what I want. That will be a nice time for me.

Okay, sure I guess. But I can't promise I won't introduce you! Arthur laughed. Somehow it seemed necessary, some laughter.

Lupe looked at him. She smiled, as if intrigued. You're a good guy, she said. It's going to be a good day. I'm glad you're doing it, even if your wife isn't coming. Is everybody else coming?

They all RSVP'd, he said. I mean, they all said they'd come.

I know what RSVP means.

Right, said Arthur.

Lupe now looked out the back window. Your tablecloths don't match, she said. Good thing I brought one that does. I'll go fix it.

Oh yeah if you want, yeah sure that makes sense, he said. I'll just put these pies in the..

No, said Lupe. Leave them for now. They're setting.

She went out the back door with the tablecloth. Arthur stood in the kitchen. Mercifully, the doorbell rang. It was Nancy and Faulkner, of course. They brought wine, a fancy kind that Arthur didn't recognize. Nancy put her hand on Arthur's shoulder and said, Doing okay?

He let out his breath, made a happy face, Great, he said. All ready, I think. Thanks for breakfast.

Faulkner slapped Arthur on the arm, gave him a nod. He said, Hey, Arthur, do you have enough beer? It occurs to me that we brought wine, but today might be a day for a beer.

I got plenty of beer, Arthur said. I think we're good, man, you guys just start enjoying okay?

Lupe returned to the kitchen. She greeted the Fuglesens, shook their hands.

Nancy said, I don't know if you remember but we met at the farmer's market.

I remember you, said Lupe. You were with your daughter.

Sheila, yes, said Nancy. She's been enjoying your honey so much. I can't wait to try these pies. She put her hands together and bent down over the counter, in the way people admire food carefully prepared.

What kind are they? she asked.

Three apple, one blueberry, said Lupe. She pointed to one of the pies—it had a cross cut into the crust and was oozing purple. But this one, she said, the blueberry. I don't think it turned out so well.

Oh I'm sure they're all delicious, Nancy said.

Yeah, you better keep those away from me, said Faulkner, patting his stomach. He was suddenly like a cartoon dad. Arthur laughed.

Lupe looked at Nancy. No, she said, It really isn't good, this one. You shouldn't eat it.

Faulkner made an 'o' with his mouth. Nancy nodded studiously. Arthur began to say something, to ask about the pie and why she'd brought it if… Then the doorbell rang again and broke the moment.

Timothy Gardner came in a sleek Audi, which he parked rakishly. He brought more wine, possibly fancier still, because there was melted wax over the top. He and Faulkner started to laugh, picking up some ongoing conversation, and it felt like the party finally started. Jamie and Vicky arrived pulling a picnic cart that Nancy called cute, and they unloaded chips and dip and homemade pickles and asked Arthur where to put them and he showed them a serving table he had set up and they talked for a minute about canning and how the dill was growing like crazy. Now here was Alfred and Jennifer Beardsley pulling up in a Subaru wagon, which they parked close to Timothy's Audi, possibly to his chagrin. Alfred thanked Arthur again for the fine work on the website and Jennifer said how great it looked and it was about time they updated that. Arthur asked them how it had been in Florida and they said it was crazy as usual and frankly nice to be back in the Midwest. By now the party was humming, people mixing nicely, so Arthur could turn his attention to cooking. Now and then Lupe appeared at his side, anticipating needs. There were things he had forgotten but she remembered—dishes for serving, a lawn umbrella for shade, salt and pepper. He noticed she had put on an apron. Other times, she seemed to vanish. It was hard to keep track in all the action.

The grill was ready and it was time to put the chicken on. But not all the guests were there—specifically, the Martins. If he started the chicken too soon and had to wait for them it would be ruined. Well they could spare a few minutes. They didn't have to eat exactly at 2. And everyone was having fun it seemed, and there was already a lot of food. But still, it was irritating to get behind schedule. Maybe they weren't coming. When would he decide they weren't coming? This was the hardest part about being a chef—the timing. How had Grandma done it, year after year, for

Thanksgiving? Always everything was ready exactly when it should be.

Then a white Ram pickup pulled down the driveway slowly. The doors opened, and there was Bradley and Karen Martin. They carried things as they approached the party. They seemed older, a rickety walk. Bradley had a bowl of punch with plastic wrap over it. Karen had a casserole dish with what looked like Jell-o dessert. As they approached, Arthur saw that Bradley had a pistol in a holster on his hip. That didn't seem necessary. But he had worn that every time Arthur had seen him, so. Part of his outfit, apparently. This would be the worst part of the party, as the weird Martins joined the group and everyone had to act naturally. This was the moment it had to go well, to put everybody at ease, and it was the host's job to do it.

Welcome, welcome, Arthur said, glad you could come. He took the casserole dish from Karen, and introduced himself. She just nodded.

Sorry we're late, said Bradley. There's always something. He glanced at Karen, and back at Arthur, an implied accusation.

Not at all, said Arthur. I love a good Jell-o dessert.

I brought punch, said Bradley. He presented the bowl, then whispered, It's just a little spiked.

Perfect, Arthur said. Thanks so much for bringing all this, you guys.

You're welcome, said Karen. There was something vacant about her, as if she had been programmed, was an android maybe. She darted glances at Bradley, who ignored her.

Did Lupe see that they had arrived? How would she act? Stoically probably. But would the Martins know who she was? Surely they would—it was a small town. Arthur looked around. Then Lupe was there, carrying drinks. In a smooth flow, she set down the drinks, took Bradley's punch bowl, then handed the drinks to them—a beer for Bradley and a white wine for Karen. Then she vanished.

Bradley drank half the beer in one go, and released a happy groan. Now we're talking, he said.

Arthur couldn't think of what to say. He said, Gorgeous day.

Sposed to rain, said Karen.

Nonsense, said Bradley. He gripped Arthur's arm and leaned forward. I see you got some help, he said. He looked past Arthur's shoulder, toward Lupe pouring wine into Timothy's glass. He said, I'm impressed.

It was troubling. Oh, no, said Arthur, that's just… But he stopped short of explaining. That was Lupe's request, wasn't it? Also, what would he say? There were so many people to please at once—you had to trust it would all sort out.

Jamie and Vicky came over to say hello to the Martins and they began talking about some issue they were debating on the Chamber of Commerce. What good luck—they knew each other then. Timothy Gardner overheard and joined the conversation with a case he had years ago where there were two Chambers of Commerce in one town because the business owners couldn't get along and so made factions and it was only a town of 300 people!

Nancy found Arthur, pulled him aside. Could I just ask, she said, What's Lupe doing?

There came an embarrassment and an overwhelming sadness. It felt cruel having her come to this party with these people, these awful Martins. But she had asked him to do this. But none of this would have happened if Arthur had done the right thing on that day. He should have called the police. That was his first instinct and probably the right one. But he was confused and overcome with dread on that horrible day. He felt paralyzed. How could he continue with this party, as the host, with his mood crashing like an old tree rotten at the core in a windstorm?

He stared at Nancy. It's what she wanted, he said.

Nancy studied on this, surveying the party. I see, she said. Well.

It wasn't the reassurance he needed. What was he supposed to do now?

He would get to work, is what he'd do. There was chicken to cook, and dishes to bring out, and toasts to make, and all the requirements of a party he had promised his friends. Or, his friends plus two… not friends. Nancy moved away. He got to work.

When he put the chicken on the grill, he looked up aimlessly and saw that the living chickens were gone from their yard. They must be back in the house. He checked his phone and confirmed the door was open. The automation was working. But also, the goats—they were huddled beneath their perches. That was strange too, but you never knew with animals. He continued cooking.

Just as the chicken was seared properly, as he prepared to take it from the grill, Arthur became aware that the party had grown quiet. Not totally quiet—Bradley Martin was laughing at something. But the other voices had hushed. Something was wrong.

Arthur turned. He saw the Fuglesens looking toward the driveway. He followed their gaze.

There stood Morgan.

She wore a pale blue dress with a white sweater and a breeze flicked her dress and her hair. She held a bouquet of flowers in one hand and a pastry box in the other. Arthur could tell she didn't quite know what to do. He had seen this posture before, the way she paused before entering a loud bar or a church. She hated that she suffered this hesitancy, struck with a senseless anxiety. He understood that anxiety, the revulsion at the crowd, the yearning to remain in the shelter of your thoughts. In those days Arthur would take her hand and they would go together and then they'd be all right. They would rise to the occasion. And although they were exhausted later, they were glad they went.

But here she was—here was Morgan, on this one perfect day.

Arthur dropped his tongs and walked to her. Morgan waited. When he got close, he stopped. He should hug her. But should he hug her? There she was the actual person with her legs and her arms and her wild hair pulled back in some clip and those incredible, miraculous eyes.

Hello Art, she said.

Morgan, he said. You came.

I did, she said and laughed a little.

Oh shit, said Arthur. I didn't make a vegetarian entrée.

TWENTY SIX

On her drive down to Middling, Morgan considered turning back, over and over. But each time, she said, One more mile. Then she went another mile, and another, more than a hundred times, and then she was on the road to the little farm she shared with Arthur. It was sunny as she drove, but the whole way it seemed a storm followed her. That was funny because it was too symbolic, but sometimes life makes symbolism that would be ridiculous in a work of art. In her rear view mirror she could see dark, towering clouds coming down from the northwest. They were gorgeous, menacing clouds with a sharp line of contrast against the blue sky to the south. When storms come in like this, they are always violent. It would be nice to sit in the old house and listen to the storm outside. But also, Arthur, and what would they say to each other?

She rehearsed conversations in her mind. Maybe she would say she was sorry for that hurtful message she sent. Saying sorry always put people at ease. But wouldn't her being there be proof of how sorry she was? Was she really sorry? Not entirely. She was still kind of angry. But also forgiving. She wanted his friendship. She wanted someone she could talk to, someone who understood her, someone who could help her make these big decisions. The two jobs and Mrs Vogel's house and her marriage—her marriage, for goodness sakes! Yes, decisions were probably what she should concentrate on. She would say, Arthur I think it's time we made some decisions, and they could talk it all through like adults. Then they could have sex. Haha, no but maybe? God she missed sex. She missed Arthur's big body and his mouth. But no of course there wouldn't be sex. Not yet.

When she arrived and saw all the cars in the driveway, all that thinking vanished. Arthur must be having a party. Was it good that he was having the party? On this, the day she was supposed to visit? Well it was impressive, at least, much more respectable than pouting. But also was it insulting to her? Was he moving on? Maybe it would be pathetic that she showed up during a party he threw after giving up on her. Now there was much less than one more mile. Now it was one more foot, and then another, and she was stepping out of her car and getting the flowers and the donuts he liked and she was on the driveway looking at all these people. All these people down in the yard having some kind of picnic?

And here was Arthur.

He wore a nice shirt that must be new and some slip-on shoes that were more stylish than she'd expect and he had lost a lot of weight and his hair was cut very short the way she liked and his face. Oh god that Arthur face, big and Celtic, framed with ginger hair—he looked so happy to see her! His face was full of love, for christ's sake—there was no doubt. But also trepidation and surprise and so many emotions. For a moment her awareness collapsed down to just the face of her husband and there was no sound and no light.

It's fine, she said, I'm sure there are a lot of vegetables I can eat. I brought donuts.

Why were they talking about this? The wind picked up.

I thought, Arthur said, I thought you weren't coming. Just that, you said We're done.

I know, said Morgan. I changed my mind. If that's okay.

The wind grew stronger, a sudden gust.

Well of course, he said. I mean of course. Come on in. It's just that…

He had turned halfway, looking at the party, looking at her, at what she carried. He said, It's really good to see you.

I know, she said, and laughed. Why couldn't she hold a thought? Sorry, I meant to say…

Then the full force of the wind arrived. The big cold front that followed Morgan all the way down, it came like bison. Her dress whipped up, pressed against her back, and the flowers were nearly ripped from her hands and as she clung to them, she tipped the pastry box and donuts fell out.

I got it, I got it, Arthur said, and he collected the donuts and shook them, like that mattered, and put them in the box. And the wind blew harder and now, beyond the trees across the river, thunder rolled out like pounding hooves. Here was the storm.

Arthur looked up at the sound. Now a flash of lightning and another bark of thunder and it began to spit rain. He looked with curiosity, as if he couldn't quite understand what was happening. Then, calm realization. Then, resolution. He always was good in an emergency.

Oh wow, Arthur said, I guess the forecast was right.

He took the box of donuts and put a hand, lightly, on her back and said, Let's get you inside. I need to bring in the food.

They ran, crouching from the rain as if that would help, down to the patio. The guests were scurrying up the back stairs into the house. A tall, older man brought up the rear, his long arms out, herding them. Except for an athletic woman, with hair as wild as Morgan's, who stacked dishes in her arms to bring inside. And a small dark-haired woman in an apron, folding up the tablecloths.

Morgan followed the group to the stairs. But Arthur wasn't coming. He was at the grill with tongs, flipping chicken into a serving dish.

Morgan went to him. It was hard to speak against the wind and thunder.

How can I help? She cried.

Arthur smiled at her, his face shining wet. Thanks, no, he yelled back. You should get inside.

No I should help, Morgan said. Her sweater and dress were soaked through, sticking to her skin. She couldn't get any wetter now so might as well. She grabbed some pies from the table and put them into a cardboard box she found underneath but the box was ruined so she balanced the pies on her arms and ran them inside.

Who were all these people? Oh there was Jamie and Vicky at least. Vicky was handing out dish towels so people could dry off and Jamie was checking the radar on his phone, announcing, It won't last long. Morgan waved to them, Hi! Sorry, I'll talk with you soon! she said and returned to the back door. The athletic woman came in carrying vases and said, I'll get things organized in here, Morgan, you go to him. How did this woman know her name? Where was Arthur? She went outside.

Morgan shielded her eyes and saw all the food was taken in and the grill was closed and the umbrellas were dropped. There he was, out by the chicken coop, reaching up with the handle of a hoe. When had he done all this with the chicken coop? And those gardens?

She ran out, calling, How can I help?

He kept reaching but called back, It's okay honey I got it – go back inside so you don't get hit by lightning.

Yeah but what about you? she asked. He had called her honey.

Arthur hooked a wire flying loose and pulled it down with the hoe. He tucked it under his shoe and then dropped a rock on it. He said, This electric wire came loose and it's fucking up my automation!

She could see now that the little hatch door of the chicken house was opening and closing, like the mouth of a ventriloquist's dummy. The wire pulled loose of the rock and flipped back against the chicken fence.

I can take that wire while you fix it, Morgan said. She reached for it.

No! That's a live wire—you could get shocked.

Morgan pulled back but said, Yeah but if it pulled loose it doesn't make a circuit right?

There was a crack and boom of thunder. Rain like a waterfall.

Arthur squinted. Oh you're probably right, he said. I just don't want to risk it. Also the lightning!

Morgan put the rock back on the wire and held it with her foot. There! she said.

Arthur ran through the gate into the chicken yard and slammed the hatch door down. He pulled a tool from his pocket and fiddled with the perimeter of the door and it stayed shut. He yelled back to her, I can't control the automation because the rain keeps fucking up my phone!

Why did he need automation on a coop with a dozen chickens? Morgan didn't ask this. She reached and touched the wire, then pulled away quickly, then touched it again for longer. She was right. It wasn't live.

Now the storm was subsiding, almost as quickly as it started. Summer storms were like that. Thunder rumbled from the southeast, ruining more parties down there no doubt. Now the sky was a lighter shade of gray. Still the wind gusted, and still it rained, but Morgan could hear the chickens in an uproar inside the house. Arthur had gone round to the human door and closed himself inside. Morgan went to that door.

What's going on? she said.

A mink! Arthur shouted. A fucking mink got in! It's right here freaking out.

I didn't think there were still minks, Morgan called through the door.

Well I'm looking at one here! I just can't get the fucker. It killed two chickens.

Let me in and I'll help.

Arthur didn't respond, but the door cracked and she slid inside and they closed the door together, for fear the chickens would rush out and be lost, and in that moment their bodies touched, all soggy with rain and now a little perspired from the action and she could feel the presence of him. The chickens were shrieking, cowering up on their laying racks. The air was strong with musk. There was the mink, backed into a corner, looking sinister and beautiful. A big dark weasel with black eyes, a chicken-killing machine. It was amazing to see.

Arthur said, Okay I'll chase him round and you open the door just for a sec but try not to let chickens out okay?

And so they did it—the mink darted away from Arthur's looming chase, just two arcing leaps and the creature was out the door. The chickens never made a move, so it was easy. Now the birds settled down into a kind of cathartic croaking.

Arthur reached up and petted one hen, then another. Oh there you are, he said. It's over.

He looked to Morgan, chagrined. They won't lay for a week. My stupid automation.

The two dead hens lay on the straw on the floor, feathers shredded, flesh bloody.

Arthur stepped in front to obscure her view. I'm sorry, he said.

He must be thinking of the grackles. So he remembered that. So that was important to him.

It's all right, she said. I'll help you get them out.

While Morgan held the door, Arthur grabbed the birds by the legs, tucked them behind his back and scooted around, keeping them from her view.

I've seen lots of dead chickens you know, she said. I'm not squeamish.

Well that's true, said Arthur, but still.

They walked to the hedge beyond the goat yard. He had built this goat yard too? The rain ceased. The four goats stood on grassy perches, chewing simultaneously, as if there had been no storm.

Arthur held the chickens, unsure. He said, This probably isn't best practice, leaving these birds here, but I have a bunch of guests inside.

In the goat yard Morgan saw five-gallon paint buckets—maybe for the goats to play with? She said, How about we put them in one of those buckets and then we can deal with them later?

Yeah okay, Arthur said. That makes sense.

When the chickens were put away, they stood beside the goat fence. The sun came through a hole in the clouds for a moment and it was hot. Back at the house you could see the dark-haired woman wiping the tables. The athletic woman snapped open tablecloths, followed by the other guests, bringing dishes.

Helpful guests, said Morgan.

That's Nancy Fuglesen, he said. And Lupe.

Lupe Gallardo? Morgan asked. She wondered, how could this be? There were so many questions. She should have let him know she was coming, so they could get on the same page. Maybe they could linger a moment more.

Yes, Arthur said. She asked me to have this party, after you… declined. Also she doesn't want to be noticed for some reason. And she doesn't want us to eat the blueberry pie. I'll fill you in later, I promise.

He wiped his dirty hands on the grass, looked at them, wiped them on his pants. He looked at the party, then at her.

I think we need to get back, he said. Sorry, I gotta host.

Right, said Morgan. But somehow she couldn't move. A goat trotted over and butted the fence by her. She put her hand on its head.

They're so beautiful, she said.

I made cheese, he said. You can try it.

Have you named them, the goats?

Arthur paused. Not really, he said. Maybe you can.

Morgan kept petting the goat, her hand pinched between the fence. We have a lot to talk about, you know?

Yeah, said Arthur. He looked at his hands, still dirty, and made a look of comical defeat. He said, I'm glad you came, Morgan. Like, really glad.

How is it that men can be so dazzling and capable and brilliant and also just little boys? But then she probably looked like a little girl just now, hair a mess, clothes hanging all weird, her new mary jane shoes probably ruined on her soaking feet. Why can't people be less complicated and just be their own authentic selves like they are as children? Why do we make life into a monster that chases us around like, like chickens. Those poor chickens.

Morgan said, I'm glad too.

Arthur turned to the party reassembling on the patio, his gaze sharp and determined. He said, It's gonna be weird, because the Martins are here too. Maybe you can help, with the weirdness?

Of course, said Morgan. He had taken a step closer to her. She said, But maybe first—maybe first we should hug?

For a moment, Arthur looked like he might cry, or maybe fall down. Then he put his arms out wide and enveloped her around the shoulders and she rested her head against his chest and wrapped his back and felt his ribs with her hands. Now she thought she might fall too—it was like drinking when you didn't realize how thirsty you were and then you just drink and drink.

Someone hooted from the patio. She and Arthur had been seen. Someone shushed the hooter.

They pulled apart but kept their hands on each other. It was awkward like a middle school dance but who gave a shit.

Arthur said, Do you know what I called this day?

I don't know, said Morgan. The Grand Opening?

Oh you mean like the farm, he said. He laughed. No. There's nothing grand about it.

I saw your sign, she said.

You should have seen the first one.

What did that say?

It was dumb, he replied. That was a long time ago, feels like.

What did you call this day?

Arthur let her arms drop, gently. He let out a long breath, and looked up toward the sky. That was probably dumb too, he said. Or, maybe profound? I don't know.

For a moment he was lost in his thoughts. Then he looked her directly into her eyes and held it. She held it too. It was like there was nothing to lose anymore. She had no fear. Or maybe, she wasn't afraid of her fear.

I'll tell you later, he said.

All right, said Morgan.

They walked, side by side, back to the house.

TWENTY SEVEN

Morgan and Arthur found dry clothes in the bedroom they had shared for years. Through the window they could hear bebop jazz playing and the guests laughing, while Nancy and Lupe got the dishes out and Faulkner reheated the chicken on the grill. Arthur held his clothes in a neat stack and said, I can change in the bathroom.

You don't have to do that, said Morgan, I can go.

She opened her closet and drew in a breath.

What? he asked.

Well, just that everything is how I left it.

Arthur looked at her. She seemed a long way away across the room. He said, I might have moved a few things, just to dust.

Morgan imagined now, in a rush of images, Arthur living alone in that house for so many months, taking care of all the daily things, respecting her spaces, dusting. He seemed far away across the room, holding his clothes. He was so much thinner now.

Arthur, she said. I'm not seeing anyone. I made that up. Because I was so upset. But there's no one. I have this friend, I mean, a pretty good friend, or maybe not. But there's no one else.

Okay, said Arthur. He forced a smile. It should have been a tremendous relief, but there was no feeling. Maybe it was the sensory overload of the day or maybe he had grown callouses in the emotional parts of his brain and couldn't feel through them. Or maybe, he couldn't trust her anymore.

I just wanted to get that out there, said Morgan.

Thanks, said Arthur. I appreciate that. We should probably get dressed and go huh?

When he left, Morgan put on some shorts and found they were a little too big for her now, and also a blouse that seemed faintly musty from being in the closet too long. What was she expecting? For Arthur to run over and embrace her? That was ridiculous. But he didn't have to be so mysterious either. So reserved. Well, obviously things would never be the same after everything that happened, but still that was sad. She tried to arrange her hair using the mirror over the dresser, but it was a lost cause. In the reflection, looking at the room behind her, Morgan looked for Mr Vogel watching in all his sadness. But she wasn't at Mrs Vogel's house right now. She was at Arthur's farm. Or her farm. Or their farm. It felt like she was floating.

After the storm, the party had a new life to it, an extra energy. The guests sat around the table, food piled on their plates, glasses full of wine and beer, music playing, laughter. Nothing like a storm passing to elevate the souls of Midwesterners. Faulkner was at one head of the table, professing to Bradley Martin on one side and Jennifer Beardsley on the other. Arthur had offered Morgan the other head of the table, but she said don't be ridiculous you're the host, and he said he wished the table were round, so no one had to sit at the head, but he sat down and she sat next to him, and she drew Lupe over to sit next to her. Lupe, who had been pouring waters. That was insane that Lupe was there—how had Arthur conjured all this?—and why did Lupe want to just serve, like some kind of help, that was inappropriate, and why were the Martins there—was there some new development that Arthur hadn't told Morgan? She had no right to know, honestly, since she had broken things off, so she would just have to watch it all unfold. But it was good to be sitting next to Arthur, it felt grounded, and also Nancy was a hoot, sitting across from Morgan like your best friend's hilarious mom.

Lupe tapped Morgan's arm. She said, So this is your farm. But you live in Chicago.

Yes, said Morgan. I work in Chicago, so.

How often do you come down? asked Lupe.

Well to be honest, said Morgan, We're kind of separated, working some things out.

Yes, said Lupe. Your husband told me that. It must be difficult.

Morgan touched Lupe's arm. She said, Your husband—I heard about it. I'm so sorry.

Lupe looked in Morgan's eyes, unblinking. Was there meaning? Morgan felt for a moment like she might be sick. When all this was over she would be honest with this woman, somehow.

I know, said Lupe.

Well, said Morgan, I'm so glad you could come. Arthur has made some great new friends.

Lupe nodded, and began to cut into her chicken.

As they began to eat, it occurred to Arthur that he should say something, make some kind of toast, but just then Faulkner was clinking his wine glass. Timothy continued sharing a lively story with the Martins, who had piled their plates to overflowing but seemed rapt by Timothy's words. And Jennifer was asking questions about children to Jamie and Vicky, who sat across from her. Faulkner stood up and shouted, hey! And the table went silent.

I would like to propose a toast, said Faulkner. A toast for our host.

He laughed. Toast for the host! Did I just make that up?

Nancy hissed, Fawk!

No, seriously, Fawk laughed. He paused reflectively. You know, he said, The struggle of a lifetime can be healed by one day with friends.

Hear hear! cried Timothy, raising his glass.

No, no! Faulkner scolded. I'm not done.

Better sit back, muttered Nancy, but she smiled at her husband.

Fawk continued. I want to greet our other neighbor, Morgan, who we have been waiting so long to meet. Welcome back, Morgan. And also our new friend Lupe. And all you other lovely neighbors.

Amen, said Bradley Martin, and he tipped his glass of punch to his mouth.

Faulkner held out his hand. No no—wait.

Bradley sighed in disappointment and put his glass down. Karen stared at her plate of food. She looked so uncomfortable—why was she uncomfortable? It was so strange that the Martins were here. They didn't seem like murderers. But now wasn't the time to consider that. For a moment Arthur saw flashes of scenes—Armando on the bank of the river, all the people wearing animal masks, lunch with Bradley in the café, Lupe turning her back in her farm stand. Faulkner and Nancy must see that this is very strange, possibly volatile. How were they acting so normally? Well, that's what they do. But now wasn't time to give in to anxious thoughts. Maybe there was healing here, maybe there was peace. Now was time to summon the strength to bring some joy to the good people here, and leave penance for some later time. Also Morgan was here, just beside him, and that was almost impossible to believe.

And as for our host, said Faulkner, I wish to thank Arthur Prendergast for his friendship and his selfless effort in bringing us all together today. You know, a person who faces a stubborn challenge, despite all odds and advice against it, who succeeds despite the inexorable drag of entropy— that person makes us all better. And I'll say no one embodies that piece of wisdom more than Arthur, our lovable goofy, brilliant neighbor. Look at what you've done here—taking this recalcitrant piece of land and coaxing it into something extraordinary. Where gardens yield this delicious food, where goats cavort on perches, where chickens lay lovely eggs, where bees buzz and birds chirp all among native plants—there's hope yet, for all of us and for our planet, I say, when you look around Prendergast Acres. And where there's hope, there's wine. And where there's wine, there's love, and where there's love…

To Arthur! Nancy cried.

They all toasted and drank, and Arthur nodded with embarrassment and shifted his eyes from one to another, and there were comments on how good the wine was, and Timothy began explaining how the wine he brought was from a vineyard in Sonoma where there was a perfect replica of a French château. The guests started to dig into their meals. This wasn't right.

Wait! Arthur said. He stood up with his glass.

If you can stand just one more minute, he said, I would also like to propose a toast.

The eating stopped and people reached back for their glasses.

I want to thank you all for coming, of course, Arthur said. And sorry about the weather. That wasn't planned. But my toast, he said, is to Morgan. He looked at her, blinking.

All those eyes on her, it was unnerving. They must know she and Arthur were separated, and that she had left and gone to Chicago and not come back for this long. That wasn't honoring her, it was judging her, maybe? Maybe this was cruel, Arthur calling her out. Or maybe it was kind—how were you supposed to know these things? You thought you wanted to be treated special until you were and then it's too much.

To Morgan, Arthur said, who came a long way today. And without her, well. Without her this day wouldn't be complete. And, anyway… sorry… Here's to Morgan.

It was a horrible toast, he felt it, but even so people cried aww. Arthur sat down and looked over and saw Morgan looking at her plate, her brow lowered.

Timothy began clinking his now empty wine glass. Kiss! he cried. A few joined him in a chant to Kiss!

Morgan turned toward Timothy. She fixed her enchanted eyes on him and it was terrifying and Timothy put down his fork and the table grew silent. Awkwardness hung. Then Morgan smiled and said, Thank you so much everyone it's great to see you all, now let's eat! And so they did.

With the conversation rumbling, Arthur said to Morgan, Sorry.

Yeah no I'm sorry, she said. No offense but…

No yeah, he said. It makes sense.

I appreciate what you said. I don't know how to respond.

Arthur shrugged. He really didn't expect her to respond. He had just wanted to say it.

Is the food bad? he asked.

Of course not, she said. I can't speak for the chicken but all of this is lovely. The whole day is lovely… except, I mean, I wish I knew a little more…

Arthur looked briefly at the Martins. They were eating with rigor, scooping their food with forks held wrong, listening to Timothy.

So do I, he said. Maybe it's all right. I'm just trying to do what I promised.

It feels wrong, said Morgan.

Arthur nodded agreement but had no words.

The dinner went on. Maybe it was the lightness of the air after the storm, or the mildness of the late afternoon sunshine, or the gentle rush of the river back through the trees, now swelling with all the rain. Maybe it was the quality of the company—but whatever the reason, people kept talking and laughing and filling each other's glasses and getting up for seconds and the dinner just kept going. After a while no one talked with Arthur and Morgan, an envelope of privacy wrapped around them.

How long do you think you'll stay? Arthur asked.

I don't know, she said. I didn't come with a plan.

You said we had a lot to talk about. Like, more than the obvious things?

Yes, said Morgan. Do you want me to start now?

I'm trying to get better with patience. But yes.

Morgan twisted the stem of her glass, round and round, and looked at her hand. She was anxious. He didn't want her to be anxious. She was pausing too long.

He said. It's fine I'm sure, whatever it is.

She looked up at him, her face now so awake, bursting. I have a lot of decisions to make, she said. I mean, really big decisions.

I know, Arthur said. He thought he knew but actually maybe he didn't. He assumed it was about him but then maybe it wasn't about him. You had to think of that sometimes.

No you don't, Morgan said. I mean, you couldn't know some of these things.

Well, he said, okay.

I came down because I need someone to talk to. I want some advice I guess, or a sounding board. There's nobody else.

Morgan was now turned toward him, her hand on the table, her face upward to his. Had she forgotten they were surrounded by all these people? But the people didn't seem to notice. They were all drunk, probably. It was loud. Did he hear a goat bleat? He glanced over, saw all four of the goats okay, and turned back to Morgan. Cripes, what a day.

I have a job offer, Morgan said. Two job offers, actually.

She watched his face cloud, and clear, and consider, and then form words.

You mean instead of Mrs Vogel?

Yes, she said. Proper jobs as an RN at a hospital. The thing is. One of them is Illinois Masonic, going back there. And the other is at Middling. Like, here. They contacted me, out of the blue, with an offer to return and a signing bonus. That was the letter you forwarded to me. No idea why they reached out to me now, but.

Something became clear to Arthur.

Nancy, he said.

You mean this Nancy, she asked, and pointed discreetly with her hand.

Yes, he said. She's on the hospital board.

Why would she do that? Morgan asked. You could tell she wanted to look at Nancy but she restrained herself.

She's nice, Arthur said. He shrugged. Probably as simple as that. Also, she heard how good you were. So, actually, she was just doing her job. As a board member.

Fuck, Morgan said, and then, Sorry. She covered her mouth. It just kind of blows me away.

So are you going to take one of the jobs? Arthur asked. If you don't mind my asking.

Of course I don't mind you asking—that's why I'm bringing it up, stupid.

They both laughed at her rudeness. It was good she felt comfortable to call him stupid.

There's more, she said.

Arthur waited, sipping wine and nodding. He noticed, momentarily, Lupe answering a question about bees to Vicky. He heard Bradley and Timothy laugh loudly. It was difficult, all this restraint. So many words kept bubbling up into his mouth and he had to keep clamping them down. He wanted to say, Morgan, come home, come home to me and we'll be so happy and everything will be perfect, Morgan, just like this perfect day. But you can't always just say what comes into your mind, even when it's someone you know and love so well, because words are these horribly imperfect tools that have to be handled carefully like nitroglycerin.

Morgan said, Mrs. Vogel left her house to me.

She realized this was too blunt a way to say it, and also not the right moment—she should have waited until later. But she couldn't wait. All these months of restraint, this persistent but vague fear of consequences. She had to let it out. Arthur assumed a kind of astonished smile, a perplexion. Was perplexion a word? That's what his face looked like.

Well, congratulations, I guess, he said. I mean that's great. What about her kids—she has kids, right?

They don't get along. She's giving them money. And other things, I guess. I hope so.

Arthur began to speak, but paused, frozen it seemed, in perplexion. Neither of them knew what he was thinking. A mind can only process so much in a day.

Let's talk about it later, Morgan said. Thanks for letting me unload that.

Mmm, said Arthur.

Now Lupe was standing beside him. I'll set out dessert, she said.

I'll help, said Arthur.

No, sit, said Lupe. I got it.

All the guests formed a line at the side table, where Lupe stood serving pie. They took plates and held them out and she cut them slices. Amazing, said Timothy. So good of you, said Vicky. It was a polite ritual, the serving and receiving of pie. Faulkner pointed to the blueberry, now missing two slices. That one looks good, he said. I don't think so, said Lupe, and she gave him apple. Arthur poured coffee and Lupe took her seat and they sat eating.

Goddamn that's good pie, said Bradley. Don't you think, Karen?

It's good pie, said Karen.

The party grew quiet, so full-bellied and talked-out and satisfied.

When dessert was ended, Lupe took her cup, raised it to the dinner guests, saying, I would like to say something. Her voice was quiet, and she cleared her throat and continued. My name is Lupe Gallardo. Maybe some of you know me. I have lived and worked in this place for many years.

Arthur could see that her hand was trembling. He didn't want her to be nervous. But she had something to say. Now they would know.

She said, I raised three children, and made good friends, and ran a business. I grew food for people. Done my best, for many years. This is my home. I'm grateful for the life I've had here. Thank you, Arthur, for inviting me to this party. I think you are a good man.

It sounded to Arthur like a question. But the group mumbled approval. Timothy started to clap. Lupe shook her head no. Her expression narrowed to a point. She raised her voice,

But I'm sorry to say I have some bad news to share. She pointed at Bradley and Karen. Bad news for you, I'm afraid. Do you know what that is? I'll tell you. You have eaten poison in that pie.

It took a moment for the group to react to her words. A confusion swirling. Of course, Arthur thought, he should have seen this coming. But also, Lupe poisoned them? Right in front of everyone? That couldn't be. But then, she had asked for all this to happen. Oh, no.

Bradley Martin grimaced at Lupe, then turned a hard stare toward Arthur. He said, What's going on here?

No, Lupe said firmly. I'm talking. Esto es lo que está pasando. Maybe there is poison in your pie. Or maybe not. Maybe I forgot to put poison in that pie. You don't know. But you ate it. You are the only ones who ate it, and if it is poisoned, you don't have much time left. Now you know what it means to live in uncertainty, whether you will see tomorrow.

Karen spit the remainder of pie on her plate, fingering her mouth, and looked sideways, angrily at Bradley.

What…the… fuck! he said. Who the fuck do you think you are?

Morgan had the sense of a dream, the surreality of it, people saying things like, Okay, Hold on now, Lupe you're joking right… There was too much talking at once.

But over the voices Lupe continued, now commandingly, saying, You killed my husband. Armando Gallardo. Now you see me. Now you know what it feels like to fear death. Maybe you are dying, you don't know.

Are you for real? cried Bradley. What the fuck is going on here?

You don't know, said Lupe, fiercely. That is the point.

Morgan thought, if they had been poisoned, Bradley and Karen would need medical attention immediately. They'd need their stomachs pumped. Or maybe she could induce vomiting.

Now Bradley stood, his chair falling, unsnapping his holster, pulling his pistol, pointing it at Lupe. He said, You're gonna tell me right now if these pies have poison—you have ten seconds!

Now people were saying Whoa, whoa, Hey, Bradley, put that…

Bradley was counting, seven, six, five…

Morgan watched Arthur walking around the table. He knew guns, that was good. But you don't approach a guy with a gun. But, there was that boy in the alley, with the gun. He had run.

Arthur heard himself saying, Nope, nope, as he walked around the table. This wouldn't do. This wasn't the plan. It felt easy, to walk toward Bradley Martin brandishing a gun, who now turned and brandished it toward him, Arthur. But Bradley wasn't a scary man, he was the man who hid inside a mask, the head of a deer, and a deer isn't a predator, it's prey, deer are fearful things, and sometimes fearful things are actually dangerous, but it was too late now to worry about that. Also he could see the safety was still on. Arthur put his hand on Bradley's shoulder, and felt a rage in the muscle, and he put his hand over the hand with the gun and slid it until he felt the barrel and gripped it and there was resistance, and maybe people shouting, but then the gun was released and he had it.

For a moment Arthur felt obliged to shoot the pistol, to point it aloft and fire it, because once the gun was there it had to be fired. But instead, he released the clip, and drained the cartridges from it, and put them in his pocket, quite heavy in there, and snapped the empty clip back in, and handed the gun to Bradley. He said, We better get you some help.

Arthur turned to Morgan and asked, What do we do?

Lupe stared at Bradley, who now looked at Karen, who held her stomach, rocking in her chair.

Lupe said, Now you see. Now you see.

Morgan said, Somebody call 911. But I think you guys better throw up.

Now Karen was beside Bradley, pulling at his shirt, saying, We have to go, we have to get to the hospital. Bradley swatted at her, Stop it, he said, there's no poison. But Karen was persistent, now actually screaming, We are going! she cried. We are going now!

Together they marched away, staggering slightly, Bradley looking back saying, There's no poison! You'll regret this! You lying bitch!

That's right, said Lupe. You go.

The white truck peeled out of the driveway and roared away—that familiar exhaust note.

Then they were all standing, looking at each other.

Nancy whispered, I have 911 on the phone. What should I say?

Lupe stared at where the truck had been. Her shoulders were down, her exhaustion plain. You can hang up, she said. There's no poison. I'm going home.

Now the full weight of all the atrocities bore down on them, the shame of it, the hopelessness.

So ended the one perfect day.

TWENTY EIGHT

In the morning they put the canoe into the river at the Lincoln Trail Homestead, because the body must have come that far, according to the pictures. Arthur held the boat against the bank so they could get the feel of it. There was a nice eddy here and the water was calm. Beyond that, the river was running high thanks to the storm yesterday.

Feel all right? Arthur asked.

It's been a while, said Morgan. But yeah. I've canoed before.

I remember, said Arthur. Do you want some coffee? Sit here for a minute?

Actually I do, she said, and set the paddle down and turned in her seat to face him.

The sunlight came dappled through the maple trees over the bank and made shifting shapes on their faces. They were both puffy-eyed from staying up most of the night. They drank coffee out of plastic camp cups while the boat rocked in the eddy. Morgan chewed her lip. It felt like it was necessary to lighten the mood.

Maybe we'll see your ghost friend, Morgan said. She looked up the bank through some hawthorn trees.

Arthur watched her expression. You're teasing me, he said.

I'm no longer a doubter, she said.

Really, Arthur said. Did you see him that time when we sat on the swing…

I remember the time, she said. You've asked me this before, Arthur.

He shrugged and sat, splaying this feet against the sides of the aluminum canoe, to keep it stable.

I'm probably crazier than you, she said. There's a ghost at Mrs Vogel's too.

Seriously? It sounded too eager.

Oh yes, seriously. It's the ghost of Mr Vogel.

No kidding. Her husband?

He's quite a character.

Is he like Hanacek, I mean how he appeared? I just wonder if ghosts have common qualities.

Pretty much, Morgan said. He's very real and concrete, but also transparent. Kind of shimmery, like an illuminated haze.

That's a beautiful way to say it.

Thank you. It just came to me.

What does he do, Mr Vogel?

He was really anxious, she said, and also angry. But now he's much calmer. He kind of hangs near Mrs Vogel but then vanishes.

Why do you think he changed, in his attitude?

That's a whole nother story, she said. I'll save it for later.

It was good to hear her say later, because that implied there would be a later time when she would share that story and they would still be together. And Morgan knew this, and also that saying it so casually suggested later might be a long time from now—that there was no hurry.

Do other people see Mr Vogel?

Mrs Vogel sees him. Nakeisha does too, I think. But not Devin.

I wonder why, Arthur said. He took his paddle and poked it against the bank, to point the bow back downriver. It was probably time to get going.

Morgan saw this and turned in her seat and lifted her paddle too. She began to tread water with it.

I don't know, she said. Of course it's ridiculous. I mean, people just die. We see their physical bodies die and decompose.

Unless you're like Armando, said Arthur. Maybe he shouldn't have said it, but you had to laugh because otherwise. Also there were the pictures.

Morgan laughed. Except for Armando, she said. Still, it's worth considering. I've thought about it. We know a person's physical self goes back into the kind of molecular soup of the universe. But the idea of a person, the concept of a person—that doesn't go away. It's stored in everybody's brain who knew that person. And so sometimes, in some cases, some of us can actually see that idea of a person. Maybe it's really there, but just a projection of our brain and a trick of our senses. But it doesn't matter, because in any case, it's fundamentally the idea of a person, which you can't dispute. Just a theory.

Arthur looked down the river. That's nice, he said. But then how about people we never met in life?

You mean like Hanacek.

So you did see him!

Maybe. Maybe not. I don't see him now.

He's super unreliable, said Arthur. Drives me nuts.

They were paddling out into the center of the river and the current seized the boat and tugged it forward. They worked to avoid snags and hazards in the river, to keep them in the main channel, if you could call it that on such a gnarly waterway.

They scanned the banks for Armando, and looked into the water, but you couldn't see a thing through the brown silt that churned up. All that precious topsoil, the world's most fertile earth, forged over millennia on the prairie, now draining away toward the polluted gulf. It was depressing if you thought too much about it.

This must be the crookedest river in the world, Morgan said.

Or at least in Illinois, he replied. But come to think of it, what was a crookeder river? How could you quantify crookedness? A total, collective radius of curves, probably. Someone must have done this by now. If you thought of it, someone must have done it.

So your ghost theory, Arthur said. Do you think that if two people see the same ghost, it means there's a special connection between them? Meaning, if they both create the same image of the idea of that person, they must share a common way of perception?

Morgan turned her head so he could see her smile. He liked her dimple so she showed it to him, and also it was nice that he was thinking of her theory. She resumed paddling. Probably, she said. But if what you're getting at is whether you and I share a special connection, well I guess there's more proof than that we see the same ghosts.

It felt good to say that to him. It was true and he'd like it and there was no risk in saying it.

Arthur parked his paddle across his lap and took binoculars and searched higher past the bank. It gave him vertigo, immediately, with the boat in motion, and he could only look for a few seconds. That wasn't going to yield anything. Somehow it seemed appropriate and maybe cool to be scanning with binoculars. Not that Morgan could see him, with her back turned. She had said they had a special connection. Well of course they did. But still she had said it.

They stopped for lunch on the river, tucked into another eddy, held fast by a fallen cottonwood. So many fallen trees. Were they falling faster than new ones could grow? That wasn't something to think about now. They ate leftovers from the big dinner, now in plastic containers. The corn was rubbery but the potatoes were better.

How long do you think we'll go? Morgan asked.

Until we find him.

She looked up from her dish to see how he meant that. Arthur smiled, and shrugged. This newfound confidence, this equanimity—it suited him.

Okay, Morgan said. She closed her eyes and lifted her face to the sun. It was getting milder these days, especially this day, which had a whiff of autumn to it. Midwestern people are funny how they start looking for autumn in August. Wonder why that is—does it make us gloomy people, yearning for the end of the happy time, or is it a harvest thing?

That was beautiful how she lifted her face to the sun. Arthur thought about how nice it would be to kiss her. But also would it be strange, kissing again after so long? Maybe it would be great, like when they were first dating and kissed every chance they got and couldn't get enough of each other. But he shouldn't be thinking of kissing—there was a solemn job to do now.

Morgan leaned forward and put her arms on her knees. She said, Arthur what are we going to do if we find the body?

When we find the body.

Sure, when we find the body. What are we going to do with it?

We're going to bring it back to Lupe, like she asked.

Yeah, but practically. How does that work? I don't know if I can touch it.

I think we'll just know how, Arthur said. That's what I'm counting on. But also, it won't be like a regular corpse. Armando's body isn't decaying. Because of the mushrooms.

Right, she said. That's just crazy.

A crow flew up the river, calling. It darted around them, so effortlessly. Crows know more than we think they do.

Morgan asked, Do you think Lupe considered actually poisoning that pie?

She must have, to then decide not to.

But other people might have eaten it then. Faulkner almost took a piece.

Probably why she didn't poison it.

I don't think Lupe is capable of poisoning someone, killing them.

We don't know what she's capable of, just what she did.

It still seems wrong, Morgan said. For them to get away with murder.

Arthur closed the lid of his container and began to put things away. He said, I guess it's up to Lupe to decide what's justice.

Morgan leaned back, her arms against the bow. That's an interesting concept, she said, letting victims decide what a punishment should be.

Oh, said Arthur. He leaned forward, elbows on his knees. I wasn't thinking of it that way. More like victims get to decide when they're at peace with things.

True. She paused and felt the boat rocking on the water. She said, I guess there's no way we can really understand what she's feeling.

No, said Arthur. We can't know what it's like to be Lupe.

Morgan drank from her water bottle and put that in the cooler between them. It makes me feel, she said, I feel simultaneously very fortunate and very guilty.

Like why do we fight all the time, when we're so lucky.

Yes, Morgan said, like why are we wasting our precious time.

We're having a little epiphany here, Arthur said. I guess we're all fixed.

They laughed. And then were quiet.

She said she forgave you, Morgan said.

Yeah, she did.

So then did you feel better?

No, I felt worse.

Well, I was very angry with you too. But for what it's worth, I kind of understand how everything happened and why you did things.

Thanks, said Arthur. I had thought that if I had the party for Lupe, and then found Armando's body, my debt would be paid.

That sounds like penance.

Something like that.

But now?

Arthur sighed. It surprised him to hear it, like such a weary man. To be honest, I have no idea, he said. Not a clue how I should feel...

She could see in his face a hint of pain, still. Things weren't going to be all fixed. Maybe things were never fixed, just faded. Everything Morgan could think of to say now seemed trivial. She put her hand out, and he reached and touched it, hooking fingertips, releasing.

They sat while the boat rocked in the echo of the current coming around the bend past the great fallen cottonwood tree. A squirrel chattered in the canopy.

But seriously, said Morgan. What are we going to do when we find Armando's body?

Ah, Arthur said. That's easy. I have some towing straps we'll put around him so we can pull him to shore, if that's necessary. And then I have a sleeping bag we can put him in. His body will be rigid, so not too hard to carry. Then we'll call Faulkner to bring the truck and we'll haul him to Lupe's house.

Are you serious? She studied Arthur. There was this new quality to him, Morgan had noticed, where he was just a little less earnest. A little more detached and maybe ironic. It made him seem spicy. Why did women like men who were a little spicy, rather than just plain sweet?

Arthur shook his head and smiled. A rueful smile. No, he said. If we find Armando's body we're going to call Lupe and let her decide what to do, and we'll help however she says.

I didn't believe you, Morgan said.

Yes you did, he said.

They pushed the boat back into the stream and paddled it straight, scanning the waters for a body.

In late afternoon, they passed a series of houses up on a bluff, with elaborate stairs that came down to the water and small docks.

What town is this? Morgan asked.

I don't know.

Weird how different everything is from the river.

Yeah, he said. I think if we were up on the road, we'd know where we are.

I guess I could check my phone, she said.

You could. Personally, I don't want to, because we'd realize how not very far we've come.

The sun is low, maybe I should check my phone.

Sure, he said.

Morgan held her paddle for a while. But then she didn't check her phone. Why did that seem like it would spoil it, if she checked their location? Why did it feel like that would prevent them from finding Armando?

We're going to have to find a place to camp, said Arthur.

Maybe there will be a park? she said.

Hopefully, he said. Or just some field far from anything. Last thing we need is to get arrested for trespassing.

Well I don't think we'd be arrested. Just kicked out.

That's probably true.

They kept paddling until there were no houses, just broad banks and hardwood forest. What the locals called timber. They had to get out once, to portage around a big snag. They sunk to their ankles in the mud. Afterward, they tried to rinse off their feet by hanging them over the side of the canoe but it was difficult to balance that way and also steer, and so eventually they gave up and accepted muddy feet.

With the last light of day fading, they came around a broad bend to an island. The river was in the process of making a new course here, and eventually there would be an ox bow pond. But for now, there was an island. Just in time.

Wow that's lucky, Morgan said. She got up in the bow so she could jump out and pull while Arthur paddled hard.

Be careful, he said, probably poison ivy on the bank. Might be poison ivy over this whole island.

The bank was gravelly, with some sand that made it less muddy. You could even see through the water a little here. There was no poison ivy, but there were nettles.

The canoe made a satisfying crunching sound as it nosed up the bank and they pulled it in and tied it to a young locust tree just to be safe.

I think we can have a fire here, Arthur said. Technically an island is no one's land. It's public property, because rivers are a federal waterway.

Is that true?

I don't know, actually, he said. It's something I read or heard once, but to be honest I don't know.

Well, it seems fair, she said. And here we are.

They made a fire of fallen sticks, which were abundant on the island. They took out what was left of the leftovers. They sat on a blanket beside the fire and ate.

After a while, Morgan set down her dish. I'm kind of sick of this, she said. No offense.

Me too, he said. He put his dish down. It seemed kind of pathetic now, these plastic containers of yesterday's dinner. And after that, what?

We're not exactly intrepid explorers, are we? Arthur said.

Not really, said Morgan. She had her arms wrapped around her legs and she was staring into the fire.

Do you want some whiskey, he said. I brought a little.

Not really, said Morgan.

Can I put my arm around you? he asked.

Of course, she said. Please. Morgan still looked into the fire. There were so many shapes in there, in that tiny inferno. She waited to feel Arthur's touch.

He crawled over and sat right beside her and put his arm around her shoulders and held her. She raised a hand, held it for a moment, and then put it on his knee. They sat there for a while.

It's nice, she said. Sitting here.

I'm so glad you came, he said.

I am too. But I never imagined this.

I did.

You did?

No.

Enough joking.

Okay, sorry.

How long are we going to do this, looking for Armando.

Until we find him.

When will that be?

Tomorrow.

Really?

Yes. Somehow I feel like we'll find him tomorrow, but it won't be easy.

And then we'll call Lupe?

That's the plan.

It was getting tiring sitting that way, so he took his arm from around her and reached for her hand. They interwove their fingers and leaned against each other and that was more comfortable.

Morgan? he said.

Yes, Arthur.

I want to ask you something.

Good, she said. Go ahead.

Do you think there's hope? For us? Will we make it past all this?

She pressed her fingers more tightly around his. There were stars in the firmament and crickets sang in the darkness and somewhere in that river a man awaited.

Maybe, she said.

And maybe was the best they could hope for.

About the Author

Kipling Knox has worked as an engineering manager at Microsoft, an editor at World Book Publishing, and Director of Web Services at the University of Illinois. He is the author of *Under the Moon in Illinois,* an interconnected collection whose stories have won the Chris O'Malley Prize in Fiction and the Wild Women Fiction Award. He also writes *Small Talk,* a series of essays covering science, philosophy, culture, and the arts—all with a touch of humor—at http://kiplingknox.com.

www.ingramcontent.com/pod-product-compliance
Lightning Source LLC
Chambersburg PA
CBHW020240010826
48973CB00006B/1600